Dreamers of the Ghetto by Israel Zangwill

Israel Zangwill was born in London on 21st January 1864, to a family of Jewish immigrants from the Russian Empire.

Zangwill was initially educated in Plymouth and Bristol. At age 9 he was enrolled in the Jews' Free School in Spitalfields in east London. Zangwill excelled here. He began to teach part-time at the school and eventually full time. Whilst teaching he also studied with the University of London and by 1884 had earned his BA with triple honours in philosophy, history, and the sciences.

His writing earned him the sobriquet "the Dickens of the Ghetto" primarily based on his much lauded novel 'Children of the Ghetto: A Study of a Peculiar People' in 1892 and its glimpse of the poverty-stricken life in London's Jewish quarter.

As a writer he was keen to reflect on his political and social outlooks. His simulation of Yiddish sentence structure in English aroused great interest. His mystery work, 'The Big Bow Mystery' (1892) was the first locked room mystery novel.

Zangwill was also involved with narrowly focused Jewish issues as an assimilationist, an early Zionist, and later a territorialist. In the early 1890s he had joined the Lovers of Zion movement in England. In 1897 he joined Theodor Herzl (considered the father of modern political Zionism) in founding the World Zionist Organization.

Zangwill quit the established philosophy of Zionism when his plan for a homeland in Uganda was rejected and founded his own organisation; the Jewish Territorialist Organization. Its stated goal was to create a Jewish homeland in whatever territory in the world could be found for them.

Amongst the challenges in his life he found time to write poetry. He had translated a medieval Jewish poet in 1903 and his volume 'Blind Children' in 1908 shows his promise in this new endeavour.

'The Melting Pot' in 1909 made Zangwill's name as an admired playwright. When the play opened in Washington D.C., former President Theodore Roosevelt leaned over the edge of his box and shouted, "That's a great play, Mr. Zangwill, that's a great play."

Israel Zangwill died on 1st August 1926 in Midhurst, West Sussex.

Index of Contents

PREFACE

This is a Chronicle of Dreamers, who have arisen in the Ghetto from its establishment in the sixteenth century to its slow breaking-up in our own day. Some have become historic in Jewry, others have penetrated to the ken of the greater world and afforded models to illustrious artists in letters, and but for the exigencies of my theme and the faint hope of throwing some new light upon them, I should not have ventured to treat them afresh; the rest are personally known to me or are, like "Joseph the Dreamer," the artistic typification of many souls through which the great Ghetto dream has passed. Artistic truth is for me literally the highest truth: art may seize the essence of persons and movements no less truly, and certainly far more vitally, than a scientific generalization unifies a chaos of phenomena. Time and Space are only the conditions through which spiritual facts straggle. Hence I have here and there permitted myself liberties with these categories. Have I, for instance, misplaced the moment of Spinoza's obscure love-episode—I have only followed his own principle, to see things sub specie æternitatis, and even were his latest Dutch editor correct in denying the episode altogether, I should still hold it true as summarizing the emotions with which even the philosopher must reckon. Of Heine I have attempted a sort of composite conversation-photograph, blending, too, the real heroine of the little episode with "La Mouche." His own words will be recognized by all students of him—I can only hope the joins with mine are not too obvious. My other sources, too, lie sometimes as plainly on the surface, but I have often delved at less accessible quarries. For instance, I owe the celestial vision of "The Master of the Name" to a Hebrew original kindly shown me by my friend Dr. S. Schechter, Reader in Talmudic at Cambridge, to whose luminous essay on the Chassidim, in his Studies in Judaism, I have a further indebtedness. My account of "Maimon the Fool" is based on his own (not always reliable) autobiography, of which I have extracted the dramatic essence, though in the supplementary part of the story I have had to antedate slightly the publication of Mendelssohn's "Jerusalem" and the fame of Kant. In fine, I have never hesitated to take as an historian or to focus and interpret as an imaginative artist.

I have placed "A Child of the Ghetto" first, not only because the Venetian Jewry first bore the name of Ghetto, but because this chapter may be regarded as a prelude to all the others. Though the Dream pass through Smyrna or Amsterdam, through Rome or Cairo, through Jerusalem or the Carpathians, through London or Berlin or New York, almost all the Dreamers had some such childhood, and it may serve to explain them. It is the early environment from which they all more or less emerged.

And there is a sense in which the stories all lead on to that which I have placed last. The "Child of the Ghetto" may be considered "father to the man" of "Chad Gadya" in that same city of the sea.

For this book is the story of a Dream that has not come true.

I.Z.

MOSES AND JESUS

In dream I saw two Jews that met by chance,
One old, stern-eyed, deep-browed, yet garlanded
With living light of love around his head,
The other young, with sweet seraphic glance.
Around went on the Town's satanic dance,
Hunger a-piping while at heart he bled.
Shalom Aleichem mournfully each said,
Nor eyed the other straight but looked askance.

Sudden from Church out rolled an organ hymn,
From Synagogue a loudly chaunted air,
Each with its Prophet's high acclaim instinct.
Then for the first time met their eyes, swift-linked
In one strange, silent, piteous gaze, and dim
With bitter tears of agonized despair.

A CHILD OF THE GHETTO

I

The first thing the child remembered was looking down from a window and seeing, ever so far below, green water flowing, and on it gondolas plying, and fishing-boats with colored sails, the men in them looking as small as children. For he was born in the Ghetto of Venice, on the seventh story of an ancient house. There were two more stories, up which he never went, and which remained strange regions, leading towards the blue sky. A dusky staircase, with gaunt whitewashed walls, led down and down— past doors whose lintels all bore little tin cases containing holy Hebrew words—into the narrow court of the oldest Ghetto in the world. A few yards to the right was a portico leading to the bank of a canal, but a grim iron gate barred the way. The water of another canal came right up to the back of the Ghetto, and cut off all egress that way; and the other porticoes leading to the outer world were likewise provided with gates, guarded by Venetian watchmen. These gates were closed at midnight and opened in the morning, unless it was the Sabbath or a Christian holiday, when they remained shut all day, so that no Jew could go in or out of the court, the street, the big and little square, and the one or two tiny alleys that made up the Ghetto. There were no roads in the Ghetto, any more than in the rest of Venice; nothing but pavements ever echoing the tramp of feet. At night the watchmen rowed round and round its canals in large barcas, which the Jews had to pay for. But the child did not feel a prisoner. As he had no wish to go outside the gates, he did not feel the chain that would have drawn him back again, like a dog to a kennel; and although all the men and women he knew wore yellow hats and large O's on their breasts when they went into the world beyond, yet for a long time the child scarcely realized that there were people in the world who were not Jews, still less that these hats and these rounds of yellow cloth were badges of shame to mark off the Jews from the other people. He did not even know that all little boys did not wear under their waistcoats "Four-corners," colored shoulder-straps with squares of stuff at each end, and white fringes at each corner, and that they did not say, "Hear, O Israel, the Lord is our God, the Lord is One," as they kissed the fringes. No, the Ghetto was all his world, and a mighty universe it was, full of everything that the heart of a child could desire. What an eager swarm of life in the great sunny square where the Venetian mast towered skywards, and pigeons sometimes strutted among the crowd that hovered about the countless shops under the encircling colonnade—pawnshops, old-clo' shops, butcher-shops, wherein black-bearded men with yellow turbans bargained in Hebrew! What a fascination in the tall, many-windowed houses, with their peeling plastered fronts and patches of bald red brick, their green and brown shutters, their rusty balconies, their splashes of many-colored washing! In the morning and evening, when the padlocked well was opened, what delight to watch the women drawing water, or even to help tug at the chain that turned the axle. And on the bridge that led from the Old Ghetto to the New, where the canal, though the view was brief, disappeared round two corners, how absorbing to stand and speculate on what might be coming round either corner, and which would yield a vision first! Perhaps there would come along a sandolo rowed by a man standing at the back, his two oars crossed gracefully; perhaps a floating raft with barefooted boys bestriding it; perhaps a barca punted by men in blue blouses, one at front and two at the back, with a load of golden hay, or with provisions for the Ghetto—glowing fruit and picturesque vegetables, or bleating sheep and bellowing bulls, coming to be killed by the Jewish method. The canal that bounded the Ghetto at the back offered a much more extended view, but one hardly dared to stand there, because the other shore was foreign, and the strange folk called Venetians lived there, and some of these heathen roughs might throw stones across if they saw you. Still, at night one could creep there and look along the moonlit water and up at the stars. Of the world that lay on the other side of the water, he only knew that it was large and hostile and cruel, though from his high window he loved to look out towards its great unknown spaces, mysterious with the domes and spires of mighty buildings, or towards those strange mountains that rose seawards, white and misty, like the hills of dream, and which he thought must be like Mount Sinai, where God spake to Moses. He never thought that fairies might live in them, or gnomes or pixies, for he had never heard of such creatures. There were good spirits and bad spirits in the world, but they floated invisibly in the air, trying to make little boys good or sinful. They were always fighting with one another for little boys' souls. But on the Sabbath your bad angel had no power, and your guardian Sabbath angel hovered triumphantly around, assisting your every-day good angel, as you might tell by noticing how you cast two shadows instead of one when the two Sabbath candles were lighted. How beautiful were those Friday evenings, how snowy the table-cloth, how sweet everything tasted, and how restful the atmosphere! Such delicious peace for father and mother after the labors of the week!

It was the Sabbath Fire-woman who forced clearly upon the child's understanding—what was long but a dim idea in the background of his mind—that the world was not all Jews. For while the people who lived inside the gates had been chosen and consecrated to the service of the God of Israel, who had brought them out of Egyptian bondage and made them slaves to Himself, outside the gates were people who were not expected to obey the law of Moses; so that while he might not touch the fire—nor even the candlesticks which had held fire—from Friday evening to Saturday night, the Fire-woman could poke and poke at the logs to her heart's content. She poked her way up from the ground-floor through all the seven stories, and went on higher, a sort of fire-spirit poking her way skywards. She had other strange privileges, this little old woman with the shawl over her head, as the child discovered gradually. For she could eat pig-flesh or shell-fish or fowls or cattle killed anyhow; she could even eat butter directly after meat, instead of having to wait six hours—nay, she could have butter and meat on the same plate, whereas the child's mother had quite a different set of pots and dishes for meat things or butter things. Yes, the Fire-woman was indeed an inferior creature, existing mainly to boil the Ghetto's tea-kettles and snuff its candles, and was well rewarded by the copper coin which she gathered from every hearth as soon as one might touch money. For when three stars appeared in the sky the Fire-woman sank back into her primitive insignificance, and the child's father made the Habdalah, or ceremony of division between week-day and Sabbath, thanking God who divideth holiday from working-day, and light from darkness. Over a brimming wine-cup he made the blessing, holding his bent fingers to a wax taper to make a symbolical appearance of shine and shadow, and passing round a box of sweet-smelling spices. And, when the chanting was over, the child was given to sip of the wine. Many delicious mouthfuls of wine were associated in his mind with religion. He had them in the synagogue itself on Friday nights and on Festival nights, and at home as well, particularly at Passover, on the first two evenings of which his little wine-glass was replenished no less than four times with mild, sweet liquid. A large glass also stood ready for Elijah the Prophet, which the invisible visitor drank, though the wine never got any lower. It was a delightful period altogether, this feast of Passover, from the day before it, when the last crumbs of bread and leavened matter were solemnly burnt (for no one might eat bread for eight days) till the very last moment of the eighth day, when the long-forbidden bread tasted as sweet and strange as cake. The mere change of kitchen vessels had a charm: new saucepans, new plates, new dishes, new spoons, new everything, in harmony with the Passover cakes that took the place of bread—large thick biscuits, baked without yeast, full of holes, or speckled and spotted. And when the evening table was laid for the Seder service, looking oh! so quaint and picturesque, with wine-cups and strange dishes, the roasted shank-bone of a lamb, bitter herbs, sweet spices, and what not, and with everybody lolling around it on white pillows, the child's soul was full of a tender poetry, and it was a joy to him to ask in Hebrew:—"Wherein doth this night differ from all other nights? For on all other nights we may eat leavened and unleavened, but to-night only unleavened?" He asked the question out of a large thin book, gay with pictures of the Ten Plagues of Egypt and the wicked Pharaoh sitting with a hard heart on a hard throne. His father's reply, which was also in Hebrew, lasted some two or three hours, being mixed up with eating and drinking the nice things and the strange dishes; which was the only part of the reply the child really understood, for the Hebrew itself was very difficult. But he knew generally what the Feast was about, and his question was only a matter of form, for he grew up asking it year after year, with a feigned surprise. Nor, though he learned to understand Hebrew well, and could even translate his daily prayers into bad Italian, a corruption of the Venetian dialect finding its way into the Ghetto through the mouths of the people who did business with the outside world, did he ever really think of the sense of his prayers as he gabbled them off, morning, noon, and night. There was so much to say—whole books full. It was a great temptation to skip the driest pages, but he never yielded to it, conscientiously scampering even through the passages in the tiniest type that had a diffident air of expecting attention from only able-bodied adults. Part of the joy of Sabbaths and Festivals was the change of prayer-diet. Even the Grace—that long prayer chanted after bodily diet—had refreshing little variations. For, just as the child put on his best clothes for Festivals, so did his prayers seem to clothe themselves in more beautiful words, and to be said out of more beautiful books, and with more beautiful tunes to them. Melody played a large part in the synagogue services, so that, although he did not think of the meaning of the prayers, they lived in his mind as music, and, sorrowful or joyous, they often sang themselves in his brain in after years. There were three consecutive "Amens" in the afternoon service of the three Festivals—Passover, Pentecost, Tabernacles—that had a quaint charm for him. The first two were sounded staccato, the last rounded off the theme, and died away, slow and lingering. Nor, though there were double prayers to say on these occasions, did they weigh upon him as a burden, for the extra bits were insinuated between the familiar bits, like hills or flowers suddenly sprung up in unexpected places to relieve the monotony of a much-travelled road. And then these extra prayers were printed so prettily, they rhymed so profusely. Many were clever acrostics, going right through the alphabet from Aleph, which is A, to Tau, which is T, for Z comes near the beginning of the Hebrew alphabet. These acrostics, written in the Middle Ages by pious rabbis, permeated the Festival prayer-books, and even when the child had to confess his sins—or rather those of the whole community, for each member of the brotherhood of Israel was responsible for the rest—he sinned his sin with an "A," he sinned his sin with a "B," and so on till he could sin no longer. And, when the prayers rhymed, how exhilarating it was to lay stress on each rhyme and double rhyme, shouting them fervidly. And sometimes, instead of rhyming, they ended with the same phrase, like the refrain of a ballad, or the chorus of a song, and then what a joyful relief, after a long breathless helter-skelter through a strange stanza, to come out on the old familiar ground, and to shout exultantly, "For His mercy endureth for ever," or "The appearance of the priest!" Sometimes the run was briefer—through one line only—and ended on a single word like "water" or "fire." And what pious fun it was to come down sharp upon fire or water! They stood out friendly and simple, the rest was such curious and involved Hebrew that sometimes, in an audacious moment, the child wondered whether even his father understood it all, despite that he wept freely and bitterly over certain acrostics, especially on the Judgment Days. It was awe-inspiring to think that the angels, who were listening up in heaven, understood every word of it. And he inclined to think that the Cantor, or minister who led the praying, also understood; he sang with such feeling and such fervid roulades. Many solos did the Cantor troll forth, to which the congregation listened in silent rapture. The only time the public prayers bored the child was on the Sabbath, when the minister read the Portion of the Week; the Five Books of Moses being read through once a year, week by week, in a strange sing-song with only occasional flights of melody. The chant was determined by curious signs printed under the words, and the signs that made nice music were rather rare, and the nicest sign of all, which spun out the word with endless turns and trills, like the carol of a bird, occurred only a few times in the whole Pentateuch. The child, as he listened to the interminable incantation, thought he would have sprinkled the Code with bird-songs, and made the Scroll of the Law warble. But he knew this could not be. For the Scroll was stern and severe and dignified, like the high members of the congregation who bore it aloft, or furled it, and adjusted its wrapper and its tinkling silver bells. Even the soberest musical signs were not marked on it, nay, it was bare of punctuation, and even of vowels. Only the Hebrew consonants were to be seen on the sacred parchment, and they were written, not printed, for the printing-press is not like the reverent hand of the scribe. The child thought it was a marvellous feat to read it, much less know precisely how to chant it. Seven men—first a man of the tribe of Aaron the High Priest, then a Levite, and then five ordinary Israelites—were called up to the platform to stand by while the Scroll was being intoned, and their arrivals and departures broke the monotony of the recitative. After the Law came the Prophets, which revived the child's interest, for they had another and a quainter melody, in the minor mode, full of half tones and delicious sadness that ended in a peal of exultation. For the Prophets, though they thundered against the iniquities of Israel, and preached "Woe, woe," also foretold comfort when the period of captivity and contempt should be over, and the Messiah would come and gather His people from the four corners of the earth, and the Temple should be rebuilt in Jerusalem, and all the nations would worship the God who had given His law to the Jews on Mount Sinai. In the meantime, only Israel was bound to obey it in every letter, because only the Jews—born or unborn—had agreed to do so amid the thunders and lightnings of Sinai. Even the child's unborn soul had been present and accepted the yoke of the Torah. He often tried to recall the episode, but although he could picture the scene quite well, and see the souls curling over the mountains like white clouds, he could not remember being among them. No doubt he had forgotten it, with his other pre-natal experiences—like the two Angels who had taught him Torah and shown him Paradise of a morning and Hell every evening—when at the moment of his birth the Angel's finger had struck him on the upper lip and sent him into the world crying at the pain, and with that dent under the nostrils which, in every human face, is the seal of oblivion of the celestial spheres. But on the anniversary of the great Day of the Decalogue—on the Feast of Pentecost—the synagogue was dressed with flowers. Flowers were not easy to get in Venice—that city of stones and the sea—yet every synagogue (and there were seven of them in that narrow Ghetto, some old and beautiful, some poor and humble) had its pillars or its balconies twined with roses, narcissi, lilies, and pansies. Prettier still were the customs of "Tabernacles," when the wooden booths were erected in the square or the courtyards of the synagogues in commemoration of the days when the Children of Israel lived in tents in the wilderness. The child's father, being particularly pious, had a booth all to himself, thatched with green boughs, and hung with fruit, and furnished with chairs and a table at which the child sat, with the blue sky playing peep-bo through the leaves, and the white table-cloth astir with quivering shadows and glinting sunbeams. And towards the last days of the Festival he began to eat away the roof, consuming the dangling apples and oranges, and the tempting grapes. And throughout this beautiful Festival the synagogue rustled with palm branches, tied with boughs of willows of the brook and branches of other pleasant trees—as commanded in Leviticus—which the men waved and shook, pointing them east and west and north and south, and then heavenwards, and smelling also of citron kept in boxes lined with white wool. As one could not breakfast before blessing the branches and the citron, a man carried them round to such of the women-folk as household duties kept at home—and indeed, home was a woman's first place, and to light the Sabbath lamp a woman's holiest duty, and even at synagogue she sat in a grated gallery away from the men downstairs. On the seventh day of Tabernacles the child had a little bundle of leafy boughs styled "Hosannas," which he whipped on the synagogue bench, his sins falling away with the leaves that flew to the ground as he cried, "Hosanna, save us now!" All through the night his father prayed in the synagogue, but the child went home to bed, after a gallant struggle with his closing eyelids, hoping not to see his headless shadow on the stones, for that was a sign of death. But the ninth day of Tabernacles was the best, "The Rejoicing of the Law," when the fifty-second portion of the Pentateuch was finished and the first portion begun immediately all over again, to show that the "rejoicing" was not because the congregation was glad to be done with it. The man called up to the last portion was termed "The Bridegroom of the Law," and to the first portion "The Bridegroom of the Beginning," and they made a wedding-feast to which everybody was invited. The boys scrambled for sweets on the synagogue floor. The Scrolls of the Law were carried round and round seven times, and the boys were in the procession with flags and wax tapers in candlesticks of hollow carrots, joining lustily in the poem with its alternative refrain of "Save us, we pray Thee," "Prosper us, we pray Thee." So gay was the minister that he could scarcely refrain from dancing, and certainly his voice danced as it sang. There was no other time so gay, except it was Purim—the feast to celebrate Queen Esther's redemption of her people from the wicked Haman—when everybody sent presents to everybody else, and the men wore comic masks or dressed up as women and performed little plays. The child went about with a great false nose, and when the name of "Haman" came up in the reading of the Book of Esther, which was intoned in a refreshingly new way, he tapped vengefully with a little hammer or turned the handle of a little toy that made a grinding noise. The other feast in celebration of a Jewish redemption—Chanukah, or Dedication—was almost as impressive, for in memory of the miracle of the oil that kept the perpetual light burning in the Temple when Judas Maccabæus reconquered it from the Greek gods, the Ghetto lighted candles, one on the first night and two on the second, and so on till there were eight burning in a row, to say nothing of the candle that kindled the others and was called "The Beadle," and the child sang hymns of praise to the Rock of Salvation as he watched the serried flames. And so, in this inner world of dreams the child lived and grew, his vision turned back towards ancient Palestine and forwards towards some vague Restoration, his days engirdled with prayer and ceremony, his very games of ball or nuts sanctified by Sandalphon, the boy-angel, to whom he prayed: "O Sandalphon, Lord of the Forest, protect us from pain."

There were two things in the Ghetto that had a strange attraction for the child: one was a large marble slab on the wall near his house, which he gradually made out to be a decree that Jews converted to Christianity should never return to the Ghetto nor consort with its inhabitants, under penalty of the cord, the gallows, the prison, the scourge, or the pillory; the other was a marble figure of a beautiful girl with falling draperies that lay on the extreme wall of the Ghetto, surveying it with serene eyes.

Relic and emblem of an earlier era, she co-operated with the slab to remind the child of the strange vague world outside, where people of forbidden faith carved forbidden images. But he never went outside; at least never more than a few streets, for what should he do in Venice? As he grew old enough to be useful, his father employed him in his pawn-shop, and for recreation there was always the synagogue and the study of the Bible with its commentaries, and the endless volumes of the Talmud, that chaos of Rabbinical lore and legislation. And when he approached his thirteenth year, he began to prepare to become a "Son of the Commandment." For at thirteen the child was considered a man. His sins, the responsibility of which had hitherto been upon his father's shoulders, would now fall upon his own, and from counting for as little as a woman in the congregation, he would become a full unit in making up the minimum of ten men, without which public worship could not be held. And so, not only did he come to own a man's blue-striped praying-shawl to wrap himself in, but he began to "lay phylacteries," winding the first leather strap round his left arm and its fingers, so that the little cubical case containing the holy words sat upon the fleshy part of the upper arm, and binding the second strap round his forehead with the black cube in the centre like the stump of a unicorn's horn, and thinking the while of God's Unity and the Exodus from Egypt, according to the words of Deuteronomy xi. 18, "And these my words ... ye shall bind for a sign upon your hand, and they shall be as frontlets between your eyes." Also he began to study his "Portion," for on the first Sabbath of his thirteenth year he would be summoned, as a man, to the recitation of the Sacred Scroll, only instead of listening, he would have to intone a section from the parchment manuscript, bare of vowels and musical signs. The boy was shy, and the thought of appearing brazenly on the platform before the whole congregation was terrifying. Besides, he might make mistakes in the words or the tunes. It was an anxious time, scarcely redeemed by the thought of new clothes, "Son-of-the-Commandment" presents, and merry-makings. Sometimes he woke up in the middle of the night in a cold sweat, having dreamed that he stood on the platform in forgetful dumbness, every eye fixed upon him. Then he would sing his "Portion" softly to himself to reassure himself. And, curiously enough, it began, "And it was in the middle of the night." In verity he knew it as glibly as the alphabet, for he was infinitely painstaking. Never a lesson unlearnt, nor a duty undone, and his eager eyes looked forward to a life of truth and obedience. And as for Hebrew without vowels, that had long since lost its terrors; vowels were only for children and fools, and he was an adept in Talmud, cunning in dispute and the dovetailing of texts—quite a little Rabbi, they said in the Ghetto! And when the great moment actually came, after a few timid twists and turns of melody he found his voice soaring aloft triumphantly, and then it became to him a subtle pleasure to hold and dominate all the listening crowd. Afterwards his father and mother received many congratulations on the way he had "said his Portion."

And now that he was a man other parts of Judaism came into prominence in his life. He became a member of the "Holy Society," which washed and watched the bodies of the dead ere they were put to rest in the little island cemetery, which was called "The House of Life" because there is no death in the universe, for, as he sang triumphantly on Friday evenings, "God will make the dead alive in the abundance of His kindness." And now, too, he could take a man's part in the death services of the mourners, who sat for seven days upon the ground and said prayers for the souls of the deceased. The boy wondered what became of these souls; some, he feared, went to perdition, for he knew their owners had done and eaten forbidden things. It was a comfort to think that even in hell there is no fire on the Sabbath, and no Fire-woman. When the Messiah came, perhaps they would all be forgiven. Did not the Talmud say that all Israel—with the good men of all nations—would have a part in the world to come?

There were many fasts in the Ghetto calendar, most of them twelve hours long, but some twenty-four. Not a morsel of food nor a drop of water must pass the lips from the sunset of one day to nightfall on the next. The child had only been allowed to keep a few fasts, and these only partially, but now it was for his own soul to settle how long and how often it would afflict itself, and it determined to do so at every opportunity. And the great opportunity came soon. Not the Black Fast when the congregation sat shoeless on the floor of the synagogue, weeping and wailing for the destruction of Jerusalem, but the great White Fast, the terrible Day of Atonement commanded in the Bible. It was preceded by a long month of solemn prayer, ushering in the New Year. The New Year itself was the most sacred of the Festivals, provided with prayers half a day long, and made terrible by peals on the ram's horn. There were three kinds of calls on this primitive trumpet—plain, trembling, wailing; and they were all sounded in curious mystic combinations, interpolated with passionate bursts of prayer. The sinner was warned to repent, for the New Year marked the Day of Judgment. For nine days God judged the souls of the living, and decided on their fate for the coming year—who should live and who should die, who should grow rich and who poor, who should be in sickness and who in health. But at the end of the tenth day, the day of the great White Fast, the judgment books were closed, to open no more for the rest of the year. Up till twilight there was yet time, but then what was written was finally sealed, and he who had not truly repented had missed his last chance of forgiveness. What wonder if early in the ten penitential days, the population of the Ghetto flocked towards the canal bridge to pray that its sins might be cast into the waters and swept away seawards!

'Twas the tenth day, and an awful sense of sacred doom hung over the Ghetto. In every house a gigantic wax taper had burnt, white and solemn, all through the night, and fowls or coins had been waved round the heads of the people in atonement for their iniquities. The morning dawned gray and cold, but with the dawn the population was astir, for the services began at six in the morning and lasted without intermission till seven at night. Many of the male worshippers were clad in their grave-clothes, and the extreme zealots remained standing all day long, swaying to and fro and beating their breasts at the confessions of sin. For a long time the boy wished to stand too, but the crowded synagogue reeked with heavy odors, and at last, towards mid-day, faint and feeble, he had to sit. But to fast till nightfall he was resolved. Hitherto he had always broken his fast at some point in the services, going home round the corner to delicious bread and fish. When he was seven or eight this breakfast came at mid-day, but the older he grew the longer he fasted, and it became a point of honor to beat his record every successive year. Last time he had brought his breakfast down till late in the afternoon, and now it would be unforgivable if he could not see the fast out and go home, proud and sinless, to drink wine with the men. He turned so pale, as the afternoon service dragged itself along, that his father begged him again and again to go home and eat. But the boy was set on a full penance. And every now and again he forgot his headache and the gnawing at his stomach in the fervor of passionate prayer and in the fascination of the ghostly figures weeping and wailing in the gloomy synagogue, and once in imagination he saw the heavens open overhead and God sitting on the judgment throne, invisible by excess of dazzling light, and round him the four-winged cherubim and the fiery wheels and the sacred creatures singing "Holy, holy, holy is the Lord of Hosts, the whole earth is full of His glory." Then a great awe brooded over the synagogue, and the vast forces of the universe seemed concentred about it, as if all creation was awaiting in tense silence for the terrible words of judgment. And then he felt some cool, sweet scent sprinkled on his forehead, and, as from the far ends of the world, he heard a voice that sounded like his father's asking him if he felt better. He opened his eyes and smiled faintly, and said nothing was the matter, but now his father insisted that he must go home to eat. So, still dazed by the glories he had seen, he dragged himself dreamily through the press of swaying, weeping worshippers, over whom there still seemed to brood some vast, solemn awe, and came outside into the little square and drew in a delicious breath of fresh air, his eyes blinking at the sudden glare of sunlight and blue sky. But the sense of awe was still with him, for the Ghetto was deserted, the shops were shut, and a sacred hush of silence was over the stones and the houses, only accentuated by the thunder of ceaseless prayer from the synagogues. He walked towards the tall house with the nine stories, then a great shame came over him. Surely he had given in too early. He was already better, the air had revived him. No, he would not break his fast; he would while away a little time by walking, and then he would go back to the synagogue. Yes, a brisk walk would complete his recovery. There was no warder at the open gate; the keepers of the Ghetto had taken a surreptitious holiday, aware that on this day of days no watching was needed. The guardian barca lay moored to a post unmanned. All was in keeping with the boy's sense of solemn strangeness. But as he walked along the Cannaregio bank, and further and further into the unknown city, a curious uneasiness and surprise began to invade his soul. Everywhere, despite the vast awe overbrooding the world, shops were open and people were going about unconcernedly in the quaint alleys; babies laughed in their nurses' arms, the gondoliers were poised as usual on the stern of their beautiful black boats, rowing imperturbably. The water sparkled and danced in the afternoon sun. In the market-place the tanned old women chattered briskly with their customers. He wandered on and on in growing wonder and perturbation. Suddenly his trouble ceased, a burst of wonderful melody came to him; there was not only a joyful tune, but other tunes seemed to blend with it, melting his heart with unimaginable rapture; he gave chase to the strange sounds, drawing nearer and nearer, and at last he emerged unexpectedly upon an immense square bordered by colonnades, under which beautifully dressed signori and signore sat drinking at little tables, and listening to men in red with great black cockades in their hats who were ranged on a central platform, blowing large shining horns; a square so vast and so crowded with happy chattering people and fluttering pigeons that he gazed about in blinking bewilderment. And then, uplifting his eyes, he saw a sight that took his breath away—a glorious building like his dream of the Temple of Zion, glowing with gold and rising in marvellous domes and spires, and crowned by four bronze animals, which he felt sure must be the creatures called horses with which Pharaoh had pursued the Israelites to the Red Sea. And hard by rose a gigantic tower, like the Tower of Babel, leading the eye up and up. His breast filled with a strange pleasure that was almost pain. The enchanted temple drew him across the square; he saw a poor bare-headed woman going in, and he followed her. Then a wonderful golden gloom fell upon him, and a sense of arches and pillars and soaring roofs and curved walls beautiful with many-colored pictures; and the pleasure, that was almost pain, swelled at his heart till it seemed as if it must burst his breast. Then he saw the poor bare-headed woman kneel down, and in a flash he understood that she was praying—ay, and in the men's quarter— and that this was no Temple, but one of those forbidden places called churches, into which the abhorred deserters went who were spoken of on that marble slab in the Ghetto. And, while he was wrestling with the confusion of his thoughts, a splendid glittering being, with a cocked hat and a sword, marched terrifyingly towards him, and sternly bade him take off his hat. He ran out of the wonderful building in a great fright, jostling against the innumerable promenaders in the square, and not pausing till the merry music of the big shining horns had died away behind him. And even then he walked quickly, as if pursued by the strange vast world into which he had penetrated for the first time. And suddenly he found himself in a blind alley, and knew that he could not find his way back to the Ghetto. He was about to ask of a woman who looked kind, when he remembered, with a chill down his spine, that he was not wearing a yellow O, as a man should, and that, as he was now a "Son of the Commandment," the Venetians would consider him a man. For one forlorn moment it seemed to him that he would never find himself back in the Ghetto again; but at last he bethought himself of asking for the Cannaregio, and so gradually, cold at heart and trembling, he reached the familiar iron gate and slipped in. All was as before in the Ghetto. The same sacred hush in court and square, accentuated by the rumble of prayer from the synagogues, the gathering dusk lending a touch of added solemnity.

"Well, have you eaten?" asked the father. The boy nodded "Yes." A faint flush of exultation leapt into his pale cheek. He would see the fast out after all. The men were beating their breasts at the confession of sin. "For the sin we have committed by lying," chimed in the boy. But although in his attention to the wailful melody of the words he scarcely noticed the meaning, something of the old passion and fervor had gone out of his voice. Twilight fell; the shadows deepened, the white figures, wailing and weeping in their grave-clothes, grew mystic; the time for sealing the Books of Judgment drew nigh. The figures threw themselves forward full length, their foreheads to the floor, proclaiming passionately again and again, "The Lord He is God; the Lord He is God!" It was the hour in which the boy's sense of overbrooding awe had always been tensest. But he could not shake off the thought of the gay piazza and the wonderful church where other people prayed other prayers. For something larger had come into his life, a sense of a vaster universe without, and its spaciousness and strangeness filled his soul with a nameless trouble and a vague unrest. He was no longer a child of the Ghetto.

JOSEPH THE DREAMER

I

"We must not wait longer, Rachel," said Manasseh in low, grave, but unfaltering accents. "Midnight approaches."

Rachel checked her sobs and assumed an attitude of reverence as her husband began to intone the benedictions, but her heart felt no religious joy in the remembrance of how the God of her fathers had saved them and their Temple from Hellenic pollution. It was torn by anxiety as to the fate of her boy, her scholar son, unaccountably absent for the first time from the household ceremonies of the Feast of Dedication. What was he doing—outside the Ghetto gates—in that great, dark, narrow-meshed city of Rome, defying the Papal law, and of all nights in the year on that sinister night when, by a coincidence of chronology, the Christian persecutor celebrated the birth of his Saviour? Through misty eyes she saw her husband's face, stern and rugged, yet made venerable by the flowing white of his locks and beard, as with the supernumerary taper he prepared to light the wax candles in the nine-branched candlestick of silver. He wore a long, hooded mantle reaching to the feet, and showing where it fell back in front a brown gaberdine clasped by a girdle. These sombre-colored robes were second-hand, as the austere simplicity of the Pragmatic required. The Jewish Council of Sixty did not permit its subjects to ruffle it like the Romans of those days of purple pageantry. The young bloods, forbidden by Christendom to style themselves signori, were forbidden by Judea to vie with signori in luxury.

"Blessed art Thou, O Lord, our God," chanted the old man. "King of the Universe, who hast sanctified us with Thy commandments, and commanded us to kindle the light of Chanukah."

It was with a quavering voice that Rachel joined in the ancient hymn that wound up the rite. "O Fortress, Rock of my salvation," the old woman sang. "Unto Thee it is becoming to give praise; let my house of prayer be restored, and I will there offer Thee thanksgivings; when Thou shalt have prepared a slaughter of the blaspheming foe, I will complete with song and psalm the dedication of the altar."

But her imagination was roving in the dim oil-lit streets of the tenebrous city, striving for the clairvoyance of love. Arrest by the sbirri was certain; other dangers threatened. Brawls and bravos abounded. True, this city of Rome was safer than many another for its Jews, who, by a miracle, more undeniable than that which they were now celebrating, had from the birth of Christ dwelt in the very heart of Christendom, the Eternal People in the Eternal City. The Ghetto had witnessed no such sights as Barcelona or Frankfort or Prague. The bloody orgies of the Crusaders had raged far away from the Capital of the Cross. In England, in France, in Germany, the Jew, that scapegoat of the nations, had poisoned the wells and brought on the Black Death, had pierced the host, killed children for their blood, blasphemed the saints, and done all that the imagination of defalcating debtors could suggest. But the Roman Jews were merely pestilent heretics. Perhaps it was the comparative poverty of the Ghetto that made its tragedy one of steady degradation rather than of fitful massacre. Nevertheless bloodshed was not unknown, and the song died on Rachel's lips, though the sterner Manasseh still chanted on.

"The Grecians were gathered against me in the days of the Hasmoneans; they broke down the walls of my towers and defiled all the oils; but from one of the last remaining flasks a miracle was wrought for Thy lily, Israel; and the men of understanding appointed these eight days for songs and praises."

They were well-to-do people, and Rachel's dress betokened the limit of the luxury allowed by the Pragmatic—a second-hand silk dress with a pin at the throat set with only a single pearl, a bracelet on one arm, a ring without a bezel on one finger, a single-stringed necklace round her neck, her hair done in a cheap net.

She looked at the nine-branched candlestick, and a mystical sadness filled her. Would she had nine scions of her house like Miriam's mother, a true mother in Israel; but, lo! she had only one candle—one little candle. A puff and it was gone, and life would be dark.

That Joseph was not in the Ghetto was certain. He would never have caused her such anxiety wilfully, and, indeed, she and her husband and Miriam had already run to all the likely places in the quarter, even to those marshy alleys where every overflow of the Tiber left deposits of malarious mud, where families harbored, ten in a house, where stunted men and wrinkled women slouched through the streets, and a sickly spawn of half-naked babies swarmed under the feet. They had had trouble enough, but never such a trouble as this. Manasseh and Rachel, with this queer offspring of theirs, this Joseph the Dreamer, as he had been nicknamed, this handsome, reckless black-eyed son of theirs, with his fine oval face, his delicate olive features; this young man, who could not settle down to the restricted forms of commerce possible in the Ghetto, who was to be Rabbi of the community one day, albeit his brilliance was occasionally dazzling to the sober tutors upon whom he flashed his sudden thought, which stirred up that which had better been left asleep. Why was he not as other sons, why did he pace the street with unobservant eyes, why did he weep over the profane Hebrew of the Spanish love-singers as if their songs were Selichoth or Penitential Verses? Why did he not marry Miriam, as one could see the girl wished? Why did he set at naught the custom of the Ghetto, in silently refraining from so obvious a match between the children of two old friends, equally well-to-do, and both possessing the Jus Gazzaga or leasehold of the houses in which they lived; tall, quaint houses, separated only by an ancient building with a carved porch, and standing at the end of the great Via Rua where it adjoined the narrow little street, Delle Azzimelle, in which the Passover cakes were made. Miriam's family, being large, had their house to themselves, but a good deal of Manasseh's was let out; for room was more and more precious in the Ghetto, which was a fixed space for an ever-expanding population.

II

They went to bed. Manasseh insisted upon that. They could not possibly expect Joseph till the morning. Accustomed as Rachel was to lean upon her husband's strength, at this moment his strength seemed harshness. The night was long. A hundred horrid visions passed before her sleepless eyes. The sun rose upon the Ghetto, striving to slip its rays between the high, close-pressed tops of opposite houses. The five Ghetto gates were thrown open, but Joseph did not come through any. The Jewish pedlars issued, adjusting their yellow hats, and pushing before them little barrows laden with special Christmas wares. "Heb, heb," they shouted as they passed through the streets of Rome. Some sold simples and philtres, and amulets in the shape of miniature mandores or four-stringed lutes to preserve children from maladies. Manasseh, his rugged countenance grown harder, went to his place of business. He had forbidden any inquiries to be made outside the pale till later in the day; it would be but to betray to the enemy Joseph's breach of the law. In the meantime, perhaps, the wanderer would return. Manasseh's establishment was in the Piazza Giudea. Numerous shops encumbered the approaches, mainly devoted to the sale of cast-off raiment, the traffic in new things being prohibited to Jews by Papal Bull, but anything second-hand might be had here from the rough costume of a shepherd of Abruzzo to the faded fripperies of a gentleman of the Court. In the centre a new fountain with two dragons supplied the Ghetto with water from the Aqueduct of Paul the Fifth in lieu of the loathly Tiber water, and bore a grateful Latin inscription. About the edges of the square a few buildings rose in dilapidated splendor to break the monotony of the Ghetto barracks; the ancient palace of the Boccapaduli, and a mansion with a high tower and three abandoned churches. A monumental but forbidding gate, closed at sundown, gave access to a second Piazza Giudea, where Christians congregated to bargain with Jews—it was almost a suburb of the Ghetto. Manasseh had not far to go, for his end of the Via Rua debouched on the Piazza Giudea; the other end, after running parallel to the Via Pescheria and the river, bent suddenly near the Gate of Octavius, and finished on the bridge Quattro Capi. Such was the Ghetto in the sixteen hundreds.

Soon after Manasseh had left the house, Miriam came in with anxious face to inquire if Joseph had returned. It was a beautiful Oriental face, in whose eyes brooded the light of love and pity, a face of the type which painters have given to the Madonna when they have remembered that the Holy Mother was a Jewess. She was clad in a simple woollen gown, without lace or broidery, her only ornament a silver bracelet. Rachel wept to tell her the lack of news, but Miriam did not join in her tears. She besought her to be of good courage.

And very soon indeed Joseph appeared, with an expression at once haggard and ecstatic, his black hair and beard unkempt, his eyes glittering strangely in his flushed olive face, a curious poetic figure in his reddish-brown mantle and dark yellow cap.

"Pax vobiscum," he cried, in shrill, jubilant accents.

"Joseph, what drunken folly is this?" faltered Rachel.

"Gloria in altissimis Deo and peace on earth to all men of goodwill," persisted Joseph. "It is Christmas morning, mother." And he began to troll out the stave of a carol, "Simeon, that good saint of old—"

Rachel's hand was clapped rudely over her son's mouth.

"Blasphemer!" she cried, an ashen gray overspreading her face.

Joseph gently removed her hand. "It is thou who blasphemest, mother," he cried. "Rejoice, rejoice, this day the dear Lord Christ was born—He who was to die for the sins of the world."

Rachel burst into fresh tears. "Our boy is mad—our boy is mad. What have they done to him?" All her anticipations of horror were outpassed by this.

Pain shadowed the sweet silence of Miriam's face as she stood in the recess of the window.

"Mad! Oh, my mother, I am as one awakened. Rejoice, rejoice with me. Let us sink ourselves in the universal joy, let us be at one with the human race."

Rachel smiled tentatively through her tears. "Enough of this foolery," she said pleadingly. "It is the feast of Dedication, not of Lots. There needs no masquerading to-day."

"Joseph, what ails thee?" interposed the sweet voice of Miriam. "What hast thou done? Where hast thou been?"

"Art thou here, Miriam?" His eyes became conscious of her for the first time. "Would thou hadst been there with me!"

"Where?"

"At St. Peter's. Oh, the heavenly music!"

"At St. Peter's!" repeated Rachel hoarsely. "Thou, my son Joseph, the student of God's Law, hast defiled thyself thus?"

"Nay, it is no defilement," interposed Miriam soothingly. "Hast thou not told us how our fathers went to the Sistine Chapel on Sabbath afternoons?"

"Ay, but that was when Michel Angelo Buonarotti was painting his frescoes of the deliverances of Israel. And they went likewise to see the figure of our Lawgiver in the Pope's mausoleum. And I have even heard of Jews who have stolen into St. Peter's itself to gaze on that twisted pillar from Solomon's temple, which these infidels hold for our sins. But it is the midnight mass that this Epicurean has been to hear."

"Even so," said Joseph in dreamy undertones, "the midnight mass—incense and lights and the figures of saints, and wonderful painted windows, and a great multitude of weeping worshippers and music that wept with them, now shrill like the passionate cry of martyrs, now breathing the peace of the Holy Ghost."

"How didst thou dare show thyself in the cathedral?" whimpered Rachel.

"Who should dream of a Jew in the immense throng? Outside it was dark, within it was dim. I hid my face and wept. They looked at the cardinals in their splendid robes, at the Pope, at the altar. Who had eyes for me?"

"But thy yellow cap, Joseph!"

"One wears not the cap in church, mother."

"Thou didst blasphemously bare thy head, and in worship?"

"I did not mean to worship, mother mine. A great curiosity drew me—I desired to see with my own eyes, and hear with mine own ears, this adoration of the Christ, at which my teachers scoff. But I was caught up in a mighty wave of organ-music that surged from this low earth heavenwards to break against the footstool of God in the crystal firmament. And suddenly I knew what my soul was pining for. I knew the meaning of that restless craving that has always devoured me, though I spake not thereof, those strange hauntings, those dim perceptions—in a flash I understood the secret of peace."

"And that is—Joseph?" asked Miriam gently, for Rachel drew such laboring breath she could not speak.

"Sacrifice," said Joseph softly, with rapt gaze. "To suffer, to give one's self freely to the world; to die to myself in delicious pain, like the last tremulous notes of the sweet boy-voice that had soared to God in the Magnificat. Oh, Miriam, if I could lead our brethren out of the Ghetto, if I could die to bring them happiness, to make them free sons of Rome."

"A goodly wish, my son, but to be fulfilled by God alone."

"Even so. Let us pray for faith. When we are Christians the gates of the Ghetto will fall."

"Christians!" echoed Rachel and Miriam in simultaneous horror.

"Ay, Christians," said Joseph unflinchingly.

Rachel ran to the door and closed it more tightly. Her limbs shook. "Hush!" she breathed. "Let thy madness go no further. God of Abraham, suppose some one should overhear thee and carry thy talk to thy father." She began to wring her hands.

"Joseph, bethink thyself," pleaded Miriam, stricken to the heart. "I am no scholar, I am only a woman. But thou—thou with thy learning—surely thou hast not been befooled by these jugglers with the sacred text? Surely thou art able to answer their word-twistings of our prophets?"

"Ah, Miriam," replied Joseph tenderly. "Art thou, too, like our brethren? They do not understand. It is a question of the heart, not of texts. What is it I feel is the highest, divinest in me? Sacrifice! Wherefore He who was all sacrifice, all martyrdom, must be divine."

"Bandy not words with him, Miriam," cried his mother. "Oh, thou infidel, whom I have begotten for my sins. Why doth not Heaven's fire blast thee as thou standest there?"

"Thou talkest of martyrdom, Joseph," cried Miriam, disregarding her. "It is we Jews who are martyrs, not the Christians. We are penned here like cattle. We are marked with shameful badges. Our Talmud is burnt. Our possessions are taxed away from us. We are barred from every reputable calling. We may not even bury our dead with honor or carve an epitaph over their graves." The passion in her face matched his. Her sweetness was exchanged for fire. She had the air of a Judith or a Jael.

"It is our own cowardice that invites the spittle, Miriam. Where is the spirit of the Maccabæans whom we hymn on this feast of Chanukah? The Pope issues Bulls, and we submit—outwardly. Our resistance is silent, sinuous. He ordains yellow hats; we wear yellow hats, but gradually the yellow darkens; it becomes orange, then ochre, till at last we go capped in red like so many cardinals, provoking the edict afresh. We are restricted to one synagogue. We have five for our different country-folk, but we build them under one roof and call four of them schools."

"Hush, thou Jew-hater," cried his mother. "Say not such things aloud. My God! my God! how have I sinned before Thee?"

"What wouldst thou have, Joseph?" said Miriam. "One cannot argue with wolves. We are so few—we must meet them by cunning."

"Ah, but we set up to be God's witnesses, Miriam. Our creed is naught but prayer-mumbling and pious mummeries. The Christian Apostles went through the world testifying. Better a brief heroism than this long ignominy." He burst into sudden tears and sank into a chair overwrought.

Instantly his mother was at his side, bending down, her wet face to his.

"Thank Heaven! thank Heaven!" she sobbed. "The madness is over."

He did not answer her. He had no strength to argue more. There was a long, strained silence. Presently the mother asked—

"And where didst thou find shelter for the night?"

"At the palace of Annibale de' Franchi."

Miriam started. "The father of the beautiful Helena de' Franchi?" she asked.

"The same," said Joseph flushing.

"And how camest thou to find protection there, in so noble a house, under the roof of a familiar of the Pope?"

"Did I not tell thee, mother, how I did some slight service to his daughter at the last Carnival, when, adventuring herself masked among the crowd in the Corso, she was nigh trampled upon by the buffaloes stampeding from the race-course?"

"Nay, I remember naught thereof," said Rachel, shaking her head. "But thou mindest me how these Christians make us race like the beasts."

He ignored the implied reproach.

"Signor de' Franchi would have done much for me," he went on. "But I only begged the run of his great library. Thou knowest how hard it is for me that the Christians deny us books. And there many a day have I sat reading till the vesper bell warned me that I must hasten back to the Ghetto."

"Ah! 'twas but to pervert thee."

"Nay, mother, we talked not of religion."

"And last night thou wast too absorbed in thy reading?" put in Miriam.

"That is how it came to pass, Miriam."

"But why did not Helena warn thee?"

This time it was Joseph that started. But he replied simply—

"We were reading in Tasso. She hath rare parts. Sometimes she renders Plato and Sophocles to me."

"And thou, our future Rabbi, didst listen?" cried Rachel.

"There is no word of Christianity in these, mother, nor do they satisfy the soul. Wisely sang Jehudah Halevi, 'Go not near the Grecian wisdom.'"

"Didst thou sit near her at the mass?" inquired Miriam.

He turned his candid gaze towards her.

"She did not go," he said.

Miriam made a sudden movement to the door.

"Now that thou art safe, Joseph, I have naught further to do here. God keep thee."

Her bosom heaved. She hurried out.

"Poor Miriam!" sighed Rachel. "She is a loving, trustworthy maiden. She will not breathe a whisper of thy blasphemies."

Joseph sprang from his feet as if galvanized.

"Not breathe a whisper! But, mother, I shall shout them from the housetops."

"Hush! hush!" breathed his mother in a frenzy of alarm. "The neighbors will hear thee."

"It is what I desire."

"Thy father may come in at any moment to know if thou art safe."

"I will go allay his anxiety."

"Nay." She caught him by the mantle. "I will not let thee go. Swear to me thou wilt spare him thy blasphemies, or he may strike thee dead at his feet."

"Wouldst have me lie to him? He must know what I have told thee."

"No, no; tell him thou wast shut out, that thou didst remain in hiding."

"Truth alone is great, mother. I go to bring him the Truth." He tore his garment from her grasp and rushed without.

She sat on the floor and rocked to and fro in an agony of apprehension. The leaden hours crept along. No one came, neither son nor husband. Terrible images of what was passing between them tortured her. Towards mid-day she rose and began mechanically preparing her husband's meal. At the precise minute of year-long habit he came. To her anxious eye his stern face seemed more pallid than usual, but it revealed nothing. He washed his hands in ritual silence, made the blessing, and drew chair to table. A hundred times the question hovered about Rachel's lips, but it was not till near the end of the meal that she ventured to say, "Our son is back. Hast thou not seen him?"

"Son? What son? We have no son." He finished his meal.

III

The scholarly apostle, thus disowned by his kith and kin, was eagerly welcomed by Holy Church, the more warmly that he had come of his own inward grace and refused the tribute of annual crowns with which the Popes often rewarded true religion—at the expense of the Ghetto, which had to pay these incomes to its recreants. It was the fashion to baptize converted Jews in batches—for the greater glory—procuring them from without when home-made catechumens were scarce, sometimes serving them up with a proselyte Turk. But in view of the importance of the accession, and likewise of the closeness of Epiphany, it was resolved to give Joseph ben Manasseh the honor of a solitary baptism. The intervening days he passed in a monastery, studying his new faith, unable to communicate with his parents or his fellow Jews, even had he or they wished. A cardinal's edict forbade him to return to the Ghetto, to eat, drink, sleep, or speak with his race during the period of probation; the whip, the cord, awaited its violation. By day Rachel and Miriam walked in the precincts of the monastery, hoping to catch sight of him; nearer than ninety cubits they durst not approach under pain of bastinado and exile. A word to him, a message that might have softened him, a plea that might have turned him back—and the offender was condemned to the galleys for life.

Epiphany arrived. A great concourse filled the Basilica di Latran. The Pope himself was present, and amidst scarlet pomp and swelling music, Joseph, thrilled to the depths of his being, received the sacraments. Annibale de' Franchi, whose proud surname was henceforth to be Joseph's, stood sponsor. The presiding cardinal in his solemn sermon congratulated the congregants on the miracle which had taken place under their very eyes, and then, attired in white satin, the neophyte was slowly driven through the streets of Rome that all might witness how a soul had been saved for the true faith. And in the ecstasy of this union with the human brotherhood and the divine fatherhood, and with Christ, its symbol, Giuseppe de' Franchi saw not the dark, haggard faces of his brethren in the crowd, the hate that smouldered in their dusky eyes as the festal procession passed by. Nor while he knelt before crucifix and image that night, did he dream of that other ceremonial in the Synagogue of the Piazza of the Temple, half-way from the river; a scene more impressive in its sombreness than all the splendor of the church pageant.

The synagogue was a hidden building, indistinguishable externally from the neighboring houses; within, gold and silver glistened in the pomegranates and bells of the Scrolls of the Law or in the broidery of the curtain that covered the Ark; the glass of one of the windows, blazing with a dozen colors for the Twelve Tribes, represented the Urim and the Thummim. In the courtyard stood a model of the ancient Temple of Jerusalem, furnished with marvellous detail, memorial of lost glories.

The Council of Sixty had spoken. Joseph ben Manasseh was to suffer the last extremity of the Jewish law. All Israel was called together to the Temple. An awful air of dread hung over the assemblage; in a silence as of the grave each man upheld a black torch that flared weirdly in the shadows of the synagogue. A ram's horn sounded shrill and terrible, and to its elemental music the anathema was launched, the appalling curse withdrawing every human right from the outlaw, living or dead, and the congregants, extinguishing their torches, cried, "Amen." And in a spiritual darkness as black, Manasseh tottered home to sit with his wife on the floor and bewail the death of their Joseph, while a death-light glimmering faintly swam on a bowl of oil, and the prayers for the repose of the soul of the deceased rose passionately on the tainted Ghetto air. And Miriam, her Madonna-like face wet with hot tears, burnt the praying-shawl she was weaving in secret love for the man who might one day have loved her, and went to condole with the mourners, holding Rachel's rugged hand in those soft, sweet fingers that no lover would ever clasp.

But Rachel wept for her child, and would not be comforted.

IV

Helena de' Franchi gave the news of the ban to Giuseppe de' Franchi. She had learned it from one of her damsels, who had had it from Shloumi the Droll, a graceless, humorous rogue, steering betwixt Jews and Christians his shifty way to profit.

Giuseppe smiled a sweet smile that hovered on the brink of tears. "They know not what they do," he said.

"Thy parents mourn thee as dead."

"They mourn the dead Jew; the living Christian's love shall comfort them."

"But thou mayst not approach them, nor they thee."

"By faith are mountains moved; my spirit embraces theirs. We shall yet rejoice together in the light of the Saviour, for weeping may endure for a night, but joy cometh in the morning." His pale face gleamed with celestial radiance.

Helena surveyed him in wondering compassion. "Thou art strangely possessed, Ser Giuseppe," she said.

"It is not strange, Signora, it is all simple—like a child's thought," he said, meeting her limpid eyes with his profound mystic gaze.

She was tall and fair, more like those Greek statues which the sculptors of her day imitated than like a Roman maiden. A simple dress of white silk revealed the beautiful curves of her figure. Through the great oriel window near which they stood the cold sunshine touched her hair and made spots of glory on the striped beast-skins that covered the floor, and on the hanging tapestries. The pictures and ivories, the manuscripts and the busts all contributed to make the apartment a harmonious setting for her noble figure. As he looked at her he trembled.

"And what is thy life to be henceforward?" she asked.

"Surrender, sacrifice," he said half in a whisper. "My parents are right. Joseph is dead. His will is God's, his heart is Christ's. There is no life for me but service."

"And whom wilt thou serve?"

"My brethren, Signora."

"They reject thee."

"I do not reject them."

She was silent for a moment. Then more passionately she cried: "But, Ser Giuseppe, thou wilt achieve nothing. A hundred generations have failed to move them. The Bulls of all the Popes have left them stubborn."

"No one has tried Love, Signora."

"Thou wilt throw away thy life."

He smiled wistfully. "Thou forgettest I am dead."

"Thou art not dead—the sap is in thy veins. The spring-time of the year comes. See how the sun shines already in the blue sky. Thou shalt not die—it is thine to be glad in the sun and in the fairness of things."

"The sunshine is but a symbol of the Divine Love, the pushing buds but prefigure the Resurrection and the Life."

"Thou dreamest, Giuseppe mio. Thou dreamest with those wonderful eyes of thine open. I do not understand this Love of thine that turns from things earthly, that rends thy father's and mother's heart in twain."

His eyes filled with tears. "Pazienza! earthly things are but as shadows that pass. It is thou that dreamest, Signora. Dost thou not feel the transitoriness of it all—yea, even of this solid-seeming terrestrial plain and yon overhanging roof and the beautiful lights set therein for our passing pleasure! This sun which swims daily through the firmament is but a painted phantasm compared with the eternal rock of Christ's Love."

"Thy words are tinkling cymbals to me, Ser Giuseppe."

"They are those of thy faith, Signora."

"Nay, not of my faith," she cried vehemently. "Thou knowest I am no Christian at heart. Nay, nor are any of our house, though they perceive it not. My father fasts at Lent, but it is the Pagan Aristotle that nourishes his thought. Rome counts her beads and mumbles her paternosters, but she has outgrown the primitive faith in Renunciation. Our pageants and processions, our splendid feasts, our gorgeous costumes, what have these to do with the pale Christ, whom thou wouldst foolishly emulate?"

"Then there is work for me to do, even among the Christians," he said mildly.

"Nay, it is but mischief thou wouldst do, with thy passionless ghost of a creed. It is the artists who have brought back joy to the world, who have perceived the soul of beauty in all things. And though they have feigned to paint the Holy Family and the Crucifixion and the Dead Christ and the Last Supper, it is the loveliness of life that has inspired their art. Yea, even from the prayerful Giotto downwards, it is the pride of life, it is the glory of the human form, it is the joy of color, it is the dignity of man, it is the adoration of the Muses. Ay, and have not our nobles had themselves painted as Apostles, have they not intruded their faces into sacred scenes, have they not understood for what this religious art was a pretext? Is not Rome full of Pagan art? Were not the Laocoon and the Cleopatra and the Venus placed in the very orange garden of the Vatican?"

"Natheless it is the Madonna and the Child that your painters have loved best to paint."

"'Tis but Venus and Cupid over again."

"Nay, these sneers belie the noble Signora de' Franchi. Thou canst not be blind to the divine aspiration that lay behind a Madonna of Sandro Botticelli."

"Thou hast not seen his frescoes in the Villa Lemmi, outside Firenze, the dainty grace of his forms, the charming color, else thou wouldst understand that it was not spiritual beauty alone that his soul coveted."

"But Raffaello da Urbino, but Leonardo—"

"Leonardo," she repeated. "Hast thou seen his Bacchus, or his battle-fresco? Knowest thou the later work of Raffaello? And what sayest thou to our Fra Lippo Lippi? A Christian monk he, forsooth! What sayest thou to Giorgione of Venice and his pupils, to this efflorescence of loveliness, to our statuaries and our builders, to our goldsmiths and musicians? Ah, we have rediscovered the secret of Greece. It is Homer that we love, it is Plato, it is the noble simplicity of Sophocles; our Dante lied when he said it was Virgil who was his guide. The poet of Mantua never led mortal to those dolorous regions. He sings of flocks and bees, of birds and running brooks, and the simple loves of shepherds; and we listen to him again and breathe the sweet country air, the sweeter for the memory of those hell-fumes which have poisoned life for centuries. Apollo is Lord, not Christ."

"It is Apollyon who tempts Rome thus with the world and the flesh."

"Thou hast dethroned thy reason, Messer Giuseppe. Thou knowest these things dignify, not degrade our souls. Hast thou not thrilled with me at the fairness of a pictured face, at the glow of luminous color, at the white radiance of a statue?"

"I sinned if I loved beauty for itself alone, and—forgive me if I wound thee, lady—this worship of beauty is for the rich, the well-fed, the few. What of the poor and the down-trodden who weep in darkness? What comfort holds thy creed for such? All these wonders of the human hand and the human brain are as straws weighed against a pure heart, a righteous deed. The ages of Art have always been the ages of abomination, Signora. It is not in cunning but in simplicity that our Lord is revealed. Unless ye become as little children, ye shall not enter the Kingdom of Heaven."

"Heaven is here." Her eyes gleamed. Her bosom heaved. The fire of her glance passed to his. Her loveliness troubled him, the matchless face and form that now blent the purity of a statue with the warmth of living woman.

"Verily, where Christ is Heaven is. Thou hast moved in such splendor of light, Signora de' Franchi, thou dost not realize thy privilege. But I, who have always walked in darkness, am as a blind man restored to sight. I was ambitious, lustful, torn by doubts and questionings; now I am bathed in the divine peace, all my questions answered, my riotous blood assuaged. Love, love, that is all; the surrender of one's will to the love that moves the sun and all the stars, as your Dante says. And sun and stars do but move to this end, Signora—that human souls may be born and die to live, in oneness with Love. Oh, my brethren"— he stretched out his arms yearningly, and his eyes and his voice were full of tears—"why do ye haggle in the market-place? Why do ye lay up store of gold and silver? Why do ye chase the futile shadows of earthly joy? This, this is the true ecstasy, to give yourself up to God, all in all, to ask only to be the channel of His holy will."

Helena's face was full of a grave wonder; for a moment an answering light was reflected on it as though she yearned for the strange raptures she could not understand.

"All this is sheer folly. Thy brethren hear thee now as little as they will ever hear thee."

"I shall pray night and day that my lips may be touched with the sacred fire."

"Love, too, is a sacred fire. Dost thou purpose to live without that?" She drew nearer. Her breath stirred the black lock on his forehead. He moved back a pace, thrilling.

"I shall have divine Love, Signora."

"Thou art bent on becoming a Dominican?"

"I am fixed."

"The cloister will content thee?"

"It will be Heaven."

"Ay, where there is no marrying nor giving in marriage. What Samson-creed is this that pulls down the pillars of human society?"

"Nay, marriage is in the scheme. 'Tis the symbol of a diviner union. But it is not for all men. It is not for those who symbolize divine things otherwise, who typify to their fellow-men the flesh crucified, the soul sublimed. It is not for priests."

"But thou art not a priest."

"'Tis a question of days. But were I even refused orders I should still remain celibate."

"Still remain celibate! Wherefore?"

"Because mine own people are cut off from me. And were I to marry a Christian, like so many Jewish converts, the power of my example would be lost. They would say of me, as they say of them, that it was not the light of Christ but a Christian maiden's eyes that dazzled and drew. They are hard; they do not believe in the possibility of a true conversion. Others have enriched themselves by apostasy, or, being rich, have avoided impoverishing mulcts and taxes. But I have lost all my patrimony, and I will accept nothing. That is why I refused thy father's kind offices, the place in the Seal-office, or even the humbler position of mace-bearer to his Holiness. When my brethren see, moreover, that I force from them no pension nor moneys, not even a white farthing, that I even preach to them without wage, verily for the love of Heaven, as your idiom hath it, when they see that I live pure and lonely, then they will listen to me. Perchance their hearts will be touched and their eyes opened." His face shone with wan radiance. That was, indeed, the want, he felt sure. No Jew had ever stood before his brethren an unimpeachable Christian, above suspicion, without fear, and without reproach. Oh, happy privilege to fill this apostolic rôle!

"But suppose—" Helena hesitated; then lifting her lovely eyes to meet his in fearless candor, "she whom you loved were no Christian."

He trembled, clenching his hands to drive back the mad wave of earthly emotion that flooded him, as the tide swells to the moon, under the fervor of her eyes.

"I should kill my love all the same," he said hoarsely. "The Jews are hard. They will not make fine distinctions. They know none but Jews and Christians."

"Methinks I see my father galloping up the street," said Helena, turning to the oriel window. "That should be his feather and his brown Turkey horse. But the sun dazzles my eyes! I will leave thee."

She passed to the door without looking at him. Then turning suddenly so that his own eyes were dazzled, she said—

"My heart is with thee whatsoever thou choosest. Only bethink thee well, ere thou donnest cowl and gown, that unlovely costume which, to speak after thine own pattern, symbolizes all that is unlovely. Addio!"

He followed her and took her hand, and, bending down, kissed it reverently. She did not withdraw it.

"Hast thou the strength for the serge and the cord, Giuseppe mio?" she asked softly.

He drew himself up, holding her hand in his.

"Yes," he said. "Thou shalt inspire me, Helena. The thought of thy radiant purity shall keep me pure and unfaltering."

A fathomless expression crossed Helena's face. She drew away her hand.

"I cannot inspire to death," she said. "I can only inspire to life."

He closed his eyes in ecstatic vision. "'Tis not death. He is the Resurrection and the Life," he murmured.

When he opened his eyes she was gone. He fell on his knees in a passion of prayer, in the agony of the crucifixion of the flesh.

V

During his novitiate, before he had been admitted to monastic vows, he preached a trial "Sermon to the Jews" in a large oratory near the Ghetto. A church would have been contaminated by the presence of heretics, and even from the Oratory any religious objects that lay about had been removed. There was a goodly array of fashionable Christians, resplendent in gold-fringed mantles and silk-ribboned hats; for he was rumored eloquent, and Annibale de' Franchi was there in pompous presidency. One Jew came— Shloumi the Droll, relying on his ability to wriggle out of the infraction of the ban, and earn a meal or two by reporting the proceedings to the fattori and the other dignitaries of the Ghetto, whose human curiosity might be safely counted upon. Shloumi was rich in devices. Had he not even for months flaunted a crimson cap in the eye of Christendom, and had he not when at last brought before the Caporioni, pleaded that this was merely an ostensive sample of the hats he was selling, his true yellow hat being unintentionally hidden beneath? But Giuseppe de' Franchi rejoiced at the sight of him now.

"He is a gossip, he will scatter the seed," he thought.

Late in the afternoon of the next day the preacher was walking in the Via Lepida, near the Monastery of St. Dominic. There was a touch on his mantle. He turned. "Miriam!" he cried, shrinking back.

"Why shrinkest thou from me, Joseph?"

"Knowest thou not I am under the ban? Look, is not that a Jew yonder who regards us?"

"I care not. I have a word to say to thee."

"But thou wilt be accursed."

"I have a word to say to thee."

His eyes lit up. "Ah, thou believest!" he cried exultantly. "Thou hast found grace."

"Nay, Joseph, that will never be. I love our fathers' faith. Methinks I have understood it better than thou, though I have not dived like thee into holy lore. It is by the heart alone that I understand."

"Then why dost thou come? Let us turn down towards the Coliseum. 'Tis quieter, and less frequented of our brethren."

They left the busy street with its bustle of coaches, and water-carriers with their asses, and porters, and mounted nobles with trains of followers, and swash-buckling swordsmen, any of whom might have insulted Miriam, conspicuous by her beauty and by the square of yellow cloth, a palm and a half wide, set above her coiffure. They walked on in silence till they came to the Arch of Titus. Involuntarily both stopped, for by reason of the Temple candlestick that figured as spoil in the carving of the Triumph of Titus, no Jew would pass under it. Titus and his empire had vanished, but the Jew still hugged his memories and his dreams.

An angry sulphur sunset, streaked with green, hung over the ruined temples of the ancient gods and the grass-grown fora of the Romans. It touched with a glow as of blood the highest fragment of the Coliseum wall, behind which beasts and men had made sport for the Masters of the World. The rest of the Titanic ruin seemed in shadow.

"Is it well with my parents?" said Joseph at last.

"Hast thou the face to ask? Thy mother weeps all day, save when thy father is at home. Then she makes herself as stony as he. He—an elder of the synagogue!—thou hast brought down his gray hairs in sorrow to the grave."

He swallowed a sob. Then, with something of his father's stoniness, "Suffering chastens, Miriam," he said. "It is God's weapon."

"Accuse not God of thy cruelty. I hate thee." She went on rapidly, "It is rumored in the Ghetto thou art to be a friar of St. Dominic. Shloumi the Droll brought the news."

"It is so, Miriam. I am to take the vows at once."

"But how canst thou become a priest? Thou lovest a woman."

He stopped in his walk, startled.

"What sayest thou, Miriam?"

"Nay, this is no time for denials. I know her. I know thy love for her. It is Helena de' Franchi."

He was white and agitated. "Nay, I love no woman."

"Thou lovest Helena."

"How knowest thou that?"

"I am a woman."

They walked on silently.

"And this is what thou camest to say?"

"Nay, this. Thou must marry her and be happy."

"I—I cannot, Miriam. Thou dost not understand."

"Not understand! I can read thee as thou readest the Law—without vowels. Thou thinkest we Jews will point the finger of scorn at thee, that we will say it was Helena thou didst love, not the Crucified One, that we will not listen to thy gospel."

"But is it not so?"

"It is so."

"Then—"

"But it will be so, do what thou wilt. Cut thyself into little pieces and we would not believe in thee or thy gospel. I alone have faith in thy sincerity, and to me thou art as one mad with over-study. Joseph, thy dream is vain. The Jews hate thee. They call thee Haman. Willingly would they see thee hanged on a high tree. Thy memory will be an execration to the third and fourth generation. Thou wilt no more move them than the seven hills of Rome. They have stood too long."

"Ay, they have stood like stones. I will melt them. I will save them."

"Thou wilt destroy them. Save rather thyself—wed this woman and be happy."

He looked at her.

"Be happy," she repeated. "Do not throw away thy life for a vain shadow. Be happy. It is my last word to thee. Henceforth, as a true daughter of Judah, I obey the ban, and were I a mother in Israel my children should be taught to hate thee even as I do. Peace be with thee!"

He caught at her gown. "Go not without my thanks, though I must reject thy counsel. To-morrow I am admitted into the Brotherhood of Righteousness." In the fading light his face shone weird and unearthly amid the raven hair. "But why didst thou risk thy good name to tell me thou hatest me?"

"Because I love thee. Farewell."

She sped away.

He stretched out his arms after her. His eyes were blind with mist. "Miriam, Miriam!" he cried. "Come back, thou too art a Christian! Come back, my sweet sister in Christ!"

A drunken Dominican lurched into his open arms.

The Jews would not come to hear Fra Giuseppe. All his impassioned spirituality was wasted on an audience of Christians and oft-converted converts. Baffled, he fell back on scholastic argumentation, but in vain did he turn the weapons of Talmudic dialectic against the Talmudists themselves. Not even his discovery by cabbalistic calculations that the Pope's name and office were predicted in the Old Testament availed to draw the Jews, and it was only in the streets that he came upon the scowling faces of his brethren. For months he preached in patient sweetness, then one day, desperate and unstrung, he sought an interview with the Pope, to petition that the Jews might be commanded to come to his sermons; he found the Pontiff in bed, unwell, but chatting blithely with the Bishop of Salamanca and the Procurator of the Exchequer, apparently of a droll mishap that had befallen the French Legate. It was a pale scholarly face that lay back on the white pillow under the purple skull-cap, but it was not devoid of the stronger lines of action. Giuseppe stood timidly at the door, till the Wardrobe-Keeper, a gentleman of noble family, told him to advance. He moved forward reverently, and kneeling down kissed the Pope's feet. Then he rose and proffered his request. But the ruler of Christendom frowned. He was a scholar and a gentleman, a great patron of letters and the arts. Wiser than that of temporal kings, his Jewish policy had always been comparatively mild. It was his foreign policy that absorbed his zeal, considerably to the prejudice of his popularity at home. While Giuseppe de' Franchi was pleading desperately to a bored Prelate, explaining how he could solve the Jewish question, how he could play upon his brethren as David upon the harp, if he could only get them under the spell of his voice, a gentleman of the bed-chamber brought in a refection on a silver tray, the Preguste tasted of the food to ensure its freedom from poison, though it came from the Papal kitchen, and at a sign from his Holiness, Giuseppe had to stand aside. And ere the Pope had finished there were other interruptions; the chief of his band of musicians came for instructions for the concert at his Ferragosto on the first of August; and—most vexatious of all—a couple of goldsmiths came with their work, and with rival models of a button for the Pontifical cope. Giuseppe fumed and fretted while the Holy Father put on his spectacles to examine the great silver vase which was to receive the droppings from his table, its richly chased handles and its festoons of acanthus leaves, and its ingenious masks; and its fellow which was to stand in his cupboard and hold water, and had a beautiful design representing St. Ambrogio on horseback routing the Arians. And when one of the jewellers had been dismissed, laden with ducats by the Pope's datary, the other remained an intolerable time, for it appeared his Holiness was mightily pleased with his wax model, marvelling how cunningly the artist had represented God the Father in bas-relief, sitting in an easy attitude, and how elegantly he had set the fine edge of the biggest diamond exactly in the centre. "Speed the work, my son," said His Holiness, dismissing him at last, "for I would wear the button myself before I die." Then, raising a beaming face, "Wouldst thou aught further with me, Fra Giuseppe? Ah, I recall! Thou yearnest to preach to thy stiff-necked kinsmen. Ebbene, 'tis a worthy ambition. Luigi, remember me to-morrow to issue a Bull."

With sudden-streaming eyes the Friar fell at the Pontiff's feet again, kissing them and murmuring incoherent thanks. Then he bowed his way out, and hastened back joyfully to the convent.

The Bull duly appeared. The Jews were to attend his next sermon. He awaited the Sabbath afternoon in a frenzy of spiritual ecstasy. He prepared a wonderful sermon. The Jews would not dare to disobey the Edict. It was too definite. It could not be evaded. And their apathetic resistance never came till later, after an obedient start. The days passed. The Bull had not been countermanded, although he was aware backstairs influence had been tried by the bankers of the community; it had not even been modified under the pretence of defining it, as was the manner of Popes with too rigorous Bulls. No, nothing could save the Jews from his sermon.

On the Thursday a plague broke out in the Ghetto; on the Friday a tenth of the population was dead. Another overflow of the Tiber had co-operated with the malarious effluvia of those congested alleys, those strictly limited houses swarming with multiplying broods. On the Saturday the gates of the Ghetto were officially closed. The plague was shut in. For three months the outcasts of humanity were pent in their pestiferous prison day and night to live or die as they chose. When at length the Ghetto was opened and disinfected, it was the dead, not the living, that were crowded.

VII

Joseph the Dreamer was half stunned by this second blow to his dreams. An earthly anxiety he would not avow to himself consumed him during the progress of the plague, which in spite of all efforts escaped from the Ghetto as if to punish those who had produced the conditions of its existence. But his anxiety was not for himself—it was for his mother and father, it was for the noble Miriam. When he was not in fearless attendance upon plague-stricken Christians he walked near the city of the dead, whence no news could come. When at last he learned that his dear ones were alive, another blow fell. The Bull was still to be enforced, but the Pope's ear was tenderer to the survivors. He respected their hatred of Fra Giuseppe, their protest that they would more willingly hear any other preacher. The duty was to be undertaken by his brother Dominicans in turn. Giuseppe alone was forbidden to preach. In vain he sought to approach his Holiness; he was denied access. Thus began that strange institution, the Predica Coattiva, the forced sermon.

Every Sabbath after their own synagogue sermon, a third of the population of the Ghetto, including all children above the age of twelve, had to repair in turn to receive the Antidote at the Church of San Benedetto Alla Regola, specially set apart for them, where a friar gave a true interpretation of the Old Testament portion read by their own cantor. His Holiness, ever more considerate than his inferiors, had enjoined the preachers to avoid the names of Jesus and the Holy Virgin, so offensive to Jewish ears, or to pronounce them in low tones; but the spirit of these recommendations was forgotten by the occupants of the pulpit with a congregation at their mercy to bully and denounce with all the savage resources of rhetoric. Many Jews lagged reluctant on the road churchwards. A posse of police with whips drove them into the holy fold. This novel church procession of men, women, and children grew to be one of the spectacles of Rome. A new pleasure had been invented for the mob. These compulsory services involved no small expense. By a refinement of humor the Jews had to pay for their own conversion. Evasion of the sermon was impossible; a register placed at the door of the church kept account of the absentees, whom fine and imprisonment chastised. To keep this register a neophyte was needed, one who knew each individual personally and could expose substitutes. What better man than the new brother? In vain Giuseppe protested. The Prior would not hearken. And so in lieu of offering the sublime spectacle of an unpaid apostleship, the powerless instigator of the mischief, bent over his desk, certified the identity of the listless arrivals by sidelong peeps, conscious that he was adding the pain of contact with an excommunicated Jew to the sufferings of his brethren, for whose Sabbath his writing-pen was shamelessly expressing his contempt. Many a Sabbath he saw his father, a tragic, white-haired wreck, touched up with a playful whip to urge him faster towards the church door. It was Joseph whom that whip stung most. When the official who was charged to see that the congregants paid attention, and especially that they did not evade the sermon by slumber, stirred up Rachel with an iron rod, her unhappy son broke into a cold sweat. When, every third Sabbath, Miriam passed before his desk with steadfast eyes of scorn, he was in an ague, a fever of hot and cold. His only consolation was to see rows of devout faces listening for the first time in their life to the gospel. At least he had achieved something. Even Shloumi the Droll had grown regenerate; he listened to the preachers with sober reverence.

Joseph the Dreamer did not know that, adopting the whimsical device hit on by Shloumi, all these devout Jews had wadding stuffed deep into their ears.

But, meanwhile, in other pulpits, Fra Giuseppe was gaining great fame. Christians came from far and near to hear him. He went about among the people and they grew to love him. He preached at executions, his black mantle and white scapulary were welcomed in loathsome dungeons, he absolved the dying, he exorcised demons. But there was one sinner he could not absolve, neither by hair-shirt nor flagellation, and that was himself. And there was one demon he could not exorcise—that in his own breast, the tribulation of his own soul, bruising itself perpetually against the realities of life and as torn now by the shortcomings of Christendom as formerly by those of the Ghetto.

VIII

It was the Carnival week again—the mad blaspheming week of revelry and devilry. The streets were rainbow with motley wear and thunderous with the roar and laughter of the crowd, recruited by a vast inflow of strangers; from the windows and roofs, black with heads, frolicsome hands threw honey, dirty water, rotten eggs, and even boiling oil upon the pedestrians and cavaliers below. Bloody tumults broke out, sacrilegious masqueraders invaded the churches. They lampooned all things human and divine; the whip and the gallows liberally applied availed naught to check the popular licence. Every prohibitory edict became a dead letter. In such a season the Jews might well tremble, made over to the facetious Christian; always excellent whetstones for wit, they afforded peculiar diversion in Carnival times. On the first day a deputation of the chief Jews, including the three gonfaloniers and the rabbis, headed the senatorial cortége, and, attired in a parti-colored costume of red and yellow, marched across the whole city, from the Piazza of the People to the Capitol, through a double fire of scurrilities. Arrived at the Capitol, the procession marched into the Hall of the Throne, where the three Conservators and the Prior of the Caporioni sat on crimson velvet seats with the fiscal advocate of the Capitol in his black toga and velvet cap. The Chief Rabbi knelt upon the first step of the throne, and, bending his venerable head to the ground, pronounced a traditional formula: "Full of respect and of devotion for the Roman people, we, chiefs and rabbis of the humble Jewish community, present ourselves before the exalted throne of Your Eminences to offer them respectfully fidelity and homage in the name of our co-religionists, and to implore their benevolent commiseration. For us, we shall not fail to supplicate the Most High to accord peace and a long tranquillity to the Sovereign Pontiff, who reigns for the happiness of all; to the Apostolic Holy Seat, as well as to Your Eminences, to the most illustrious Senate, and to the Roman people."

To which the Chief of the Conservators replied: "We accept with pleasure the homage of fidelity, of vassalage, and of respect, the expression of which you renew to-day in the name of the entire Jewish community, and, assured that you will respect the laws and orders of the Senate, and that you will pay, as in the past, the tribute and the dues which are incumbent upon you, we accord you our protection in the hope that you will know how to make yourself worthy of it." Then, placing his foot upon the Rabbi's neck, he cried: "Andate!" (Begone!)

Rising, the Rabbi presented the Conservators with a bouquet and a cup containing twenty crowns, and offered to decorate the platform of the Senator on the Piazza of the People. And then the deputation passed again in its motley gear through the swarming streets of buffoons, through the avenue of scurrilities, to renew its hypocritical protestations before the throne of the Senator.

Mock processions parodied this march of Jews. The fishmongers, who, from their proximity to the Ghetto, were aware of its customs, enriched the Carnival with divers other parodies; now it was a travesty of a rabbi's funeral, now a long cavalcade of Jews galloping upon asses, preceded by a mock rabbi on horseback, with his head to the steed's tail, which he grasped with one hand, while with the other he offered an imitation Scroll of the Law to the derision of the mob. Truly, the baiting of the Jews added rare spice to the fun of the Carnival; their hats were torn off, filth was thrown in their faces. This year the Governor of Rome had interfered, forbidding anything to be thrown at them except fruit. A noble marquis won facetious fame by pelting them with pineapples. But it was not till the third day, after the asses and buffaloes had raced, that the Jews touched the extreme of indignity, for this was the day of the Jew races.

The morning dawned blue and cold; but soon the clouds gathered, and the jostling revellers scented with joy the prospect of rain. At the Arch of San Lorenza, in Lucina, in the long narrow street of the Via Corso, where doorways and casements and roofs and footways were agrin with faces, half a dozen Jews or so were assembled pell-mell. They had just been given a hearty meal, but they did not look grateful. Almost naked, save for a white cloak of the meagrest dimensions, comically indecent, covered with tinsel and decorated with laurels, they stood shivering, awaiting the command to "Go!" to run the gauntlet of all this sinister crowd, overwelling with long-repressed venom, seething with taunts and lewdness. At last a mounted officer gave the word, and, amid a colossal shout of glee from the mob, the half-naked, grotesque figures, with their strange Oriental faces of sorrow, started at a wild run down the Corso. The goal was the Castle of St. Angelo. Originally the race-course ended with the Corso, but it had been considerably lengthened to gratify a recent Pope who wished to have the finish under his windows as he sat in his semi-secret Castle chamber amid the frescoed nudes of Giulio Romano. Fast, fast flew the racers, for the sooner the goal was reached the sooner would they find respite from this hail of sarcasm mixed with weightier stones, and these frequent proddings from the lively sticks of the bystanders, or of the fine folk obstructing the course in coaches in defiance of edict. And to accelerate their pace still further, the mounted officer, with a squad of soldiers armed cap-à-pie, galloped at their heels, ever threatening to ride them down. They ran, ran, puffing, panting, sweating, apoplectic; for to the end that they might nigh burst with stitches in the side had a brilliant organizer of the fête stuffed them full with preliminary meat. Oh, droll! oh, delicious! oh, rare for Antony! And now a young man noticeable by his emaciated face and his premature baldness was drawing to the front amid ironic cheers. When the grotesque racers had passed by, noble cavaliers displayed their dexterity at the quintain, and beautiful ladies at the balconies—not masked, as in France, but radiantly revealed— changed their broad smiles to the subtler smiles of dalliance. And then suddenly the storm broke— happy ally of the fête—jocosely drenching the semi-nude runners. On, on they sped, breathless, blind, gasping, befouled by mud, and bruised by missiles, with the horses' hoofs grazing their heels; on, on along the thousand yards of the endless course; on, on, sodden and dripping and stumbling. They were nearing the goal. They had already passed San Marco, the old goal. The young Jew was still leading, but a fat old Jew pressed him close. The excitement of the crowd redoubled. A thousand mocking voices encouraged the rivals. They were on the bridge. The Castle of St. Angelo, whose bastions were named after the Apostles, was in sight. The fat old Jew drew closer, anxious, now that he was come so far, to secure the thirty-six crowns that the prize might be sold for. But the favorite made a mighty spurt. He passed the Pope's window, and the day was his. The firmament rang with laughter as the other candidates panted up. A great yell greeted the fall of the fat old man in the roadway, where he lay prostrate.

An official tendered the winner the pallio which was the prize—a piece of red Venetian cloth. The young Jew took it, surveying it with a strange, unfathomable gaze, but the Judge interposed.

"The captain of the soldiers tells me they did not start fair at the Arch. They must run again to-morrow." This was a favorite device for prolonging the fun. But the winner's eyes blazed ominously.

"Nay, but we started as balls shot from a falconet."

"Peace, peace, return him the pallio," whispered a racer behind him, tugging apprehensively at his one garment.

"They always adjudge it again to the first winner." But the young man was reckless.

"Why did not the captain stop us, then?" he asked.

"Keep thy tongue between thy dog's teeth," retorted the Judge. "In any event the race must be run again, for the law ordains eight runners as a minimum."

"We are eight," replied the young Jew.

The Judge glared at the rebel; then, striking each rueful object with a stick, he counted out, "One—two—three—four—five—six—seven!"

"Eight," persisted the young man, perceiving for the first time the old Jew on the ground behind him, and stooping to raise him.

"That creature! Basta! He does not count. He is drunk."

"Thou hell-begotten hound!" and straightening himself suddenly, the young Jew drew a crucifix from within his cloak. "Thou art right!" he cried in a voice of thunder. "There are only seven Jews, for I—I am no Jew. I am Fra Giuseppe!" And the crucifix whirled round, clearing a space of awe about him.

The Judge cowered back in surprise and apprehension. The soldiers sat their horses in stony amazement, the seething crowd was stilled for a moment, struck to silent attention. The shower had ceased and a ray of watery sunlight glistened on the crucifix.

"In the name of Christ I denounce this devil's mockery of the Lord's chosen people," thundered the Dominican. "Stand back all. Will no one bring this poor old man a cup of cold water?"

"Hasn't Heaven given him enough cold water?" asked a jester in the crowd. But no one stirred.

"Then may you all burn eternally," said the Friar. He bent down again and raised the old man's head tenderly. Then his face grew sterner and whiter. "He is dead," he said. "The Christ he denied receive him into His mercy." And he let the corpse fall gently back and closed the glassy eyes. The bystanders had a momentary thrill. Death had lent dignity even to the old Jew. He lay there, felled by an apoplectic stroke, due to the forced heavy meal, the tinsel gleaming grotesquely on his white sodden cloak, his naked legs rigid and cold. From afar the rumors of revelry, the brouhaha of a mad population, saluted his deaf ears, the distant music of lutes and viols. The captain of the soldiers went hot and cold. He had harried the heels of the rotund runner in special amusement, but he had not designed murder. A wave of compunction traversed the spectators. But the Judge recovered himself.

"Seize this recreant priest!" he cried. "He is a backslider. He has gone back to his people. He is become a Jew again—he shall be flayed alive."

"Back, in the name of Holy Church!" cried Fra Giuseppe, veering round to face the captain, who, however, had sat his horse without moving. "I am no Jew. I am as good a Christian as his Holiness, who but just now sat at yon jalousie, feasting his eyes on these heathen saturnalia."

"Then why didst thou race with the Jews? It is contamination. Thou hast defiled thy cloth."

"Nay, I wore not my cloth. Am I not half naked? Is this the cloth I should respect—this gaudy frippery, which your citizens have made a target for filth and abuse?"

"Thou hast brought it on thyself," put in the captain mildly. "Wherefore didst thou race with this pestilent people?"

The Dominican bowed his head. "It is my penance," he said in tremulous tones. "I have sinned against my brethren. I have aggravated their griefs. Therefore would I be of them at the moment of their extremest humiliation, and that I might share their martyrdom did I beg his place from one of the runners. But penance is not all my motive." And he lifted up his eyes and they blazed terribly, and his tones became again a thunder that rolled through the crowd and far down the bridge. "Ye who know me, faithful sons and daughters of Holy Church, ye who have so often listened to my voice, ye into whose houses I have brought the comfort of the Word, join with me now in ending the long martyrdom of the Jews, your brethren. It is by love, not hate, that Christ rules the world. I deemed that it would move your hearts to see me, whom I know ye love, covered with filth, which ye had never thrown had ye known me in this strange guise. But lo, this poor old man pleadeth more eloquently than I. His dead lips shake your souls. Go home, go home from this Pagan mirth, and sit on the ground in sackcloth and ashes, and pray God He make you better Christians."

There was an uneasy stir in the crowd: the fantastic mud-stained tinsel cloak, the bare legs of the speaker, did but add to his impressiveness; he seemed some strange antique prophet, come from the far ends of the world and time.

"Be silent, blasphemer," said the Judge. "The sports have the countenance of the Holy Father. Heaven itself hath cursed these stinking heretics. Pah!" he spurned the dead Jew with his foot. The Friar's bosom swelled. His head was hot with blood.

"Not Heaven but the Pope hath cursed them," he retorted vehemently. "Why doth he not banish them from his dominions? Nay, he knows how needful they are to the State. When he exiled them from all save the three cities of refuge, and when the Jewish merchants of the seaports of the East put our port of Ancona under a ban, so that we could not provision ourselves, did not his Holiness hastily recall the Jews, confessing their value? Which being so, it is love we should offer them, not hatred and a hundred degrading edicts."

"Thou shalt burn in the Forum for this," spluttered the Judge. "Who art thou to set thyself up against God's Vicar?"

"He God's Vicar? Nay, I am sooner God's Vicar. God speaks through me."

His wan, emaciated face had grown rapt and shining; to the awed mob he loomed gigantic.

"This is treason and blasphemy. Arrest him!" cried the Judge.

The Friar faced the soldiers unflinchingly, though only the body of the old Jew divided him from their prancing horses.

"Nay," he said softly, and a sweet smile mingled with the mystery of his look. "God is with me. He hath set this bulwark of death between you and my life. Ye will not fight under the banner of the Anti-Christ."

"Death to the renegade!" cried a voice in the crowd. "He calls the Pope Anti-Christ."

"Ay, he who is not for us is against us. Is it for Christ that he rules Rome? Is it only the Jews whom he vexes? Hath not his rage for power brought the enemy to the gates of Rome? Have not his companies of foreign auxiliaries flouted our citizens? Ye know how Rome hath suffered through the machinations of his bastard son, with his swaggering troop of cut-throats. Is it for Christ that he hath begotten this terror of our streets?"

"Down with Baccio Valori!" cried a stentorian voice, and a dozen enthusiastic throats echoed the shout.

"Ay, down with Baccio Valori!" cried the Dominican.

"Down with Baccio Valori!" repeated the ductile crowd, its holiday humor subtly passing into another form of recklessness. Some who loved the Friar were genuinely worked upon, others in mad, vicious mood were ready for any diversion. A few, and these the loudest, were swashbucklers and cutpurses.

"Ay, but not Baccio Valori alone!" thundered Fra Giuseppe. "Down with all those bastard growths that flourish in the capital of Christendom. Down with all that hell-spawn, which is the denial of Christ; down with the Pardoner! God is no tradesman that he should chaffer for the forgiveness of sins. Still less—oh blasphemy!—of sins undone. Our Lady wants none of your wax candles. It is a white heart, it is the flame of a pure soul that the Virgin Mother asks for. Away with your beads and mummeries, your paternosters and genuflections! Away with your Carnivals, your godless farewells to meat! Ye are all foul. This is no city of God, it is a city of hired bravos and adulterous abominations and gluttonous feasts, and the lust of the eye, and the pride of the flesh. Down with the foul-blooded Cardinal, who gossips at the altar, and borrows money of the despised Jews for his secret sins! Down with the monk whose missal is Boccaccio! Down with God's Vicegerent who traffics in Cardinals' hats, who dare not take the Eucharist without a Pretaster, who is all absorbed in profane Greek texts, in cunning jewel-work, in political manœuvres and domestic intrigues, who comes caracoling in crimson and velvet upon his proud Neapolitan barb, with his bareheaded Cardinals and his hundred glittering horsemen. He the representative of the meek Christ who rode upon an ass, and said, 'Sell that thou hast and give to the poor, and come follow me'! Nay," and the passion of righteousness tore his frame and thralled his listeners, "though he inhabit the Vatican, though a hundred gorgeous bishops abase themselves to kiss his toe, yet I proclaim here that he is a lie, a snare, a whited sepulchre, no protector of the poor, no loving father to the fatherless, no spiritual Emperor, no Vicar of Christ, but Anti-Christ himself."

"Down with Anti-Christ!" yelled a pair of Corsican cut-throats.

"Down with Anti-Christ!" roared the crowd, the long-suppressed hatred of the ruling power finding vent in a great wave of hysteric emotion.

"Captain, do thy duty!" cried the Judge.

"Nay, but the Friar speaks truth. Bear the old man away, Alessandro!"

"Is Rome demented? Haste for the City Guards, Jacopo!"

Fra Giuseppe swiftly tied the pallio to his crucifix, and, waving the red cloth on high, "This is the true flag of Christ!" he cried. "This, the symbol of our brethren's martyrdom! See, 'tis the color of the blood He shed for us. Who is for Jesus, follow me!"

"For Christ, for Jesus! Viva Gesú!" A far-rumbling thunder broke from the swaying mob. His own fire caught extra flame from theirs.

"Follow me! This day we will bear witness to Christ, we will establish His kingdom in Rome."

There was a wild rush, the soldiers spurred their horses, people fell under their hoofs, and were trampled on. It was a moment of frenzy. The Dominican ran on, waving the red pallio, his followers contagiously swollen at every by-street. Unchecked he reached the great Piazza, where a new statue of the Pope gleamed white and majestic.

"Down with Anti-Christ!" shouted a cutpurse.

"Down with Anti-Christ!" echoed the mob.

The Friar waved his hand, and there was silence. He saw the yellow gleam of a Jew's head in the crowd, and called upon him to fling him his cap. It was hurled from hand to hand. Fra Giuseppe held it up in the air. "Men of Rome, Sons of Holy Church, behold the contumelious mark we set upon our fellow-men, so that every ruffian may spit upon them. Behold the yellow—the color of shame, the stigma of women that traffic in their womanhood—with which we brand the venerable brows of rabbis and the heads of honorable merchants. Lo! I set it upon the head of this Anti-Christ, a symbol of our hate for all that is not Love." And raising himself on the captain's stirrup, he crowned the statue with the yellow badge.

A great shout of derision rent the air. There was a multifarious tumult of savage voices.

"Down with Anti-Christ! Down with the Pope! Down with Baccio Valori! Down with the Princess Teresa!"

But in another moment all was a wild mêlée. A company of City Guards—pikemen, musketeers, and horsemen with two-handed swords dashed into the Piazza from one street, the Pope's troops from another. They charged the crowd. The soldiers of the revolting captain, revolting in their turn, wheeled round and drove back their followers. There was a babel of groans and shrieks and shouts, muskets rang out, daggers flashed, sword and pike rang against armor, sparks flew, smoke curled, and the mob broke and scurried down the streets, leaving the wet, scarlet ground strewn with bodies.

And long ere the roused passions of the riffraff had assuaged themselves by loot and outrage in the remoter streets, in the darkest dungeon of the Nona Tower, on a piece of rotten mattress, huddled in his dripping tinselled cloak, and bleeding from a dozen cuts, Joseph the Dreamer lay prostrate, too exhausted from the fierce struggle with his captors to think on the stake that awaited him.

IX

He had not long to wait. To give the crowd an execution was to crown the Carnival. Condemned criminals were often kept till Shrove Tuesday, and keen was the disappointment when there was only the whipping of courtesans caught masked. The whipping of a Jew, found badgeless, was the next best thing to the execution of a Christian, for the flagellator was paid double (at the cost of the culprit), and did not fail to double his zeal. But the execution of a Jew was the best of all. And that Fra Giuseppe was a Jew there could be no doubt. The only question was whether he was a backslider or a spy. In either case death was his due. And he had lampooned the Pope to boot—in itself the unpardonable sin. The unpopular Pontiff sagely spared the others—the Jew alone was to die.

The population was early astir. In the Piazza of the People—the centre of the Carnival—where the stake had been set up, a great crowd fought for coigns of vantage—a joyous, good-humored tussle. The great fountain sent its flashing silver spirts towards a blue heaven. As the death-cart lumbered into the Piazza ribald songs from the rabble saluted the criminal's ears, and his wild, despairing eyes lighted on many a merry face that but a few hours before had followed him to testify to righteousness; and, mixed with theirs, the faces of his fellow-Jews, sinister with malicious glee. No brother friar droned consolation to him or held the cross to his eyes—was he not a pestilential infidel, an outcast from both worlds? The chief of the Caporioni was present. Troops surrounded the stake lest, perchance, the madman might have followers who would yet attempt a rescue. But the precautions were superfluous. Not a face that showed sympathy; those who, bewitched by the Friar, had followed his crucifix and pallio now exaggerated their jocosity lest they should be recognized; the Jews were joyous at the heavenly vengeance which had overtaken the renegade.

The Dominican Jew was tied to the timber. They had dressed him in a gaberdine and set the yellow cap on his shaven poll. Beneath it his face was calm, but very sad. He began to speak.

"Gag him!" cried the Magistrate. "He is about to blaspheme."

"Prithee not," pleaded a bully in the crowd. "We shall lose the rascal's shrieks."

"Nay, fear not. I shall not blaspheme," said Joseph, smiling mournfully. "I do but confess my sin and my deserved punishment. I set out to walk in the footsteps of the Master—to win by love, to resist not evil. And lo, I have used force against my old brethren, the Jews, and force against my new brethren, the Christians. I have urged the Pope against the Jews, I have urged the Christians against the Pope. I have provoked bloodshed and outrage. It were better I had never been born. Christ receive me into His infinite mercy. May He forgive me as I forgive you!" He set his teeth and spake no more, an image of infinite despair.

The flames curled up. They began to writhe about his limbs, but drew no sound to vie with their crackling. But there was weeping heard in the crowd. And suddenly from the unobservedly overcast heavens came a flash of lightning and a peal of thunder followed by a violent shower of rain. The flames were extinguished. The spring shower was as brief as it was violent, but the wood would not relight.

But the crowd was not thus to be cheated. At the order of the Magistrate the executioner thrust a sword into the criminal's bowels, then, unbinding the body, let it fall upon the ground with a thud: it rolled over on its back, and lay still for a moment, the white, emaciated face staring at the sky. Then the executioner seized an axe and quartered the corpse. Some sickened and turned away, but the bulk remained gloating.

Then a Franciscan sprang on the cart, and from the bloody ominous text patent to all eyes, passionately preached Christ and dissolved the mob in tears.

X

In the house of Manasseh, the father of Joseph, there were great rejoicings. Musicians had been hired to celebrate the death of the renegade as tradition demanded, and all that the Pragmatic permitted of luxury was at hand. And they danced, man with man and woman with woman. Manasseh gravely handed fruits and wine to his guests, but the old mother danced frenziedly, a set smile on her wrinkled face, her whole frame shaken from moment to moment by peals of horrible laughter.

Miriam fled from the house to escape that laughter. She wandered outside the Ghetto, and found the spot of unconsecrated ground where the mangled remains of Joseph the Dreamer had been hastily shovelled. The heap of stones thrown by pious Jewish hands, to symbolize that by Old Testament Law the renegade should have been stoned, revealed his grave. Great sobs swelled Miriam's throat. Her eyes were blind with tears that hid the beauty of the world. Presently she became aware of another bowed figure near hers—a stately female figure—and almost without looking knew it for Helena de' Franchi.

"I, too, loved him, Signora de' Franchi," she said simply.

"Art thou Miriam? He hath spoken of thee." Helena's silvery voice was low and trembling.

"Ay, Signora."

Helena's tears flowed unrestrainedly. "Alas! Alas! the Dreamer! He should have been happy—happy with me, happy in the fulness of human love, in the light of the sun, in the beauty of this fair world, in the joy of art, in the sweetness of music."

"Nay, Signora, he was a Jew. He should have been happy with me, in the light of the Law, in the calm household life of prayer and study, of charity, and pity, and all good offices. I would have lit the Sabbath candles for him and set our children on his knee that he might bless them. Alas! Alas! the Dreamer!"

"Neither of these fates was to be his, Miriam. Kiss me, let us comfort each other."

Their lips met and their tears mingled.

"Henceforth, Miriam, we are sisters."

"Sisters," sobbed Miriam.

They clung to each other—the noble Pagan soul and the warm Jewish heart at one over the Christian's grave.

Suddenly bells began to ring in the city. Miriam started and disengaged herself.

"I must go," she said hurriedly.

"It is but Ave Maria," said Helena. "Thou hast no vespers to sing."

Miriam touched the yellow badge on her head. "Nay, but the gates will be closing, sister."

"Alas, I had forgotten. I had thought we might always be together henceforth. I will accompany thee so far as I may, sister."

They hastened from the lonely, unblessed grave, holding each other's hand.

The shadows fell. It was almost dark by the time they reached the Ghetto.

Miriam had barely slipped in when the gates shut with a harsh clang, severing them through the long night.

URIEL ACOSTA

PART I

GABRIEL DA COSTA

I

Gabriel Da Costa pricked his horse gently with the spur, and dashing down the long avenue of cork-trees, strove to forget the torment of spiritual problems in the fury of physical movement, to leave theology behind with the monasteries and chapels of Porto. He rode with grace and fire, this beautiful youth with the flashing eyes, and the dark hair flowing down the silken doublet, whom a poet might have feigned an image of the passionate spring of the South, but for whose own soul the warm blue sky of Portugal, the white of the almond blossoms, the pink of the peach sprays, the delicate odors of buds, and the glad clamor of birds made only a vague background to a whirl of thoughts.

No; it was impossible to believe that by confessing his sins as the Church prescribed he could obtain a plenary absolution. If salvation was to be secured only by particular rules, why, then, one might despair of salvation altogether. And, perhaps, eternal damnation was indeed his destiny, were it only for his doubts, and in despite of all his punctilious mechanical worship. Oh, for a deliverer—a deliverer from the questionings that made the splendid gloom of cathedrals a darkness for the captive spirit! Those cursed Jesuits, zealous with the zealotry of a new order! His blood flamed as he thought of their manœuvrings, and putting his hand to his holster, where hung a pair of silver-mounted pistols marked with his initial, he drew out one and took flying aim at a bird on a twig, pleasing himself with the foolish fancy that 'twas Ignatius Loyola. But though a sure marksman, he had not the heart to hurt any living thing, and changing with the swiftness of a flash he shot at the twig instead, snapping it off.

Why had his dead father set him to study ecclesiastical law? True, for a wealthy youth of the upper middle classes 'twas the one road to distinction, to social equality with the nobility—and whose fault but his own that even after the first stirrings of scepticism he had accepted semi-sacerdotal office as chief treasurer of a clerical college? But how should he foresee that these uneasinesses of youth would be aggravated rather than appeased by deeper study, more passionate devotion? Strange! All around him, in college or cathedral, was faith and peace; in his spirit alone a secret disquiet and a suppressed ferment that not all the soaring music of fresh-voiced boys could soothe or allay.

He felt his horse slacken suddenly under him, and had used his spurs viciously without effect, ere he became conscious that he had come to the steep, clayey bank of a ravine through which a tiny stream trickled, and that the animal's flanks were stained with blood. Instantly his eyes grew humid.

"Pobre!" he cried, leaping from the saddle and caressing the horse's nostrils. "To be shamed before men have I always dreaded, but 'tis worse to be shamed before myself."

And leading his steed by the bridle, the young cavalier turned back towards Porto by winding grassy paths purpled with anemones and bordered by gray olive-trees, with here and there the vivid gleam of oranges peeping amid deep green foliage that tore the sky into a thousand azure patches.

II

He remounted his horse as he approached the market-place, from which the town climbed up; but he found his way blocked, for 'twas market-day, and the great square, bordered with a colonnade that made an Eastern bazaar, was thickly planted with stalls, whose white canvas awnings struck a delicious note of coolness against the throbbing blue sky and the flaming costumes of the peasants come up from the environs. Through a corner of the praça one saw poplars and elms and the fresh gleam of the river. The nasal hum of many voices sounded blithe and busy. At the bazaar entrance, where old women vended flowers and fruit, Gabriel reined in his horse.

"How happy these simple souls!" he mused. "How sure of their salvation! To count their beads and mutter their Ave Marias; 'tis all they need. Yon fisher, with his great gold ear-rings, who throws his nets and cuddles his Juanita and carouses with his mates, hath more to thank the saints for than miserable I, who, blessed with wealth, am cursed with loneliness, and loving my fellow-men, yet know they are but sheep. God's sheep, natheless, silly and deaf to the cry of their true shepherd, and misled by priestly wolves."

A cripple interrupted his reflections by a whining appeal. Gabriel shuddered with pity at the sight of his sores, and, giving him a piece of silver, lost himself in a new reverie on the mystery of suffering.

"Thine herbs sold out too!" cheerily grumbled a well-known voice, and, turning his head, Gabriel saw that the burly old gentleman addressing the wrinkled market-woman from the vantage-point of a mule's back was, indeed, Dom Diego de Balthasar, late professor of the logics at the University of Coimbra, and newly settled in Porto as a physician.

"Ay, indeed, ere noon!" the dried-up old dame mumbled. "All Porto seems hungry for bitter herbs to-day. But thus it happens sometimes about Eastertide, though I love not such salads myself."

"Naturally. They are good for the blood," laughed Dom Diego, as his eye caught Gabriel's. "And thou hast none, good dame."

There seemed almost a wink in the professorial eye, and the young horseman smiled in good-natured response to the physician's estimate of the jest.

"Then are the eaters sensible," he said.

"Ay, the only sensible people in Portugal," rejoined Dom Diego, changing his speech to Latin, but retaining his smile. "And the only good blood, Da Costa," he added, with what was now an unmistakable wink. But this time Gabriel failed to see the point.

"The only good blood?" he repeated. "Dost thou then hold with the Trappists that meat is an evil?"

A strange, startled look flashed across the physician's face, sweeping off its ruddy hue, and though his smile returned on the instant, it was as though forced back.

"In a measure," he replied. "Too much flesh generateth humors and distempers in the blood. Hence Holy Church hath ordained Lent. She is no friend to us physicians. Adeos!" and he ambled off on his mule, waving the young horseman a laughing farewell.

But Gabriel, skirting the market, rode up the steep streets troubled by a vague sense of a mystery, and later repeated the conversation to a friar at the college.

III

A week later he heard in the town that Dom Diego de Balthasar had been arrested by the Inquisition for Judaism. The news brought him a more complex thrill than that shock of horror at the treacherous persistence of a pestilent heresy which it excited in the breast of his fellow-citizens. He recalled to mind now that there were thirty-four traces by which the bloodhounds of the Holy Office scented out the secret Jew, and that one of the tests ran: "If he celebrates the Passover by eating bitter herbs and lettuces." But the shudder which the thought of the Jew had once caused him was, to his own surprise, replaced by a secret sympathy. In his slowly-matured, self-evolved scepticism, he had forgotten that a whole race had remained Protestant from the first, rejecting at any and every cost the corner-stone of the Christian scheme. And this race—he remembered suddenly with a leap of the heart and a strange tingling of the blood—had once been his own! The knowledge that had lurked in the background of consciousness, like the exiled memory of an ancient shame, sprang up, strong and assertive. The far-off shadowy figures of those base-born ancestors of his who had prayed in the ancient synagogues in the days before the Great Expulsion, shook off the mists of a hundred years and stood forth solid, heroic, appealing.

And then recalling the dearth of bitter herbs in the market-place on what he now understood was the eve of Passover, he had a sudden intuition of a great secret brotherhood of the synagogue ramifying beneath all the outward life of Church and State; of a society honeycombed with Judaism that persisted tenaciously and eternally though persecution and expulsion, not in stray units, such as the Inquisition ferreted out, but in ineradicable communities. It was because the incautious physician had mistaken him for a member of the brotherhood of Israel that he had ventured upon his now transparent jests. "Good God!" thought Da Costa, sickening as he remembered the auto-da-fé he had seen at Lisbon in his boyhood, when De la Asunçao, the Franciscan Jew monk, clothed in the Sanbenito, was solemnly burnt in the presence of the king, the queen, the court, and the mob. "What if 'twas my tale to Frei José that led to Dom Diego's arrest! But no, that were surely evidence too trivial, and ambiguous at the best." And he put the painful suspicion aside and hastened to shut himself up in his study, sending down an excuse to his mother and brother by Pedro, the black slave-boy.

In the beautiful house on the hilltop, built by Gabriel's grandfather, and adorned with fine panelings and mosaics of many-colored woods from the Brazils, this study, secluded by its position at the head of the noble staircase, was not the least beautiful room. The floor and the walls were of rich-hued tiles, the arched ceiling was ribbed with polished woods to look like the scooped-out interior of a half-orange. Costly hangings muffled the noise of the outer world, and large shutters excluded, when necessary, the glare of the sun. The rays of Reason alone could not be shut out, and in this haunt of peace the young Catholic had known his bitterest hours of unrest. Here he now cast himself feverishly upon the perusal of the Old Testament, neglected by him, as by the Church.

"This book, at least, must be true," ran his tumultuous thoughts. "For this Testament do both creeds revere that wrangle over the later." He had a Latin text, and first he turned to the fifty-third chapter of Isaiah, and, reading it critically, he seemed to see that all these passages of prediction he had taken on trust as prognostications of a Redeemer might prophesy quite other and more intelligible things. And long past midnight he read among the Prophets, with flushed cheek and sparkling eye, as one drunk with new wine. What sublime truths, what aspirations after peace and justice, what trumpet-calls to righteousness!

He thrilled to the cry of Amos: "Take thou away from me the noise of thy songs, for I will not hear the melody of thy viols. But let judgment run down as waters, and righteousness as a mighty stream." And to the question of Micah: "What doth the Lord require of thee but to do justly and to love mercy and to walk humbly with thy God?" Ay, justice and mercy and humbleness—not paternosters and penances. He was melted to tears, he was exalted to the stars.

He turned to the Pentateuch and to the Laws of Moses, to the tender ordinances for the poor, the stranger, the beast. "Thou shalt love thy neighbor as thyself." "Thou shalt be unto me a holy people."

Why had his ancestors cut themselves off from this great people, whose creed was once so sublime and so simple? There had reached down to him some vague sense of the nameless tragedies of the Great Expulsion when these stiff-necked heretics were confronted with the choice of expatriation or conversion; but now he searched his book-shelves eagerly for some chronicle of those days of Torquemada. The native historians had little, but that little filled his imagination with horrid images of that second Exodus—famine, the plague, robbery, slaughter, the violation of virgins.

And all on account of the pertinacious ambition of a Portuguese king to rule Spain through an alliance with a Spanish princess—an ambition as pertinaciously foiled by the irony of history. No, they were not without excuse, those ancestors of his who had been left behind clinging to the Church. Could they have been genuine converts, these Marranos, or New Christians? he asked himself. Well, whatever his great-grandfathers had felt, his father's faith had been ardent enough, of that he could not doubt. He recalled the long years of ritual; childish memories of paternal pieties. No, the secret conspiracy had not embraced the Da Costa household. And he would fain believe that his more distant progenitors, too, had not been hypocrites; for aught he knew they had gone over to the Church even before the Expulsion; at any rate he was glad to have no evidence for an ancestry of deceit. None of the Da Costas had been cowards, thank Heaven! And he—he was no coward, he told himself.

IV

In the morning, though only a few hours of sleep had intervened, the enthusiasm of the night had somewhat subsided. "Whence came the inspiration of Moses?" flew up to his mind almost as soon as he opened his eyes on the sunlit world. He threw open the protrusive casement of his bedroom to the balmy air, tinged with a whiff of salt, and gazed pensively at the white town rambling down towards the shining river. Had God indeed revealed Himself on Mount Sinai? But this fresh doubt was banished by the renewed suspicion which, after having disturbed his dreams in nebulous distortions, sprang up in daylight clearness. It was his babbling about Dom Diego that had ruined the genial old physician. After days of gathering uneasiness, being unable to gain any satisfaction from the friar, he sought the secretary of the Inquisition in his bureau at a monastery of the Dominicans. The secretary rubbed his hands at the sight of the speechful face. "Aha! What new foxes hast thou scented?" The greeting stung like a stab.

"None," he replied, with a tremor in his speech and in his limbs. "I did but desire to learn if I am to blame for Dom Diego's arrest."

"To blame?" and the secretary looked askance at him. "Say, rather, to praise."

"Nay, to blame," repeated Gabriel staunchly. "Mayhap I mistook or misrendered his conversation. 'Tis scant evidence to imprison a man on. I trust ye have found more."

"Ay, thou didst but set Frei José on the track. We did not even trouble thee to appear before the Qualifiers."

"And he is, indeed, a Jew!"

"A Hebrew of Hebrews, by his stiff-neckedness. But 'twas not quite proven; the fox is a cunning beast. Already he hath had the three 'first audiences,' but he will not confess and be made a Penitent. This morning we try other means."

"Torture?" said Gabriel, paling. The secretary nodded.

"But if he is innocent."

"No fear of that; he will confess at the first twinge. Come, unknit thy brow. Wouldst make sure thou hast served Heaven? Thou shalt hear his confession—as a reward for thy zeal."

"He will deem I have come to gloat."

"Here is a mask for thee."

Gabriel took it hesitatingly, repelled, but more strongly fascinated, and after a feverish half-hour of waiting he found himself with the secretary, the judge of the Inquisition, the surgeon, and another masked man in an underground vault faintly lit by hanging lamps. On one side were the massive doors studded with rusty knobs, of airless cells; on the rough, spider-webbed wall opposite, against which leaned an iron ladder, were fixed iron rings at varying heights. A thumbscrew stood in the corner, and in the centre was a small writing-table, at which the judge seated himself.

The secretary unlocked a dungeon door, and through the holes of his mask Gabriel had a glimpse of the despondent figure of the burly physician crouching in a cell nigh too narrow for turning room.

"Stand forth, Dom Abraham de Balthasar!" said the judge, ostentatiously referring to a paper.

The physician blinked his eyes at the increased light, but did not budge.

"My name is Dom Diego," he said.

"Thy baptismal name imports no more to us than to thee. Perchance I should have said Dom Isaac. Stand forth!"

The physician straightened himself sullenly. "A pretty treatment for a loyal son of Holy Church who hath served his Most Faithful and Catholic Sovereign at the University," he grumbled. "Who accuses me of Judaism? Confront me with the rogue!"

"'Tis against our law," said the secretary.

"Let me hear the specific charges. Read me the counts."

"In the audience-chamber. Anon."

"Confess! confess!" snapped the judge testily.

"To confess needs a sin. I have none but those I have told the priest. But I know my accuser—'tis Gabriel da Costa, a sober and studious young senhor with no ear for a jest, who did not understand that I was rallying the market-woman upon the clearance of her stock by these stinking heretics. I am no more a Jew than Da Costa himself." But even as he spoke, Gabriel knew that they were brother-Jews—he and the prisoner.

"Thou hypocrite!" he cried involuntarily.

"Ha!" said the secretary, his eye beaming triumph.

"This persistent denial will avail thee naught," said the judge, "'twill only bring thee torture."

"Torture an innocent man! 'Tis monstrous!" the physician protested. "Any tyro in the logics will tell thee that the onus of proving lies with the accuser."

"Tush! tush! This is no University. Executioner, do thy work."

The other masked man seized the old physician and stripped him to the skin.

"Confess!" said the judge warningly.

"If I confessed I was a Jew, I should be doubly a bad Christian, inasmuch as I should be lying."

"None of thy metaphysical quibbles. If thou expirest under the torture (let the secretary take note), thy death shall not be laid at the door of the Holy Office, but of thine own obstinacy."

"Christ will avenge His martyrs," said Dom Diego, with so sublime a mien that Gabriel doubted whether, after all, instinct had not misled him.

The judge made an impatient sign, and the masked man tied the victim's hands and feet together with a thick cord, and winding it around the breast, placed the hunched, nude figure upon a stool, while he passed the ends of the cord through two of the iron rings in the wall. Then, kicking away the stool, he left the victim suspended in air by cords that cut into his flesh.

"Confess!" said the judge.

But Dom Diego set his teeth. The executioner drew the cords tighter and tighter, till the blood burst from under his victim's nails, and ever and anon he let the sharp-staved iron ladder fall against his naked shins.

"O Sancta Maria!" groaned the physician at length.

"These be but the beginning of thy tortures, an thou confessest not," said the judge, "Draw tighter."

"Nay," here interrupted the surgeon. "Another draw and he may expire."

Another tightening, and Gabriel da Costa would have fainted. Deadly pale beneath his mask, he felt sick and trembling—the cords seemed to be cutting into his own flesh. His heart was equally hot against the torturers and the tortured, and he admired the physician's courage even while he abhorred his cowardice. And while the surgeon was busying himself to mend the victim for new tortures, Gabriel da Costa had a shuddering perception of the tragedy of Israel—sublime and sordid.

V

It was with equally mingled feelings, complicated by astonishment, that he learned a week or so later that Dom Diego had been acquitted of Judaism and set free. Impulse drove him to seek speech with the sufferer. He crossed the river to the physician's house, but only by extreme insistence did he procure access to the high vaulted room in which the old man lay abed, surrounded by huge tomes on pillow and counterpane, and overbrooded by an image of the Christ.

"Pardon that I have been reluctant to go back without a sight of thee," said Gabriel. "My anxiety to see how thou farest after thy mauling by the hell-hounds must be my excuse."

Dom Diego cast upon him a look of surprise and suspicion.

"The hounds may follow a wrong scent; but they are of heaven, not hell," he said rebukingly. "If I suffered wrongly, 'tis Christian to suffer, and Christian to forgive."

"Then forgive me," said Gabriel, mazed by this persistent masquerading, "for 'twas I who innocently made thee suffer. Rather would I have torn out my tongue than injured a fellow Jew."

"I am no Jew," cried the physician fiercely.

"But why deny it to me when I tell thee I am one?"

"'In vain is the net spread in the sight of any bird,'" quoted Dom Diego angrily. "Thou art as good a Christian as I,—and a worse fowler. A Jew, indeed, who knows not of the herbs! Nay, the bird-lime is smeared too thick, and there is no cord between the holes of the net."

"True, I am neither Jew nor Christian," said the young man sadly. "I was bred a Christian, but my soul is torn with questionings. See, I trust my life in thy hand."

But Dom Diego remained long obdurate, even when Gabriel made the candid admission that he was the masked man who had cried "Hypocrite!" in the torture-vault; 'twas not till, limping from the bed, he had satisfied himself that the young man had posted no auditors without, that he said at last: "Well, 'tis my word against thine. Mayhap I am but feigning so as to draw thee out." Then, winking, he took down the effigy of the Christ and thrust it into a drawer, and filling two wine-glasses from a decanter that stood at the bedside, he cried jovially, "Come! Confusion to the Holy Office!"

A great weight seemed lifted off the young man's breast. He smiled as he quaffed the rich wine.

"Meseems thou hast already wrought confusion to the Holy Office."

"Ha! ha!" laughed the physician, expanding in the glow of the wine. "Yea, the fox hath escaped from the trap, but not with a whole skin."

"No, alas! How feel thy wounds?"

"I meant not my corporeal skin," said the physician, though he rubbed it with rueful recollection. "I meant the skin whereof my purse was made. To prove my loyalty to Holy Church I offered her half my estate, and the proof was accepted. 'Twas the surgeon of the Inquisition who gave me the hint. He is one of us!"

"What! a Jew!" cried Gabriel, thunderstruck.

"Hush! hush! or we shall have him replaced by an enemy. 'Twas his fellow-feeling to me, both as a brother and a medicus, that made him declare me on the point of death when I was still as lusty as a false credo. For the rest, I had sufficient science to hold in my breath while the clown tied me with cords, else had I been too straitened to breathe. But thou needest a biscuit with thy wine. Ianthe!"

A pretty little girl stepped in from an adjoining room, her dark eyes drooping shyly at the sight of the stranger.

"Thou seest I have a witness against thee," laughed the physician; "while the evidence against me which the fools could not find we will eat up. The remainder of the Motsas, daughterling!" And drawing a key from under his pillow, he handed it to her. "Soft, now, my little one, and hide them well."

When the child had gone, the father grumbled, over another glass of wine, at having to train her to a double life. "But it sharpens the wits," said he. "Ianthe should grow up subtle as the secret cupboard within a cupboard which she is now opening. But a woman scarcely needs the training." He was yet laughing over his jape when Ianthe returned, and produced from under a napkin some large, thick biscuits, peculiarly reticulated. Gabriel looked at them curiously.

"Knowest thou not Passover cakes?" asked Dom Diego.

Gabriel shook his head.

"Thou hast never eaten unleavened bread?"

"Unleavened bread! Ah, I was reading thereof in the Pentateuch but yesterday. Stay, is it not one of the Inquisition's tests? But I figured it not thus."

"'Tis the immemorial pattern, smuggled in from Amsterdam," said the wine-flushed physician, throwing caution to the winds. "Taste! 'Tis more palatable than the Host."

"Is Amsterdam, then, a Jewish town?"

"Nay, but 'tis the Jerusalem of the West. Little Holland, since she shook off Papistry, hath no persecuting polity like the other nations. And natural enough, for 'tis more a ship than a country. Half my old friends have drifted thither—'tis a sad drain for our old Portuguese community."

Gabriel's bosom throbbed. "Then why not join them?"

The old physician shook his head. "Nay, I love my Portugal. 'Tis here that I was born, and here will I die. I love her—her mountains, her rivers, her valleys, her medicinal springs—always love Portugal, Ianthe—"

"Yes, father," said the little girl gravely.

"And, oh, her poets—her Rubeiro, her Falcão, her Camoëns—my own grandfather was thought worthy of a place in the 'Cancioneiro Geral'; and I too have made a Portuguese poem on the first aphorism of Hippocrates, though 'tis yet in manuscript."

"But if thou darest not profess thy faith," said Gabriel, "'tis more than all the rest. To live a daily lie—intolerable!"

"Hoity-toity! Thou art young and headstrong. The Catholic religion! 'Tis no more than fine manners; as we say in Hebrew, derech eretz, the way of the country. Why do I wear breeches and a cocked hat— when I am abroad, videlicet? Why does little Ianthe trip it in a petticoat?"

"Because I am a girl," said Ianthe.

Dom Diego laughed. "There's the question rhetorical, my little one, and the question interrogative. However, we'll not puzzle thee with Quintilian. Run away to thy lute. And so it is, Senhor da Costa. I love my Judaism more than my Portugal; but while I can keep both my mistresses at the cost of a little finesse—"

"But the danger of being burnt alive!"

"'Tis like hell to the Christian sinner—dim and distant."

"Thou hast been singed, methinks."

"Like a blasted tree. The lightning will not strike twice. Help thyself to more wine. Besides, my stomach likes not the Biscay Bay. God made us for land animals."

But Gabriel was not to be won over to the worthy physician's view, and only half to the man himself. Yet was not this his last visit, for he clung to Dom Diego as to the only Jew he knew, and borrowed from him a Hebrew Bible and a grammar, and began secretly to acquire the sacred tongue, bringing toys and flowers to the little Ianthe, and once a costlier lute than her own, in return for her father's help with the idioms. Also he borrowed some of Dom Diego's own works, issued anonymously from the printing presses of Amsterdam; and from his new friend's "Paradise of Earthly Vanity," and other oddly entitled volumes of controversial theology, the young enthusiast sucked instruction and confirmation of his doubts. To Dom Diego's Portuguese fellow-citizens the old gentleman was the author of an erudite essay on the treatment of phthisis, emphatically denouncing the implicit reliance on milk.

But Gabriel could not imitate this comfortable self-adjustment to surroundings. 'Twas but a half fight for the Truth, he felt, and ceased to cultivate the semi-recreant physician. For as he grew more and more in love with the Old Testament, with its simple doctrine of a people, chosen and consecrate, so grew his sense of far-reaching destinies, of a linked race sprung from the mysterious East and the dawn of history, defying destruction and surviving persecution, agonizing for its faith and its unfaith—a conception that touched the springs of romance and the source of tears—and his vision turned longingly towards Amsterdam, that city of the saints, the home of the true faith, of the brotherhood of man, and the fatherhood of God.

VI

"Mother," said Gabriel, "I have something to say to thee." They were in the half-orange room, and she had looked in to give her good-night kiss to the lonely student, but his words arrested her at the door. She sat down and gazed lovingly at her handsome eldest-born, in whom her dead husband lived as in his prime. "'Twill be of Isabella," she thought, with a stir in her breast, rejoiced to think that the brooding eyes of the scholar had opened at last to the beauty and goodness of the highborn heiress who loved him.

"Mother, I have made a great resolution, and 'tis time to tell thee."

Her eyes grew more radiant.

"My blessed Gabriel!"

"Nay, I fear thou wilt hate me."

"Hate thee!"

"Because I must leave thee."

"'Tis the natural lot of mothers to be left, my Gabriel."

"Ah, but this is most unnatural. Oh, my God! why am I thus tried?"

"What meanest thou? What has happened?" The old woman had risen.

"I must leave Portugal."

"Wherefore? in Heaven's name! Leave Portugal?"

"Hush, or the servants will hear. I would become," he breathed low, "a Jew!"

Dona da Costa blenched, and stared at him breathless, a strange light in her eyes, but not that which he had expected.

"'Tis the finger of God!" she whispered, awestruck.

"Mother!" He was thrilled with a wild suspicion.

"Yes, my father was a Jew. I was brought up as a Jewess."

"Hush! hush!" he cautioned her again, and going to the door peered into the gloom. "But my father?" he asked, shutting the door carefully.

She shook her head.

"His family, though likewise Marranos, were true believers. It was the grief of my life that I dared never tell him. Often since his death, memories from my girlhood have tugged at my heart. But I durst not influence my children's faith—it would have meant deadly peril to them. And now—O Heaven!— perchance torture—the stake—!"

"No, mother, I will fly to where faith is free."

"Then I shall lose thee all the same. O God of Israel, Thy vengeance hath found me at last!" And she fell upon the couch, sobbing, overwrought. He stood by, helpless, distracted, striving to hush her.

"How did this thing happen to you?" she sobbed.

Briefly he told her of his struggles, of the episode of Dom Diego, of his conviction that the Old Testament was the true and sufficient guide to life.

"But why flee?" she asked. "Let us all return to Judaism; thy brother Vidal is young and malleable, he will follow us. We will be secret; from my girlhood I know how suspicion may be evaded. We will gradually change all the servants save Pedro, and have none but blacks. Why shouldst thou leave this beautiful home of thine, thy friends, thy station in society, thy chances of a noble match?"

"Mother, thou painest me. What is all else beside our duty to truth, to reason, to God? I must worship all these under the naked sky."

"My brave boy! forgive me!" And she sprang up to embrace him. "We will go with thee; we will found a new home at Amsterdam."

"Nay, not at thy years, mother." And he smoothed her silver hair.

"Yea; I, too, have studied the Old Testament." And her eyes smiled through their tears. "'Wherever thou goest, I will go. Thy country shall be my country, and thy God my God.'"

He kissed her wet cheek.

Ere they separated in the gray dawn they had threshed out ways and means; how to realize their property with as little loss and as little observation as possible, and how secretly to ship for the Netherlands. The slightest imprudence might betray them to the Holy Office, and so Vidal was not told till 'twas absolutely essential.

The poor young man grew pale with fright.

"Wouldst drive me to Purgatory?" he asked.

"Nay, Judaism hath no Purgatory." Then seeing the consolation was somewhat confused, Gabriel added emphatically, to ease the distress of one he loved dearly, "There is no Purgatory."

Vidal looked more frightened than ever. "But the Church says—" he began.

"The Church says Purgatory is beneath the earth; but the world being round, there is no beneath, and, mayhap, men like ourselves do inhabit our Antipodes. And the Church holds with Aristotle that the heavens be incorruptible, and contemns Copernicus his theory; yet have I heard from Dom Diego de Balthasar, who hath the science of the University, that a young Italian, hight Galileo Galilei, hath just made a wondrous instrument which magnifies objects thirty-two times, and that therewith he hath discovered a new star. Also doth he declare the Milky Way to be but little stars; for the which the Holy Office is wroth with him, men say."

"But what have I to make with the Milky Way?" whimpered Vidal, his own face as milk.

Gabriel was somewhat taken aback. "'Tis the infallibility of the Pope that is shaken," he explained. "But in itself the Christian faith is more abhorrent to Reason than the Jewish. The things it teaches about God have more difficulties."

"What difficulties?" quoth Vidal. "I see no difficulties."

But in the end the younger brother, having all Gabriel's impressionability, and none of his strength to stand alone, consented to accompany the refugees.

During those surreptitious preparations for flight, Gabriel had to go about his semi-ecclesiastical duties and take part in Church ceremonies as heretofore. This so chafed him that he sometimes thought of proclaiming himself; but though he did not shrink from the thought of the stake, he shrank from the degradation of imprisonment, from the public humiliation, foreseeing the horror of him in the faces of all his old associates. And sometimes, indeed, it flashed upon him how dear were these friends of his youth, despite reason and religion; how like a cordial was the laughter in their eyes, the clasp of their hands, the well-worn jests of college and monastery, market-place and riding-school! How good it was, this common life, how sweet to sink into the general stream and be borne along effortless! Even as he knelt, in conscious hypocrisy, the emotion of all these worshippers sometimes swayed him in magnetic sympathy, and the crowds of holiday-makers in the streets, festively garbed, stirred him to yearning reconciliation. And now that he was to tear himself away, how dear was each familiar haunt—the woods and waters, the pleasant hills strewn with grazing cattle! How caressingly the blue sky bent over him, beseeching him to stay! And the town itself, how he loved its steep streets, the massive Moorish gates, the palaces, the monasteries, the whitewashed houses, the old-fashioned ones, quaint and windowless, and the newer with their protrusive balcony-windows—ay, and the very flavor of garlic and onion that pervaded everything; how oft he had sauntered in the Rua das Flores, watching the gold-workers! And as he moved about the old family home he had a new sense of its intimate appeal. Every beautiful panel and tile, every gracious curve of the great staircase, every statue in its niche, had a place, hitherto unacknowledged, in his heart, and called to him.

But greater than the call of all these was the call of Reason.

PART II

URIEL ACOSTA

VII

With what emotion, as of a pilgrim reaching Palestine, Gabriel found himself at last in the city where a synagogue stood in the eye of day! The warmth at his heart annulled whatever of chill stole in at the grayness of the canaled streets of the northern city after the color and glow of Porto. His first care as soon as he was settled in the great, marble-halled house which his mother's old friends and relatives in the city had purchased on his behalf, was to betake himself on the Sabbath with his mother and brother to the Portuguese synagogue. Though his ignorance of his new creed was so great that he doffed his hat on entering, nor knew how to don the praying-shawl lent him by the beadle, and was rather disconcerted to find his mother might not sit at his side, but must be relegated to a gallery behind a grille, yet his attitude was too emotional to be critical. The prayer-book interested him keenly, and though he strove to follow the service, his conscious Hebrew could not at all keep pace with the congregational speed, and he felt unreasonably shamed at his failures to rise or bow. Vidal, who had as yet no Hebrew, interested himself in picking out ancient denizens of Porto and communicating his discoveries to his brother in a loud whisper, which excited Gabriel's other neighbor to point out scions of the first Spanish families, other members of which, at home, were props of Holy Church, bishops, and even archbishops. A curious figure, this red-bearded, gross-paunched neighbor, rocking automatically to and fro in his taleth, but evidently far fainer to gossip than to pray.

Friars and nuns of almost every monastic order were, said he, here regathered to Judaism. He himself, Isaac Pereira, who sat there safe and snug, had been a Jesuit in Spain.

"I was sick of the pious make-believe, and itched to escape over here. But the fools had let me sell indulgences, and I had a goodly stock on hand, and trade was slack"—here he interrupted himself with a fervent "Amen!" conceded to the service—"in Spain just then. It's no use carrying 'em over to the Netherlands, thinks I; they're too clever over there. I must get rid of 'em in some country free for Jews, and yet containing Catholics. So what should I do but slip over from Malaga to Barbary, where I sold off the remainder of my stock to some Catholics living among the Moors. No sooner had I pocketed the— Amen!—money than I declared myself a Jew. God of Abraham! The faces those Gentiles pulled when they found what a bad bargain they had made with Heaven! They appealed to the Cadi against what they called the imposition. But"—and here an irrepressible chuckle mingled with the roar of the praying multitude—"I claimed the privilege of a free port to sell any description of goods, and the Cadi had to give his ruling in accordance with the law."

In the exhilaration of his mood this sounded amusing to Gabriel, an answering of fools according to their folly. But 'twas not long before it recurred to him to add to his disgust and his disappointment with his new brethren and his new faith. For after he had submitted himself, with his brother, to circumcision, replaced his baptismal name by the Hebrew Uriel, and Vidal's by Joseph, Latinizing at the same time the family name to Acosta, he found himself confronted by a host of minute ordinances far more galling than those of the Church. Eating, drinking, sleeping, dressing, washing, working; not the simplest action but was dogged and clogged by incredible imperatives.

Astonishment gave place to dismay, and dismay to indignation and abhorrence, as he realized into what a network of ceremonial he had entangled himself. The Pentateuch itself, with its complex codex of six hundred and thirteen precepts, formed, he discovered, but the barest framework for a parasitic growth insinuating itself with infinite ramifications into the most intimate recesses of life.

What! Was it for this Rabbinic manufacture that he had exchanged the stately ceremonial of Catholicism? Had he thrown off mental fetters but to replace them by bodily?

Was this the Golden Age that he had looked to find—the simple Mosaic theocracy of reason and righteousness?

And the Jews themselves, were these the Chosen People he had clothed with such romantic glamour?— fat burghers, clucking comfortably under the wing of the Protestant States-General; merchants sumptuously housed, vivifying Dutch trade in the Indies; their forms and dogmas alone distinguishing them from the heathen Hollanders, whom they aped even to the very patronage of painters; or, at the other end of this bastard brotherhood of righteousness, sore-eyed wretches trundling their flat carts of second-hand goods, or initiating a squalid ghetto of diamond-cutting and cigar-making in oozy alleys and on the refuse-laden borders of treeless canals. Oh! he was tricked, trapped, betrayed!

His wrath gathered daily, finding vent in bitter speeches. If this was what had become of the Mosaic Law and the Holy People, the sooner a son of Israel spoke out the better for his race. Was it not an inspiration from on high that had given him the name of Uriel—"fire of God"? So, when his private thunders had procured him a summons before the outraged Rabbinic court, he was in no wise to be awed by the Chacham and his Rabbis in their solemn robes.

"Pharisees!" he cried, and, despite his lost Christianity, all the scorn of his early training clung to the word.

"Epicurean!" they retorted, with contempt more withering still.

"Nay, Epicurus have I never read, and what I know of his doctrine by hearsay revolteth me. I am for God and Reason, and a pure Judaism."

"Even so talked Elisha Ben Abuya in Palestine of old," put in the second Rabbi more mildly. "He with his Greek culture, who stalked from Sinai to Olympus, and ended in Atheism."

"I know not of Elisha, but I marvel not that your teaching drove him to Atheism."

"Said I not 'twas Atheism, not Judaism, thou talkedst? And an Atheist in our ranks we may not harbor: our community is young in Amsterdam. 'Tis yet on sufferance, and these Dutchmen are easily moved to riot. We have won our ground with labor. Traitor! wouldst thou cut the dykes?"

"Traitor thou!" retorted Uriel. "Traitor to God and His holy Law."

"Hold thy peace!" thundered the Chacham, "or the ban shall be laid upon thee."

"Hold my peace!" answered Uriel scornfully. "Nay, I expatriated myself for freedom; I shall not hold my peace for the sake of the ban."

Nor did he. At home and abroad he exhausted himself in invective, in exhortation.

"Be silent, Uriel," begged his aged mother, dreading a breach of the happiness her soul had found at last in its old spiritual swathings. "This Judaism thou deridest is the true, the pure Judaism, as I was taught it in my girlhood. Let me go to my grave in peace."

"Be silent, Uriel," besought his brother Joseph. "If thou dost not give over, old Manasseh and his cronies will bar me out from those lucrative speculations in the Indies, wherein also I am investing thy money for thee. They have already half a hundred privateers, and the States-General wink at anything that will cripple Spain, so if we can seize its silver fleet, or capture Portuguese possessions in South America, we shall reap revenge on our enemies and big dividends. And he hath a comely daughter, hath Manasseh, and methinks her eye is not unkindly towards me. Give over, I beg of thee! This religion liketh me much—no confession, no damnation, and 'tis the faith of our fathers."

"No damnation—ay, but no salvation either. They teach naught of immortality; their creed is of the earth, earthy."

"Then why didst thou drag me from Portugal?" inquired Joseph angrily.

But Uriel—the fire of God—was not to be quenched; and so, not without frequent warning, fell the fire of man. In a solemn conclave in the black-robed synagogue, with awful symbolisms of extinguished torches, the ban was laid upon Uriel Acosta, and henceforth no man, woman, or child dared walk or talk with him. The very beggars refused his alms, the street hawkers spat out as he passed by. His own mother and brother, now completely under the sway of their new Jewish circle, removed from the pollution of his presence, leaving him alone in the great house with the black page. And this house was shunned as though marked with the cross of the pestilence. The more high-spirited Jew-boys would throw stones at its windows or rattle its doors, but it was even keener sport to run after its tenant himself, on the rare occasions when he appeared in the streets, to spit out like their elders at the sight of him, to pelt him with mud, and to shout after him, "Epicurean!" "Bastard!" "Sinner in Israel!"

VIII

But although by this isolation the Rabbis had practically cut out the heretic's tongue—for he knew no Dutch, nor, indeed, ever learned to hold converse with his Christian neighbors—yet there remained his pen, and in dread of the attack upon them which rumor declared him to be inditing behind the shuttered windows of his great lonely house, they instigated Samuel Da Silva, a physician equally skilled with the lancet and the quill, to anticipate him by a counterblast calculated to discredit the thunderer. He denied immortality, insinuated the horrified Da Silva, in his elegant Portuguese treatise, Tradado da Immortalide, probably basing his knowledge of Uriel's "bestial and injurious opinions" on the confused reports of the heretic's brother, but refraining from mentioning his forbidden name.

"False slanders!" cried Uriel in his reply—completed—since he had been anticipated—at his leisure; but he only confirmed the popular conception of his materialistic errors, seeming, indeed, of wavering mind on the subject of the future life. His thought had marched on: and whereas it had been his complaint to Joseph that Rabbinism laid no stress on immortality, further investigation of the Pentateuch had shown him that Moses himself had taken no account whatsoever of the conception, nor striven to bolster up the morality of to-day by the terrors of a posthumous to-morrow.

So Uriel stood self-condemned, and the Rabbis triumphed, superfluously justified in the eyes of their flock against this blaspheming materialist. Nay, Uriel should fall into the pit himself had digged. The elders of the congregation appealed to the magistrates; they translated with bated breath passages from the baleful book, Tradiçoens Phariseas conferidos con a Ley escrida. Uriel was summoned before the tribunal, condemned to pay three hundred guldens, imprisoned for eight days. The book was burnt.

No less destructive a flame burnt at the prisoner's heart, as, writhing on his dungeon pallet, biting his lips, digging his nails into his palms, he cursed these malignant perverters of pure Judaism, who had shamed him even before the Hollanders. He, the proud and fearless gentleman of Portugal, had been branded as a criminal by these fish-blooded Dutchmen. Never would he hold intercourse with his fellow-creatures again—never, never! Alone with God and his thoughts he would live and die.

And so for year after year, though he lingered in the city that held his dear ones, he abode in his cold marble-pillared house, save for his Moorish servant, having speech with man nor woman. Nor did he ever emerge, unless at hours when his childish persecutors were abed, so that in time they turned to fresher sport. But at night he would sometimes be met wandering by the dark canals, with eyes that kept the inward look of the sequestered student, seeming to see nothing of the sombre many-twinkling beauty of starlit waters, or the tender coloring of mist and haze, but full only of the melancholy of the gray marshes, and sometimes growing wet with bitter yearning for the sun and the orange-trees and the warmth of friendly faces. And sometimes in the cold dawn the early market-people met him riding madly in the environs, in the silk doublet of a Portuguese grandee, his sword clanking, and in his hand a silver-mounted pistol, with which he snapped off the twigs as he flew past. And when his beloved brother was married to the daughter of Manasseh, the millionaire and the president of the India Company—which in that wonderful year paid its shareholders a dividend of seventy-five in the hundred—some of the wedding-guests averred that they had caught a glimpse of Uriel's dark, yearning face amid the motley crowd assembled outside the synagogue to watch the arrival of Joseph Acosta and his beautiful bride; and there were those who said that Uriel's hands were raised as in blessing. And once on a moonless midnight, when the venerable Dona Acosta had passed away, the watchman in the Jews' cemetery, stealing from his turret at a suspicious noise, turned his lantern upon—no body-snatcher, but—O more nefarious spectacle!—the sobbing figure of Uriel Acosta across a new-dug grave, polluting the holy soil of the Beth-Chayim!

IX

And so the seasons and the years wore on, each walling in the lonely thinker with more solid ice, and making it only the more difficult ever to break through or to melt his prison walls. Nigh fifteen long winter years had passed in a solitude tempered by theological thought, and Uriel, nigh forgotten by his people, had now worked his way even from the religion of Moses. It was the heart alone that was the seat of religion; wherefore, no self-styled Revelation that contradicted Nature could be true. Right Religion was according to Right Reason; but no religion was reasonable that could set brother against brother. All ceremonies were opposed to Reason. Goodness was the only true religion. Such bold conclusions sometimes affrighted himself, being alone in the world to hold them. "All evils," his note-book summed it up in his terse Latin, "come from not following Right Reason and the Law of Nature."

And thinking such thoughts in the dead language that befitted one cut off from life, to whom Dutch was never aught but the unintelligible jargon of an unspiritual race, he was leaving his house on a bleak evening when one clapped him on the shoulder, and turning in amaze, he was still more mazed to find, for the first time in fifteen years, a fellow-creature tendering a friendly smile and a friendly hand. He drew back instinctively, without even recognizing the aged, white-bearded, yet burly figure.

"What, Senhor Da Costa! thou hast forgotten thy victim?"

With a strange thrill he felt the endless years in Amsterdam slip off him like the coils of some icy serpent, as he recognized the genial voice of the Porto physician, and though he was back again in the dungeon of the Holy Office, it was not the gloom of the vault that he felt, but sunshine and blue skies and spring and youth. Through the soft mist of delicious tears he gazed at the kindly furrowed face of the now hoary-headed physician, and clasped his great warm hand, holding it tight, forgetting to drop it, as though it were drawing him back to life and love and fellowship.

The first few words made it clear that Dom Diego had not heard of Uriel's excommunication. He was new in the city, having been driven there, pathetically enough, at the extreme end of his life by the renewed activity of the Holy Office. "I longed to die in Portugal," he said, with his burly laugh; "but not at the hands of the Inquisition."

Uriel choked back the wild impulse to denounce the crueller Inquisition of Jewry, from the sudden recollection that Dom Diego might at once withdraw from him the blessed privilege of human speech.

"Didst make a good voyage?" he asked instead.

"Nay, the billows were in the Catholic League," replied the old man, making a wry face. "However, the God of Israel neither slumbers nor sleeps, and I rejoice to have chanced upon thee, were it only to be guided back to my lodgings amid this water labyrinth."

On the way, Uriel gave what answers he could to the old man's questionings. His mother was dead; his brother Vidal had married, though his wife had died some years later in giving birth to a boy, who was growing up beautiful as a cherub. Yes, he was prospering in worldly affairs, having long since intrusted them to Joseph—that was to say, Vidal—who had embarked all the family wealth in a Dutch enterprise called the West India Company, which ran a fleet of privateers, to prey upon the treasure-ships in the war with Spain. He did not say that his own interests were paid to him by formal letter through a law firm, and that he went in daily fear that his estranged and pious brother, now a pillar of the synagogue, would one day religiously appropriate the heretic's property, backed by who knew what devilish provision of Church or State, leaving him to starve. But he wondered throughout their walk why Dom Diego, who had such constant correspondence with Amsterdam, had never heard of his excommunication, and his bitterness came back as he realized that the ban had extended to the mention of his name, that he was as one dead, buried, cast down to oblivion. Even before he had accepted the physician's invitation to cross his threshold, he had resolved to turn this silence to his own profit: he, whose inward boast was his stainless honor, had resolved to act a silent lie. Was it not fair to outwit the rogues with their own weapon? He had faded from human memory—let it be so. Was he to be cut off from this sudden joy of friendship with one of his blood and race, he whose soul was perishing with drought, though, until this moment, he had been too proud to own it to himself?

But when he entered Dom Diego's lodging and saw the unexpected, forgotten Ianthe—Ianthe grown from that sweet child to matchless grace of early womanhood; Ianthe with her dark smiling eyes and her caressing voice and her gentle movements—then this resolution of passive silence was exchanged for a determination to fight desperately against discovery. In the glow of his soul, in the stir of youth and spring in his veins, in the melting rapture of his mood, that first sight of a beautiful girl's face bent smilingly to greet her father's guest had sufficed to set his heart aflame with a new emotion, sweet, riotous, sacred. What a merry supper-party was that; each dish eaten with the sauce of joyous memories! How gaily he rallied Ianthe on her childish ways and sayings! Of course, she remembered him, she said, and the toys and flowers, and told how comically he had puckered his brow in argumentation with her father. Yes, he had the same funny lines still, and once she touched his forehead lightly for an instant with her slender fingers in facetious demonstration, and he trembled in painful rapture. And she played on her lute, too, on the lute he had given her of old, those slender fingers making ravishing music on the many-stringed instrument, though her pose as she played was more witching still. What a beautiful glimpse of white shoulders and dainty lace her straight-cut black bodice permitted!

He left the house drunk, exalted, and as the cold night air smote the forehead she had touched he was thrilled with fiery energy. He was young still, thank God, though fifteen years had been eaten out of his life, and he had thought himself as old and gray as the marshes. He was young still, he told himself fiercely, defiantly. At home his note-book lay open, as usual, on his desk, like a friend waiting to hear what thoughts had come to him in his lonely walk. How far off and alien seemed this cold confidant now, how irrelevant, and yet, when his eye glanced curiously at his last recorded sentence, how relevant! "All evils come from not following Right Reason and the Law of Nature." How true! How true! He had followed neither Right Reason nor the Law of Nature.

X

In the morning, when the cold, pitiless eye of the thinker penetrated through the sophisms of desire as clearly as his bodily eye saw the gray in his hair and the premature age in his face, he saw how impossible it was to keep the secret of his situation from Dom Diego. Honor forbade it, though this, he did not shrink from admitting to himself, might have counted little but for the certainty of discovery. If he went to the physician's abode he could not fail to meet fellow-Jews there. To some, perhaps, of the younger generation, his forgotten name would convey no horrid significance; but then, Dom Diego's cronies would be among the older men. No; he must himself warn Dom Diego that he was a leper—a pariah. But not—since that might mean final parting—not without a farewell meeting. He sent Pedro with a note to the physician's lodgings, begging to be allowed the privilege of returning his hospitality that same evening; and the physician accepting for himself and daughter, a charwoman was sent for, the great cobwebbed house was scrubbed and furbished in the living chambers, the ancient silver was exhumed from mildewed cupboards, the heavy oil-paintings were dusted, a lively canary in a bright cage was hung on a marble pillar of the dining-room, over the carven angels; flowers were brought in, and at night, in the soft light of the candles, the traces of year-long neglect being subdued and hidden, a spirit of festivity and gaiety pervaded the house as of natural wont, while the Moorish attendant's red knee-breeches, gold-braided coat, and blue-feathered turban, hitherto so incongruous in the general grayness, now seemed part of the normal color. And Uriel, too, grown younger with the house, made a handsome be-ruffed figure as he sat at the board, exchanging merry sallies with the physician and Ianthe.

After the meal and the good wine that alone had not had its cobwebs brushed shamefacedly away, Dom Diego fell conveniently asleep, looking so worn and old when the light of his lively fancy had died out of his face, that the speech of Uriel and Ianthe took a tenderer tone for fear of disturbing him. Presently, too, their hands came together, and—such was the swift sympathy between these shapely creatures— did not dispart. And suddenly, kindled to passion by her warm touch and breathing presence, stabbed with the fear that this was the last time he would see her, he told her that for the first time in his life he knew the meaning of love.

"Oh, if thou wouldst but return my love!" he faltered with dry throat. "But no! that were too much for a man of my years to hope. But whisper at least, that I am not repugnant to thee."

She was about to reply, when he dropped her hand and stayed her with a gesture as abrupt as his avowal.

"Nay, answer me not. Not till I have told thee what honor forbids I should withhold."

And he told the story of his ban and his long loneliness, her face flashing 'twixt terror and pity.

"Answer me, now," he said, almost sternly. "Couldst thou love such a man, proscribed by his race, a byword and a mockery, to whom it is a sin against Heaven even to speak?"

"They would not marry us," she breathed helplessly.

"But couldst thou love me?"

Her eyes drooped as she breathed, "The more for thy sufferings."

But even in the ecstasy of this her acknowledgment, he had a chill undercurrent of consciousness that she did not understand; that, never having lived in an unpersecuted Jewish community, she had no real sense of its own persecuting power. Still, there was no need to remain in Amsterdam now: they would live together in some lonely spot, in the religion of Right Reason that he would teach her. So their hands came together again, and once their lips met. But the father was yet to be told of their sudden-born, sudden-grown love, and this with characteristic impulse Uriel did as soon as the old physician awoke.

"God bless my soul!" said Dom Diego, "am I dreaming still?"

His sense of dream increased when Uriel went on to repeat the story of his excommunication.

"And the ban—is it still in force?" he interrupted.

"It has not been removed," said Uriel sadly.

The burly graybeard sprang to his feet. "And with such a brand upon thy brow thou didst dare speak to my daughter!"

"Father!" cried Ianthe.

"Father me not! He hath beguiled us here under false pretences. He hath made us violate the solemn decree of the synagogue. He is outlawed—he and his house and his food—Sinner! The viands thou hast given us, what of them? Is thy meat ritually prepared?"

"Thou, a man of culture, carest for these childish things?"

"Childish things? Wherefore, then, have I left my Portugal?"

"All ceremonies are against Right Reason," said Uriel in low tones, his face grown deadly white.

"Now I see that thou hast never understood our holy and beautiful religion. Men of culture, forsooth! Is not our Amsterdam congregation full of men of culture—grammarians, poets, exegetes, philosophers, jurists, but flesh and blood, mark you, not diagrams, cut out of Euclid? Whence the cohesion of our race? Ceremony! What preserves and unifies its scattered atoms throughout the world? Ceremony! And what is ceremony? Poetry. 'Tis the tradition handed down from hoary antiquity; 'tis the color of life."

"'Tis a miserable thraldom," interposed Uriel more feebly.

"Miserable! A happy service. Hast never danced at the Rejoicing of the Law? Who so joyous as our brethren? Where so cheerful a creed? The trouble with thee is that thou hast no childish associations with our glorious religion, thou camest to it in manhood with naught but the cold eye of Reason."

"But thou dost not accept every invention of Rabbinism. Surely in Porto thou didst not practise everything."

"I kept what I could. I believe what I can. If I have my private doubts, why should I set them up to perplex the community withal? There's a friend of mine in this very city—not to mention names—but a greater heretic, I ween, than even thou. But doth he shatter the peace of the vulgar? Nay, not he: he hath a high place in the synagogue, is a blessing to the Jewry, and confideth his doubts to me in epistles writ in elegant Latin. Nay, nay, Senhor Da Costa, the world loves not battering-rams."

And as the old physician spoke, Uriel began dimly to suspect that he had misconceived human life, taken it too earnestly, and at his heart was a hollow aching sense of futile sacrifice. And with it a suspicion that he had mistaken Judaism, too—missed the poetry and humanity behind the forms, and, as he gazed wistfully at Ianthe's tender clouded face, he felt the old romantic sense of brotherhood stirring again. How wonderful to be reabsorbed into his race, fused with Ianthe!

But Right Reason resurged in relentless ascendency, and he knew that his thought could never more go back on itself, that he could never again place faith in any Revelation.

"I will be an ape among apes," he thought bitterly.

XI

And the more he pondered upon this resolution, after Dom Diego had indignantly shaken off the dust of his threshold, the more he was confirmed in it. To outwit the Jewry would be the bitterest revenge, to pay lip-service to its ideals and laugh at it in his sleeve. And thus, too, he would circumvent its dreaded design to seize upon his property. Deception? Ay, but the fault was theirs who drove him to it, leaving him only a leper's life. In the Peninsula they had dissembled among Christians; he would dissemble among Jews, aping the ancient apes. He foresaw no difficulty in the recantation. And—famous idea!— his brother Joseph, poor, dear fool, should bring it about under the illusion that he was the instrument of Providence: for to employ Dom Diego as go-between were to risk the scenting of his real motive. Then, when the Synagogue had taken him to its sanctimonious arms, Ianthe—overwhelming thought!— would become his wife. He had little doubt of that; her farewell glance, after her father's back was turned, was sweet with promises and beseechments, and a brief note from her early the next morning dissipated his last doubts.

"My poor Senhor Da Costa," she wrote, "I have lain awake all night thinking of thee. Why ruin thy life for a mere abstraction? Canst thou not make peace!—Thy friend, Ianthe."

He kissed the note; then, his wits abnormally sharpened, he set to work to devise how to meet his brother, and even as he was meditating how to trick him, his heart was full of affection for his little Vidal. Poor Vidal! How he must have suffered to lose his beautiful wife!

There were days on which Joseph's business or pleasure took him past his brother's house, though he always walked on the further side, and Uriel now set himself to keep watch at his study window from morning to night, the pair of Dutch mirrors fixed slantingly outside the window enabling him to see all the street life without being seen. After three days, his patience was rewarded by the reflected image of the portly pillar of the synagogue, and with him his little boy of six. He ran downstairs and into the street and caught up the boy in his arms—

"Oh, Vidal!" he said, real affection struggling in his voice.

"Thou!" said Joseph, staggering with the shock, and trembling at the sound of his submerged name. Then, recovering himself, he said angrily, "Pollute not my Daniel with thy touch."

"He is my nephew. I love him, too! How beautiful he is!" And he kissed the wondering little fellow. He refused to put him down. He ran towards his own door. He begged Vidal to give him a word in pity of his loneliness. Joseph looked fearfully up and down the street. No Jew was in sight. He slipped hastily through the door. From that moment Uriel played his portly brother like a chess-piece, which should make complicated moves and think it made them of its own free will. Gradually, by secret conversations, daily renewed, Joseph, fired with enthusiasm and visions of the glory that would redound upon him in the community—for he was now a candidate for the dignity of treasurer—won Uriel back to Judaism. And when the faith of the revert was quite fixed, Joseph made great talk thereof, and interceded with the Rabbis.

Uriel Acosta was given a document of confession of his errors to sign; he promised to live henceforward as a true Jew, and the ban was removed. On the Sabbath he went to the synagogue, and was called up to read in the Law. The elders came to shake him by the hand; a wave of emotion traversed the congregation. Uriel, mentally blinking at all this novel sunshine, had moments of forgetfulness of his sardonic hypocrisy, thrilled to be in touch with humanity again, and moved by its forgiving good-will. The half-circle of almond and lemon trees from Portugal, planted in gaily-painted tubs before the Holy Ark, swelled his breast with tender, tearful memories of youth and the sun-lands. And as Ianthe's happy eyes smiled upon him from the gallery, the words of the Prophet Joel sang in his ears: "And I will restore to you the years that the locust hath eaten."

It was a glad night when Dom Diego and Ianthe sat again at his table, religiously victualled this time, and with them his beloved brother Joseph, not the least happy of the guests in the reconciliation with Uriel and the near prospect of the treasuryship. What a handsome creature he was! thought Uriel fondly. How dignified in manners, yet how sprightly in converse!—no graven lines of suffering on his brow, no gray in his hair. The old wine gurgled, the old memories glowed. Joseph was let into the secret of the engagement—which was not to be published for some months—but was too sure of the part he had played to suspect he had been played with. He sang the Hebrew grace jubilantly after the meal, and Ianthe's sweet voice chimed in happily. Ere the brothers parted, Uriel had extracted a promise that little Daniel should be lent him for a few days to crown his happiness and brighten the great lonely house for the coming of the bride.

XII

Uriel Acosta sat at dinner with little Daniel, feasting his eyes on the fresh beauty of the boy, whose prattle had made the last two days delightful. Daniel had been greatly exercised to find that his great big uncle could not talk Dutch, and that he must talk Portuguese—which was still kept up in families—to be understood. He had hitherto imagined that grown-up people knew everything. Pedro, his black face agrin with delight, waited solicitously upon the little fellow.

He changed his meat plate now, and helped him lavishly to tart. "Cream?" said Uriel, tendering the jug.

"No, no!" cried Daniel, with a look of horror and a violent movement of repulsion.

Uriel chuckled. "What! Little boys not like cream! We shall find cats shuddering at milk next." And pouring the contents of the jug lavishly over his own triangle of tart, he went on with his meal.

But little Daniel was staring at him with awe struck vision, forgetting to eat.

"Uncle," he cried at last, "thou art not a Jew."

Uriel laughed uneasily. "Little boys should eat and not talk."

"But, Uncle! We may not eat milk after meat."

"Well, well, then, little Rabbi!" And Uriel pushed his plate away and pinched the child's ear fondly.

But when the child went home he prattled of his uncle's transgressions, and Joseph hurried down, storming at this misleading of his boy, and this breach of promise to the synagogue. Uriel retorted angrily with that native candor of his which made it impossible for him long to play a part.

"I am but an ape among apes," he said, using his pet private sophism.

"Say rather an ape among lynxes, who will spy thee out," said Joseph, more hotly. "Thy double-dealing will be discovered, and I shall become the laughing-stock of the congregation."

It was the beginning of a second quarrel—fiercer, bitterer than the first. Joseph denounced Uriel privily to Dom Diego, who thundered at the heretic in his turn.

"I give not my daughter to an ape," he retorted, when Uriel had expounded himself as usual.

"Ianthe loves the ape; 'tis her concern," Uriel was stung into rejoining.

"Nay, 'tis my concern. By Heaven, I'll grandsire no gorillas!"

"Methinks in Porto thou wast an ape thyself," cried Uriel, raging.

"Dog!" shrieked the old physician, his venerable countenance contorted; "dost count it equal to deceive the Christians and thine own brethren?" And he flung from the house.

Uriel wrote to Ianthe. She replied—

"I asked thee to make thy peace. Thou hast made bitterer war. I cannot fight against my father and all Israel. Farewell!"

Uriel's face grew grim: the puckers in his brow that her fingers had touched showed once more as terrible lines of suffering; his teeth were clenched. The old look of the hunted man came back. He took out her first note, which he kept nearest his heart, and re-read it slowly—

"Why ruin thy life for a mere abstraction? Canst thou not make peace?"

A mere abstraction! Ah! Why had that not warned him of the woman's calibre? Nay, why had he forgotten—and here he had a vivid vision of a little girl bringing in Passover cakes—her training in a double life? Not that woman needed that—Dom Diego was right. False, frail creatures! No sympathy with principles, no recognition of the great fight he had made. Tears of self-pity started to his eyes. Well, she had, at least, saved him from cowardly surrender. The old fire flamed in his veins. He would fight to the death.

And as he tore up her notes, a strange sense of relief mingled with the bitterness and fierceness of his mood; relief to think that never again would he be called upon to jabber with the apes, to grasp their loathly paws, to join in their solemnly absurd posturings, never would he be tempted from the peace and seclusion of his book-lined study. The habits of fifteen years tugged him back like ropes of which he had exhausted the tether.

He seated himself at his desk, and took up his pen to resume his manuscript. "All evils come from not following Right Reason and the Law of Nature." He wrote on for hours, pausing from time to time to select his Latin phrases. Suddenly a hollow sense of the futility of his words, of Reason, of Nature, of everything, overcame him. What was this dreadful void at his breast? He leaned his tired, aching head on his desk and sobbed, as little Daniel had never sobbed yet.

XIII

To the congregation at large, ignorant of these inner quarrels, the backsliding of Uriel was made clear by the swine-flesh which the Christian butcher now openly delivered at the house. Horrified zealots remonstrated with him in the streets, and once or twice it came to a public affray. The outraged elders pressed for a renewal of the ban; but the Rabbis hesitated, thinking best, perhaps, henceforward to ignore the thorn in their sides.

It happened that a Spaniard and an Italian came from London to seek admission into the Jewish fold, Christian sceptics not infrequently finding peace in the bosom of the older faith. These would-be converts, hearing the rumors anent Uriel Acosta, bethought themselves of asking his advice. When the House of Judgment heard that he had bidden them beware of the intolerable yoke of the Rabbis, its members felt that this was too much. Uriel Acosta was again excommunicated.

And now began new years of persecution, more grievous, more determined than ever. Again his house was stoned, his name a byword, his walks abroad a sport to the little ones of a new generation. And now even the worst he had feared came to pass. Gradually his brother, who had refused on various pretexts to liberate his capital, encroached on his property. Uriel dared not complain to the civil magistrates, by whom he was already suspect as an Atheist; besides, he still knew no Dutch, and in worldly matters was as a child. Only his love for his brother turned to deadly hate, which was scarcely intensified when Joseph led Ianthe under the marriage canopy.

So seven terrible years passed, and Uriel, the lonely, prematurely aged, found himself sinking into melancholia. He craved for human companionship, and the thought that he could find it save among Jews never occurred to him. And at last he humbled himself, and again sought forgiveness of the synagogue.

But this time he was not to be readmitted into the fold so lightly. Imitating the gloomy forms of the Inquisition, from which they had suffered so much, the elders joined with the Rabbis in devising a penance, which would brand the memory of the heretic's repentance upon the minds of his generation.

Uriel consented to the penance, scarcely knowing what they asked of him. Anything rather than another day of loneliness; so into the great synagogue, densely filled with men and women, the penitent was led, clothed in a black mourning garb and holding a black candle. He whose earliest dread had been to be shamed before men, was made to mount a raised stage, wherefrom he read a long scroll of recantation, confessing all his ritual sins and all his intellectual errors, and promising to live till death as a true Jew. The Chacham, who stood near the sexton, solemnly intoned from the seventy-eighth Psalm: "But He, being full of compassion, forgave their iniquity and destroyed them not: yea, many a time turned He his anger away and did not stir up all his wrath. For He remembered that they were but flesh: a wind that passeth away and cometh not again."

He whispered to Uriel, who went to a corner of the synagogue, stripped as far as the girdle, and received with dumb lips thirty-nine lashes from a scourge. Then, bleeding, he sat on the ground, and heard the ban solemnly removed. Finally, donning his garments, he stretched himself across the threshold, and the congregation passed out over his body, some kicking it in pious loathing, some trampling on it viciously. The penitent remained rigid, his face pressed to the ground. Only, when his brother Joseph trampled upon him, he knew by subtle memories of his tread and breathing who the coward was.

When the last of the congregants had passed over his body, Uriel arose and went through the pillared portico, speaking no word. The congregants, standing in groups about the canal-bridge, still discussing the terrible scene, moved aside, shuddering, silenced, as like a somnambulist that strange figure went by, the shoulders thrown back, the head high, in superb pride, the nostrils quivering, but the face as that of the dead. Never more was he seen of men. Shut up in his study, he worked feverishly day and night, writing his autobiography. Exemplar Humanae Vitae—an Ensample of Human Life, he called it, with tragic pregnancy. Scarcely a word of what the world calls a man's life—only the dry account of his abstract thought, of his progress to broader standpoints, to that great discovery—"All evils come from not following Right Reason and the Law of Nature." And therewith a virulent denunciation of Judaism and its Rabbis: "They would crucify Jesus even now if He appeared again." And, garnering the wisdom of his life-experience, he bade every man love his neighbor, not because God bids him, but by virtue of being a man. What Judaism, what Christianity contains of truth belongs not to revealed, but to natural religion. Love is older than Moses; it binds men together. The Law of Moses separates them: one brings harmony, the other discord into human society.

His task was drawing to an end. His long fight with the Rabbis was ending, too. "My cause is as far superior to theirs as truth is more excellent than falsehood: for whereas they are advocates for a fraud that they may make a prey and slaves of men, I contend nobly in the cause of Truth, and assert the natural rights of mankind, whom it becomes to live suitably to the dignity of their nature, free from the burden of superstitions and vain ceremonies."

It was done. He laid down his quill and loaded his pair of silver-mounted pistols. Then he placed himself at the window as of yore, to watch in his two mirrors for the passing of his brother Joseph. He knew his hand would not fail him. The days wore on, but each sunrise found him at his post, as it was reflected sanguinarily in those fatal mirrors.

One afternoon Joseph came, but Daniel was with him. And Uriel laid down his pistol and waited, for he yet loved the boy. And another time Joseph passed by with Ianthe. And Uriel waited.

But the third time Joseph came alone. Gabriel's heart gave a great leap of exultation. He turned, took careful aim, and fired. The shot rang through the startled neighborhood, but Joseph fled in panic, uninjured, shouting.

Uriel dropped his pistol, half in surprise at his failure, half in despairing resignation.

"There is no justice," he murmured. How gray the sky was! What a cold, bleak world!

He went to the door and bolted it. Then he took up the second pistol. Irrelevantly he noted the "G." graven on it. Gabriel! Gabriel! What memories his old name brought back! There were tears in his eyes. Why had he changed to Uriel? Gabriel! Gabriel! Was that his mother's voice calling him, as she had called him in sunny Portugal, amid the vines and the olive-trees?

Worn out, world-weary, aged far beyond his years, beaten in the long fight, despairing of justice on earth and hopeless of any heaven, Uriel Acosta leaned droopingly against his beloved desk, put the pistol's cold muzzle to his forehead, pressed the trigger, and fell dead across the open pages of his Exemplar Humanae Vitae, the thin, curling smoke lingering a little ere it dissipated, like the futile spirit of a passing creature—"a wind that passeth away and cometh not again."

THE TURKISH MESSIAH

SCROLL THE FIRST

I

In the year of the world five thousand four hundred and eight, sixteen hundred and forty-eight years after the coming of Christ, and in the twenty-third year of his own life on earth, Sabbataï Zevi, men said, declared himself at Smyrna to his disciples—the long-expected Messiah of the Jews. They were gathered together in the winter midnight, a little group of turbaned, long-robed figures, the keen stars innumerable overhead, the sea stretching sombrely at their feet, and the swarming Oriental city, a black mystery of roofs, minarets, and cypresses, dominated by the Acropolis, asleep on the slopes of its snow-clad hill.

Anxiously they had awaited their Prophet's emergence from his penitential lustration in the icy harbor, and as he now stood before them in naked majesty, the water dripping from his black beard and hair, a perfect manly figure, scarred only by self-inflicted scourgings, awe and wonder held them breathless with expectation. Inhaling that strange fragrance of divinity that breathed from his body, and penetrated by the kingliness of his mien, the passionate yet spiritual beauty of his dark, dreamy face, they awaited the great declaration. Some common instinct told them that he would speak to-night, he, the master of mystic silences.

The Zohar—that inspired book of occult wisdom—had long since foretold this year as the first of the epoch of regeneration, and ever since the shrill ram's horn had heralded its birth, the souls of Sabbataï Zevi's disciples had been tense for the great moment. Surely it was to announce himself at last that he had summoned them, blessed partakers in the greatest moment of human and divine history.

What would he say?

Austere, silent, hedged by an inviolable sanctity, he stood long motionless, realizing, his followers felt, the Cabalistic teaching as to the Messiah, incarnating the Godhead through the primal Adam, pure, sinless, at one with himself and elemental Nature. At last he raised his luminous eyes heavenwards, and said in clear, calm tones one word—

YAHWEH!

He had uttered the dread, forbidden Name of God. For an instant the turbaned figures stood rigid with awe, their blood cold with an ineffable terror, then as they became conscious again of the stars glittering on, the sea plashing unruffled, the earth still solid under their feet, a great hoarse shout of holy joy flew up to the shining stars. "Messhiach! Messhiach! The Messiah!"

The Kingdom was come.

The Messianic Era had begun.

II

How long, O Lord, how long?

That desolate cry of the centuries would be heard no more.

While Israel was dispersed and the world full of sin, the higher and lower worlds had been parted, and the four letters of God's name had been dissevered, not to be pronounced in unison. For God Himself had been made imperfect by the impeding of His moral purpose.

But the Messiah had pronounced the Tetragrammaton, and God and the Creation were One again. O mystic transport! O ecstatic reunion! The joyous shouts died into a more beatific silence.

From some near mosque there broke upon the midnight air the solemn voice of the muëddin chanting the adán—

"God is most great. I testify that there is no God but God. I testify that Mohammed is God's Prophet."

Sabbataï shivered. Was it the cold air or some indefinable foreboding?

It was the day of Messianic dreams. In the century that was over, strange figures had appeared of prophets and martyrs and Hebrew visionaries. From obscurity and the far East came David Reubeni, journeying to Italy by way of Nubia to obtain firearms to rid Palestine of the Moslem—a dark-faced dwarf, made a skeleton by fasts, riding on his white horse up to the Vatican to demand an interview, and graciously received by Pope Clement. In Portugal—where David Reubeni, heralded by a silken standard worked with the Ten Commandments, had been received by the King with an answering pageantry of banners and processions—a Marrano maiden had visions of Moses and the angels, undertook to lead her suffering kinsfolk to the Holy Land, and was burnt by the Inquisition. Diogo Pires—handsome and brilliant and young, and a Christian by birth—returned to the faith of his fathers, and, under the name of Solomon Molcho, passed his brief life in quest of prophetic ecstasies and the pangs of martyrdom. He sought to convert the Pope to Judaism, and predicting a great flood at Rome, which came to pass, with destructive earthquakes at Lisbon, was honored by the Vatican, only to meet a joyful death at Mantua, where, by order of the Emperor, he was thrown upon the blazing funeral pyre. And in these restless and terrible times for the Jews, inward dreams mingled with these outward portents. The Zohar—the Book of Illumination, composed in the thirteenth century—printed now for the first time, shed its dazzling rays further and further over every Ghetto.

The secrets reserved for the days of the Messiah had been revealed in it: Elijah, all the celestial conclave, angels, spirits, higher souls, and the Ten Spiritual Substances had united to inspire its composers, teach them the bi-sexual nature of the World-Principle, and discover to them the true significance of the Torah (Law), hitherto hidden in the points and strokes of the Pentateuch, in its vowels and accents, and even in the potential transmutations of the letters of its words. Lurya, the great German Egyptian Cabalist, with Vital, the Italian alchemist, sojourned to the grave of Simon bar Yochai, its fabled author. Lurya himself, who preferred the silence and loneliness of the Nile country to the noise of the Talmud-School, who dressed in white on Sabbath, and wore a fourfold garment to signify the four letters of the Ineffable Name, and who by permutating these, could draw down spirits from Heaven, passed as the Messiah of the Race of Joseph, precursor of the true Messiah of the Race of David. The times were ripe. "The kingdom of heaven is at hand," cried the Cabalists with one voice. The Jews had suffered so much and so long. Decimated for not dying of the Black Death, pillaged and murdered by the Crusaders, hounded remorselessly from Spain and Portugal, roasted by thousands at the autos-da-fé of the Inquisition, everywhere branded and degraded, what wonder if they felt that their cup was full, that redemption was at hand, that the Lord would save Israel and set His people in triumph over the heathen! "I believe with a perfect faith that the Messiah will come, and though His coming be delayed, nevertheless will I daily expect Him."

So ran their daily creed.

In Turkey what time the Jews bore themselves proudly, rivalling the Venetians in the shipping trade, and the Grand Viziers in the beauty of their houses, gardens, and kiosks; when Joseph was Duke of Naxos, and Solomon Ashkenazi Envoy Extraordinary to Venice; when Tiberias was turned into a new Jerusalem and planted with mulberry-trees; when prosperous physicians wrote elegant Latin verses; in those days the hope of the Messiah was faint and dim. But it flamed up fiercely enough when their strength and prestige died down with that of the Empire, and the harem and the Janissaries divided power with the Prætorians of the Spahis, and the Jews were the first objects of oppression ready to the hand of the unloosed pashas, and the black turban marked them off from the Moslem. It was a Rabbi of the

Ottoman Empire who wrote the religious code of "The Ordered Table" to unify Israel and hasten the coming of the Messiah, and his dicta were accepted far and wide.

And not only did Israel dream of the near Messiah, the rumor of Him was abroad among the nations. Men looked again to the mysterious Orient, the cradle of the Divine. In the far isle of England sober Puritans were awaiting the Millennium and the Fifth Monarchy of the Apocalypse—the four "beasts" of the Babylonian, Persian, Greek, and Roman monarchies having already passed away—and when Manasseh ben Israel of Amsterdam petitioned Cromwell to readmit the Jews, his plea was that thereby they might be dispersed through all nations, and the Biblical prophecies as to the eve of the Messianic age be thus fulfilled. Verily, the times were ripe for the birth of a Messiah.

IV

He had been strange and solitary from childhood, this saintly son of the Smyrniote commission agent. He had no playmates, none of the habits of the child. He would wander about the city's steep bustling alleys that seemed hewn in a great rock, or through the long, wooden-roofed bazaars, seeming to heed the fantastically colored spectacle as little as the garbage under foot, or the trains of gigantic camels, at the sound of whose approaching bells he would mechanically flatten himself against the wall. And yet he must have been seeing, for if he chanced upon anything that suffered—a child, a lean dog, a cripple, a leper—his eyes filled with tears. At times he would stand on the brink of the green gulf and gaze seawards long and yearningly, and sometimes he would lie for hours upon the sudden plain that stretched lonely behind the dense port.

In the little congested school-room where hundreds of children clamored Hebrew at once he was equally alone; and when, a brilliant youth, he headed the lecture-class of the illustrious Talmudist, Joseph Eskapha, his mental attitude preserved the same aloofness. Quicker than his fellows he grasped the casuistical hair-splittings in which the Rabbis too often indulged, but his contempt was as quick as his comprehension. A note of revolt pierced early through his class-room replies, and very soon he threw over these barren subtleties to sink himself—at a tenderer age than tradition knew of—in the spiritual mysticisms, the poetic fervors, and the self-martyrdoms of the Cabalistic literature. The transmigrations of souls, mystic marriages, the summoning of spirits, the creation of the world by means of attributes, or how the Godhead had concentrated itself within itself in order to unfold the finite Many from the infinite One; such were the favorite studies of the brooding youth of fifteen.

"Learning shall be my life," he said to his father.

"Thy life! But what shall be thy livelihood?" replied Mordecai Zevi. "Thy elder brothers are both at work."

"So much more need that one of thy family should consecrate himself to God, to call down a blessing on the work of the others."

Mordecai Zevi shook his head. In his olden days, in the Morea, he had known the bitterness of poverty. But he was beginning to prosper now, like so many of his kinsmen, since Sultan Ibrahim had waged war against the Venetians, and, by imperilling the trade of the Levant, had driven the Dutch and English merchants to transfer their ledgers from Constantinople to Smyrna. The English house of which Mordecai had obtained the agency was waxing rich, and he in its wake, and so he could afford to have a scholar-son. He made no farther demur, and even allowed his house to become the seat of learning in which Sabbataï and nine chosen companions studied the Zohar and the Cabalah from dawn to darkness. Often they would desert the divan for the wooden garden-balcony overlooking the oranges and the prune-trees. And the richer Mordecai grew, the greater grew his veneration for his son, to whose merits, and not to his own diligence and honesty, he ascribed his good fortune.

"If the sins of the fathers are visited on the children," he was wont to say, "then surely the good deeds of the children are repaid to the fathers." His marked reverence for his wonderful son spread outwards, and Sabbataï became the object of a wistful worship, of a wild surmise.

Something of that wild surmise seemed to the father to flash into his son's own eyes one day when, returned from a great journey to his English principals, Mordecai Zevi spoke of the Fifth Monarchy men who foretold the coming of the Messiah and the Restoration of the Jews in the year 1666.

"Father!" said the boy. "Will not the Messiah be born on the ninth of Ab?"

"Of a surety," replied Mordecai, with beating heart. "He will be born on the fatal date of the destruction of both our Temples, in token of consolation, as it is written; 'and I will cause the captivity of Judah and the captivity of Israel to return, and will build them, as at the first.'"

The boy relapsed into his wonted silence. But one thought possessed father and son. Sabbataï had been born on the ninth of Ab—on the great Black Fast.

The wonder grew when the boy was divorced from his wife—the beautiful Channah. Obediently marrying—after the custom of the day—the maiden provided by his father, the young ascetic passionately denied himself to the passion ripened precociously by the Eastern sun, and the marvelling Beth-Din (House of Judgment) released the virgin from her nominal husband. Prayer and self-mortification were the pleasures of his youth. The enchanting Jewesses of Smyrna, picturesque in baggy trousers and open-necked vests, had no seduction for him, though no muslin veil hid their piquant countenances as with the Turkish women, though no prescription silenced their sweet voices in the psalmody of the table, as among the sin-fearing congregations of the West. In vain the maidens stuck roses under their ear or wore honeysuckle in their hair to denote their willingness to be led under the canopy. But Mordecai, anxious that he should fulfil the law, according to which to be celibate is to live in sin, found him a second mate, even more beautiful; but the youth remained silently callous, and was soon restored afresh to his solitary state.

"Now shall the Torah (Law) be my only bride," he said.

Blind to the beauty of womanhood, the young, handsome, and now rich Sabbataï, went his lonely, parsimonious way, and a wondering band followed him, scarcely disturbing his loneliness by their reverential companionship. When he entered the sea, morning and night, summer and winter, all stood far off; by day he would pray at the fountain which the Christians called Sancta Veneranda, near to the cemetery of the Jews, and he would stretch himself at night across the graves of the righteous in a silent agony of appeal, while the jackals barked in the lonely darkness and the wind soughed in the mountain gorges.

But at times he would speak to his followers of the Divine mysteries and of the rigorous asceticism by which alone these were to be reached and men to be regenerated and the Kingdom to be won; and sometimes he would sing to them Spanish songs in his sweet, troubling voice—strange Cabalistic verses, composed by himself or Lurya, and set to sad, haunting melodies yearning with mystic passion. And in these songs the womanhood he had rejected came back in amorous strains that recalled the Song of Songs, which is Solomon's, and seemed to his disciples to veil as deep an allegory:—

"There the Emperor's daughter
Lay agleam in the water,
Melisselda.
And its breast to her breast
Lay in tremulous rest,
Melisselda.
From her bath she arose
Pure and white as the snows,
Melisselda.
Coral only at lips
And at sweet finger-tips,
Melisselda.
In the pride of her race
As a sword shone her face,
Melisselda.
And her lips were steel bows,
But her mouth was a rose,
Melisselda."

And in the eyes of the tranced listeners were tears of worship for Melisselda as for the Messiah's mystic Bride.

V

And while the silent Sabbataï said no word of Messiah or mission, no word save the one word on the seashore, his disciples, first secret, then bold, spread throughout Smyrna the news of the Messiah's advent.

They were not all young, these first followers of Sabbataï. No one proclaimed him more ardently than the grave, elderly man of science, Moses Pinhero. But the sceptics far outnumbered the believers. Sabbataï was scouted as a madman. The Jewry was torn by dissensions and disturbances. But Sabbataï took no part in them. He had no communion with the bulk of his brethren, save in religious ceremonies, and for these he would go to the poorest houses in the most noisome courts. It was in a house of one room, the raised part of which, covered with a strip of carpet, made the bed-and living-room, and the unraised part the kitchen, that his next manifestation of occult power was made. The ceremony was the circumcision of the first-born son, but as the Mohel (surgeon) was about to operate he asked him to stay his hand awhile. Half an hour passed.

"Why are we waiting?" the guests ventured to ask of him at last.

"Elijah the Prophet has not yet taken his seat," he said.

Presently he made a sign that the proceedings might be resumed. They stared in reverential awe at the untenanted chair, where only the inspired vision of Sabbataï could perceive the celestial form of the ancient Prophet.

But the ancient Talmudical college frowned upon the new Prophet, particularly when his disciples bruited abroad his declaration on the sea-shore. He was cited before the Chachamim (Rabbis).

"Thou didst dare pronounce the ineffable Name" cried Joseph Eskapha, his old Master. "What! Shall thy unconsecrated lips pollute the sacred letters that even in the time of Israel's glory only the High Priest might breathe in the Holy of Holies on the Day of Atonement!"

"'Tis a divine mystery known to me alone," said Sabbataï.

But the Rabbis shook their heads and laid the ban upon him and his disciples. A strange radiance came in Sabbataï's face. He betook himself to the fountain and prayed.

"I thank Thee, O my Father," he said, "inasmuch as Thou hast revealed myself to myself. Now I know that my own penances have not been in vain."

But the excommunication of the Sabbatians did not quiet the commotion in the Jewish quarter of Smyrna, fed by Millennial dreams from the West. In England, indeed, a sect of Old Testament Christians had arisen, working for the adoption of the Mosaic Code as the law of the State.

From land to land of Christendom, on the feverish lips of eager believers, passed the rumor of the imminence of the Messiah of the Jews. According to some he would appear before the Grand Seignior in June, 1666, take from him his crown by force of music only, and lead him in chains like a captive. Then for nine months he would disappear, the Jews meanwhile enduring martyrdom, but he would return, mounted on a Celestial Lion, with his bridle made of seven-headed serpents, leading back the lost ten tribes from beyond the river Sambatyon, and he should be acknowledged for Solomon, King of the Universe, and the Holy Temple should descend from Heaven already built, that the Jews might offer sacrifice therein for ever. But these hopes found no lodgment in the breasts of the Jewish governors of the Smyrniote quarter, where hard-headed Sephardim were busy in toil and traffic, working with their hands, or shipping freights of figs or valonea; as for the Schnorrers, the beggars who lived by other people's wits, they were even more hard-headed than the workers. Hence constant excitements and wordy wars, till at last the authorities banished the already outlawed Sabbataï from Smyrna. When he heard the decree he said, "Is Israel not in exile?" He took farewell of his brothers and of his father, now grown decrepit in his body and full of the gout and other infirmities.

"Thou hast brought me wealth," said old Mordecai, sobbing; "but now I had rather lose my wealth than thee. Lo, I am on the brink of the grave, and my saintly son will not close mine eyes, nor know when to say Kaddish (mourning prayer) over my departed soul."

"Nay, weep not, my father," said Sabbataï. "The souls depart—but they will return."

VI

He wandered through the Orient, everywhere gaining followers, everywhere discredited. Constantinople saw him, and Athens, Thessalonica and Cairo.

For the Jew alone travel was easy in those days. The scatterings of his race were everywhere. The bond of blood secured welcome: Hebrew provided a common tongue. The scholar-guest, in especial, was hailed in flowery Hebrew as a crown sent to decorate the head of his host. Sumptuously entertained, he was laden with gifts on his departure, the caravan he was to join found for him, the cost defrayed, and even his ransom, should he unhappily be taken captive by robbers.

At the Ottoman capital the exile had a mingled reception. In the great Jewish quarter of Haskeui, with its swarming population of small traders, he found many adherents and many adversaries. Constantinople was a nest of free-lances and adventurers. Abraham Yachiny, the illustrious preacher, an early believer, was inspired to have a tomb opened in the ancient "house of life." He asked the sceptical Rabbis to dig up the earth. They found it exceedingly hard to the spade, but, persevering, presently came upon an earthen pot and therein a parchment which ran thus: "I, Abraham, was shut up for forty years in a cave. I wondered that the time of miracles did not arrive. Then a voice replied to me: 'A son shall be born in the year of the world 5386 and be called Sabbataï. He shall quell the great dragon; he is the true Messiah, and shall wage war without weapons.'"

Verily without weapons did Sabbataï wage war, almost without words. Not even the ancient Parchment convinced the scoffers, but Sabbataï took note of it as little as they. To none did he proclaim himself. His tall, majestic figure, with its sweeping black beard, was discerned in the dusk, passionately pleading at the graves of the pious. He was seen at dawn standing motionless upon his bulging wooden balcony that gave upon the Golden Horn. When he was not fasting, none but the plainest food passed his lips. He flagellated himself daily. Little children took to him, and he showered sweetmeats upon them and winning smiles of love. When he walked the refuse-laden, deep-rutted streets, slow and brooding, jostled by porters, asses, dervishes, sheiks, scribes, fruit-pedlars, shrouded females, and beggars, something more than the sombreness of his robes marked him out from the medley of rainbow-colored pedestrians. Turkish beauties peered through their yashmaks, cross-legged craftsmen smoking their narghiles raised their heads as he passed through the arched aisles of the Great Bazaar. Once he wandered into the slave-market, where fair Circassians and Georgians were being stripped to furnish the Kiosks of the Bosphorus, and he grew hot-eyed for the corrupt chaos of life in the capital, with its gorgeous pachas and loathly cripples, its countless mosques and brothels, its cruel cadis and foolish dancing dervishes. And when an angry Mussulman, belaboring his ass, called it "Jew!" his heart burnt with righteous anger. Verily, only Israel had chosen Righteousness—one little nation, the remnant that would save the world, and bring about the Kingdom of God. But alas! Israel herself was yet full of sin, hard and unbelieving.

"Woe! woe!" he cried aloud to his brethren as he entered the Jewish quarter. "Your sins shall be visited upon you. For know that when God created the world, it was not from necessity but from pure love, and to be recognized by men as their Creator and Master. But ye return Him not love for love. Woe! woe! There shall come a fire upon Constantinople and a great burning upon your habitations and substance."

Then his breast swelled with sobs; in a strange ecstasy his spirit seemed to soar from his body, and hover lovingly over all the motley multitude. All that night his followers heard him praying aloud with passionate tears, and singing the Psalms of David in his sweet melancholy voice as he strode irregularly up and down the room.

At Constantinople a messenger brought him a letter of homage from Damascus from his foremost disciple, Nathan of Gaza.

Nathan was a youthful enthusiast, son of a Jerusalem begging-agent, and newly married to the beautiful, but one-eyed daughter of a rich Portuguese, who had migrated from Damascus to Gaza. Opulent and zealous, he devoted himself henceforth to preaching the Messiah, living and dying his apostle and prophet—no other in short than the Elijah who was to be the Messiah's harbinger. Nor did he fail to work miracles in proof of his mission. Merely on reading a man's name, he would recount his life, defaults and sins, and impose just correction and penance. Evil-doers shunned his eye. More readily than on Sabbataï men believed on him, inasmuch as he claimed but the second place, and an impostor, said they, would have claimed the first. Couched in the tropes and metaphors of Rabbinical Hebrew, Nathan's letter ran thus:—

"22ND CHESVAN OF THIS YEAR.

"To the King, our King, Lord of our Lords, who gathers the Dispersed of Israel, who redeems our Captivity, the Man elevated to the Height of all sublimity, the Messiah of the God of Jacob, the true Messiah, the Celestial Lion, Sabbataï Zevi, whose honor be exalted and his dominion raised in a short time, and for ever, Amen. After having kissed thy hands and swept the dust from thy feet, as my duty is to the King of Kings, whose Majesty be exalted and His Empire enlarged. These are to make known to the Supreme Excellency of that Place, which is adorned with the beauty of thy Sanctity, that the Word of the King and of His Law hath enlightened our Faces; that day hath been a solemn day unto Israel and a day of light unto our Rulers, for immediately we applied ourselves to perform thy Commands as our duty is. And though we have heard of many strange things, yet we are courageous, and our heart is as the heart of a Lion; nor ought we to inquire or reason of thy doings; for thy works are marvellous and past finding out. And we are confirmed in our Fidelity without all exception, resigning up our very souls for the Holiness of thy Name. And now we are come as far as Damascus, intending shortly to proceed in our journey to Scanderone, according as thou hast commanded us: that so we may ascend and see the face of God in light, as the light of the face of the King of life. And we, servants of thy servants, shall cleanse the dust from thy feet, beseeching the majesty of thine excellency and glory to vouchsafe from thy habitation to have a care of us, and help us with the Force of thy Right Hand of Strength, and shorten our way which is before us. And we have our eyes towards Jah, Jah, who will make haste to help us and to save us, that the Children of Iniquity shall not hurt us; and towards whom our hearts pant and are consumed within us: who shall give us Talons of Iron to be worthy to stand under the shadow of thine ass. These are the words of thy Servant of Servants, who prostrates himself to be trod on by the soles of thy feet—NATHAN BENJAMIN."

VIII

But it was at Thessalonica—now known as Salonica—that Sabbataï gained the greatest following. For Thessalonica was the chief stronghold of the Cabalah; and though the triangular battlemented town, sloping down the mountain to the gulf, was in the hands of the Turks, who had built four fortresses and set up twelve little cannons against the Corsairs, yet Jews were largely in the ascendant, and their thirty synagogues dominated the mosques of their masters and the churches of the Greeks, even as the crowns they received for supplying the cloths of the Janissaries far exceeded their annual tribute. Castilians, Portuguese, Italians, they were further recruited by an influx of students from all parts of the Empire, for here were two great colleges teaching more than ten thousand scholars. In this atmosphere of pious warmth Sabbataï found consolation for the apathy of Constantinople. Not only men were of his devotees now, but women, and maidens, in all their Eastern fervor, raising their face-veils and putting off their shrouding izars as they sat at his feet. Virgins, untaught to love or to dissemble, lifted adoring eyes. But Sabbataï's vision was still inwards and heavenwards; and one day he made a great feast, and invited all his friends to his wedding in the chief synagogue. They came with dancing and music and lighted torches, but racked by curiosity, full of guesses as to the bride. Through the close lattice-work of the ladies' balcony peered a thousand eager eyes. When the moment came, Sabbataï, in festal garments, took his stand under the canopy. But no visible bride stood beside him. Moses Pinhero reverently drew a Scroll of the Law from the ark, vested in purple and gold broideries, and hung with golden chains and a breastplate and bells that made sweet music, and he bore it beneath the canopy, and Sabbataï, placing a golden ring on a silver peak of the Scroll, said solemnly:

"I betroth thee unto me according to the Law of Moses and Israel."

A buzz of astonishment swelled through the synagogue, blent with heavier murmurs of protest from shocked pietists. But the more poetic Cabalists understood. They explained that it was the union of the Torah, the Daughter of Heaven, with the Messiah, the Son of Heaven, who was never to mate with a mortal.

But a Chacham (Rabbi), unappeased, raised a loud plaint of blasphemy.

"Nay, the blasphemy is thine," replied the Bridegroom of the law quietly. "Say not your prophets that the Truth should be the spouse of those who love the Truth?"

But the orthodox faction prevailed, and he was driven from the city.

He went to the Morea, to his father's relatives; he wandered to and fro, and the years slipped by. Worn by fasts and penances, living in inward dreams of righteousness and regeneration, he grew towards middle age, and always on his sweet scholarly face an air of patient waiting through the slow years. And his train of disciples grew and changed; some died, some wearied of the long expectation. But Samuel Primo, of Jerusalem, became his devoted secretary, and Abraham Rubio was also ever at his side, a droll, impudent beggar, professing unlimited faith in the Messiah, and feasting with unbounded appetite on the good things sent by the worshippers, and put aside by the persistent ascetic.

"Tis fortunate I shall be with thee when thou carvest the Leviathan," he said once. "Else would the heathen princesses who shall wait upon us come in for thy pickings."

"In those days of the Kingdom there shall be no more need for abnegation," said Sabbataï. "As it is written, 'And thy fast-days shall become feast-days.'"

"Nay, then, thy feast-days shall become my fast-days," retorted Rubio.

Sabbataï smiled. The beggar was the only man who could make him smile. But he smiled—a grim, bitter smile—when he heard that the great fire he had predicted had devastated Constantinople, and wrought fierce mischief in the Jewish quarter.

"The fire will purify their hearts," he said.

IX

Nathan the Prophet did not fail to enlarge upon the miraculous prediction of his Master, and through all the lands of the Exile a tremor ran.

It reached that hospitable table in Cairo where each noon half a hundred learned Cabalists dined at the palace of the Saraph-Bashi, the Jewish Master of the Mint, himself given to penances and visions, and swathed in sackcloth below the purple robes with which he drove abroad in his chariot of state.

"He who is sent thee," wrote Nathan to Raphael Joseph Chelebi, this pious and open-handed Prince in Israel, "is the first man in the world—I may say no more. Honor him, then, and thou shalt have thy reward in his lifetime, wherein thou wilt witness miracles beyond belief. Whatever thou shouldst see, be not astonied. It is a divine mystery. When the time shall come I will give up all to serve him. Would it were granted me to follow him now!"

Chelebi was prepared to follow Sabbataï forthwith; he went to meet Sabbataï's vessel, and escorted him to his palace with great honor. But Sabbataï would not lodge therein.

"The time is not yet," he said, and sought shelter with a humble vendor of holy books, whose stall stood among the money-changers' booths, that led to the chief synagogue, and his followers distributed themselves among the quaint high houses of the Jewry, and walked prophetic in its winding alleys, amid the fantastic chaos of buyers and sellers and donkeys, under the radiant blue strip of Egyptian sky. Only at mid-day did they repair to the table of the Saraph-Bashi.

"Hadst any perils at sea?" asked the host on the first day. "Men say the Barbary Corsairs are astir again."

Sabbataï remained silent, but Samuel Primo, his secretary, took up the reply.

"Perils!" quoth he. "My Master will not speak of them, but the Captain will tell thee a tale. We never thought to pass Rhodes!"

"Ay," chimed in Abraham Rubio, "we were pursued all night by two pirates, one on either side of us like beggars."

"And the Captain," said Isaac Silvera, "despairing of escape, planned to take to the boats with his crew, leaving the passengers to their fate."

"But he did not?" quoth a breathless Cabalist.

"Alas, no," said Abraham Rubio, with a comical grimace. "Would he had done so! For then we should have owned a goodly vessel, and the Master would have saved us all the same."

"But righteousness must needs be rewarded," protested Samuel Primo. "And inasmuch as the Captain wished to save the Master in the boats—"

"The Master was reading," put in Solomon Lagnado. "The Captain cries out, 'The Corsairs are upon us!' 'Where?' says the Master. 'There!' says the Captain. The Master stretches out his hands, one towards each vessel, and raises his eyes to heaven, and in a moment the ships tack and sail away on the high sea."

Sabbataï sat eating his meagre meal in silence.

But when the rumor of his miracle spread, the sick and the crippled hastened to him, and, protesting he could do naught, he laid his hands on them, and many declared themselves healed. Also he touched the lids of the sore-eyed and they said his fingers were as ointment. But Sabbataï said nothing, made no pretensions, walking ever the path of piety with meek and humble tread. Howbeit he could not linger in Egypt. The Millennial Year was drawing nigh—the mystic 1666.

Sabbataï Zevi girded up his loins, and, regardless of the rumors of Arab robbers, nay, wearing his phylacteries on his forehead as though to mark himself out as a Jew, and therefore rich, joined a caravan for Jerusalem, by way of Damascus.

X

O the ecstasy with which he prostrated himself to kiss for the first time the soil of the sacred city! Tears rolled from his eyes, half of rapture, half of passionate sorrow for the lost glories of Zion, given over to the Moslem, its gates guarded by Turkish sentries, and even the beauty of his first view of it—domes, towers, and bastions bathed in morning sunlight—fading away in the squalor of its steep alleys.

Nathan the Prophet had apprised the Jews of the coming of their King, and the believers welcomed him with every mark of homage, even substituting Sabbataï Zevi for Sultan Mehemet in the Sabbath prayer for the Sovereign, and at the Wailing Place the despairing sobs of the Sons of the Law were tempered by a great hope.

Poor, squeezed to famishing point by the Turkish officials, deprived of their wonted subsidies from the pious Jews of Poland, who were decimated by Cossack massacres, they had had their long expectation of the Messiah intensified by the report which Baruch Gad had brought back to them from Persia—how the Sons of Moses, living beyond the river Sambatyon (that ceased to run on the Sabbath), were but awaiting, amid daily miracles, the word of the Messiah to march back to Jerusalem. The lost Ten Tribes would reassemble: at the blast of the celestial horn the dispersed of Israel would be gathered together from the four corners of the Earth. But Sabbataï deprecated the homage; of Redemption he spake no word.

And verily his coming seemed to bode destruction rather than salvation. For a greedy Pacha, getting wind of the disloyalty of the synagogue to the Sultan, made it a pretext for an impossible fine.

The wretched community was dashed back to despair. Already reduced to starvation, whence were they to raise this mighty sum? But, recovering, all hearts turned at once to the strange sorrowful figure that went humbly to and fro among them.

"Money?" said he. "Whence should I take so much money?"

"But thou art Messiah?"

"I Messiah?" He looked at them wistfully.

"Forgive us—we know the hour of thy revelation hath not yet struck. But wilt thou not save us by thy human might?"

"How so?"

"Go for us, we pray thee, on a mission to the friendly Saraph-Bashi of Cairo. His wealth alone can ransom us."

"All that man can do I will do," said Sabbataï.

"May thy strength increase!" came the grateful ejaculation, and white-bearded sages stooped to kiss the hem of his garment.

So Sabbataï journeyed back to Cairo by caravan through the desert, preceded, men said, by a pillar of fire, and accompanied when he travelled at night by myriads of armed men that disappeared in the morning, and wheresoever he passed all the Jewish inhabitants flocked to gaze upon him. In Hebron they kept watch all night around his house.

From his casement Sabbataï looked up at the silent stars and down at the swaying sea of faces.

"What if the miracle be not wrought!" he murmured. "If Chelebi refuses to sacrifice so much of his substance! But they believe on me. It must be that Jerusalem will be saved, and that I am the Messiah indeed."

At Cairo the pious Master of the Mint received him with ecstasy, and granted his request ere he had made an end of speaking.

That night Sabbataï wandered away from all his followers, beyond the moonlit Nile, towards the Great Pyramid, on, on, unto the white desert, his eyes seeing only inward visions.

"Yea, I am Messiah," he cried at length to the vast night, "I am G—!"

The sudden shelving of the sand made him stumble, and in that instant he became aware of the Sphinx towering over him, its great granite Face solemn in the moonlight. His voice died away in an awed whisper. Long, long he gazed into the great stone eyes.

"Speak!" he whispered. "Thou, Abou-el-Hol, Father of Terror, thou who broodedst over the silences ere Moses ben Amram led my people from this land of bondage, shall I not lead them from their dispersal to their ancient unity in the day when God shall be One, and His Name One?"

The Sphinx was silent. The white sea of sand stretched away endlessly with noiseless billows. The Pyramids threw funereal shadows over the arid waste.

"Yea," he cried, passionately. "My Father hath not deceived me. Through me, through me flow the streams of grace to recreate and rekindle. Hath He not revealed it to me, even ere this day of Salvation for Jerusalem, by the date of my birth, by the ancient parchment, by the homage of Nathan, by the faith of my brethren and the rumor of the nations, by my sufferings, by my self-appointed martyrdoms, by my long, weary years of forced wanderings to and fro upon the earth, by my loneliness—ah, God—my loneliness!"

The Sphinx brooded solemnly under the brooding stars. Sabbataï's voice was as the wail of a wind.

"Yea, I will save Israel, I will save the world. Through my holiness the world shall be a Temple. Sin and evil and pain shall pass. Peace shall sit under her fig-tree, and swords shall be turned into pruning-hooks, and gladness and brotherhood shall run through all the earth, even as my Father declared unto Israel by the mouth of his prophet Hosea. Yea, I, even I, will allure her and bring her into the desert, and speak comfortably unto her. And I will give her vineyards from thence, and the Valley of Achor for a door of hope; and she shall sing there as in the days of her youth and as in the days when she came up out of the land of Egypt. And I will say to them which were not my people, 'Thou art my people'; and they shall say, 'Thou art my God.'"

The Sphinx was silent. And in that silence there was the voice of dead generations that had bustled and dreamed and passed away, countless as the grains of desert sand.

Sabbataï ceased and surveyed the Face in answering silence, his own face growing as inscrutable.

"We are strong and lonely—thou and I," he whispered at last. But the Sphinx was silent.

SCROLL THE SECOND

XI

In a little Polish town, early one summer morning, two Jewish women, passing by the cemetery, saw a spirit fluttering whitely among the tombs.

They shrieked, whereupon the figure turned, revealing a beautiful girl in her night-dress, her face, albeit distraught, touched unmistakably with the hues of life.

"Ah, ye be daughters of Israel!" cried the strange apparition. "Help me! I have escaped from the nunnery."

"Who art thou?" said they, moving towards her.

"The Messiah's Bride!" And her face shone. They stood rooted to the soil. A fresh thrill of the supernatural ran through them.

"Nay, come hither," she cried. "See." And she showed them nail-marks on her naked flesh. "Last night my father's ghostly hands dragged me from the convent."

At this the women would have run away, but each encouraged the other.

"Poor creature! She is mad," they signed and whispered to each other. Then they threw a mantle over her.

"Ye will hide me, will ye not?" she said, pleadingly, and her wild sweetness melted their hearts.

They soothed her and led her homewards by unfrequented byways.

"Where are thy friends, thy parents?"

"Dead, scattered—what know I? O those days of blood!" She shuddered violently. "Baptism or death! But they were strong. I see a Cossack dragging my mother along with a thong round her neck. 'Here's a red ribbon for you, dear,' he cries with laughter; they betrayed us to the Cossacks, those Greek Christians within our gates—the Zaporogians dressed themselves like Poles—we open the gates—the gutters run blood—oh, the agonies of the tortured!—oh! father!"

They hushed her cries. Too well they remembered those terrible days of the Chmielnicki massacres, when all the highways of Europe were thronged with haggard Polish Jews, flying from the vengeance of the Cossack chieftain with his troops of Haidamaks, and a quarter of a million of Jewish corpses on the battle-fields of Poland were the blunt Cossack's reply to the casuistical cunning engendered by the Talmud.

"They hated my father," the strange beautiful creature told them, when she was calmer. "He was the lessee of the Polish imposts; and in order that he might collect the fines on Cossack births and marriages, he kept the keys of the Greek church, and the Pope had to apply to him, ere he could celebrate weddings or baptisms—they offered to baptize him free of tax, but he held firm to his faith; they impaled him on a stake and lashed him—oh, my God! And the good sisters found me weeping, a little girl, and they took me to the convent and were kind to me, and spoke to me of Christ. But I would not believe, no, I could not believe. The psalms and lessons of the synagogue came back to my lips; in visions of the night I saw my father, blood-stained, but haloed with light.

"'Be faithful,' he would say, 'be faithful to Judaism. A great destiny awaits thee. For lo! our long persecution draws to an end, the days of the Messiah are at hand, and thou shalt be the Messiah's bride,' And the glory of a great hope came into my life, and I longed to escape from my prison into the sunlit world. I, the bride of the cloister!" she cried, and revolt flung roses into her white face. "Nay, the bride of the Messiah am I, who shall restore joy to the earth, who shall wipe the tears from off all faces. Last night my father came to me again, and said, 'Be faithful to Judaism.' Then I replied, 'If thou wert of a truth my father, thou wouldst cease thy exhortations, thou wouldst know I would rather die than renounce my faith, thou wouldst rescue me from these hated walls, and give me unto my Bridegroom.' Thereupon he said, 'Stretch out thine hand,' and I stretched out my hand, and I felt an invisible hand clasp it, and when I awoke I found myself by his grave-side, where ye came upon me. Oh, take me to the Woman's Bath forthwith, I pray ye, that I may wash off the years of pollution."

They took her to the Woman's Bath, admiring her marvellous beauty.

"Where is the Messiah?" she asked.

"He is not come yet," they made answer, for the rising up of Sabbataï was as yet known to but a few disciples.

"Then I will go find Him," she answered.

She wandered to Amsterdam—the capital of Jewry—and thence to Frankfort-on-the-Main, and thence, southwards, in vain search to Livorne.

And there in the glory of the Italian sunshine, her ardent, unbalanced nature, starved in the chilly convent, yielded to passion, for there were many to love her. But to none would she give herself in marriage. "I am the Messiah's destined bride," she said, and her wild eyes had always an air of waiting.

XII

And in the course of years the news of her and of her prophecy travelled to Sabbataï Zevi, and found him at Cairo the morning after he had spoken to the Sphinx in the great silences. And to him under the blue Egyptian sky came an answering throb of romance. The womanhood that had not moved him in the flesh thrilled him, vaguely imaged from afar, mystically, spiritually.

"Let her be sent for," he said, and his disciples noted an unwonted restlessness in the weary weeks while his ambassadors were away.

"Dost think she will come?" he said once to Abraham Rubio.

"What woman would not come to thee?" replied the beggar. "What dainty is not offered thee? I trow natheless that thou wilt refuse, and that I shall come in for thy leavings."

Sabbataï smiled faintly.

"What have I to do with women?" he murmured. "But I would fain know what hath been prophetically revealed to her!"

One afternoon his ambassadors returned, and announced that they had brought her. She was resting after the journey, and would visit him on the morrow. He appointed their meeting in the Palace of the Saraph-Bashi. Then, unable to rest, he mounted the hill of the citadel and saw an auspicious golden glow over the mosques and houses of Cairo, illumining even the desert and the Pyramids. He stood watching the sun sink lower and lower, till suddenly it went out like a snuffed candle.

XIII

On the morrow he left his mean brick dwelling in the Jewry, and received her alone in a marble-paved chamber in the Palace, the walls adorned with carvings of flowers and birds, minutely worked, the ceiling with arabesques formed of thin strips of painted wood, the air cooled by a fantastic fountain playing into a pool lined with black and white marbles and red tiling. Lattice-work windows gave on the central courtyard, and were supplemented by decorative windows of stained glass, wrought into capricious patterns.

"Peace, O Messiah!" Her smile was dazzling, and there was more of gaiety than of reverence in her voice. Her white teeth flashed 'twixt laughing lips. Sabbataï's heart was beating furiously at the sight of the lady of his dreams. She was clad in shimmering white Italian silk, which, draped tightly about her bosom, showed her as some gleaming statue. Bracelets glittered on her white wrists, gems of fire sparkled among her long, white fingers, a network of pearls was all her head-dress. Her eyes had strange depths of passion, perfumes breathed from her skin, lustreless like dead ivory. Not thus came the maidens of Israel to wedlock, demure, spotless, spiritless, with shorn hair, priestesses of the ritual of the home.

"Peace, O Melisselda," he replied involuntarily.

"Nay, wherefore Melisselda?" she cried, ascending to the leewán on which he stood.

"And wherefore Messiah?" he answered.

"I have seen thee in visions—'tis the face, the figure, the prophetic beauty—But wherefore Melisselda?"

He laughed into her eyes and hummed softly:—

"'From her bath she arose, Pure and white as the snows,
Melisselda.'"

"Ay, that did I, when I washed off the convent. But my name is Sarah."

"Nay, not Sarah, but Saraï—my Princess!" His voice was hoarse and faltering. This strange new sense of romance that, like a callow-bird, had been stirring in his breast ever since he had heard of her quest of him, spread its wings and soared heavenwards. She had been impure—but her impurity swathed her in mystic seductiveness. The world's law bound her no more than him—she was free and elemental, a spirit to match his own; purified perpetually by its own white fire. She came nearer, and her eyes wrapped him in flame.

"My Prince!" she cried.

He drew backward towards the divan. "Nay, but I must know no woman."

"None but thy true mate," she answered. "Thou hast kept thyself pure for me even as I have kept myself passionate for thee. Come, thou shalt make me pure, and I will make thee passionate."

He looked at her wistfully. The cool plash of the fountain was pleasant in the silence.

"I make thee pure!" he breathed.

"Ay," and she repeated softly:—

"'Pure and white as the snows,
Melisselda.'"

"Melisselda!" he whispered.

"Messiah!" she cried, with heaving bosom. "Come, I will teach thee the joy of life. Together we will rule the world. What! when thou hast redeemed the world, shall it not rejoice, shall not the morning stars sing together? My King, my Sabbataï."

Her figure was a queen's, her eyes were stars, her lips a woman's.

"Kiss me!" they pleaded. "Thy long martyrdom is over. Now begins my mission—to bring thee joy. So hath it been revealed to me."

"Hath it been indeed revealed to thee?" he demanded hoarsely.

"Yea, again and again, in dreams of the night. The bride of the Messiah—so runs my destiny. Embrace thy bride."

His eyes kindled to hers. He seemed in a circle of dazzling white flame that exalted and not destroyed.

"Then I am Messiah, indeed," he thought, glowing, and, stooping, he knew for the first time the touch of a woman's lips.

XIV

The Master of the Mint was overjoyed to celebrate the Messiah's marriage under his own gilded roof. To the few who shook their heads at the bride's past, Sabbataï made answer that the prophecies must be fulfilled, and that he; too, had had visions in which he was commanded, like the prophet Hosea, to marry an unchaste wife. And his disciples saw that it was a great mystery, symbolizing what the Lord had spoken through the mouth of Jeremiah: "Again I will build thee and thou shalt be built, O virgin of Israel: thou shalt again be adorned with thy tabrets and shall go forth in the dances of them that make merry." So the festivities set in, and the Palace was filled with laughter and dancing and merrymaking.

And Melisselda inaugurated the reign of joy. Her advent brought many followers to Sabbataï. Thousands fell under the spell of her beauty, her queenly carriage, gracious yet gay. A new spirit of romance was born in ritual-ridden Israel. Men looked upon their wives distastefully, and the wives caught something of her fire and bearing and learnt the movement of abandon and the glance of passion. And so, with a great following, enriched by the beauty of Melisselda and the gold of the Master of the Mint, Sabbataï returned to redeem Jerusalem.

Jerusalem was intoxicated with joy: the prophecies of Elijah the Tishbite, known on earth as Nathan of Gaza, were borne on wings of air to the four corners of the world.

"To the Remnant of the Israelites," he wrote, "Peace without end. Behold I go to meet the face of our Lord, whose majesty be exalted, for he is the Sovereign of the King of Kings, whose empire be enlarged. And now I come to make known unto you that though ye have heard strange things of our Lord, yet let not your hearts faint or fear, but rather fortify yourselves in your Faith because all his actions are miraculous and secret, which human understanding cannot comprehend, and who can penetrate into the depth of them? In a brief time all things shall be manifested to you clearly in their purity, and ye shall know and consider and be instructed by the Inventor himself. Blessed is he who can expect and arrive to the Salvation of the true Messiah, who will speedily publish his Authority and Empire over us now and for ever.

"NATHAN."

In the Holy City the aged Rabbis of the Sacred Colleges alone betrayed misgivings, fearing that the fine would be annually renewed, and even the wealth of Chelebi exhausted. Elsewhere, the Jewries were divided into factions, that fought each other with texts, and set the Word against the Word. This verse clearly proved the Messiah had come, and that verse that the signs were not yet fulfilled; and had not Solomon, the wise king, said that the fool gave belief at once to all indifferently, while the wise man weighed and considered before believing? Fiercely waged the battle of texts, and a comet appeared on behalf of the believers. Demoniacles saw Sabbataï Zevi in heaven with three crowns, one for Messiah, one for King, and one for Conqueror of the Peoples. But the Jerusalem Rabbis remaining sceptical, Nathan proclaimed in an ecstasy that she was no longer the sacred city, the primacy had passed to Gaza. But Sabbataï was fain to show himself at Smyrna, his native city, and hither he marched, preceded by apostles who kindled the communities he was to pass through. Raphael, another Greek beggar, rhapsodized interminably, and Bloch, a Cabalist from Germany, a meek, simple soul, had frenzies of fiery inspiration. Samuel Primo, the untiring secretary, scattered ceaseless letters and mysterious manifestoes. But to none did Sabbataï himself claim to be the Messiah—he commanded men not to speak of it till the hour should come. Yet was his progress one long triumphal procession. At Aleppo the Jews hastened to meet him with songs and dances; "the gates of joy are opened," they wrote to Constantinople. At Smyrna itself the exile was received with delirium, with cries of "Messhiach! Messiah!" which he would not acknowledge, but to which Melisselda responded with seductive smiles. His aged father fell upon his neck.

"The souls depart," said Sabbataï, kissing him. "But they return."

He was brought before the Cadi, who demanded a miracle.

"Thou askest a miracle?" said Sabbataï scornfully. "Wouldst see a pillar of fire?"

The Sabbatians who thronged the audience chamber uttered a cry and covered their faces with their hands.

"Yea, we see, we see," they shouted; the word was passed to the dense crowd surging without, and it swayed madly. Husbands ran home to tell their wives and children, and when Sabbataï left the presence chamber he was greeted with delirious acclamations.

And while Smyrna was thus seething, and its Jews were preparing themselves by purification and prayer for the great day, a courier, dark as a Moor with the sunburn of unresting travel, arrived in the town with a letter from the Holy City. It was long before he could obtain audience with Sabbataï, who, with his inmost disciples, was celebrating a final fast, and meantime the populace was in a ferment of curiosity, the messenger recounting how he had tramped for weeks and weeks through the terrible heat to see the face of the Messiah and kiss his feet and deliver the letter from the holy men of Jerusalem, who were too poor to pay for his speedier journeying. But when at last Sabbataï read the letter, his face lit up, though he gave no sign of the contents. His disciples pressed for its publication, and, after much excitement, Sabbataï consented that it should be read from the Al Memor of the synagogue. When they learned that it bore the homage of repentant Jerusalem, their joy was tumultuous to the point of tears. Sabbataï threw twenty silver crowns on a salver for the messenger, and invited others to do the same, so that the happy envoy could scarce stagger away with his reward.

Nevertheless Sabbataï still delayed to declare himself.

But at last the long silence drew to an end. The great year of 1666 was nigh, before many moons the New Year of the Christians would dawn. Under the direction of Melisselda men were making sleeved robes of white satin for the Messiah. And one day, thus arrayed in gleaming white, at the head of a great procession walking two by two, Sabbataï Zevi marched to the House of God.

XV

In the gloom of the great synagogue, while the worshippers swayed ghostly, and the ram's horn sounded shrill and jubilant, Sabbataï, standing before the Ark, where the Scrolls of the Law stood solemn, proclaimed himself, amid a tense awe as of heavens opening in ineffable vistas, the Righteous Redeemer, the Anointed of Israel.

A frenzied shout of joy, broken by sobs, answered him from the vast assembly.

"Long live our King! Our Messiah!" Many fell prostrate on the ground, their faces to the floor, kissing it, weeping, screaming, shouting in ecstatic thankfulness; others rocked to and fro, blinded by their tears, hoarse with exultation.

"Messhiach! Messhiach!"

"The Kingdom has come!"

"Blessed be the Messiah!"

In the women's gallery there were shrieks and moans: some swooned, others fell a-prophesying, contorting themselves spasmodically, uttering wild exclamations; the spirit seized upon little children, and they waved their arms and shouted frantically.

"Messhiach! Messhiach!"

The long exile of Israel was over—the bitter centuries of the badge and the byword, slaughter and spoliation; no longer, O God! to cringe in false humility, the scoff of the street-boy, the mockery of mankind, penned in Ghettos, branded with the wheel or the cap—but restored to divine favor as every Prophet had predicted, and uplifted to the sovereignty of the peoples.

"Messhiach! Messhiach!"

They poured into the narrow streets, laughing, chattering, leaping, dancing, weeping hysterically, begging for forgiveness of their iniquities. They fell at Sabbataï feet, women spread rich carpets for him to tread (though he humbly skirted them), and decked their windows and balconies with costly hangings and cushions. Some, conscious of sin that might shut them out from the Kingdom, made for the harbor and plunged into the icy waters; some dug themselves graves in the damp soil and buried themselves up to their necks till they were numb and fainting; others dropped melted wax upon their naked bodies. But the most common way of mortification was to prick their backs and sides with thorns and then give themselves thirty-nine lashes. Many fasted for days upon days and kept Cabalistic watches by night, intoning Tikkunim (prayers).

And, blent with these penances, festival after festival, riotous, delirious, whenever Sabbataï Zevi, with his vast train of followers, and waving a fan, showed himself in the street on his way to a ceremony or to give Cabalistic interpretations of Scripture in the synagogue. The shop-keepers of the Jewish bazaar closed their doors, and followed in the frenzied procession, singing "The right hand of the Lord is exalted, the right hand bringeth victory," jostling, fighting, in their anxiety to be touched with the fan and inherit the Kingdom of Heaven. And over these vast romping crowds, drunk with faith, Melisselda queened it with her voluptuous smiles and the joyous abandon of her dancing, and men and women, boys and girls, embraced and kissed in hysterical frenzy. The yoke of the Law was over, the ancient chastity forgotten. In the Cabalistic communities of Thessalonica, where the pious began at once to do penance, some dying of a seven-days' fast, and others from rolling themselves naked in the snow, parents hastened to marry young children so that all the unborn souls which through the constant re-incarnations, necessary to enable the old sinful souls to work out their Perfection, had not yet been able to find bodies, might enter the world, and so complete the scheme of creation. Seven hundred children were thus joined in wedlock. Business, work was suspended; the wheel of the cloth-workers ceased; the camels no longer knelt in the Jewish quarter of Smyrna, the Bridge of Caravans ceased to vibrate with their passing, the shops remained open only so long as was necessary to clear off the merchandise at any price; whoso of private persons had any superfluity of household stuff sold it off similarly, but yet not to Jews, for these were interdicted from traffic, business being the mark of the unbeliever, and punishable by excommunication, pecuniary mults, or corporeal chastisements. Everybody prepared for the imminent return to Palestine, when the heathen should wait at the table of the Saints and the great Leviathan deck the Messianic board. In the interim the poor were supported by the rich. In Thessalonica alone four thousand persons lived on gifts; truly Messianic times for the Abraham Rubios. In Smyrna the authority of the Cadi was ignored or silenced by purses; when the Turks complained, the Seraglio swallowed gold on both sides. The Chacham Aaron de la Papa, being an unbeliever and one of those who had originally driven him from his birthplace, was removed by Sabbataï, and Chayim Benvenisti appointed Chacham instead. The noble Chayim Penya, the one sceptic of importance left in Smyrna, was wellnigh torn to pieces in the synagogue by the angry multitude, but when his own daughters went into prophetic trances and saw the glory of the Kingdom he went over to Sabbataï's side, and reports flew everywhere that the Messiah's enemies were struck with frenzies and madness, till, restored by him to their former temper and wits, they became his friends, worshippers, and disciples. Four hundred other men and women fell into strange ecstasies, foamed at the mouth, and recounted their visions of the Lion of Judah, while infants, who could scarcely stammer out a syllable plainly, repeated the name of Sabbataï, the Messiah; being possessed, and voices sounding from their stomachs and entrails. Such reports, bruited through the world by the foreign ambassadors at Smyrna, the clerks of the English and Dutch houses, the resident foreigners, and the Christian ministers, excited a prodigious sensation, thrilling civilized mankind. On the Exchanges of Europe men took the odds for and against a Jewish kingdom.

Upon the Jews of the world the news that the Messiah had passed from a far-off aspiration into a reality fell like a thunderbolt; they were dazed with joy; then they began to prepare for the great journey. Everywhere self-flagellation, almsgiving, prophetic ecstasies and trances, the scholars and the mob at one in joyous belief. And everywhere also profligacy, adultery, incest, through the spread of a mystical doctrine that the sinfulness of the world could only be overcome by the superabundance of sin.

XVI

Amsterdam and Hamburg—the two wealthiest communities—receiving constant prophetic messages from Nathan of Gaza, became eager participators in the coming Kingdom. In the Dutch capital, the houses of prayer grew riotous with music and dancing, the dwelling-houses gloomy with penitential rigors. The streets were full of men and women prophesying spasmodically, the printing presses panted, turning out new prayer-books with penances and formulæ for the faithful. And in these Tikkunim, starred with mystic emblems of the Messiah's dominance, the portrait of Sabbataï appeared side by side with that of King David. At Hamburg the Jews were borne heavenwards on a wave of exultation; they snapped their fingers at the Christian tormentor, refused any longer to come to the compulsory Christian services. Their own services became pious orgies. Stately Spanish Jews, grave blue-blooded Portuguese, hitherto smacking of the Castilian hidalgo, noble seigniors like Manuel Texeira, the friend of a Queen of Sweden, erudite physicians like Bendito de Castro, president of the congregation, shed their occidental veneer and might have been seen in the synagogue skipping like harts upon the mountains, dancing wild dances with the Holy Scroll clasped to their bosoms.

"Hi diddi hulda hi ti ti!" they carolled in merry meaninglessness.

"Nay, but this is second childhood," quoth the venerable Jacob Sasportas, chief Rabbi of the English Jews, as he sat in the presidential pew, an honored visitor at Hamburg. "Surely thy flock is demented."

De Castro's brow grew black.

"Have a care, or my sheep may turn dog. An they overhear thee, it were safer for thee even to go back to thy London."

Sasportas shook his head with a humorous twinkle.

"Yea, if Sabbataï will accompany me. An he be Messiah let him face the Plague, let him come and prophesy in London and outdo Solomon Eagle; let him heal the sick and disburden the death-carts."

"He should but lay his hands on the sick and they were cured!" retorted De Castro. "But his mission is not in the isles of the West; he establisheth the throne in Zion."

"Well for thee not in Hamburg, else would thy revenues dwindle, O wise physician. But the Plague is wellnigh spent now; if he come now he may take the credit of the cure."

"Rabbi as thou art, thou art an Epicurean; thou sittest in the seat of the scorner."

"'Twas thou didst invite me thereto," murmured Sasportas, smiling.

"The Plague is but a sign of the Messianic times, and the Fire that hath burnt thy dwelling-place is but the castigation for thine incredulity."

"Yea, there be those who think our royal Charles the Messiah, and petition him to declare himself," said Sasportas, with his genial twinkle. "Hath he not also his Melisseldas?"

"Hush, thou blasphemer!" cried De Castro, looking anxiously at the howling multitude. "But thou wilt live to eat thy words."

"Be it so," said Sasportas, with a shrug of resignation. "I eat nothing unclean."

But it was vain for the Rabbi of the little western isle to contend by quip or reason against the popular frenzy. England, indeed, was a hotbed of Christian enthusiasts awaiting the Jewish Millennium, the downfall of the Pope and Anti-Christ, and Jews and Christians caught mutual fire.

From the far North of Scotland came a wonderful report of a ship with silken sails and ropes, worked by sailors who spoke with one another in the solemn syllables of the sacred tongue, and flying a flag with the inscription, "The Twelve Tribes of Israel!" And a strange rumor told of the march of multitudes from unknown parts into the remote deserts of Arabia. Fronted with sceptics, believers offered wagers at ten to one that within two years Sabbataï would be anointed King of Jerusalem; bills of exchange were drawn in Threadneedle Street upon the issue.

And, indeed, Sabbataï was already King of the Jews. From all the lands of the Exile crowds of the devout came to do him homage and tender allegiance—Turkish Jews with red fez or saffron-yellow turban; Jerusalem Jews in striped cotton gowns and soft felt hats; Polish Jews with foxskin caps and long caftans; sallow German Jews, gigantic Russian Jews, high-bred Spanish Jews; and with them often their wives and daughters—Jerusalem Jewesses with blue shirts and head-veils, Egyptian Jewesses with sweeping robes and black head-shawls, Jewesses from Ashdod and Gaza, with white visors fringed with gold coins, Polish Jewesses with glossy wigs, Syrian Jewesses with eyelashes black as though lined with kohl, fat Jewesses from Tunis, with clinging breeches interwoven with gold and silver.

Daily he held his court, receiving deputations, advices, messengers. Young men and maidens offered him their lives to do with as he would; the rich laid their fortunes at his feet, and fought for the honor of belonging to his body-guard. That abstract deity of the Old Testament—awful in His love and His hate, without form, without humanity—had been replaced by a Man, visible, tangible, lovable; and all the yearning of their souls, all that suppressed longing for a visual object of worship which had found vent and satisfaction in the worship of the Bible or the Talmud in its every letter and syllable, now went out towards their bodily Redeemer. From the Ancient of Days a new divine being had been given off—the Holy King, the Messiah, the Primal Man, Androgynous, Perfect, who would harmonize the jarring chords, restore the spiritual unity of the Universe. Before the love in his eyes sin and sorrow would vanish as evil vapors; the frozen streams of grace would flow again.

"I, the Lord your God, Sabbataï Zevi!"

Thus did Secretary Samuel Primo sign the Messianic decrees and ordinances.

XVII

The month of Ab approached—the Messiah's birthday, the day of the Black Fast, commemorating the fall of the Temples. But Melisselda protested against its celebration by gloom and penance, and the word went out to all the hosts of captivity—

"The only and just-begotten Son of God, Sabbataï Zevi, Messiah and Redeemer of the people of Israel, to all the sons of Israel, Peace! Since ye have been worthy to behold the great day, and the fulfilment of God's word to the prophets, let your lament and sorrow be changed into joy, and your fasts into festivals; for ye shall weep no more. Rejoice with drums, organs, and music, making of every day a New Moon, and change the day which was formerly dedicated to sadness and sorrow into a day of jubilee, because I have appeared; and fear ye naught, for ye shall have dominion not only over the nations, but over the creatures also in the depths of the sea."

Thereat arose a new and stranger commotion throughout all the Ghettos, Jewries, and Mellahs. The more part received the divine message in uproarious jubilation. The Messiah was come, indeed! Those terrible twenty-four hours of absolute fasting and passionate prayer—henceforward to be hours of feasting and merriment! O just and joyous edict! The Jewish Kingdom was on the eve of restoration—how then longer bewail its decay!

But the staunchest pietists were staggered, and these the most fervent of the followers of Sabbataï. What! The penances and prayers of sixteen hundred years to be swept away! The Yoke of the Torah to be abolished! Surely true religion rather demanded fresh burdens. What could more fitly mark the Redemption of the World than new and more exacting laws, if, indeed, such remained to be invented? True, God himself was now incarnate on earth—of that they had no doubt. But how could He wish to do away with the laws deduced from the Holy Book and accumulated by the zealous labors of so many generations of faithful Rabbis; how could He set aside the venerated prescriptions of the Shulchan Aruch of the pious Benjamin Caro (his memory for a blessing), and all that network of ceremonial and custom for the zealous maintenance of which their ancestors had so often laid down their lives? How could He so blaspheme?

And so—in blind passion, unreasoning, obstinate—they clung to their threatened institutions; in every Jewry they formed little parties for the defence of Judaism.

What they had prayed for so passionately for centuries had come to pass. The hopes that they had caught from the Zohar, that they had nourished and repeated day and night, the promise that sorrow should be changed into joy and the Law become null and void—here was the fulfilment. The Messiah was actually incarnate—the Kingdom of the Jews was at hand. But in their hearts was a vague fear of the dazzling present, and a blind clinging to the unhappy past.

In the Jewry of Smyrna the Messiah walked on the afternoon of the abolished fast, and a vast concourse seethed around him, dancing and singing, with flute and timbrel, harp and drum. Melisselda's voice led the psalm of praise. Suddenly a whisper ran through the mob that there were unbelievers in the city, that some were actually fasting and praying in the synagogue. And at once there was a wild rush. They found the doors shut, but the voice of wailing was heard from inside.

"Beat in the doors!" cried Isaac Silvera. "What do they within, profaning the festal day?"

The crowd battered in the doors, they tore up the stones of the street and darted inside.

The floor was strewn with worshippers, rocking to and fro.

The venerable Aaron de la Papa, shorn of his ancient Rabbinical prestige, but still a commanding figure, rose from the floor, his white shroud falling weirdly about him, his face deadly pale from the long fast.

"Halt!" he cried. "How dare you profane the House of God?"

"Blasphemers!" retorted Silvera. "Ye who pray for what God in His infinite mercy has granted, do ye mock and deride Him?"

But Solomon Algazi, a hoary-headed zealot, cried out, "My fathers have fasted before me, and shall I not fast?"

For answer a great stone hurtled through the air, just grazing his head.

"Give over!" shouted Elias Zevi, one of Sabbataï's brothers. "Be done with sadness, or thou shalt be stoned to death. Hath not the Lord ended our long persecution, our weary martyrdom? Cease thy prayer, or thy blood be on thine own head." Algazi and De la Papa were driven from the city; the Kofrim, as the heretics were dubbed, were obnoxious to excommunication. The thunder of the believers silenced the still small voice of doubt.

And from the Jewries of the world, from Morocco to Sardinia, from London to Lithuania, from the Brazils to the Indies, one great cry in one tongue rose up:—"Leshanah Haba Berushalayim—Leshanah Haba Beni Chorin. Next year in Jerusalem—next year, sons of freedom!"

XVIII

It was the eve of 1666. In a few days the first sun of the great year would rise upon the world. The Jews were winding up their affairs, Israel was strung to fever pitch. The course of the exchanges, advices, markets, all was ignored, and letters recounting miracles replaced commercial correspondence.

Elijah the Prophet, in his ancient mantle, had been seen everywhere simultaneously, drinking the wine-cups left out for him, and sometimes filling them with oil. He was seen at Smyrna on the wall of a festal chamber, and welcomed with compliments, orations, and thanksgivings. At Constantinople a Jew met him in the street, and was reproached for neglecting to wear the fringed garment and for shaving. At once fringed garments were reintroduced throughout the Empire, and heads, though always shaven after the manner of Turks and the East, now became overgrown incommodiously with hair—even the Piyos, or earlock, hung again down the side of the face, and its absence served to mark off the Kofrim.

Sabbataï Zevi, happy in the love of Melisselda, rapt in heavenly joy, now confidently expecting the miracle that would crown the miracle of his career, prepared to set out for Constantinople to take the Crown from the Sultan's head to the sound of music. He held a last solemn levée at Smyrna, and there, surrounded by his faithful followers, with Melisselda radiantly enthroned at his side, he proceeded to parcel out the world among his twenty-six lieutenants.

Of these all he made kings and princes. His brothers came first. Elias Zevi he named King of Kings, and Joseph Zevi King of the Kings of Judah.

"Into thee, O Isaac Silvera," said he, "has the soul of David, King of Israel, migrated. Therefore shalt thou be called King David and shalt have dominion over Persia. Thou, O Chayim Inegna, art Jeroboam, and shalt rule over Araby. Thou, O Daniel Pinto, art Hilkiah, and thy kingdom shall be Italia. To thee, O Matassia Aschenesi, who reincarnatest Asa, shall be given Barbary, and thou, Mokiah Gaspar, in whom lives the soul of Zedekiah, shalt reign over England." And so the partition went on, Elias Azar being appointed Vice-King or Vizier of Elias Zevi, and Joseph Inernuch Vizier of Joseph Zevi.

"And for me?" eagerly interrupted Abraham Rubio, the beggar from the Morea.

"I had not forgotten thee," answered Sabbataï. "Art thou not Josiah?"

"True—I had forgotten," murmured the beggar.

"To thee I give Turkey, and the seat of thine empire shall be Smyrna."

"May thy Majesty be exalted for ever and ever," replied King Josiah fervently. "Verily shall I sit under my own fig-tree."

Portugal fell to a Marrano physician who had escaped from the Inquisition. Even Sabbataï's old enemy, Chayim Penya, was magnanimously presented with a kingdom.

"To thee, my well-beloved Raphael Joseph Chelebi of Cairo," wound up Sabbataï, "in whose palace Melisselda became my Queen, to thee, under the style of King Joash, I give the realm of Egypt."

The Emperor of the World rose, and his Kings prostrated themselves at his feet.

"Prepare yourselves," said he. "On the morning of the New Year we set out."

When he had left the chamber a great hubbub broke out. Wealthy men who had been disappointed of kingdoms essayed to purchase them from their new monarchs. The bidding for the Ottoman Empire was particularly high.

"Away! Flaunt not your money-bags!" cried Abraham Rubio, flown with new-born majesty. "Know ye not that this Smyrna is our capital city, and we could confiscate your gold to our royal exchequer? Josiah is King here." And he took his seat upon the throne vacated by Sabbataï. "Get ye gone, or the bastinado and the bowstring shall be your portion."

XIX

Punctually with the dawn of the Millennial Year the Turkish Messiah, with his Queen and his train of Kings, took ship for Constantinople to dethrone the Grand Turk, the Lord of Palestine. He voyaged in a two-masted Levantine Saic, the bulk of his followers travelling overland. Though his object had been diplomatically unpublished, pompous messages from Samuel Primo had heralded his advent. The day of his arrival was fixed. Constantinople was in a ferment. The Grand Vizier gave secret orders for his arrest as a rebel; a band of Chiauses was sent to meet the Saic in the harbor. But the day came and went and no Messiah. Instead, thunders and lightnings and rain and gales and news of wrecks. The wind was northerly, as commonly in the Hellespont and Propontis, and it seemed as if the Saic must have been blown out of her course.

The Jews of Constantinople asked news of every vessel. The captain of a ketch from the Isles of Marmora told them that a chember had cast anchor in the isles, and a tall man, clothed in white, who bestrode the deck, being apprised that the islanders were Christians, had raised his finger, whereupon the church burnt down. When at last the Jews heard of the safety of Sabbataï's weather—beaten vessel, which had made for a point on the coast of the Dardanelles, they told how their Master had ruled the waves and the winds by the mere reading of the hundred and sixteenth Psalm. But the news of his safety was speedily followed by the news of his captivity; the Vizier's officers were bringing him to Constantinople.

It was true; yet his Mussulman captors were not without a sense of the majesty of their prisoner, for they stopped their journey at Cheknesé Kutschuk, near the capital, so that he might rest for the Sabbath, and hither, apprised in advance by messenger, the Sabbatians of Constantinople hastened with food and money. They still expected to see their Sovereign arrive with pomp and pageantry, but he came up miserably on a sorry horse, chains clanking dismally at his feet. Yet was he in no wise dismayed. "I am like a woman in labor," he said to his body-guard of Kings, "the redoubling of whose anguish marks the near deliverance. Ye should laugh merrily, like the Rabbi in the Talmud when he saw the jackal running about the ruined walls of the Temple; for till the prophecies are utterly fulfilled the glory cannot return." And his face shone with conscious deity.

He was placed in a khan with a strong guard. But his worshippers bought off his chains, and even made for him a kind of throne. On the Sunday his captors brought him, and him alone, to Constantinople. A vast gathering of Jews and Turks—a motley-colored medley—awaited him on the quay; mounted police rode about to keep a path for the disembarking officers and to prevent a riot. At length, amid clamor and tumult, Sabbataï set fettered foot on shore.

His sad, noble air, the beauty of his countenance, his invincible silence, set a circle of mystery around him. Even the Turks had a moment of awe. A man-god, surely!

The Pacha had sent his subordinate with a guard to transfer him to the Seraglio. By them he was first hastily conducted into the custom-house, the guard riding among and dispersing the crowd.

Sabbataï sat upon a chest as majestically as though it were the throne of Solomon.

But the Sub-Pacha shook off the oppressive emotion with which the sight of Sabbataï inspired him.

"Rise, traitor," said he, "it is time that thou shouldst receive the reward of thy treasons and gather the fruit of thy follies." And therewith he dealt Sabbataï a sounding box of the ear.

His myrmidons, relieved from the tension, exploded in a malicious guffaw.

Sabbataï looked at the brutal dignitary with sad, steady gaze, then silently turned the other cheek.

The Sub-Pacha recoiled with an uncanny feeling of the supernatural; the mockery of the bystanders was hushed.

Sabbataï was conducted by side ways, to avoid the mob, to the Palace of the Kaimacon, the Deputy-Vizier.

"Art thou the man," cried the Kaimacon, "whom the Jews aver to have wrought miracles at Smyrna? Now is thy time to work one, for lo! thy treason shall cost thee dear."

"Miracles!" replied Sabbataï meekly. "I—what am I but a poor Jew, come to collect alms for my poor brethren in Jerusalem? The Jews of this great city persuade themselves that my blessing will bring them God's grace; they flock to welcome me. Can I stay them?"

"Thou art a seditious knave."

"An arrant impostor," put in the Sub-Pacha, "with the airs of a god. I thought to risk losing my arm when I cuffed him on the ear, but lo! 'tis stronger than ever." And he felt his muscle complacently.

"To gaol with the rogue!" cried the Kaimacon.

Sabbataï, his face and mien full of celestial conviction, was placed in the loathsome dungeon which served as a prison for Jewish debtors.

XX

For a day or so the Moslems made merry over the disconcerted Jews and their Messiah. The street-boys ran after the Sabbatians, shouting, "Gheldi mi? Gheldi mi?" (Is he coming? Is he coming?); the very bark of the street-dogs sounded sardonic. But soon the tide turned. Sabbataï's prophetic retinue testified unshaken to their Master—Messiah because Sufferer. Women and children were rapt in mystic visions, and miracles took place in the highways. Moses Suriel, who in fun had feigned to call up spirits, suddenly hearing strange singing and playing, fell into a foaming fury, and hollow prophecies issued from him, sublimely eloquent and inordinately rapid, so that on his recovery he went about crying, "Repent! Repent! I was a mocker and a sinner. Repent! Repent!" The Moslems themselves began to waver. A Turkish Dervish, clad in white flowing robes, with a stick in his hand, preached in the street corners to his countrymen, proclaiming the Jewish Messiah. "Think ye," he cried, "that to wash your hands stained with the blood of the poor and full of booty, or to bathe your feet which have walked in the way of unrighteousness, suffices to render you clean? Vain imagination! God has heard the prayers of the poor whom ye despise! He will raise the humble and abash the proud." Bastinadoed in vain several times, he was at last brought before the Cadi, who sent him to the Timar-Hané, the mad-house. But the doctors testified that he was sound, and he was again haled before the Cadi, who threatened him with death if he did not desist. "Kill me," said the Dervish pleadingly, "and ye will deliver me from the spirits which possess me and drive me to prophesy." Impressed, the Cadi dismissed him, and would have laden him with silver, but the Dervish refused and went his rhapsodical way. And in the heavens a comet flamed.

Soon Sabbataï had a large Turkish following. The Jews already in the debtors' dungeon hastened to give him the best place, and made a rude throne for him. He became King of the Prison. Thousands surged round the gates daily to get a glimpse of him. The keeper of the prison did not fail to make his profit of their veneration, and instead of the five aspres which friends of prisoners had to pay for the privilege of a visit, he charged a crown, and grew rapidly rich. Some of the most esteemed Jews attended a whole day before Sabbataï in the Oriental postures of civility and service—eyes cast down, bodies bending forward, and hands crossed on their breasts. Before these visitors, who came laden with gifts, Sabbataï maintained an equally sublime silence; sometimes he would point to the chapter of Genesis recounting how Joseph issued from his dungeon to become ruler of Egypt.

"How fares thy miserable prisoner?" casually inquired the Kaimacon of his Sub-Pacha one day.

"Miserable prisoner, Sire!" ejaculated the Sub-Pacha. "Nay, happy and glorious Monarch! The prison is become a palace. Where formerly reigned perpetual darkness, incessant wax tapers burn; in what was a sewer of filth and dung, one breathes now only amber, musk, aloe-wood, otto of roses, and every perfume; where men perished of hunger now obtains every luxury; the crumbs of Sabbataï's table suffice for all his fellow-prisoners."

The Deputy-Vizier was troubled, and cast about for what to do.

Meantime the fame of Sabbataï grew. It was said that every night a light appeared over his head, sometimes in stars, sometimes as an olive bough. Some English merchants in Galata visited him to complain of their Jewish debtors at Constantinople, who had ceased to traffic and would not discharge their liabilities. Sabbataï took up his quill and wrote:

"To you the Nation of Jews who expect the appearance of the Messiah and the Salvation of Israel, Peace without end. Whereas we are informed that ye are indebted to several of the English nation: It seemeth right unto us to order you to make satisfaction to these your just debts: which if you refuse to do, and not obey us herein, know ye that then ye are not to enter with us into our Joys and Dominions."

The debts were instantly paid, and the glory of the occupant of the debtors' prison waxed greater still. The story of his incarceration and of the homage paid him, even by Mussulmans, spread through the world. What! The Porte—so prompt to slay, the maxim of whose polity was to have the Prince served by men he could raise without envy and destroy without danger—the Turk, ever ready with the cord and the sack, the sword and the bastinado, dared not put to death a rebel, the vaunted dethroner of the Sultan. A miracle and a Messiah indeed!

XXI

But the Kaimacon was embarking for the war with Crete; in his absence he feared to leave Sabbataï in the capital. The prisoner was therefore transferred to the abode of State prisoners, the Castle of the Dardanelles at Abydos, with orders that he was to be closely confined, and never to go outside the gates. But, under the spell of some strange respect, or in the desire to have a hold upon them, too, the Kaimacon allowed his retinue of Kings to accompany him, likewise his amanuensis, Samuel Primo, and his consort, Melisselda.

The news of his removal to better quarters did not fail to confirm the faith of the Sabbatians. It was reported, moreover, that the Janissaries sent to take him fell dead at a word from his mouth, and being desired to revive them he consented, except in the case of some who, he said, were not true Turks. Then he went of his own accord to the Castle, but the shackles they laid on his feet fell from him, converted into gold with which he gratified his true and faithful believers, and, spite of steel bars and iron locks, he was seen to walk through the streets with a numerous attendance. Nor did the Sabbatians fail to find mystic significance in the fact that their Messiah arrived at his new prison on the Eve of Passover—of the anniversary of Freedom.

Sabbataï at once proceeded to kill the Paschal lamb for himself and his followers, and eating thereof with the fat, in defiance of Talmudic Law, he exclaimed:—"Blessed be God who hath restored that which was forbidden."

To the Tower of Strength, as the Sabbatians called the castle at Abydos, wherein the Messiah held his Court, streamed treasure-laden pilgrims from Poland, Germany, Italy, Vienna, Amsterdam, Cairo, Morocco, thinking by the pious journey to become worthy of seeing his face; and Sabbataï gave them his benediction, and promised them increase of their stores and enlargement of their possessions in the Holy Land. The ships were overburdened with passengers; freights rose. The natives grew rich by accommodating the pilgrims, the castellan (interpreting liberally the Kaimacon's instructions to mean that though the prisoner might not go out visitors might come in) by charging them fifteen to thirty marks for admission to the royal precincts. A shower of gold poured into Abydos. Jew, Moslem, Christian—the whole world wondered, and half of it believed. The beauty and gaiety of Melisselda witched the stubbornest sceptics. Men's thoughts turned to "The Tower of Strength," from the far ends of the world. Never before in human history had the news of a Messiah travelled so widely in his own lifetime. To console those who could not make the pilgrimage to him or to Jerusalem, Sabbataï promised equal indulgence and privilege to all who should pray at the tombs of their mothers. His initials, S.Z., were ornamentally inscribed in letters of gold over almost every synagogue, with a crown on the wall, in the circle of which was the ninety-first Psalm, and a prayer for him was inserted in the liturgy: "Bless our Lord and King, the holy and righteous Sabbataï Zevi, the Messiah of the God of Jacob."

The Ghettos began to break up. Work and business dwindled in the most sceptical. In Hungary the Jews commenced to demolish their houses. The great commercial centres, which owed their vitality to the Jews, were paralyzed. The very Protestants wavered in their Christianity. Amsterdam, under the infection of Jewish enthusiasm, effervesced with joy. At Hamburg, despite the epistolary ironies of Jacob Sasportas, the rare Kofrim, or Anti-Sabbatians, were forced, by order of Bendito de Castro, to say Amen to the Messianic prayer. At Livorne commerce dried up. At Venice there were riots, and the Kofrim were threatened with death. In Moravia the Governor had to interfere to calm the tumult. At Salee, in Algeria, the Jews so openly displayed their conviction of their coming dominance that the Emir decreed a persecution of them. At Smyrna, on the other hand, a Chacham who protested to the Cadi against the vagaries of his brethren, was, by the power of their longer purse, shaved of his beard and condemned to the galleys.

Three months of princely wealth and homage for Sabbataï had passed. In response to the joyous inspiration of Melisselda, he had abandoned all his ascetic habits, and lived the life of a king, ruling a world never again to be darkened with sin and misery. The wine sparkled and flowed, the choicest dishes adorned the banqueting-table, flowers and delicate odors made grateful the air, and the beautiful maidens of Israel danced voluptuously before him, shooting out passionate glances from under their long eyelashes. The fast of the seventeenth of Tammuz came round. Sabbataï abolished it, proclaiming that on that day the conviction that he was the Messiah had been borne in upon him. The ninth of Ab—the day of his Nativity—was again turned from a fast to a festival, the royal edict, promulgated throughout the world, quoting the exhortation of Zephaniah: "Sing and rejoice, O daughter of Zion; for lo I come, and I will dwell in the midst of thee, saith the Lord." Detailed prescriptions as to the order of the services and the psalmody accompanied the edict.

And in this supreme day of jubilation and merrymaking, of majesty and splendor, crowned with the homage and benison of his race, deputations of which came from all climes and soils to do honor to his nativity, the glory of Sabbataï culminated.

XXII

In the hour of his triumph, two Poles, who had made the pious pilgrimage, told him of a new Prophet who had appeared in far-off Lemberg, one Nehemiah Cohen, who announced the advent of the Kingdom, but not through Sabbataï Zevi.

That night, when his queen and his courtiers were sleeping, Sabbataï wrestled sore with himself in his lonely audience-chamber. The spectre of self-doubt—long laid to rest by music and pageantry—was raised afresh by this new and unexpected development. It was a rude reminder that this pompous and voluptuous existence was, after all, premature, that the Kingdom had yet to be won.

"O my Father in Heaven!" he prayed, falling upon his face. "Thou hast not deceived me. Tell me that this Prophet is false, I beseech Thee, that it is through me that Thy Kingdom is to be established on earth. I await the miracle. The days of the great year are nigh gone, and lo! I languish here in mock majesty. A sign! A sign!"

"Sabbataï!" A ravishing voice called his name. He looked up. Melisselda stood in the doorway, come from her chamber as lightly clad as on that far-off morning in the cemetery.

There was a strange rapt expression in her face, and, looking closer, he saw that her laughing eyes were veiled in sleep.

"It is the sign," he muttered in awe.

He sprang to his feet and took her white hand, that burnt his own, and she led him back to her chamber, walking unerringly.

"It is the sign," he murmured, "the sign that Melisselda hath truly led me to the Kingdom of Joy."

But in the morning he awoke still troubled. The meaning of the sign seemed less clear than in the silence of the night; the figure of the new Prophet loomed ominous.

When the Poles went back they bore a royal letter, promising the Polish Jews vengeance on the Cossacks, and commanding Nehemiah to come to the Messiah with all speed.

The way was long, but by the beginning of September Nehemiah arrived in Abydos. He was immediately received in private audience. He bore himself independently.

"Peace to thee, Sabbataï."

"Peace to thee, Nehemiah. I desired to have speech with thee; men say thou deniest me."

"That do I. How should Messiah—Messiah of the House of David, appear and not his forerunner, Messiah of the House of Ephraim, as our holy books foretell?" Sabbataï answered that the Ben Ephraim had already appeared, but he could not convince Nehemiah, who proved highly learned in the Hebrew, the Syriac, and the Chaldean, and argued point by point and text by text. The first Messiah was to be a preacher of the Law, poor, despised, a servant of the second. Where was he to be found?

Three days they argued, but Nehemiah still went about repeating his rival prophecies. The more zealous of the Sabbatians, angry at the pertinacious and pugnacious casuist, would have done him a mischief, but the Prophet of Lemberg thought it prudent to escape to Adrianople. Here in revenge he sought audience with the Kaimacon.

"Treason, O Mustapha, treason!" he announced. He betrayed the fantastic designs upon the Sultan's crown, still cherished by Sabbataï and known to all but the Divan; the Castellan of Abydos, for the sake of his pocket, having made no report of the extraordinary doings at the Castle.

Nehemiah denounced Sabbataï as a lewd person, who endeavored to debauch the minds of the Jews and divert them from their honest course of livelihood and obedience to the Grand Seignior. And, having thus avenged himself, the Prophet of Lemberg became a Mohammedan.

A Chiaus was at once dispatched to the Sultan, and there was held a Council. The problem was grave. To execute Sabbataï—beloved as he was by Jew and Turk alike—would be but to perpetuate the new sect. The Mufti Vanni—a priestly enthusiast—proposed that they should induce him to follow in the footsteps of Nehemiah, and come over to Islam. The suggestion seemed not only shrewd, but tending to the greater glory of Mohammed, the one true Prophet. An aga set out forthwith for Abydos. And so one fine day when the Castle of the Dardanelles was besieged by worshippers, when the Tower of Strength was gay with brightly clad kings, and filled with pleasant plants and odors and the blended melodies of instruments and voices, a body of moustachioed Janissaries flashed upon the scene, dispersing the crowd with their long wands; they seized the Messiah and his queen, and brought them to Adrianople.

XXIII

The Hakim Bashi, the Sultan's physician, who as a Jew-Turk himself, was thought to be the fittest to approach Sabbataï, laid the decision of the Grand Seignior before him on the evening of his arrival at Adrianople. The released prisoner was lodged with mocking splendor in a commodious apartment in the palace, overlooking the river, and lay upon a luxurious divan, puffing at a chibouque with pretended calm.

"What reverences is it customary to make to the Grand Seignior?" he asked, with affected nonchalance, when the first salutations with the physician had been exchanged. "I would not be wanting in the forms when I appear before his exalted majesty."

"An end to the farce, Sabbataï Zevi!" said the Hakim Bashi, sternly. "The Sultan demands of thee not posturings, but a miracle."

"Have not miracles enough been witnessed?" asked Sabbataï, in a low tone.

"Too many," returned the ex-Jew drily. "Yet if thou wouldst save thy life there needs another."

"What miracle?"

"That thou turn Turk!" And a faint smile played about the physician's lips.

There was a long silence. Sabbataï's own lips twitched, but not with humor. The regal radiance of Abydos had died out of his face, but its sadness was rather of misery than the fine melancholy of yore.

"And if I refuse this miracle?"

"Thou must give us a substitute. The Mufti Vanni suggests that thou be stript naked and set as a mark for the archers; if thy flesh and skin are proof like armor, we shall recognize thee as the Messiah indeed, and the person designed by Allah for the dominions and greatnesses to which thou dost pretend."

"And if I refuse this miracle, too?"

"Then the stake waits at the gate of the seraglio to compel thee," thundered the Hakim Bashi; "thou shalt die with tortures. The mercy of decapitation shall be denied thee, for thou knowest well Mohammedans will not pollute their swords with the blood of a Jew. Be advised by me, Sabbataï," he continued, lowering his tone. "Become one of us. After all, the Moslem are but the posterity of Hagar. Mohammed is but the successor of Moses. We recognize the One God who rules the heavens and the earth, we eat not swine-flesh. Thou canst Messiah it in a white turban as well as in a black," he ended jocosely.

Sabbataï winced. "Renegade!" he muttered.

"Ay, and an excellent exchange," quoth the physician. "The Sultan is a generous paymaster, may his shadow never grow less. He giveth thee till the morn to decide—Turk or martyr? With burning torches attached to thy limbs thou art to be whipped through the streets with fiery scourges in the sight of the people—such is the Sultan's decree. He is a generous paymaster. After all, what need we pretend—between ourselves, two Jews, eh?" And he winked drolly. "The sun greets Mohammed every morn, say these Turks. Let to-morrow's greet another Mohammedan."

Sabbataï sprang up with an access of majesty.

"Dog of an unbeliever! Get thee gone!"

"Till to-morrow! The Sultan will give thee audience to-morrow," said the Hakim Bashi imperturbably, and, making a mock respectful salutation, he withdrew from the apartment.

Melisselda had been dosing in an inner chamber after the fatigue of the journey, but the concluding thunders of the duologue had aroused her, and she heard the physician's farewell words. She now parted the hangings and looked through at Sabbataï, her loveliness half-framed, half-hidden by the tapestry. Her face was wreathed in a heavenly smile.

"Sabbataï!" she breathed.

He turned a frowning gaze upon her. "Thou art merry!" he said bitterly.

"Is not the hour come?" she cried joyously.

"Yea, the hour is come," he murmured.

"The hour of thy final trial and triumph! The longed-for hour of thy appearance before the Sultan, when thou wilt take the crown from his head and place it on—"

Instead of completing the sentence, she ran to take his head to her bosom. But he repulsed her embracing arms. She drew back in consternation. It was the first time she had known him rough, not only with her, but with any creature.

"Leave me! Leave me!" he cried huskily.

"Nay, thou needest me." And her forgiving arms spread towards him in fresh tenderness.

He looked at her without moving to meet them.

"Ay, I need thee," he said pathetically. "Therefore," and his voice rose firm again, "leave me to myself."

"Thou hast become a stranger," she said tremulously. "I do not understand thee."

"Would thou hadst ever been a stranger, that I had never understood thee."

"Sabbataï, thou ravest."

"I have come to my senses. O my God! my God!" and he fell a-weeping on the divan.

Melisselda's alarm grew greater.

"Rouse thyself, they will hear thee."

"Let them hear. God hears me not."

"Hears thee not? Thou art He!"

"I God!" He laughed bitterly. "Thou believest that! Thou who knowest me man!"

"I know thee all divine. I have worshipped thee in joy. Art thou not Messiah?"

"Messiah! Who cannot save myself!"

"Who can hurt thee? Who hath ever hurt thee from thy youth up? The Angels watch over thy footsteps. Is not thy life one long miracle?"

He shook his head hopelessly. "All this year I have waited the miracle—all those weary months in the dungeon of Constantinople, in the Castle of Abydos—but what sure voice hath spoken? To-morrow I shall be disembowelled, lashed with fiery scourges—who knows what these dogs may do?"

"Hush! hush!"

"Ah, thou fearest for me!" he cried, in perverse triumph. "Thou knowest I am but mortal man!"

The roses of her beautiful cheek had faded, but she spoke, unflinching.

"Nay, I believe on thee still. I followed thee to thy prison, unwitting it would turn into a palace. I follow thee to thy torture to-morrow, trusting it will be the crowning miracle and the fiery scourges will turn into angels' feathers. It is the word of Zechariah fulfilled. 'In that day will I make the governors of Judah like an hearth of fire among the wood, and like a torch of fire in a sheaf.'"

His eyes grew humid as he looked up at her. "Yea, Melisselda, thou hast been true and of good courage. And now, when I am alone, when the shouts of the faithful have died away, when the King of the World lies here alone in darkness and ashes, thou hast faith still?"

"Ay, I believe—'tis but a trial, the final trial of my faith."

She smiled at him confidently; hope quickened within him. "If this were but a trial, the final trial of my faith!" he murmured. "But no—ere that white strip of moon rises again in the heavens I shall be a mangled corpse, the feast of wolves, unless—I have prayed for a sign—oh, how I have prayed, and now—ah, see! A star is falling. O my God, that this should be the end of my long martyrdom! But the punishment of my arrogance is greater than I can bear. God, God, why didst Thou send me those divine-seeming whispers, those long, long thoughts that thrilled my soul? Why didst Thou show me the sin of Israel and his suffering, the sorrow and evil of the world, inspiring me to redeem and regenerate?" His breast swelled with hysteric sobs.

"My Sabbataï!" Melisselda's warm arms were round him. He threw her off with violence. "Back, back!" he cried. "I understand the sign; I understand at last. 'Tis through thee that I have forfeited the divine grace."

"Through me?" she faltered.

"Yea; thy lips have wooed mine away from prayer, thine arms have drawn me down from the steeps of righteousness. Thou hast made me unfaithful to my bride, the Law. For nigh forty years I lived hard and lonely, steeped my body in ice and snow, lashed myself—ay, lashed myself, I who now fear the lash—till the blood ran from a dozen wounds, and now, O God! O God! Woman, thou hast polluted me! I have lost the divine spirit. It hath gone out from me; it will incarnate itself in another, in a nobler. Once I was Messiah, now I am man."

"I?—I took from thee the divine spirit!"

She looked at him in all the flush of her beauty, grown insolent again.

He sprang up, he fell upon her breast, he kissed her lips madly.

"Nay, nay, thou hast shown it me! Love! Love! 'tis Love that breathes through all things, that lifts the burden of life. But for thee I should have passed away, unknowing the glory of manhood. I am a man—a man rejoicing in his strength! O my starved youth! why did I not behold thee earlier?" Tears of self-pity rolled down his ashen cheek. "O my love! my love! my lost youth! Give me back my youth, O God! Who am I, to save? A man; yea, a man, glorying in manhood. Ah! happy are they who lead the common fate of men, happy in love, in home, in children; woe for those who would climb, who would torture and deny themselves, who would save humanity? From what? If they have Love, have they not all? It is God, it is the Kingdom. It is the Kingdom. Come, let us live—I a man, thou a woman!"

"But a Mussulman!"

"What imports? God is everywhere. Was not our Maimonides—he at whose tomb we worship in Tiberias—himself once a Mussulman? Did he not say that if it be to save our lives naught is forbidden?"

He moved to take her in his arms, but this time it was she that drew back. Her eyes flashed.

"Nay, as a man, I love thee not. Thou art divine or naught; God or Impostor!"

"Melisselda!" She ignored his stricken cry.

"Nay, this ordeal hath endured long enough," she replied sternly. "Confess, I have been proof."

"I am neither God nor Impostor," he said brokenly. "Ah! say not that thou canst not love me as a man. When thou didst first come to bless my life I had not yet declared myself Messiah."

"Who knows what I thought then? A wild girl, crazed by the convent, by the blood shed before my childish eyes, I came to thee full of lawless passions and fantastic dreams. But as I lived with thee, as I saw the beauty of thy thought, thy large compassion, the purity of thy life amid temptations that made me jealous as a woman of Damascus, then I knew thee a God indeed."

"Nay, when I knew thee I knew myself man. But as our followers grew, as faith and fortune trod in my footsteps, my blasphemous dream revived; I believed in thy vision of the Kingdom. When I divided the world I thought myself Messiah indeed. But as I sat on my throne at Abydos, with worshippers from the world's end kissing my feet, a hollow doubt came over me, a sense of dream, and hollow voices echoed ever in my ear, asking, 'Art thou Messiah? Art thou Messiah? Art thou Messiah?' I strove to drown them in the festive song; but in the stillness of the night, when thou wast sleeping at my side, the voices came back, and they cried mockingly, 'Man! Man! Man!' And when Nehemiah came—"

"Man!" interrupted Melisselda impatiently. "Cease to cozen me. Have I not known men? Ay, who more? Their weaknesses, their vanities, their lewdnesses—enough! To-morrow thou shalt assert the God."

He threw himself back on the divan and sighed wearily. "Leave me, Melisselda. Go to thy rest; to-night I must keep vigil alone. Perchance it is my last night on earth."

Her countenance lit up. "Yea, to-morrow comes the Kingdom of Heaven." And smiling ineffable trust, she stooped down and lightly kissed his hair, then glided from the room.

And in his sleepless brain and racked soul went on, through that unending night, the terrible tragedy of doubt, tempered by spells of spasmodic prayer. A God, or a Man? A Messiah undergoing his Father's last temptation; or a martyr on the eve of horrible death? And if the victim of a monstrous self-delusion, what mattered whether one lived out one's years of shame as Jew or Mussulman? Nobler, perhaps, to die, and live as an heroic memory—but then to leave Melisselda! To leave her warm breast and the sunlight and the green earth, and all that beauty of the world and of human life to which his eyes had only been unsealed after a lifetime of self-torturing blindness?

"O God! O God!" he cried, "wherefore hast Thou mocked and abandoned me?"

XXIV

Early in the forenoon the light touch of a loved hand upon his shoulder roused him from deeps of reverie.

He uplifted a white, haggard face. Melisselda stood before him in all her dazzling freshness, like a radiant spirit come to chase the demons of the night. The ancient Spanish song came into his mind, and the sweet, sad melody vibrated in his soul.

From her bath she arose, Pure and white as the snows,
Melisselda. Coral only at lips And at sweet finger-tips,
Melisselda.

His eyes filled with tears—the divine dreams of youth stirred faintly within him.

"Is it Peace with thee?" she asked.

His head drooped again on his breast.

"From the casement I saw the sun rise over the Maritza," he said, "kindling the sullen waters, but my faith is still gray and dead. Nay, rather there came into my mind the sublime poem of Moses Ibn Ezra of Granada: 'Thy days are delusive dreams and thy life as yon cloud of morning: whilst it tarries over thy tabernacle thou may'st remain therein, but at its ascent thou art dissolved and removed unto a place unknown to thee,' This is the end, Melisselda, the end of my great delusion. What am I but a man, with a man's pains and errors and self-deceptions, a man's life that blooms but once as a rose and fades while the thorn endures?" The ineffable melancholy of his accents subdued her to silence: for the moment the music of his voice, his sad brooding eyes, the infinite despair of his attitude swayed her to a mood akin to his own. "Verily it was for me," he went on, "that the Sephardic poet sang—

"'Reflect on the labor thou didst undergo under the sun, night and day, without intermission; labor which thou knowest well to be without profit; for, verily in these many years thou hast walked after vanity and become vain. Thou wast a keeper of vineyards, but thine own vineyard thou hast not kept; whilst the Eyes of the Eternal run to and fro to see if the vine hath flourished, whether the tender grapes appear, and, lo! all was grown over with thorns; nettles had covered the face thereof. Thou hast grown old and gray, thou hast strayed but not returned.' Yea, I have strayed, but is the gate closed for return? To be a man—only a man—how great that is!" His voice died away, and with it the sweet, soothing spell. Fire glowed in Melisselda's breast, heaving her bosom, shooting sparks from her eyes.

"Nay, if thou art only a man, thou art not even a man. My love is dead."

As he shrank beneath her contempt, another stanza of his ancient song sang itself involuntarily in his brain. Never had he seen her thus.

In the pride of her race, As a sword shone her face,
Melisselda. And her lids were steel bows, But her mouth was a rose,
Melisselda.

But her mouth was a rose. Ah, God, the pity of it, to leave the rose for the crown of thorns!

"Melisselda!" he cried, with a sob. "Have pity on me."

The door opened; two of the Imperial Guards appeared.

"Thou slayest me," he said in Hebrew.

"I worship thee," she answered him, in the same sacred tongue. Her face took on its old confident smile.

"But I am a man."

Once again her lids were steel bows.

"Then die like a man! Thinkst thou I would share thy humiliation? If I am to be a Moslem's bride, let me be the Sultan's. If I am not to share the Messiah's throne, let me share an Emperor's. Thy Spanish song made me an Emperor's daughter—I will be an Emperor's consort."

And she laughed wantonly.

The guards advanced timidly with visible awe. Melisselda's swiftly flashing face changed suddenly. She drew him to her breast.

"My King!" she murmured. "'Twas cruel to tempt my faith thus." Then releasing him, she cried, "Go to thy Kingdom."

He drew himself up; the fire in her eyes flashed into his own.

"The Sultan summons thee," said one of the guards reverently.

"I am ready," he said, calmly adjusting the folds of his black mantle.

Melisselda was left alone. The slow moments wore on, tense and terrible. Little by little the radiant faith died out of her face. Half an hour went by, and cold serpents of doubt began to coil about her own heart.

What if Sabbataï were only a man after all? With frenzied rapidity she reviewed the past; now she glowed with effulgent assurances of his divinity, the homage of his people, the awe of Turk and

Christian, Rabbis and sages at his feet, the rich and the great struggling to kiss his fan, the treasures poured into his unwilling palms; now she shivered with hideous suggestions and remembrances of frailty and mortal ineptitude. And as her faith faltered, as the exaltation, with which she had inspired him, ebbed away, alarm for his safety began to creep into her soul, till at last it was as a flood sweeping her in his traces. And the more her fears swelled the more she realized how much she had grown to love him, with his sad, dark, smooth-skinned beauty, the soft, almost magnetic touch of his hand. Messiah or man, she loved him: he was right. What if she had sent him to his death! A cold, sick horror crept about her limbs. Perhaps he had dared to put his divinity to the test, and the ribald Turk was even now gloating over the screams of the wretched self-deluded man. Oh, fool that she had been to drive him to the stake and the fiery scourge. If divine, then to turn Turk were part of the plan of Salvation; if human, he would at least be spared an agonized death. The bloody visions of her childhood came back to her, fire coursed in her fevered veins. She snatched up a mantilla and threw it over her shoulders, then dashed from the chamber. Her houri-like beauty in that palace of hidden moon-faces, her breathless explanation that the Sultan had summoned her to join her husband, carried her past breathless guards, through door after door, past the black eunuchs of the seraglio and the white eunuchs of the royal apartment, till through the interstices of purple hangings she had a far-off glimpse of the despot in his great imperial turban, sitting on his high, narrow throne, his officers around him. A page stopped her rudely. Faintness overcame her.

"Mehmed Effendi," called the page.

Dizzy, her tongue scarcely under control, she tried to proffer to the tall door-keeper who parted the hangings her request for admission. But he held out his arms to catch her swaying form, and then, as in some monstrous dream, something familiar seemed to her to waft from the figure, despite the white turban and the green mantle, and the next instant, as with the pain of a stab, she recognized Sabbataï.

"What masquerade is this?" her white lips whispered in indignant revulsion as she struggled from his hold.

"My lord, the Sultan, hath made me his door-keeper—Capigi Bashi Otorak," he replied deprecatingly. "He is merciful and forgiving. May Allah exalt his dominion. The salary is large; he is a generous paymaster. I testify that there is no God but God. I testify that Mohammed is God's prophet." He caught the swooning Melisselda in his arms and covered her face with kisses.

XXV

News travelled slowly in those days. A week later, while Agi Mehmed Effendi and his wife Fauma Kadin (born Sarah and still called Melisselda by her adoring husband, the Sultan's door-keeper) were receiving instruction in the Moslem religion from the exultant Mufti Vanni, a great Synod of Jews, swept to Amsterdam by the mighty wave of faith and joy, Rabbis and scholars and presidents of colleges, were drawing up a letter of homage to the Messiah. And while the Grand Seignior was meditating the annihilation of all the Jews of the Ottoman Empire for their rebellious projects, with the forced conversion of the orphaned children to Islam, the Jews of the world were celebrating—for what they thought the last time—the Day of Atonement, and five times during that long fast-day did the weeping worshippers, rocking to and fro in their grave-clothes, passionately pronounce the blessing over Sabbataï Zevi, the Messiah of Israel.

Nor did the fame and memory of him perish for generations; nor the dreamers of the Jewry cease to cherish the faith in him, many following him in adopting the white turban of Islam.

But by what ingenious cabalistic sophistries, by what yearning fantasies—fit to make the angels weep—his unhappy followers, obstinate not to lose the great white hope that had come to illumine the gloom of the Jewries, explained away his defection; what sects and counter-sects his appostasy gave birth to, and what new prophets arose—a guitar-playing gallant of Madrid, a tobacco dealer of Pignerol, a blue-blooded Christian millionaire of Copenhagen—to nourish that great pathetic hope (which still lives on) long after Sabbataï himself, after who knows what new spasms of self-mystification and hypocrisy, what renewed aspirations after his old greatness and his early righteousness, what fresh torment of soul and body, died on the Day of Atonement, a lonely white-haired exile in a little Albanian town, where no brother Jew dwelt to close his eyelids or breathe undying homage into his dying ears—is it not written in the chronicles of the Ghetto?

THE MAKER OF LENSES

As the lean, dark, somewhat stooping passenger, noticeable among the blonde Hollanders by his noble Spanish face with its black eyebrows and long curly locks, stepped off the trekschuyt on to the canal-bank at s' Gravenhage, his abstracted gaze did not at first take in the scowling visages of the idlers, sunning themselves as the tow-boat came in. He was not a close observer of externals, and though he had greatly enjoyed the journey home from Utrecht along the quaint water-way between green walls of trees and hedges, with occasional glimpses of flat landscapes and windmills through rifts, his sense of the peace of Nature was wafted from the mass, from a pervasive background of greenness and flowing water; he was not keenly aware of specific trees, of linden, or elm, or willow, still less of the aquatic plants and flowers that carpeted richly the surface of the canal.

Even when, pursuing broodingly his homeward path through the handsome streets of the Hague, he became at last conscious of a certain ill-will in the faces he met, he did not at first connect it with himself, but with the general bellicose excitement of the populace. Although the young Prince of Orange had rewarded their insurrectionary election of him to the Stadtholdership by redeeming them from the despair to which the French invasion and the English fleet had reduced them, although since his famous "I will die in the last ditch," Holland no longer strove to commit suicide by opening its own sluices, yet the unloosed floods of popular passion were only partially abated. A stone that grazed his cheek and plumped against the little hand-bag that held his all of luggage, startled him to semi-comprehension.

They were for him, then, these sullen glances. Cries of "Traitor!" "Godless gallows-bird!" "Down with the damned renegade!" dispelled what doubt remained. A shade of melancholy deepened the expression of the sweet, thoughtful mouth; then, as by volition, the habitual look of pensive cheerfulness came back, and he walked on, unruffled.

So it had leaked out, even in his own town—where an anonymous prophet should be without dishonor—that he was the author of the infamous Tractatus Theologico-Politicus, the "traitor to State and Church" of refuting pamphleteers, the bogey of popular theology. In vain, then, had his treatise been issued with "Hamburg" on the title-page. In vain had he tried to combine personal peace with impersonal thought, to confine his body to a garret and to diffuse his soul through the world. The forger of such a thunderbolt could not remain hid from the eyes of Europe. Perhaps the illustrious foreigners and the beautiful bluestockings who climbed his stairs—to the detriment of his day's work in grinding lenses—had set the Hague scenting sulphur. More probably the hot-headed young disciples to whom he had given oral or epistolary teaching had enthusiastically betrayed him into fame—or infamy. It had always been thus, he mused, even in those early half-forgotten days when he was emancipating himself from the Ghetto, and half-shocked admirers no less than heresy-hunters bore to the ears of the Beth-din his dreadful rejection of miracle and ceremony. Poor Saul Morteira! How his ancient master must have been pained to pronounce the Great Ban, though nothing should have surprised him in a pupil so daring of question, even at fifteen. And now that he had shaken off the Ghetto, or rather been shaken off by it, he had scandalized no less shockingly that Christendom to which the Ghetto had imagined him apostatizing: he had fearlessly contradicted every system of the century, the ruling Cartesian philosophy no less than the creed of the Church, and his plea for freedom of thought had illustrated it to the full. True, the Low Countries, when freed from the Spanish rack, had nobly declared for religious freedom, but at a scientific treatment of the Bible as sacred literature even Dutch toleration must draw the line, unbeguiled by the appeal to the State to found itself on true religion and ignore the glossing theologians. "What evil can be imagined greater for a State than that honorable men, because they have thoughts of their own and cannot act a lie, are sent as culprits into exile or led to the scaffold?" Already the States-General had attached the work containing this question and forbidden its circulation: now apparently persecution was to reach him in person, Christendom supplementing what he had long since suffered from the Jewry. He thought of the fanatical Jew whose attempt to stab him had driven him to live on the outskirts of Amsterdam even before the Jews had persuaded the civil magistrates to banish him from their "new Jerusalem," and in a flash of bitterness the picturesque Portuguese imprecations of the Rabbinic tribunal seemed to him to be bearing fruit. "According to the decision of the angels and the judgment of the saints, with the sanction of the Holy God and the whole congregation, we excommunicate, expel, curse, and execrate Baruch de Espinoza before the holy books.... Cursed be he by day, and cursed be he by night; cursed be he when he lieth down, and cursed be he when he riseth up; cursed be he when he goeth out, and cursed be he when he cometh in. May God never forgive him! His anger and His passion shall be kindled against this man, on whom rest all the curses and execrations which are written in the Holy Scriptures...." Had the words been lurking at the back of his mind, when he was writing the Tractatus? he asked himself, troubled to find them still in his memory. Had resentment colored the Jewish sections? Had his hot Spanish blood kept the memory of the dagger that had tried to spill it? Had suffering biassed the impersonality of his intellect? "This compels me to nothing which I should not otherwise have done," he had said to his Mennonite friend when the sentence reached him in the Oudekirk Road. But was it so? If he had not been cut off from his father and his brothers and sisters, and the friends of childhood, would he have treated the beauties of his ancestral faith with so grudging a sympathy? The doubt disturbed him, revealing once more how difficult was self-mastery, absolute surrender to absolute Truth. Never had he wavered under persecution like Uriel Acosta—at whose grave in unholy ground he had stood when a boy of eight,—but had it not wrought insidiously upon his spirit?

"Alas!" thought he, "the heaviest burden that men can lay upon us, is not that they persecute us with their hatred and scorn, but that they thus plant hatred and scorn in our souls. That is what does not let us breathe freely or see clearly." Retrospect softened the odiousness of his Jewish persecutors; they were but children of a persecuting age, and it was indeed hard for a community of refugees from Spain and Portugal to have that faith doubted for which they or their fathers had given up wealth and country. Even at the hour of his Ban the pyres of the Inquisition were flaming with Jewish martyrs, and his fellow-scholars were writing Latin verses to their sacred memories. And should the religion which exacted and stimulated such sacrifices be set aside by one providentially free to profess it? How should they understand that a martyr's death proved faith, not truth? Well, well, if he had not sufficiently repaid his brethren's hatred with love, it was no good being sorry, for sorrow was an evil, a passing to lesser perfection, diminished vitality. Let him rather rejoice that the real work of his life—his Ethica, which he was working out on pure geometrical principles—would have no taint of personality, would be without his name, and would not even be published till death had removed the last possibility of personal interest in its fortunes. "For," as he was teaching in the book itself, "those who desire to aid others by counsel or deed to the common enjoyment of the chief good shall in no wise endeavor themselves that a doctrine be called after them."

Another stone and a hoot of derision from a gang of roughs reminded him that death might not wait for the finishing of his work. "Strange," he reflected, "that they who cannot even read should so run to damn." And then his thoughts recurred to that horrible day not a year ago when the brutal mob had torn to pieces the noblest men in the realm—his friends, the brothers De Witt. He could scarcely retain his tears even now at the memory of the martyred patriots, whose ignominiously gibbeted bodies the police had only dared remove in the secrecy of the small hours. It was hard even for the philosopher to remember that the brutes did but express the essence of their being, even as he expressed his. Nevertheless Reason did not demand that theirs should destroy his: the reverse sooner, had he the power. So, turning the corner of the street, he slipped into his favorite book-shop in the Spuistraat and sought at once safety and delectation among the old folios and the new Latin publications and the beautiful productions of the Elzevirs of Amsterdam.

"Hast thou Stoupe's Religion des Hollandois?" he asked, with a sudden thought.

"Inquire elsewhere," snapped the bookseller surlily.

"Et tu, Brute!" said Spinoza, smiling. "Dost thou also join the hue and cry? Methinks heresy should nourish thy trade. A wilderness of counterblasts, treatises, tractlets, pasquinades—the more the merrier, eh?"

The bookseller stared. "Thou to come in and ask for Stoupe's book? 'Tis—'tis—brazen!"

Spinoza was perplexed. "Brazen? Is it because he talks of me in it?"

"Heer Spinoza," said the bookseller solemnly, "thy Cartesian commentary has brought me a many pence, and if thou thyself hast browsed more than bought, thou wast welcome to take whatever thou couldst carry away in that long head of thine. But to serve thee now is more than I dare, with the populace so wrought up against thee. What! Didst thou think thy doings in Utrecht would not penetrate hither?"

"My doings in Utrecht!"

"Ay, in the enemy's headquarters—betraying us to the periwigs!"

Spinoza was taken aback. This was even more serious than he had thought. It was for supposed leaning to the French that the De Witts had been massacred. Political odium was even more sinister than theological. Perhaps he had been unwise to accept in war-time the Prince of Condé's flattering invitation to talk philosophy. To get to the French camp with the Marshal's safe-conduct had been easy enough: to get back to his own headquarters bade fair to be another matter. But then why had the Dutch authorities permitted him to go? Surely such unique confidence was testimonial enough.

"Oh, but this is absurd!" he said. "Every burgher in Den Haag knows that I am a good republican, and have never had any aim but the honor and welfare of the State. Besides, I did not even see Condé. He had been called away, and I would not wait his return."

"Ay, but thou didst see Luxemburg; thou wast entertained by Colonel Stoupe, of the Swiss regiment."

"True, but he is theologian as well as soldier."

"He did not offer to bribe thee?"

"Ay, he did," said Spinoza, smiling. "He offered me a pension—"

The bookseller plugged his ears. "'Sh! I will not know. I'll have no hand in thy murder."

"Nay, but it will interest thee as a bookseller. The pension was to be given me by his royal master if I would dedicate a book to his august majesty."

"And thou refusedst?"

"Naturally. Louis Quatorze has flatterers enough."

The bookseller seized his hands and wrung them with tears. "I told them so, I told them so. What if they did see these French gentry visiting thee? Political emissaries forsooth! As well fear for the virtue of the ladies of quality who toil up his stairs, quoth I. They do but seek further explications of their Descartes. Ah, France may have begotten a philosopher, but it requires Holland to shelter him, a Dutchman to understand him. That musked gallant a spy! Why, that was D'Hénault, the poet. How do I know? Well, when a man inquires for D'Hénault's poems and is half-pleased because I have the book, and half-annoyed because he must needs buy it—! An epicurean rogue by his lip, a true son of the Muses. And suppose there is a letter from England, quoth I, with the seal of the Royal Society!"

"Is there a letter from England?"

"Thou hast not been to thy lodging? That Royal Society, quoth I, is a learned body—despite its name—and hath naught to do with King Charles and the company he keeps. 'Tis they who egg him on to fight us, the hussies!"

Spinoza smiled. "It must be from my good friend Oldenburg, the secretary."

"'Tis what I told them. He was in my shop when he was here—"

"Asking for his book?"

"Nay, for thine." And the bookseller's smile answered Spinoza's. "He bade me despatch copies of the Principia Philosophiae Cartesianae to sundry persons of distinction. I would to Heaven thou wouldst write a new book!"

"Heaven may not share thy view," murmured Spinoza, who was just turning over the pages of an attack on his "new book," and reading of himself as "a man of bold countenance, fanatical, and estranged from all religion."

"A good book thou hast there," said the bookseller. "By Musæus, the Jena Professor. The Tractatus Theologico-Politicus ad Veritatis Lancem Examinatus—weighed in Truth's balance, indeed. A title that draws. They say 'tis the best of all the refutations of the pernicious and poisonous Tractate."

"Of which I see sundry copies here masked in false titles."

"'Sh! Forbidden fruit is always in demand. But so long as I supply the antidote too—"

"Needs fruit an antidote?"

"Poisoned apples of Knowledge offered by the serpent."

"A serpent indeed," said Spinoza, reading the Antidote aloud. "'He has left no mental faculty, no cunning, no art untried in order to conceal his fabrication beneath a brilliant veil, so that we may with good reason doubt whether among the great number of those whom the devil himself has hired for the destruction of all human and divine right, there is one to be found who has been more zealous in the work of corruption than this traitor who was born to the great injury of the church and to the harm of the state.' How he bruises the serpent's head, this theology professor!" he cried; "how he lays him dead on his balance of Truth!" To himself he thought: "How the most ignorant are usually the most impudent and the most ready to rush into print!" He had a faint prevision of how his name—should it really leak out, despite all his precautions—would come to stand for atheism and immorality, a catchword of ill-omen for a century or two; but he smiled on, relying upon the inherent reasonableness and rightness of the universe.

"Wilt take the book?" said the bookseller.

"Nay, 'tis not by such tirades that Truth is advanced. But hast thou the Refutation by Lambert Velthuysen?"

The bookseller shook his head.

"That is worth a hundred of this. Prithee get that and commend it to thy clients, for Velthuysen wields a formidable dialectic by which men's minds may be veritably stimulated."

On his homeward way dark looks still met him, but he faced them with cheerful, candid gaze. At the end of the narrow Spuistraat the affairs of the broad market-place engrossed popular attention, and the philosopher threaded his way unregarded among the stalls and the canvas-covered Zeeland waggons, and it was not till he reached the Paviljoensgracht—where he now sits securely in stone, pencilling a thought as enduring—that he encountered fresh difficulty. There, at his own street door, under the trees lining the canal-bank, his landlord, Van der Spijck, the painter—usually a phlegmatic figure haloed in pipe-clouds—congratulated him excitedly on his safe return, but refused him entry to the house. "Here thou canst lodge no more."

"Here I lodge to-night," said Spinoza quietly, "if there be any law in Holland."

"Law! The folk will take the law into their own hands. My windows will be broken, my doors battered in. And thou wilt be murdered and thrown into the canal."

His lodger laughed. "And wherefore? An honest optician murdered! Go to, good friend!"

"If thou hadst but sat at home, polishing thy spy-glasses instead of faring to Utrecht! Customarily thou art so cloistered in that the goodwife declares thou forgettest to eat for three days together—and certes there is little thou canst eat when thou goest not abroad to buy provision! What devil must drive thee on a long journey in this hour of heat and ferment? Not that I believe a word of thy turning traitor—I'd sooner believe my mahl-stick could turn serpent like Aaron's rod—but in my house thou shalt not be murdered."

"Reassure thyself. The whole town knows my business with Stoupe; at least I told my bookseller, and 'tis only a matter of hours."

"Truly he is a lively gossip."

"Ay," said Spinoza drily. "He was even aware that a letter from the Royal Society of England awaits me."

Van der Spijck reddened. "I have not opened it," he cried hastily.

"Naturally. But the door thou mayst open."

The painter hesitated. "They will drag thee forth, as they dragged the De Witts from the prison."

Spinoza smiled sadly. "And on that occasion thou wouldst not let me out; now thou wilt not let me in."

"Both proofs that I have more regard for thee than thou for thyself. If I had let thee dash out to fix up on the public wall that denunciation thou hadst written of the barbarian mob, there had been no life of thine to risk to-day. Fly the town, I beseech thee, or find thicker walls than mine. Thou knowest I would shelter thee had I the power; do not our other lodgers turn to thee in sickness and sorrow to be soothed by thy talk? Do not our own little ones love and obey thee more than their mother and me? But if thou wert murdered in our house, how dreadful a shock and a memory to us all!"

"I know well your love for me," said Spinoza, touched. "But fear nothing on my account: I can easily justify myself. There are people enough, and of chief men in the country too, who well know the motives of my journey. But whatever comes of it, so soon as the crowd make the least noise at your door, I will go out and make straight for them, though they should serve me as they have done the unhappy De Witts."

Van der Spijck threw open the door. "Thy word is an oath!"

On the stairs shone the speckless landlady, a cheerful creature in black cap and white apron, her bodice laced with ornamental green and red ribbons. She gave a cry of joy, and flew to meet him, broom in hand. "Welcome home, Heer Spinoza! How glad the little ones will be when they get back from school! There's a pack of knaves been slandering thee right and left; some of them tried to pump Henri, but we sent them away with fleas in their ears—eh, Henri?"

Henri smiled sheepishly.

"Most pertinacious of all was a party of three—an old man and his daughter and a young man. They came twice, very vexed to find thee away, and feigning to be old friends of thine from Amsterdam; at least not the young man—his lament was to miss the celebrated scholar he had been taken to see. A bushel of questions they asked, but not many pecks did they get out of me."

A flush had mantled upon Spinoza's olive cheek. "Did they give any name?" he asked with unusual eagerness.

"It ends in Ende—that stuck in my memory."

"Van den Ende?"

"Or suchlike."

"The daughter was—beautiful?"

"A goddess!" put in the painter.

"Humph!" said the vrouw. "Give me the young man. A cold marble creature is not my idea of a goddess."

"'Tis a Greek goddess," said Spinoza with labored lightness. "They are indeed old friends of mine—saving the young man, who is doubtless a pupil of the old. He is a very learned philologist, this Dr. van den Ende: he taught me Latin—"

"And Greek goddesses," flashed the vrouw affectionately.

Spinoza tried to say something, but fell a-coughing instead, and began to ascend to his room. He was agitated: and it was his principle to quit society whenever his emotions threatened to exceed philosophical moderation.

"Wait! I have thy key," cried the goodwife, pursuing him. "And oh! what dust in thy room! No wonder thou art troubled with a phthisis!"

"Thou didst not arrange anything?" he cried in alarm.

"A flick with a feather-brush, as I took in thy letters—no more; my hand itched to be at thy papers, but see! not one is in order!"

She unlocked his door, revealing a little room in which books and papers mingled oddly with the bedroom furniture and the tools and bench of his craft. There were two windows with shabby red curtains. On nails hung a few odd garments, one of which, the doublet anciently pierced by the fanatic's dagger, merely served as a memento, though not visibly older than the rest of his wardrobe. "Who puts a mediocre article into a costly envelope?" was the philosopher's sartorial standpoint. Over the mantel (on which among some old pipes lay two silver buckles, his only jewellery) was pinned a charcoal sketch of Masaniello in shirt-sleeves, with a net on his shoulder, done by Spinoza himself, and obviously with his own features as model: perhaps in some whimsical moment when he figured himself as an intellectual revolutionary. A portfolio that leaned against a microscope contained black and white studies of some of his illustrious visitors, which caught happily their essential features without detail. The few other wall-pictures were engravings by other hands. Spinoza sat down on his truckle-bed with a great sigh of content.

"Desideratoque acquiescimus lecto," he murmured. Then his eye roving around: "My spiders' webs are gone!" he groaned.

"I could not disarrange aught in sweeping them away!" deprecated the goodwife.

"Thou hast disarranged me! I have learnt all my wisdom from watching spiders!" he said, smiling.

"Nay, thou jestest."

"In no wise. The spider and the fly—the whole of life is there. 'Tis through leaving them out that the theologies are so empty. Besides, who will now catch the flies for my microscope?"

"I will not believe thou wouldst have the poor little flies caught by the great big spiders. Never did I understand what Pastor Cordes prated of turning the other cheek till I met thee."

"Nay, 'tis not my doctrine. Mine is the worship of joy. I hold that the effort to preserve our being is virtue."

"But thou goest to church sometimes?"

"To hear a preacher."

"A strange motive." She added musingly: "Christianity is not then true?"

"Not true for me."

"Then if thou canst not believe in it, I will not."

Spinoza smiled tenderly. "Be guided by Dr. Cordes, not by me."

The goodwife was puzzled. "Dost thou then think I can be saved in Dr. Cordes' doctrine?" she asked anxiously.

"Yes, 'tis a very good doctrine, the Lutheran; doubt not thou wilt be saved in it, provided thou livest at peace with thy neighbors."

Her face brightened. "Then I will be guided by thee."

Spinoza smiled. Theology demanded perfect obedience, he thought, even as philosophy demanded perfect knowledge, and both alike were saving; for the believing mob, therefore, to which Religion meant subversion of Reason, speculative opinions were to be accounted pious or impious, not as they were true or false, but as they confirmed or shook the believer's obedience.

Refusing her solicitous offers of a warm meal, and merely begging her to buy him a loaf, he began to read his arrears of letters, picking them up one after another with no eagerness but with calm interest. His correspondence was varied. Some of it was taken up with criticisms of his thought—products of a leisurely age when the thinkers of Europe were a brotherhood, calling to each other across the dim populations; some represented the more deferential doubts of disciples or the elegant misunderstandings of philosophic dilettanti, some his friendly intercourse with empirical physicists like Boyle or like Huyghens, whose telescope had enlarged the philosopher's universe and the thinker's God; there was an acknowledgment of the last scholium from the young men's society of Amsterdam—"Nil volentibus arduum,"—to which he sent his Ethica in sections for discussion; the metropolis which had banished him not being able to keep out his thought. There was the usual demand for explanations of difficulties from Blyenbergh, the Dort merchant and dignitary, accompanied this time by a frightened yearning to fly back from Reason to Revelation. And the letter with the seal of the Royal Society proved equally faint-hearted, Oldenburg exhorting him not to say anything in his next book to loosen the practice of virtue. "Dear Heinrich!" thought Spinoza. "How curious are men! All these years since first we met at Rijnburg he has been goading and spurring me on to give my deepest thought to the world. 'Twas always, 'Cast out all fear of stirring up against thee the pigmies of the time—Truth before all—let us spread our sails to the wind of true Knowledge.' And now the tune is, 'O pray be careful not to give sinners a handle!' Well, well, so I am not to tell men that the highest law is self-imposed; that there is no virtue even in virtues that do not express the essence of one's being. Oh, and I am to beware particularly of telling them their wills are not free, and that they only think so because they are conscious of their desires, but not of the causes of them. I fear me even Oldenburg does not understand that virtue follows as necessarily from adequate knowledge as from the definition of a triangle follows that its angles are equal to two right angles. I am, I suppose, also to let men continue to think that the planetary system revolves round them, and that thunders and lightnings wait upon their wrong-doing. Oldenburg has doubtless been frighted by the extravagances of the restored Court. But 'tis not my teachings will corrupt the gallants of Whitehall. Those who live best by Revelation through Tradition must cling to it, but Revelation through Reason is the living testament of God's word, nor so liable as the dead letter to be corrupted by human wickedness. Strange that it is thought no crime to speak unworthily of the mind, the true divine light, no impiety to believe that God would commit the treasure of the true record of Himself to any substance less enduring than the human heart."

A business letter made a diversion. It concerned the estate of the deceased medical student, Simon De Vries, a devoted disciple, who knowing himself doomed to die young, would have made the Master his heir, had not Spinoza, by consenting to a small annual subsidy, persuaded him to leave his property to his brother. The grateful heir now proposed to increase Spinoza's allowance to five hundred florins.

"How unreasonable people are!" mused the philosopher again. "I agreed once for all to accept three hundred, and I will certainly not be burdened with a stuiver more."

His landlady here entered with the loaf, and Spinoza, having paid and entered the sum in his household account-book, cut himself a slice, adding thereto some fragments of Dutch cheese from a package in his hand-bag.

"Thou didst leave some wine in the bottle," she reminded him.

"Let it grow older," he answered. "My book shows more than two pints last month, and my journey was costly. To make both ends meet I shall have to wriggle," he added jestingly, "like the snake that tries to get its tail in its mouth." He cut open a packet, discovering that a friend had sent him some conserve of red roses from Amsterdam. "Now am I armed against fever," he said blithely. Then, with a remembrance, "Pray take some up to our poor Signore. I had forgotten to inquire!"

"Oh, he is out teaching again, thanks to thee. He hath set up a candle for thee in his church."

A tender smile twitched the philosopher's lip, as the door closed.

A letter from Herr Leibnitz set him wondering uneasily what had taken the young German Crichton from Frankfort, and what he was about in Paris. They had had many a discussion in this little lodging, but he was not yet sure of the young man's single-mindedness. The contents of the letter were, however, unexpectedly pleasing. For it concerned not the philosopher but the working-man. Even his intimates could not quite sympathize with his obstinate insistence on earning his living by handicraft—a manual activity by which the excommunicated Jew was brother to the great Rabbis of the Talmud; they could not understand the satisfaction of the craftsman, nor realize that to turn out his little lenses as perfectly as possible was as essential a part of his life as that philosophical activity which alone interested them. That his prowess as an optician should be invoked by Herr Leibnitz gave him a gratification which his fame as a philosopher could never evoke. The only alloy was that he could not understand what Leibnitz wanted. "That rays from points outside the optic axis may be united exactly in the same way as those in the optic axis, so that the apertures of glasses may be made of any size desired without impairing distinctness of vision!" He wrinkled his brow and fell to making geometrical diagrams on the envelope, but neither his theoretical mathematics nor his practical craftsmanship could grapple with so obscure a request, and he forgot to eat while he pondered. He consulted his own treatise on the Rainbow, but to no avail. At length in despair he took up the last letter, to find a greater surprise awaiting him. A communication from Professor Fabritius, it bore an offer from the Elector Palatine of a chair at the University of Heidelberg. The fullest freedom in philosophy was to be conceded him: the only condition that he should not disturb the established religion.

His surprise passed rapidly into mistrust. Was this an attempt on the part of Christianity to bribe him? Was the Church repeating the tactics of the Synagogue? It was not so many years since the messengers of the congregation had offered him a pension of a thousand florins not to disturb its "established religion." Fullest freedom in philosophy, forsooth! How was that to be reconciled with impeccable deference to the ruling religion? A courtier like Descartes might start from the standpoint of absolute doubt and end in a pilgrimage to Our Lady of Loretto; but for himself, who held miracles impossible, and if possible irrelevant, there could be no such compromise with a creed whose very basis was miracle. True, there was a sense in which Christ might be considered os Dei—the mouth of God,—but it was not the sense in which the world understood it, the world which caricatured all great things, which regarded piety and religion, and absolutely all things related to greatness of soul, as burdens to be laid aside after death, toils to be repaid by a soporific beatitude; which made blessedness the prize of virtue instead of the synonym of virtue. Nay, nay, not even the unexpected patronage of the Most Serene Carl Ludwig could reconcile his thoughts with popular theology.

How curious these persistent attempts of friend and foe alike to provide for his livelihood, and what mistaken reverence his persistent rejections had brought him! People could not lift their hands high enough in admiration because he followed the law of his nature, because he preferred a simple living, simply earned, while for criminals who followed equally the laws of their nature they had anger rather than pity. As well praise the bee for yielding honey or the rose for making fragrant the air. Certainly his character had more of honey than of sting, of rose than of thorn; humility was an unnecessary addition to the world's suffering; but that he did not lack sting or thorn, his own sisters had discovered when they had tried to keep their excommunicated brother out of his patrimony. How puzzled Miriam and Rebekah had been by his forcing them at law to give up the money and then presenting it to them. They could not see that to prove the outcast Jew had yet his legal rights was a duty; the money itself a burden. Yes, popular ethics was sadly to seek, and involuntarily his hand stretched itself out and lovingly possessed itself of the ever-growing manuscript of his magnum opus. His eye caressed those serried concatenated propositions, resolving and demonstrating the secret of the universe; the indirect outcome of his yearning search for happiness, for some object of love that endured amid the eternal flux, and in loving which he should find a perfect and eternal joy. Riches, honor, the pleasures of sense— these held no true and abiding bliss. The passion with which van den Ende's daughter had agitated him had been wisely mastered, unavowed. But in the Infinite Substance he had found the object of his search: the necessary Eternal Being in and through whom all else existed, among whose infinite attributes were thought and extension, that made up the one poor universe known to man; whom man could love without desiring to be loved in return, secure in the consciousness he was not outside the Divine order. His book, he felt, would change theology to theonomy, even as Copernicus and Kepler and Galileo had changed astrology to astronomy. This chain of thoughts, forged link by link, without rest, without hurry, as he sat grinding his glasses, day by day, and year by year: these propositions, laboriously polished like his telescope and microscope lenses, were no less designed for the furtherance and clarification of human vision.

And yet not primarily vision. The first Jew to create an original philosophy, he yet remained a Jew in aiming not at abstract knowledge, but at concrete conduct: and was most of all a Jew in his proclamation of the Unity. He would teach a world distraught and divided by religious strife the higher path of spiritual blessedness; bring it the Jewish greeting—Peace. But that he was typical—even by his very isolation—of the race that had cast him out, he did not himself perceive, missing by his static philosophy the sense of historical enchainment, and continuous racial inspiration.

As, however, he glanced to-day over the pages of Part Three, "The Origin and Nature of the Affects," he felt somehow out of tune with this bloodless vivisection of human emotions, this chain of quasi-mathematical propositions with their Euclidean array of data and scholia, marshalling passions before the cold throne of intellect. The exorcised image of Klaartje van den Ende—raised again by the landlady's words—hovered amid the demonstrations. He caught gleams of her between the steps. Her perfect Greek face flashed up and vanished as in coquetry, her smile flickered. How learned she was, how wise, how witty, how beautiful! And the instant he allowed himself to muse thus, she appeared in full fascination, skating superbly on the frozen canals, or smiling down at him from the ancient balustrade of the window (surely young Gerard Dou must have caught an inspiration from her as he passed by). What happy symposia at her father's house, when the classic world was opening for the first time to the gaze of the clogged Talmud-student, and the brilliant cynicism of the old doctor combined with the larger outlook of his Christian fellow-pupils to complete his emancipation from his native environment. After the dead controversies of Hillel and Shammai in old Jerusalem, how freshening these live discussions as to whether Holland should have sheltered Charles Stuart from the regicide Cromwell, or whether the doelen-stuk of Rembrandt van Rijn were as well painted as Van Ravosteyn's. In the Jewish quarter, though Rembrandt lived in it, interest had been limited to the guldens earned by dirty old men in sitting to him. What ardor, too, for the newest science, what worship of Descartes and deprecation of the philosophers before him! And then the flavor of romance—as of their own spices— wafted from the talk about the new Colonies in the Indies! Good God! had it been so wise to quench the glow of youth, to slip so silently to forty year? He had allowed her to drop out of his life—this child so early grown to winning womanhood—she was apparently dead for him, yet this sudden idea of her proximity had revitalized her so triumphantly that the philosopher wondered at the miracle, or at his own powers of self-deception.

And who was this young man?

Had he analyzed love correctly? He turned to Proposition xxxiii. "If we love a thing which is like ourselves we endeavor as much as possible to make it love us in return." His eye ran over the proof with its impressive summing-up. "Or in other words (Schol. Prop, xiii., pt. 3), we try to make it love us in return." Unimpeachable logic, but was it true? Had he tried to make Klaartje love him in return? Not unless one counted the semi-conscious advances of wit-combats and intellectual confidences as she grew up! But had he succeeded? No, impossible, and his spirits fell, and mounted again to note how truly their falling corroborated—by converse reasoning—his next Proposition. "The greater the affect with which we imagine that a beloved object is affected towards us, the greater will be our self-exaltation," No, she had never given him cause for self-exaltation, though occasionally it seemed as if she preferred his talk to that of even the high-born, foppish youths sent by their sires to sit at her father's feet.

In any case perhaps it was well he had given her maidenly modesty no chance of confession. Marriage had never loomed as a possibility for him—the life of the thinker must needs shrink from the complications and prejudices engendered by domestic happiness: the intellectual love of God more than replaced these terrestrial affections.

But now a sudden conviction that nothing could replace them, that they were of the essence of personality, wrapped him round as with flame. Some subtle aroma of emotion like the waft of the orange-groves of Burgos in which his ancestors had wandered thrilled the son of the mists and marshes. Perhaps it was only the conserve of red roses. At any rate that was useless in this fever.

He took up his tools resolutely, but he could not work. He fell back on his rough sketch for a lucid Algebra, but his lucid formulæ were a blur. He went downstairs and played with the delighted children and listened to the landlady's gossip, throwing her a word or two of shrewd counsel on the everyday matters that came up. Presently he asked her if the van den Endes had told her anything of their plans.

"Oh, they were going to stay at Scheveningen for the bathing. The second time they came up from there."

His heart leapt. "Scheveningen! Then they are practically here."

"If they have not gone back to Amsterdam."

"True," he said, chilled.

"But why not go see? Henri tramped ten miles for me every Sunday."

Spinoza turned away. "No, they are probably gone back. Besides, I know not their address."

"Address? At Scheveningen! A village where everybody's business can be caught in one net."

Spinoza was ascending the stairs. "Nay, it is too late."

Too late in sad verity! What had a philosopher of forty year to do with love?

Back in his room he took up a lens, but soon found himself re-reading his aphorism on Marriage. "It is plain that Marriage is in accordance with Reason, if the desire is engendered not merely by external form, but by a love of begetting children and wisely educating them; and if, in addition, the love both of the husband and wife has for its cause not external form merely, but chiefly liberty of mind." Assuredly, so far as he was concerned, the desire of children, who might be more rationally and happily nurtured than himself, had some part in his rare day-dreams, and it was not merely the noble form but also the noble soul he divined in Klaartje van den Ende that had stirred his pulses and was now soliciting him to a joy which like all joys would mark the passage to a greater perfection, a fuller reality. And in sooth how holy was this love of woman he allowed himself to feel for a moment, how easily passing over into the greater joy—the higher perfection—the love of God!

Why should he not marry? Means were easily to hand! He had only to accept from his rich disciples what was really the wage of tuition, though hitherto like the old Rabbis he had preferred to teach for Truth's sole sake. After all Carl Ludwig offered him ample freedom in philosophizing.

But he beat down the tempting images and sought relief in the problem posited by Leibnitz. In vain: his manuscript still lay open, Proposition xxxv. was under his eye.

"If I imagine that an object beloved by me is united to another person by the same, or by a closer bond of friendship than that by which I myself alone held the object, I shall be affected with hatred towards the beloved object itself and shall envy that other person."

Who was the young man?

He clenched his teeth: he had, then, not yet developed into the free man, redeemed by Reason from the bondage of the affects whose mechanic workings he had analyzed so exhaustively. He was, then, still as far from liberty of mind as the peasant who has never taken to pieces the passions that automatically possess him. If this fever did not leave him, he must try blood-letting on himself, as though in a tertian. He returned resolutely to his work. But when he had ground and polished for half an hour, and felt soothed, "Why should I not go to Scheveningen all the same?" he asked himself. Why should he miss the smallest chance of seeing his old friends who had taken the trouble to call on him twice?

Yes, he would walk to the hamlet and ponder the optical problem, and the terms in which to refuse the Elector Palatine's offer. He set out at once, forgetting the dangers of the streets and in reality lulling suspicion by his fearless demeanor. The afternoon was closing somewhat mistily, and an occasional fit of coughing reminded him he should have had more than a falling collar round his throat and a thicker doublet than his velvet. He thought of going back for his camelot cloak, but he was now outside the north-west gate, so, lighting his pipe, he trudged along the pleasant new-paved road that led betwixt the avenues of oak and lime to Scheveningen. He had little eye for the beautiful play of color-shades among the glooming green perspectives on either hand, scarcely noted the comely peasant-women with their scarlet-lined cloaks and glittering "head-irons," who rattled by, packed picturesquely in carts. Half-way to the hamlet the brooding pedestrian was startled to find his hand in the cordial grip of the very man he had gone out to see.

"Salve, O Benedicte," joyously cried the fiery-eyed veteran. "I had despaired of ever setting eyes again on thy black curls!" Van den Ende's own hair tossed under his wide-brimmed tapering hat as wildly as ever, though it was now as white as his ruff, his blood seemed to beat as boisterously, and a few minutes' conversation sufficed to show Spinoza that the old pedagogue's soul was even more unchanged than his body. The same hilarious atheism, the same dogmatic disbelief, the same conviction of human folly combined as illogically, as of yore, with schemes of perfect states: time seemed to have mellowed no opinion, toned down no crudity. He was coming, he said, to make a last hopeless call on his famous pupil, the others were working. The others—he explained—were his little Klaartje and his newest pupil, Kerkkrinck, a rich and stupid youth, but honest and good-hearted withal. He had practically turned him over to Klaartje, who was as good a guide to the Humanities as himself—more especially for the stupid. "She was too young in thy time, Benedict," concluded the old man jocosely.

Benedict thought that she was too young now to be left instructing good-hearted young men, but he only said, "Yes, I daresay I was stupid. One should cut one's teeth on Latin conjugations, and I was already fourteen with a full Rabbinical diploma before I was even aware there was such a person as Cicero in history."

"And now thou writest Ciceronian Latin. Shake not thy head—'tis a compliment to myself, not to thee. What if thou art sometimes more exact than elegant—fancy what a coil of Hebrew cobwebs I had to sweep out of that brain-pan of thine ere I transformed thee from Baruch to Benedict."

"Nay, some of the webs were of silk. I see now how much Benedict owes to Baruch. The Rabbinical gymnastic is no ill-training, though unmethodic. Maimonides de-anthropomorphises God, the Cabalah grapples, if confusedly, with the problem of philosophy."

"Thou didst not always speak so leniently of thy ancient learning. Methinks thou hast forgotten thy sufferings and the catalogue of curses. I would shut thee up a week with Moses Zacut, and punish you both with each other's society. The room should be four cubits square, so that he should be forced to disobey the Ban and be within four cubits of thee."

"Thou forgettest to reckon with the mathematics," laughed Spinoza. "We should fly to opposite ends of the diagonal and achieve five and two third cubits of separation."

"Ah, fuzzle me not with thy square roots. I was never a calculator."

"But Moses Zacut was not so unbearable. I mind me he also learnt Latin under thee."

"Ay, and now spits out to see me. Fasted forty days for his sin in learning the devil's language."

"What converted him?"

"That Turkish mountebank, I imagine."

"Sabbata Zevi?"

"Yes; he still clings to him though the Messiah has turned Mohammedan. He has published Five Evidences of the Faith, expounding that his Redeemer's design is to bring over the Mohammedans to Judaism. Ha! ha! What a lesson in the genesis of religions! The elders who excommunicated thee have all been bitten—a delicious revenge for thee. Ho! ho! What fools these mortals be, as the English poet says. I long to shake our Christians and cry, 'Nincompoops, Jack-puddings, feather-heads, look in the eyes of these Jews and see your own silly selves.'"

"'Tis not the way to help or uplift mankind," said Spinoza mildly. "Men should be imbued with a sense of their strength, not of their weakness."

"In other words," laughed the doctor, "the way to uplift men is to appeal to the virtues they do not possess."

"Even so," assented Spinoza, unmoved. "The virtues they may come to possess. Men should be taught to look on noble patterns, not on mean."

"And what good will that do? Moses Zacut had me and thee to look on," chuckled the old man. "No, Benedict, I believe with Solomon, 'Answer a fool according to his folly,' Thou art too half-hearted—thou deniest God like a serving-man who says his master is out—thou leavest a hope he may be there all the while. One should play bowls with the holy idols."

Spinoza perceived it was useless to make the old man understand how little their ideas coincided. "I would rather uplift than overturn," he said mildly.

The old sceptic laughed: "A wonder thou art not subscribing to uplift the Third Temple," he cried. "So they call this new synagogue they are building in Amsterdam with such to-do."

"Indeed? I had not heard of it. If I could hope it were indeed the Third Temple," and a mystic light shone in his eyes, "I would subscribe all I had."

"Thou art the only Christian I have ever known!" said van den Ende, half mockingly, half tenderly. "And thou art a Jew."

"So was Christ."

"True, one forgets that. But the rôles are becoming nicely reversed. Thou forgivest thine enemies, and in Amsterdam 'tis the Jews who are going to the Christians to borrow money for this synagogue of theirs!"

"How is the young juffrouw?" asked Spinoza at last.

"Klaartje! She blooms like a Jan de Heem flowerpiece. This rude air has made a rose of my lily. Her cheeks might have convinced the imbeciles who took away their practice from poor old Dr. Harvey. One can see her blood circulating. By the way, thy old crony, Dr. Ludwig Meyer, bade me give thee his love."

"Dost think she will remember me?"

"Remember thee, Benedict? Did she not send me to thee to-day? Thy name is ever on those rosy lips of hers—to lash dull pupils withal. How thou didst acquire half the tongues of Europe in less time that they master τυπτω." Spinoza allowed his standing desire to cough to find satisfaction. He turned his head aside and held his hand before his mouth. "We quarrel about thy Tractatus—she and I—for of course she recognized thine olden argumentations just as I recognized my tricks of style."

"She reads me then?"

"As a Lutheran his Bible. 'Twas partially her hope of threshing out certain difficulties with thee that decided us on Scheveningen. I do not say that the forest which poor Paul Potter painted was not a rival attraction."

A joy beyond the bounds of Reason was swelling the philosopher's breast. Unconsciously his step quickened. He encouraged his companion to chatter more about his daughter, how van Ter Borch had made of her one of his masterpieces in white satin, how she herself dabbled daintily in all the fine arts, but the old man diverged irrevocably into politics, breathed fire and fury against the French, spoke of his near visit to Paris on a diplomatic errand, and, growing more confidential, hinted of a great scheme, an insurrection in Normandy, Admiral Tromp to swoop down on Quillebœuf, a Platonic republic to be reared on the ruins of the French monarchy. Had Spinoza seen the shadow of a shameful death hovering over the spirited veteran, had he foreknown that the poor old gentleman—tool of two desperate roués and a femme galante,—was to be executed in Paris for this very conspiracy, the words that sounded so tediously in his ear would have taken on a tragic dignity.

They approached the village, whose huts loomed solemnly between the woods and the dunes in the softening twilight. The van den Endes were lodged with the captain of a fishing-smack in a long, narrow wooden house with sloping mossy tiles and small-paned windows. The old man threw open the door of the little shell-decorated parlor and peered in. "Klaartje!" his voice rang out. A parrot from the Brazils screamed, but Spinoza only heard the soft "Yes, father," that came sweetly from some upper region.

"Guess whom I've brought thee?"

"Benedict!" She flew down, a vision of loveliness and shimmering silk and white pearls. Spinoza's hand trembled in hers that gleamed snowily from the ruffled half-sleeve; the soft warmth burnt away philosophy. They exchanged the commonplaces of the situation.

"But where is Kerkkrinck?" said the doctor.

"At his toilette." She exchanged a half-smile with Spinoza, who thrilled deliciously.

"Then I'll go make mine," cried her father. "We sup in half an hour, Benedict. Thou'lt stay, we go to-morrow. 'Tis the last supper." And, laughing as if he had achieved a blasphemy, and unconscious of the shadow of doom, the gay old freethinker disappeared.

As Klaartje spoke of his book with sparkling eyes, and discussed points in a low, musical voice, something crude and elemental flamed in the philosopher, something called to him to fuse himself with the universal life more tangibly than through the intellect. His doubts and vacillations fled: he must speak now, or the hour and the mood would never recur. If he could only drag the conversation from the philosophical. By a side door it escaped of itself into the personal; her father did not care to take her with him to Paris, spoke of possible dangers, and hinted it was time she was off his hands. There seemed a confession trembling in her laughing eye. It gave him courage to seize her fingers, to falter a request that she would come to him—to Heidelberg! The brightness died suddenly out of her face: it looked drawn and white.

After a palpitating silence she said, "But thou art a Jew!"

He was taken aback, he let her fingers drop. From his parched throat came the words, "But thou art—no Christian."

"I know—but nevertheless—oh, I never dreamed of anything of this with thee—'twas all of the brain, the soul."

"Soul and body are but one fact."

"Women are not philosophers. I—" She stopped. Her fingers played nervously with the pearl necklace that rose and fell on her bosom. He found himself noting its details, wondering that she had developed such extravagant tastes. Then, awaking to her distress, he said quietly, "Then there is no hope for me?"

Her face retained its look of pain.

"Not ever? You could never—?" His cough shook him.

"If there had been no other," she murmured, and her eyes drooped half-apologetically towards the necklace.

The bitterness of death was in his soul. He had a sudden ironic sense of a gap in his mathematical philosophy. He had fathomed the secret of Being, had analyzed and unified all things from everlasting to everlasting, yet here was an isolated force—a woman's will—that stood obstinately between him and happiness. He seemed to visualize it, behind her serious face, perversely mocking.

The handle of the door turned, and a young man came in. He was in the pink of fashion—a mantle of Venetian silk disposed in graceful folds about his handsome person, his neckcloth of Flanders lace, his knee-breeches of satin, his shoes gold-buckled, his dagger jewelled. Energy flashed from his eye, vigor radiated from his every movement.

"Ah, Diedrich!" she cried, as her face lit up with more than relief. "Here is Heer Spinoza at last. This is Heer Kerkkrinck!"

"Spinoza!" A thrill of awe was in the young man's voice, the reverence of the consciously stupid for the great brains of the earth. He did not take Spinoza's outstretched hand in his but put it to his lips.

The lonely thinker and the happy lover stood thus for an instant, envying and admiring each other. Then Spinoza said cordially, "And now that I have had the pleasure of meeting Heer Kerkkrinck I must hurry back to town ere the road grows too dark."

"But father expects thee to sup with us," murmured Klaartje.

"'Tis a moonless night, and footpads may mistake me for a Jew." He smiled. "Make my apologies to the doctor."

It was indeed a moonless night, but he did not make for the highroad. Instinctively he turned seawards.

A slight mist brooded over the face of all things, adding to the night, blurring the village to a few gleams of fire. On the broad sandy beach he could just see the outlines of the boats and the fishing-nets. He leaned against the gunwale of a pink, inhaling the scents of tar and brine, and watching the apparent movement seawards of some dark sailing-vessel which, despite the great red anchor at his feet, seemed to sail outwards as each wave came in.

The sea stretched away, soundless, moveless, and dark, save where it broke in white foam at his feet; near the horizon a pitch-black wall of cloud seemed to rise sheer from the water and join the gray sky that arched over the great flat spaces. And in the absence of stars, the earth itself seemed to gain in vastness and mystery, its own awfulness, as it sped round, unlessened by those endless perspectives of vaster planets. And from the soundless night and sea and sky, and from those austere and solemn stretches of sand and forest, wherein forms and colors were lost in a brooding unity, there came to Spinoza a fresh uplifting sense of the infinite, timeless Substance, to love and worship which was exaltation and ecstasy. The lonely thinker communed with the lonely Being.

"Though He slay me," his heart whispered, "yet will I trust in Him."

Yea, though the wheels of things had passed over his body, it was still his to rejoice in the eternal movement that brought happiness to others.

Others! How full the world was of existences, each perfect after its kind, the laws of God's nature freely producing every conception of His infinite intellect. In man alone how many genera, species, individuals—from saints to criminals, from old philosophers to gallant young livers, all to be understood, none to be hated. And man but a fraction of the life of one little globe, that turned not on man's axis, nor moved wholly to man's ends. This sea that stretched away unheaving was not sublimely dead—even to the vulgar apprehension—but penetrated with quivering sensibility, the exquisite fresh feeling of fishes darting and gliding, tingling with life in fin and tail, chasing and chased, zestfully eating or swiftly eaten: in the air the ecstasy of flight, on the earth the happy movements of animals, the very dust palpitating pleasurably with crawling and creeping populations, the soil riddled with the sluggish voluptuousness of worms; each tiniest creature a perfect expression of the idea of its essence, individualized by its conatus, its effort to persist in existence on its own lines, though in man alone the potentiality of entering through selfless Reason into the intellectual ecstasy of the love with which God loves Himself—to be glad of the strength of the lion and the grace of the gazelle and the beauty of the woman who belongs to another. Blessings on the happy lovers, blessings on all the wonderful creation, praise, praise to the Eternal Being whose modes body forth the everlasting pageant.

Beginningless æons before his birth It had been—the great pageant to whose essence Being belonged—endless æons after his ephemeral passing It would still throb and glow, still offer to the surrendered human soul the supreme uplift. He had but a moment to contemplate It, yet to understand Its essence, to know the great laws of Its workings, to see It sub specie aeternitatis, was to partake of Its eternity. There was no need to journey either in space or time to discover Its movement, everywhere the same, as perfect in the remotest past as in the farthest future, by no means working—as the vulgar imagined—to a prospective perfection; everywhere educed from the same enduring necessities of the divine freedom. Progress! As illusory as the movement of yon little vessel that, anchored stably, seemed always sailing out towards the horizon.

And so in that trance of adoration, in that sacred Glory, in that rapturous consciousness that he had fought his last fight with the enslaving affects, there formed themselves in his soul—white heat at one with white light—the last sentences of his great work:—

"We see, then, what is the strength of the wise man, and by how much he surpasses the ignorant who is driven forward by lust alone. For the ignorant man is not only agitated by eternal causes in many ways, and never enjoys true peace of soul, but lives also ignorant, as it were, both of God and of things, and as soon as he ceases to suffer, ceases also to be. On the other hand, the wise man is scarcely ever moved in his mind, but being conscious by a certain eternal necessity of himself, of God, and of things, never ceases to be, and always enjoys true peace of soul. If the way which leads hither seem very difficult, it can nevertheless be found. It must indeed be difficult since it is so seldom discovered: for if salvation lay ready to hand and could be discovered without great labor, how could it be possible that it should be neglected almost by everybody? But all noble things are as difficult as they are rare."

So ran the words that were not to die.

Suddenly a halo on the upper edge of the black cloud heralded the struggling through of the moon: she shot out a crescent, reddish in the mist, then labored into her full orb, wellnigh golden as the sun.

Spinoza started from his reverie: his doublet was wet with dew, he felt the mist in his throat. He coughed: then it was as if the salt of the air had got into his mouth, and as he spat out the blood, he knew he would not remain long sundered from the Eternal Unity.

But there is nothing on which a free man will meditate less than on death. Desirous to write down what was in his mind, Spinoza turned from the sea and pursued his peaceful path homewards.

THE MASTER OF THE NAME

I

Now that I have come to the close of my earthly days, and that the higher circles will soon open to me, whereof I have learned the secrets from my revered Master—where there is neither eating nor drinking, but the pious sit crowned and delight themselves with the vision of the Godhead—I would fain leave some chronicle, in these confused and evil days, of him whom I have loved best on earth, for he came to teach man the true life and the true worship. To him, the ever glorious and luminous Israel Baal Shem, the one true Master of the Name, I owe my redemption from a living death. For he found me buried alive under a mountain of ashes, and he drew me out and kindled the ashes to fire, so that I cheered myself thereat. And since now the flame is like to go out again, and the Master's teaching to be choked and concealed beneath that same ash-mountain, I pray God that He inspire my unready quill to set down a true picture of the Man and his doctrine.

Of my own history I do not know that it is needful to tell very much. My grandfather came to Poland from Vienna, whence he had been expelled with all the Jews of the Arch-Duchy, to please the Jesuit-ridden Empress Margaret, who thus testified her gratitude to Heaven for her recovery from an accident that had befallen her at a court ball. I have heard the old man tell how trumpeters proclaimed in the streets the Emperor's edict, and how every petition proved as futile as the great gold cup and the silver jug and basin presented by the Jews to the Imperial couple as they came out of church, after the thanksgiving ceremony.

It was an ill star that guided my grandfather's feet towards Poland. The Jews of Poland had indeed once been paramount in Europe, but the Cossack massacres and the disruption of the kingdom had laid them low, and they spawned beggars who wandered through Europe, preaching and wheedling with equal hyper-subtlety. My father at any rate escaped mendicancy, for he managed to obtain a tiny farm in the north-east of Lithuania, though what with the exactions of the Prince of the estate, and the brutalities of the Russian regiments quartered in the neighborhood, his life was bitter as the waters of Marah. The room in which I was born constituted our whole hut, which was black as a charred log within and without, and never saw the sunlight save through rents in the paper which covered the crossed stripes of pine that formed the windows. In winter, when the stove heated the hovel to suffocation, and the wind and rain drove back the smoke through the hole in the roof that served for chimney, the air was almost as noxious to its human inhabitants as the smoke to the vermin in the half-washed garments that hung across poles. We sat at such times on the floor, not daring to sit higher, for fear of suffocation in the denser atmosphere hovering over us; and I can still feel the drip, drip, on my head, of the fat from the sausages that hung a-drying. In a corner of this living and sleeping room stood the bucket of clean water, and alongside it the slop-pail and the pail into which my father milked the cow. Poor old cow! She was quite like one of the family, and often lingered on in the room after being milked.

My mother kneaded bread with the best, and was as pious as she was deft, never omitting to throw the Sabbath dough in the fire. Not that her prowess as a cook had much opportunity, for our principal fare was corn-bread, mixed with bran and sour cabbage and red beets, which lay stored on the floor in tubs. Here we all lived together—my grandfather, my parents, my brother and sister; not so unhappy, especially on Sabbaths and festivals, when we ate fish cooked with butter in the evening, and meat at dinnertime, washed down with mead or spirits. We children—and indeed our elders—were not seldom kicked and cudgelled by the Russian soldiers, when they were in liquor, but we could be merry enough romping about ragged and unwashed, and our real life was lived in the Holy Land, with patriarchs, kings, and prophets, and we knew that we should return thither some day, and inherit Paradise.

Once, I remember, the Princess, the daughter of our Prince, being fatigued while out hunting, came to rest herself in our mean hut, with her ladies and her lackeys, all so beautiful and splendid, and glittering with gold and silver lace. I stared at the Princess with her lovely face and rich dress, as if my eyes would burst from their sockets. "O how beautiful!" I ejaculated at last, with a sob.

"Little fool!" whispered my father soothingly. "In the world to come the Princess will kindle the stove for us."

I was struck dumb with a medley of feelings. What! such happiness in store for us—for us, who were now buffeted about by drunken Cossacks! But then—the poor Princess! How she would soil her splendid dress, lighting our fire! My eyes filled with tears at the sight of her beautiful face, that seemed so unconscious of the shame waiting for it. I felt I would get up early, and do her task for her secretly. Now I have learnt from my Master the mysteries of the World-To-Come, and I thank the Name that there is a sphere in heaven for princesses who do no wrong.

My brother and I did not get nearer heaven by our transference to school, for the Cheder was a hut little larger than and certainly as smoky as our own, where a crowd of youngsters of all ages sat on hard benches or on the bare earth, according to the state of the upper atmosphere. The master, attired in a dirty blouse, sat unflinchingly on the table, so as to dominate the whole school-room, and between his knees he held a bowl, in which, with a gigantic pestle, he brayed tobacco into snuff. The only work he did many a day was to beat some child black and blue, and sometimes in a savage fit of rage he would half wring off a boy's ear, or almost gouge out an eye. The rest of the teaching was done by the ushers—each in his corner—who were no less vindictive, and would often confiscate to their own consumption the breakfasts and lunches we brought with us. What wonder if our only heaven was when the long day finished, or when Sabbath brought us a whole holiday, and new moon a half.

Of the teaching I acquired here, and later in the Beth-Hamidrash—for I was destined by my grandfather for a Rabbi—my heart is too heavy to speak. Who does not know the arid wilderness of ceremonial law, the barren hyper-subtleties of Talmudic debate, which in my country had then reached the extreme of human sharpness in dividing hairs; the dead sea fruit of learning, unquickened by living waters? And who will wonder if my soul turned in silent longing in search of green pastures, and panted for the water-brooks, and if my childish spirit found solace in the tales my grandfather told me in secret of Sabbataï Zevi, the Son of God? For my grandfather was at heart a Shab (Sabbatian). Though Sabbataï Zevi had turned Turk, the honest veteran was one of those invincibles who refused to abandon their belief in this once celebrated Messiah, and who afterwards transferred their allegiance to the successive Messiahs who reincarnated him, even as he had reincarnated King David. For the new Sabbatian doctrine of the Godhead, according to which the central figure of its Trinity found successive reincarnation in a divine man, had left the door open for a series of prophets who sprang up, now in Tripoli, now in Turkey, now in Hungary. I must do my grandfather the justice to say that his motives were purer than those of many of the sect, whose chief allurement was probably the mystical doctrine of free love, and the Adamite life: for the poor old man became more a debauchee of pain than of pleasure, inflicting upon himself all sorts of penances, to hasten the advent of the kingdom of God on earth. He denied himself food and sleep, rolled himself in snow, practised fumigations and conjurations and self-flagellations, so as to overthrow the legion of demons who, he said, barred the Messiah's advent. Sometimes he terrified me by addressing these evil spirits by their names, and attacking them in a frenzy of courage, smashing windows and stoves in his onslaught till he fell down in a torpor of exhaustion. And, though he was so advanced in years, my father could not deter him from joining in the great pilgrimage that, under Judah the Saint, set out for Palestine, to await the speedy redemption of Israel. Of this Judah the Saint, who boldly fanned the embers of the Sabbatian heresy into fierce flame, I have a vivid recollection, because, against all precedent, he mounted the gallery of the village synagogue to preach to the women. I remember that he was clad in white satin, and held under his arm a scroll of the law, whose bells jingled as he walked; but what will never fade from my recollection is the passion of his words, his wailing over our sins, his profuse tears. Lad as I was, I was wrought up to wish to join this pilgrimage, and it was with bitter tears of twofold regret that I saw my grandfather set out on that disastrous expedition, the leader of which died on the very day of its arrival in Jerusalem.

My own Sabbatian fervor did not grow cold for a long time, and it was nourished by my study of the Cabalah. But, although ere I lay down my pen I shall have to say something of the extraordinary resurgence of this heresy in my old age, and of the great suffering which it caused my beloved Master, the Baal Shem, yet Sabbatianism did not really play much part in my early life, because such severe measures were taken against it by the orthodox Rabbis that it seemed to be stamped out, and I myself, as I began to reflect upon it, found it inconceivable that a Jewish God should turn Turk: as well expect him to turn Christian. But indirectly this redoubtable movement entered largely into my life by way of the great Eibeschütz-Emden controversy. For it will not be stale in the memory of my readers that this lamentable controversy, which divided and embittered the Jews of all Europe, which stirred up Kings and Courts, originated in the accusation against the Chief Rabbi of the Three Communities that the amulets which he—the head of the orthodox tradition—wrote for women in childbirth, were tainted with the Sabbatian heresy. So bitter and widespread were the charges and counter-charges, that at one moment every Jewish community in Europe stood excommunicated by the Chief Rabbis of one side or the other—a ludicrous position, whereof the sole advantage was that it brought the Ban into contempt and disuse. It was not likely that a controversy so long-standing and so impassioned would fail to permeate Poland; and, indeed, among us the quarrel, introduced as it was by Baruch Yavan, who was agent to Bruhl, the Saxon Minister, raged in its most violent form. Every fair and place of gathering became a battle-field for the rival partisans. Bribery, paid spies, treachery, and violence—all the poisonous fruits of warfare—flourished, and the cloud of controversy seems to overhang all my early life.

Although I penetrated deeply into the Cabalah, I could never become a practical adept in the Mysteries. I thought at the time it was because I had not the stamina to carry out the severer penances, and was no true scion of my grandsire. I have still before me the gaunt, emaciated figure of the Saint, whom I found prostrate in our outhouse. I brought him to by unbuttoning his garment at the throat (thus discovering his hair shirt), but in vain did I hasten to bring him all sorts of refreshments. He let nothing pass his lips. I knew this man by repute. He had already performed the penance of Kana, which consisted in fasting daily for six years, and avoiding in his nightly breakfast whatever comes from a living being, be it flesh, fish, milk, or honey. He had likewise practised the penance of Wandering, never staying two days in the same place. I ran to fetch my father to force the poor man to eat, but when I returned the obstinate ascetic was gone. We followed his track, and found him lying dead on the road. We afterwards learnt that even his past penances had not pacified his conscience, and he wished to observe the penance of Weighing, which proportions specific punishments to particular sins. But, finding by careful calculation that his sins were too numerous to be thus atoned for, he had decided to starve himself to death. Although, as I say, I had not the strength for such asceticism, I admired it from afar. I pored over the Zohar and the Gates of Light and the Tree of Life (a work considered too holy to be printed), and I puzzled myself with the mysteries of the Ten Attributes, and the mystic symbolism of God's Beard, whereof every hair is a separate channel of Divine grace; and once I came to comical humiliation from my conceit that I had succeeded by force of incantations in becoming invisible. As this was in connection with my wife, who calmly continued looking at me and talking to me long after I thought I had disappeared, I am reminded to say something of this companion of my boyish years. For, alas! it was she that presently disappeared from my vision, being removed by God in her fifteenth year; so that I, who—being a first-born son, and allowed by the State to found a family—had been married to her by our fathers when I was nine and she was eight, had not much chance of offspring by her; and, indeed, it was in the bearing of our first child—a still-born boy—that she died, despite the old family amulet originally imported from Metz and made by Rabbi Eibeschütz. When, after her death, it was opened by a suspicious partisan of Emden, sure enough it contained a heretical inscription: "In the name of the God of Israel, who dwelleth in the adornment of His might, and in the name of His anointed Sabbataï Zevi, through whose wounds healing is come to us, I adjure all spirits and demons not to injure this woman." I need not say how this contributed to the heat of the controversy in our own little village; and I think, indeed, it destroyed my last tincture of Sabbatianism. Looking back now from the brink of the grave, I see how all is written in the book of fate: for had not my Peninah been taken from me, or had I accepted one of the many daughters that were offered me in her stead, I should not have been so free to set out on the pilgrimage to my dear Master, by whom my life has been enriched and sanctified beyond its utmost deserving.

At first, indeed, the loss of Peninah, to whom I had become quite attached—for she honored my studies and earned our bread, and was pious even to my mother's liking—threw me into a fit of gloomy brooding. My longing for the living waters and the green pastures—partially appeased by Peninah's love as she grew up—revived and became more passionate. I sought relief in my old Cabalistic studies, and essayed again to perform incantations, thinking in some vague way that now that I had a dear friend among the dead, she would help me to master the divine mysteries. Often I summoned up her form, but when I strove to clasp it, it faded away, so that I was left dubious whether I had succeeded. I had wild fits of weeping both by day and night, not of grief for Peninah, but because I seemed somehow to live in a great desert of sand. But even had I known what I desired, I could not have opened my heart to my father-in-law (in whose house, many versts from my native village, I continued to reside), for he was a good, plain man, who expected me to do posthumous honor to his daughter by my Rabbinical renown. I was indeed long since qualified as a Rabbi, and only waited for some reputable post.

But a Rabbi I was never to be. For it was then that the luminous shadow of the Baal Shem fell upon my life.

II

There came to our village one winter day a stranger who had neither the air of a Schnorrer (beggar) nor of an itinerant preacher; nor, from the brief time he spent at the Beth-Hamidrash, where I sat pursuing droningly my sterile studies, did he appear to be a scholar. He was a lean, emaciated, sickly young man, but his eyes had the fire of a lion's, and his glance was as a god's. When he spoke his voice pierced you, and when he was silent his presence filled the room. From Eliphaz the Pedlar (who knew everything but the Law) I learnt at last that he was an emissary of Rabbi Baer, the celebrated chief of the Chassidim (the pious ones).

"The Chassidim!" I cried. "They died out with Judah the Saint."

"Nay, this is a new order. Have you not heard of the Baal Shem?"

Now, from time to time I had heard vague rumors of a new wonder-working saint who had apparently succeeded far better with Cabalah than I, and had even gathered a following, but the new and obscure movement had not touched our out-of-the-way village, which was wholly given over to the old Sabbatian controversy, and so my knowledge of it was but shadowy. I thought it better to feign absolute ignorance, and thus draw out the Pedlar.

"Why, the Baal Shem by much penance has found out the Name of God," said he; "and by it he works his will on earth and in heaven, so that there is at times confusion in the other world."

"And is his name Rabbi Baer?"

"No; Rabbi Baer is a very learned man who has joined him, and whom, with the other superiors of the Order, he has initiated, so that they, too, work wonders. I chanced with this young man on the road, and he told me that his sect therefore explains the verse in the Psalms, 'Sing unto God a new song; His praise is in the congregation of Saints,' in the following wise: Since God surpasses every finite being, His praise must surpass the praise of every such being. Hitherto the praise of Him consisted in ascribing miracles to Him, and the knowledge of the hidden and the future. But since all this is now within the capacity of the saints of the Order, the Almighty has no longer any pre-eminence over them in respect of the supernatural—'His praise is in the congregation of the saints,'—and therefore it is necessary to find for Him some new praise—'Sing unto God a new song'—suitable to Him alone."

The almost blasphemous boldness of this conception, which went in a manner further even than the Cabalah or the Sabbatians, startled me, as much as the novelty of the exegesis fascinated me.

"And this young man here—can he rule the upper and lower worlds?" I asked eagerly, mindful of my own miserable failures.

"Assuredly he can rule the lower worlds," replied Eliphaz, with a smile. "For to that I can bear witness, seeing that I have stayed with him in a town where there is a congregation of Chassidim, which was in his hands as putty in the glazier's. For, you see, he travels from place to place to instruct his inferiors in the society. The elders of the congregations, venerable and learned men, trembled like spaniels before him. A great scholar who would not accept his infallibility, was thrown into such terror by his menacing look that he fell into a violent fever and died. And this I witnessed myself."

"But there are no Chassidim in our place," said I, trembling myself, half with excitement, half with sympathetic terror. "What comes he to do here?"

"Why, but there are Chassidim, and there will be more—" He stopped suddenly. "Nay, I spoke at random."

"You spoke truly," said I sternly. "But speak on—do not fear me."

"You are a Rabbi designate," he said, shaking his head.

"What of it?"

"Know you not that everywhere the Rabbis fight desperately against the new Order, that they curse and excommunicate its members."

"Wherefore?"

"I do not know. These things are too high for me. Unless it be that this Rabbi Baer has cut out of the liturgy the Piutim (Penitential Poems), and likewise prays after the fashion of the Portuguese Jews."

"Nay," I said, laughing. "If you were not such a man-of-the-earth, you would know that to cut out one line of one prayer is enough to set all the Rabbis excommunicating."

"Ay," said he; "but I know also that in some towns where the Chassidim are in the ascendant, they depose their Rabbis and appoint a minion of Baer instead."

"Ha! so that is what the young man is after," said I.

"I didn't say so," said the Pedlar nervously. "I merely tell you—though I should not have said anything—what the young man told me to beguile the way."

"And to gain you over," I put in.

"Nay," laughed Eliphaz; "I feel no desire for Perfection, which is the catchword of these gentry."

Thus put upon the alert, I was easily able to detect a secret meeting of Chassidim (consisting of that minimum of ten which the sect, in this following the orthodox practice, considers sufficient nucleus for a new community), and to note the members of the conventicle as they went in and out again.

With some of these I spake privily, but though I allayed their qualms and assured them I was no spy but an anxious inquirer after Truth, desiring nothing more vehemently than Perfection, yet either they would not impart to me the true secrets of the Order, or they lacked intelligence to make clear to me its special doctrine. Nevertheless, of the personality of the Founder they were willing to speak, and I shall here set down the story of his life as I learnt it at the first from these simple enthusiasts. It may be that, as I write, my pen unwittingly adds episodes or colors that sank into my mind afterwards, but to the best of my power I will set down here the story as it was told me, and as it passed current then—nay, what say I?—as it passes current now in the Chassidic communities.

III

Rabbi Eliezer, the Baal Shem's father, lived in Moldavia, and in his youth he was captured by the Tartars, but his wife escaped. He was taken to a far country where no Jew lived, and was sold to a Prince. He soon found favor with his master by dint of faithful service, and was made steward of his estates. But mindful of the God of Israel, he begged the Prince to excuse him from work on Saturdays, which the Prince, without understanding, granted. Still the Rabbi was not happy. He prepared to take flight, but a vision appeared to him, bidding him tarry a while longer with the Tartars. Now it happened that the Prince desired some favor from the Viceroy's counsellor, so he gave the Rabbi to the counsellor as a bribe.

Rabbi Eliezer soon found favor with his new master. He was given a separate chamber to live in, and was exempt from manual labor, save that when the counsellor came home he had to go to meet him with a vessel of water to wash his feet, according to the custom of the nobility. Hence Rabbi Eliezer had time to serve his God.

It came to pass that the King had to go to war, so he sent for the counsellor, but the counsellor was unable to give any advice to the point, and the King dismissed him in a rage. When the Rabbi went out to meet him with the vessel of water, he kicked it over wrathfully. Whereupon the Rabbi asked him why he was in such poor spirits. The counsellor remained dumb, but the Rabbi pressed him, and then he unbosomed himself.

"I will pray to God," said Rabbi Eliezer, "that the right plan of campaign may be revealed to me."

When his prayer was answered he communicated the heavenly counsel to his master, who hastened joyfully to the King. The King was equally rejoiced at the plan.

"Such counsel cannot come from a human being," he said. "It must be from the lips of a magician."

"Nay," said the counsellor; "it is my slave who has conceived the plan."

The King forthwith made the slave an officer in his personal retinue. One day the monarch wished to capture a fort with his ships, but night was drawing in, and he said—

"It is too late. We shall remain here over night, and to-morrow we shall make our attack."

But the Rabbi was told from Heaven that the fort was almost impregnable in the daytime. "Send against it at once," he advised the King, "a ship full of prisoners condemned to death, and promise them their lives if they capture the fort, for they, having nothing to lose, are the only men for a forlorn hope."

His advice was taken, and the desperadoes destroyed the fort. Then the King saw that the Rabbi was a godly man, and on the death of his Viceroy he appointed him in his stead, and married him to the late Viceroy's daughter.

But the Rabbi, remembering his marriage vows and his duty to the house of Israel, made her his wife only in name. One day when they were sitting at table together, she asked him, "Why art thou so distant towards me?"

"Swear," he answered, "that thou wilt never tell a soul, and thou shalt hear the truth."

On her promising, he told her that he was a Jew. Thereupon she sent him away secretly, and gave him gold and jewels, of which, however, he was robbed on his journey home.

After he had returned to his joyful wife, who, though she had given him up for dead, had never ceased to mourn for him, an angel appeared unto him and said, "By reason of thy good deeds, and thy unshaken fidelity to the God of Israel throughout all thy sufferings and temptations, thou shalt have a son who will be a light to enlighten the eyes of all Israel. Therefore shall his name be Israel, for in him shall the words of scripture be fulfilled! 'Thou art my servant Israel, in whom I will be glorified.'"

But the Rabbi and his wife grew older and older, and there was no son born unto them. But when they were a hundred years old, the woman conceived and bore a son, who was called Israel, and afterwards known of men as the Master of the Name—the Baal Shem. And this was in the mystic year 5459, whereof the properties of the figures are most wonderful, inasmuch as the five which is the symbol of the Pentagon is the Key of the whole, and comes also from subtracting the first two from the last two, and whereas the first multiplied by the third is the square of five, so is the second multiplied by the fourth the square of six, and likewise the first added to the third is ten, which is the number of the Commandments, and the second added to the fourth is thirteen, which is the number of the Creeds. And even according to the Christians who count this year as 1700, it is the beginning of a new era.

The child's mother died soon after he was weaned, and Rabbi Eliezer was not long in following her to the grave. On his death-bed he took the child in his arms, and blessed him, saying, "Though I am denied the blessing of bringing thee up, always think of God and fear not, for he will ever be with thee." So saying, he gave up the ghost.

Now the people of Ukop in Bukowina, where the Master was born, though they knew nothing of his glorious destiny, yet carefully tended him for the sake of his honored father. They engaged for him a teacher of the Holy Law, but though in the beginnings he seemed to learn with rare ease, he often slipped away into the forest that bordered the village, and there his teacher would find him after a long search, sitting fearlessly in some leafy glade. His dislike for the customary indoor studies became so marked that at last he was set down as stupid, and allowed to follow his own vagrant courses. No one understood that the spirits of Heaven were his teachers.

As he grew older, he was given a post as assistant to the school-master, but his office was not to teach—how could such an ignorant lad teach?—but to escort the children from their homes to the synagogue and thence to the school. On the way he taught them solemn hymns, which he had composed and which he sang with them, and the sweet voices of the children reached Heaven. And God was as pleased with them as with the singing of the Levites in the Temple, and it was a pleasing time in Heaven. But Satan, fearing lest his power on earth would thereby be lessened, disguised himself as a werwolf, which used to appear before the childish procession and put it to flight. The parents thereupon kept their children at home, and the services of song were silenced. But Israel, recalling his father's dying counsel, persuaded the parents to entrust the children to him once more. Again the werwolf bounded upon the singing children, but Israel routed him with his club.

In his fourteenth year the supposed unlettered Israel was appointed caretaker in the Beth-Hamidrash, where the scholars considered him the proverbial ignoramus who "spells Noah with seven mistakes." He dozed about the building all day and got a new reputation for laziness, but at night when the school-room was empty and the students asleep, Israel took down the Holy Books; and all the long night he pored over the sacred words. Now it came to pass that, in a far-off city, a certain holy man, Rabbi Adam, who had in his possession celestial manuscripts (which had only before him been revealed to Abraham our Father, and to Joshua, the son of Nun) told his son on his death-bed that he was unworthy to inherit them. But he was to go to the town of Ukop and deliver them to a certain man named Israel whom he would find there, and who would instruct him, if he proved himself fit. After his father's death the son duly journeyed to Ukop and lodged with the treasurer of the synagogue, who one day asked him the purpose of his visit.

"I am in search of a wife," said he.

At once many were the suitors for his hand, and finally he agreed with a rich man to bestow it on his daughter. After the wedding he pursued his search for the heir to the manuscripts, and, on seeing the caretaker of the Beth-Hamidrash, concluded he must be the man. He induced his father-in-law to have a compartment partitioned off in the school, wherein he could study by himself, and to monopolize the services of the caretaker to attend upon him.

But when the student fell asleep, Israel began to study according to his wont; and when he fell asleep, his employer took one page of the mystic manuscript and placed it near him. When Israel woke up and saw the page he was greatly moved, and hid it. Next day the man again placed a page near the sleeping Israel, who again hid it on awaking. Then was the man convinced that he had found the inheritor of the spiritual secrets, and he told him the whole story and offered all the manuscripts on condition Israel should become his teacher. Israel assented, on condition that he should outwardly remain his attendant as before, and that his celestial knowledge should not be bruited abroad. The man now asked his father-in-law to give him a room outside the town, as his studies demanded still more solitude. He needed none but Israel to attend him. His father-in-law gave him all he asked for, rejoicing to have found so studious a son-in-law. As their secret studies grew deeper, the pupil begged his master to call down the Archangel of the Law for him to study withal. But Rabbi Israel dissuaded him, saying the incantation was a very dangerous one, the slightest mistake might be fatal. After a time the man returned to the request, and his master yielded. Both fasted from one week's end to the other and purified themselves, and then went through all the ceremony of summoning the Archangel of the Law, but at the crucial moment of the invocation Rabbi Israel cried out, "We have made a slip. The Angel of Fire is coming instead. He will burn up the town. Run and tell the people to quit their dwellings and snatch up their most precious things."

Thus did Rabbi Israel's pupil leap to consideration in the town, being by many considered a man of miracles, and the saviour of their lives and treasures. But he still hankered after the Archangel of the Law, and again induced Rabbi Israel to invoke him. Again they purified and prepared themselves, but Rabbi Israel cried out—

"Alas! death has been decreed us, unless we remain awake all this night."

They sat, mutually vigilant against sleep, but at last towards dawn the fated man's eyelids closed, and he fell into that sleep from which there could be no waking.

So the Baal Shem departed thence, and settled in a little town near Brody, and became a teacher of children, in his love for the little ones. Small was his wage and scanty his fare, and the room in which he lodged he could only afford because it was haunted. When the Baal Shem entered to take possession, the landlord peeping timidly from the threshold saw a giant Cossack leaning against the mantelpiece. But as the new tenant advanced, the figure of the Cossack dwindled and dwindled, till at last the dwarf disappeared.

Though Israel did not yet reveal himself, being engaged in wrestling with the divine mysteries, and having made oath in the upper spheres not to use the power of the Name till he was forty years old save four, and though outwardly he was clad in coarse garments and broken boots, yet all his fellow-townsmen felt the purity and probity that seemed to emanate from him. He was seen to perform ablutions far oftener than of custom; and in disputes men came to him as umpire, nor was even the losing party ever dissatisfied with his decision. When there was no rain and the heathen population had gone in a sacred procession, with the priests carrying their gods, all in vain, Israel told the Rabbi to assemble the Jewish congregation in the synagogue for a day of fasting and prayer. The heathen asked them why the service lasted so long that day, and, being told, they laughed mockingly. "What! shall your God avail when we have carried ours in vain?" But the rain fell that day.

And so the fame of Israel grew and reached some people even in Brody.

One day in that great centre of learning the learned Rabbi Abraham, having a difference with a man, was persuaded by the latter to make a journey to Rabbi Israel for arbitration. When they appeared before him, the Baal Shem knew by divine light that Rabbi Abraham's daughter would be his wife. However, he said nothing but delivered adequate judgment, according to Maimonides. So delighted was the old Rabbi with this stranger's learning that he said:

"I have a daughter who has been divorced. I should love to marry thee to her."

"I desire naught better," said the Baal Shem, "for I know her soul is noble. But I must make it a condition that in the betrothal contract no learned titles are appended to my name. Let it be simply Israel the son of Eliezer."

While returning to Brody, Rabbi Abraham died. Now his son, Rabbi Gershon, was the chief of the Judgment Counsel, and a scholar of great renown; and when he found among the papers of his dead father a deed of his sister's betrothal to a man devoid of all titles of learning he was astonished and shocked.

He called his sister to him: "Art thou aware thou art betrothed again?" said he.

"Nay," she replied; "how so?"

"Our father—peace be upon him—hath betrothed thee to one Israel the son of Eliezer."

"Is it so? Then I must needs marry him."

"Marry him! But who is this Israel?"

"How should I know?"

"But he is a man of the earth. He hath not one single title of honor."

"What our father did was right."

"What?" persisted the outraged brother; "thou, my sister, of so renowned a family, who couldst choose from the most learned young men, thou wouldst marry so far beneath thee."

"So my father hath arranged."

"Well, thank Heaven, thou wilt never discover who and where this ignoramus of an Israel is."

"There is a date on the contract," said his sister calmly; "at the stipulated time my husband will come and claim me."

When the appointed wedding-day drew nigh, the Baal Shem intimated to the people of his town that he was going to leave them. They begged him to remain with their children, and offered him a higher wage. But he refused and left the place. And when he came near to Brody, he disguised himself as a peasant in a short jacket and white girdle. And he appeared at the door of the House of Judgment while Rabbi Gershon was deciding a high matter. When the Judge caught sight of him, he imagined it was a poor man asking alms. But the peasant said he had a secret to reveal to him. The Judge took him into another room, where Israel showed him his copy of the betrothal contract. Rabbi Gershon went home in alarm and told his sister that the claimant was come. "Whatever our father—peace be upon him—did was right," she replied; "perchance pious children will be the offspring of this union." Rabbi Gershon, still smarting under this dishonor to the family, reluctantly fixed the wedding-day. Before the ceremony Israel sought a secret interview with his bride, and revealed himself and his mission to her.

"Many hardships shall we endure together, humble shall be our dwelling, and by the sweat of our brow shall we earn our bread. Thou who art the daughter of a great Rabbi, and reared in every luxury, hast thou courage to face this future with me?"

"I ask no better," she replied. "I had faith in my father's judgment, and now am I rewarded."

The Baal Shem's voice trembled with tenderness. "God bless thee," he said. "Our sufferings shall be but for a time."

After the wedding Rabbi Gershon wished to instruct his new brother-in-law, who had, of course, taken up his abode in his house. But the Baal Shem feigned to be difficult of understanding, and at length, in despair, the Judge went stormily to his sister and cried out: "See how we are shamed and disgraced through thy husband, who argues ignorantly against our most renowned teachers. I cannot endure the dishonor any longer. Look thou, sister mine, I give thee the alternative—either divorce this ignoramus or let me buy thee a horse and cart and send you both packing from the place."

"We will go," she said simply.

They jogged along in their cart till they came far from Jews and remote even from men. And there in a lonely spot, on one of the spurs of the Carpathian Mountains, honeycombed by caves and thick with trees, the couple made their home. Here Israel gave himself up to prayer and contemplation. For his livelihood he dug lime in the ravines, and his wife took it in the horse and cart, and sold it in the nearest town, bringing back flour. When the Baal Shem was not fasting, which was rarely, he mixed this flour with water and earth, and baked it in the sun. That was his only fare. What else needed he—he, whose greatest joy was to make holy ablutions in the mountain waters, or to climb the summits of the mountains and to wander about wrapt in the thought of God? Once the robbers who lurked in the caves saw him approaching a precipice, his ecstatic gaze heavenwards. They halloed to him, but his ears were lent to the celestial harmonies. Then they held their breath, waiting for him to be dashed to pieces. But the opposite mountain came to him. And then the two mountains separated, re-uniting again for his return. After this the robbers revered him as a holy man, and they, too, brought him their disputes. And the Baal Shem did not refuse the office,—"For," said he, "even amid the unjust, justice must rule." But one of the gang whom he had decided against sought to slay him as he slept. An invisible hand held back the axe as it was raised to strike the fatal blow, and belabored the rogue soundly, till he fell prone, covered with blood.

Thus passed seven years of labor and spiritual vision. And the Baal Shem learned the language of birds and beasts and trees, and the healing properties of herbs and simples; and he redeemed souls that had been placed for their sins in frogs and toads and loathsome creatures of the mountains.

But at length Rabbi Gershon was sorry for his sister, and repented him of his harshness. He sought out the indomitable twain, and brought them back to Brody, and installed them in an apartment near him, and made the Baal Shem his coachman. But his brother-in-law soon disgusted him again, for, one day, when they were driving together, and Rabbi Gershon had fallen asleep, the Baal Shem, whose pure thoughts had ascended on high, let the vehicle tumble into a ditch. "This fellow is good neither for heaven nor earth," cried Rabbi Gershon.

He again begged his sister to get a divorce, but she remained steadfast and silent. In desperation Rabbi Gershon asked a friend of his, Rabbi Mekatier, to take Israel to a mad woman, who told people their good and bad qualities, and whose stigmatization, he thought, might have an effect upon his graceless brother-in-law. The audience-chamber of the possessed creature was crowded, and, as each visitor entered, a voice issued from her lips greeting them according to their qualities. As Rabbi Mekatier came in: "Welcome, holy and pure one," she cried, and so to many others. The Baal Shem entered last. "Welcome, Rabbi Israel," cried the voice; "thou deemest I fear thee, but I fear thee not. For I know of a surety that thou hast been sworn in Heaven not to make use of the Name, not till thy thirty-sixth year."

"Of what speakest thou?" asked the people in bewilderment.

Then the woman repeated what she had said, but the people understood her not. And she went on repeating the words. At length Rabbi Israel rebuked her sharply.

"Silence, or I will appoint a Council of Judgment who will empower me to drive thee out of this woman. I ask thee, therefore, to depart from this woman of thine own accord, and we will pray for thee."

So the spirit promised to depart.

Then the Baal Shem said: "Who art thou?"

"I cannot tell thee now," replied the spirit. "It will disgrace my children who are in the room. If they depart, I will tell thee."

Thereupon all the people departed in haste and spread the news that Israel could cast out devils. The respect for him grew, but Rabbi Gershon was incredulous, saying such things could only be done by a scholar; and, becoming again out of patience with this ignorant incubus upon his honorable house, he bought his sister a small inn in a village far away on the border of a forest. While his wife managed the inn, the Baal Shem built himself a hut in the forest and retired there to study the Law day and night; only on the Sabbath did he go out, dressed in white, and many ablutions did he make, as becomes the pure and the holy.

It was here that he reached his thirty-sixth year, but still he did not reveal himself, for he had not meditated sufficiently nor found out his first apostles. But in his forty-second year he began freely to speak and to gather disciples, wandering about Podolia and Wallachia, and teaching by discourse and parable, crossing streams by spreading his mantle upon the waters, and saving his disciples from freezing in the wintry frosts by touching the trees with his finger-tips, so that they burnt without being consumed.

And now he was become the chief of a mighty sect, that ramified everywhere, and the head of a school of prophets and wonder-workers to whom he had unveiled the secret of the Name.

IV

So strange and marvellous a story, so full of minute detail, and for the possible truth of which my Cabalistic studies had prepared me, roused in me again the ever-smouldering hope of becoming expert in these traditional practices of our nation. Why should not I, like other Rabbis, have the key of the worlds? Why should not I, too, fashion a fine fat calf on the Friday and eat it for my Sabbath meal? or create a soulless monster to wait upon me hand and foot? The Talmudical subtleties had kept me long enough wandering in a blind maze. I would go forth in search of light. I would gird up my loins and take my staff in my hand and seek the fountain-head of wisdom, the great Master of the Name himself; I would fall at his feet and beseech him to receive me among his pupils.

Travelling was easy enough:—in every town a Beth-Hamidrash into which the wanderer would first make his way; in every town hospitable entertainers who would board and lodge a man of learning like myself, rejoicing at the honor. Even in the poorest villages I might count upon black bread and sheep's cheese and a bed of fir branches. But when I came to make inquiries I found that the village in Volhynia, which Rabbi Baer had made his centre, was far nearer than the forest where the Master, remote and inaccessible, retired to meditate after his missionary wanderings; nay, that my footsteps must needs pass through this Mizricz, the political stronghold of Chassidism. This discovery did not displease me, for I felt that thus I should reach the Master better prepared. In my impatience I could scarcely wait for the roads to become passable, and it was still the skirt of winter when, with a light heart and a wild hope, I set my face for the wild ravines of Severia and the dreary steppes of the Ukraine. Very soon I came into parts where the question of the Chassidim was alive and burning, and indeed into towns where it had a greater living interest than the quarrel of the amulets. And in these regions the rumor of the Baal Shem began to thicken. There was not a village of log-houses but buzzed with its own miracle. Everywhere did I hear of healings of the sick and driving out of demons and summoning of spirits, and the face of the Master shining.

Of these strange stories I will set down but two. The Master and his retinue were riding on a journey, and came to a strange road. His disciples did not know the way, and the party went astray and wandered about till Wednesday night, when they put up at an inn. In the morning the host asked who they were.

"I am a wandering preacher," replied the Baal Shem. "And I wish to get to the capital before the Sabbath, for I have heard that the richest man in the town is marrying there on the Friday, and perchance I may preach at the wedding."

"That thou wilt never do," said the innkeeper, "for the capital is a week's journey."

The Master smiled. "Our horses are good," he said.

The innkeeper shook his head: "Impossible, unless you fly through the air," he said. But, presently remembering that he himself had to go some leagues on the road to the capital, he begged permission to join the party, which was cheerfully given.

The Master then retired to say his morning prayers, and gave orders for breakfast and dinner.

"But why art thou delaying?" inquired the innkeeper. "How can you arrive for Sabbath?"

The Baal Shem did not, however, abate one jot of his prayers, and it was not till eve that they set out. All through the night they travelled, and in the morning the innkeeper found himself, to his confusion, not where he had reckoned to part with the others, but in the environs of the capital. The Baal Shem took up his quarters in a humble district, while the dazed innkeeper wandered about the streets of the great city, undecided what to do. All at once he heard screams and saw a commotion, and people began to run to and fro; and then he saw men carrying a beautiful dead girl in bridal costume, and in the midst of them one, who by his Sabbath garments and his white shoes was evidently the bridegroom, mazed and ghastly pale. He heard people telling one another that death had seized her as she stood under the canopy, before the word could be said or the glass broken that should have made her the wife of the richest man in the capital. The innkeeper ran towards them and he said—

"Do not despair. Last night I was hundreds of miles from here. I came here with a great wonder-worker. Mayhap he will be able to help you." The bridegroom went with him to seek out the Baal Shem at the far end of the town, and offered a vast sum for the restoration of his beloved.

"Nay, keep thy money," said the Master. And he fared back with the twain to see the corpse, which had been laid in an apartment.

As soon as he had looked upon the face of the bride he said: "Let a grave be dug; and let the washers prepare her for the tomb. And then let her be reclad in her marriage vestments. I will go to the graveyard and await her coming."

When her body was brought, he told the bearers to lay her in the grave, earth to earth. The onlookers wept to see how, for once, that shroud which every bride wore over her fur robe was become a fitting ornament, and how the marvellous fairness of the dead face, crowned with its myrtle garlands, gleamed through the bridal veil. The Master placed two stalwart men with their faces towards the grave, and bade them, the instant they noted any change in her face, take her out. Then he leaned upon his staff and gazed at the dead face. And those who were near said his face shone with a heavenly light of pity; but his brow was wrinkled as though in grave deliberation. The moments passed, but the Master remained as motionless as she in the grave. And all the people stood around in awed suspense, scarce daring to whisper. Suddenly a slight flush appeared in the dead face. The Baal Shem gave a signal, the two men lifted out the bride from the raw earth, and he cried: "Get on with the wedding," and walked away.

"Nay, come with us," besought the weeping bridegroom, falling at his feet and kissing the hem of his garment. "Who but thou should perform the ceremony?"

So the throng swept back towards the synagogue with many rejoicings and songs, and the extinguished torches were relighted, and the music struck up again, and the bride walked, escorted by her friends, seemingly unconscious that this was not the same joyous procession which had set out in the morning, or that she had already stood under the canopy. But, when they were arrived in the synagogue courtyard, and the Baal Shem began the ceremony, then as she heard his voice, a strange light of recollection leapt into her face. She tore off her veil and cried, "This is the man that drew me out of the cold grave."

"Be silent," reprimanded the Master sternly, and proceeded with the wedding formulæ. At the wedding feast, the bride's friends asked her what she had seen and heard in the tomb. Whereupon she gave them the explanation of the whole matter. The former wife of her rich bridegroom was the bride's aunt, and when she fell ill and knew she would die, she felt that he would assuredly marry this young girl—his ward,—who was brought up in his house. She became madly jealous, and, calling her husband to her death-bed, she made him take an oath not to marry the girl. Nor would she trust him till he had sworn with his right hand in hers and his left hand in the girl's. After the wife's death neither of the parties to this oath kept faith, but wished to marry the other. Wherefore as they stood under the canopy at the marriage celebration the dead wife, seen only of the bride, killed her. While she was lying in the grave, the Baal Shem was occupied in weighing the matter, both she and the jealous woman having to state their case; and he decided that the living were in the right, and had only given their promise to the dead wife by force and out of compassion. And so he exclaimed, "Get on with the wedding!" The memory of this trial in the world of spirits had clean passed from her till she heard the Master's voice beginning to read the marriage service, when she cried out, and tore off her veil to see him plainly.

The Baal Shem spent the Sabbath in the capital; and on Sunday he was escorted out of the town with a great multitude doing him honor. And afterwards it was found that all the sick people, whose names happened to be scribbled by their relatives on the grave-stone which his robe had brushed, recovered. Nor could this be entirely owing to the merits of him who lay below, pious man though he was.

On the Tuesday night the Baal Shem and his disciples came to an inn, where he found the host sitting sadly in a room ablaze festally with countless candles and crowded with little boys, rocking themselves to and fro with prayer.

"Can we lodge here for the night?" asked the Baal Shem.

"Nay," answered the host dejectedly.

"Why art thou sad? Perchance I can help thee," said the Baal Shem.

"To-night, as thou seest, is watch-night," said the man; "for to-morrow my latest-born is to be circumcised. This is my fifth child, and all the others have died suddenly at midnight, although up to then there has been no sign of sickness. I know not why Lilith should have such a grudge against my progeny. But so it is, the devil's mother, she kills them every one, despite the many charms and talismans hung round my wife's bed. Every day since the birth, these children have come to say the Shemang and the ninety-first psalm. And to-night the elders are coming to watch and study all night. But I fear they will not cheat Lilith of her prey. Therefore am I not in the humor to lodge strangers."

"Let the little ones go home; they are falling asleep," said the Master. "And let them tell their fathers to stay at home in their beds. My pupils and I will watch and pray."

So said, so done. The Baal Shem told off two of his men to hold a sack open at the cradle of the child, and he instructed the rest of his pupils to study holy law ceaselessly, and on no account to let their eyelids close, though he himself designed to sleep. Should anything fall into the sack the two men were to close it forthwith and then awaken him. With a final caution to his disciples not to fall asleep, the Master withdrew to his chamber. The hours drew on. Naught was heard save the droning of the students and the sough of the wind in the forest. At midnight the flames of the candles wavered violently, though no breath of wind was felt within the hot room. But the watchers shielding the flames with their hands strove to prevent them being extinguished. Nevertheless they all went out, and a weird gloom fell upon the room, the firelight throwing the students' shadows horribly on the walls and ceiling. Their blood ran cold. But one, bolder than the rest, snatching a brand from the hearth, relit the candles. As the last wick flamed again, a great black cat fell into the sack. The two men immediately tied up the mouth of it and went to rouse the Baal Shem.

"Take two cudgels," said he, "and thrash the sack as hard as you can."

After they had given it a sound drubbing, he bade them unbind the sack and throw it into the street. And so the day dawned, and all was well with the child. That day they performed the ceremony of Initiation with great rejoicing, and the Baal Shem was made godfather or Sandek. But before the feasting began, the father of the child begged the Baal Shem to tarry, "for," said he, "I must needs go first to the lord of the soil and take him a gift of wine. For he is a cruel tyrant, and will visit it upon me if I fail to pay him honor on this joyous occasion."

"Go in peace," said the Baal Shem.

When the man arrived at the seigneur's house, the lackeys informed him that their master was ill, but had left instructions that he was to be told when the gift was brought. The man waited, and the seigneur ordered him to be admitted, and received him very affably, asking him how business was, and if he had guests at his inn.

"Ay, indeed," answered the innkeeper; "there is staying with me a very holy man who is from Poland, and he delivered my child from death."

"Indeed!" said the seigneur, with interest, and the man thereupon told him the whole story.

"Bring me this stranger," commanded the seigneur; "I would speak with him."

The innkeeper went home very much perturbed.

"Why so frightened an air?" the Baal Shem asked him.

"The seigneur desires thee to go to him. I fear he will do thee a mischief. I beseech thee, depart at once, and I will tell him thou hadst already gone."

"I will go to him," said the Baal Shem.

He was ushered into the sick-room. As soon as the seigneur had dismissed his lackeys he sat up in bed, thus revealing black-and-blue marks in his flesh, and sneered vengefully—

"Doubtless thou thinkest thyself very cunning to have caught me unawares."

"Would I had come before thou hadst killed the other four," replied the Baal Shem.

"Ho! ho!" hissed the magician; "so thou feelest sure thou art a greater wizard than I. Well, I challenge thee to the test."

"I have no desire to contend with thee," replied the Baal Shem calmly; "I am no wizard. I have only the power of the Holy Name."

"Bah! My witchcraft against thy Holy Name," sneered the wizard.

"The Name must be vindicated," said the Baal Shem. "I accept thy challenge. This day a month I will assemble my pupils. Do thou and thy brethren gather together your attendant spirits. And thou shalt learn that there is a God."

In a month's time the Baal Shem with all his pupils met the wizard with his fellows in an open field; and there, under the blue circle of Heaven, the Baal Shem made two circles around himself and one in another place around his pupils, enjoining them to keep their eyes fixed on his face, and, if they noticed any change in it, immediately to begin crying the Penitential Prayer. The arch-wizard also made a circle for himself and his fellow-wizards at the other end of the field, and commenced his attack forthwith. He sent against the Baal Shem swarms of animals, which swept towards the circle with clamorous fury. But when they came to the first circle, they vanished. Then another swarm took their place—and another—and then another—lions, tigers, leopards, wolves, griffins, unicorns, and unnameable creatures, all dashing themselves into nothingness against the holy circle. Thus it went on all the long day, every instant seeing some new bristling horde vomited and swallowed up again.

Towards twilight the arch-magician launched upon the Baal Shem a herd of wild boars, spitting flames; and these at last passed beyond the first circle. Then the pupils saw a change come over the Baal Shem's face, and they began to wail the Penitential Prayer.

Still the boars sped on till they reached the second circle. Then they vanished. Three times the wizard launched his boars, the flames of their jaws lighting up the gathering dusk, but going out like blown candles at the second circle. Then said the wizard, "I have done my all." He bowed his head. "Well, I know one glance of thine eyes will kill me. I bid life farewell."

"Nay, look up," said the Baal Shem; "had I wished to kill thee, thou wouldst long ago have been but a handful of ashes spread over this field. But I wish to show thee that there is a God above us. Come, lift up thine eyes to Heaven."

The wizard raised his eyes towards the celestial circle, in which the first stars were beginning to twinkle. Then two thorns came and took out his eyes. Till his death was he blind; but he saw that there was a God in Heaven.

V

Of Rabbi Baer I heard on my way nothing but eulogies, and his miracles were second only to those of his Master. He was a great man in Israel, a scholar profound as few. Even the enemies of the Chassidim—and they were many and envenomed—admitted his learning, and complained that his defection to the sect had greatly strengthened and drawn grave disciples to this ignorant movement. For, according to them, the Baal Shem was as unlettered as he gave himself out to be, nor did they credit the story of his followers that all his apparent ignorance was due to his celestial oath not to reveal himself till his thirty-sixth year. As for the followers, they were esteemed simply a set of lewd, dancing fanatics; and, of a truth, a prayer-service I succeeded in witnessing in one town considerably chilled my hopes. For the worshippers shouted, beat their breasts, struck their heads against the wall, tugged at their ear-curls, leaped aloft with wild yells and even foamed at the mouth, nor could I see any sublime idea behind these maniacal manifestations. They had their own special Zaddik (Saint) here, whom they vaunted as even greater than Baer.

"He talks with angels," one told me.

"How know you that?" I said sceptically.

"He himself admits it."

"But suppose he lies!"

"What! A man who talks with angels be capable of a lie!"

I did not pause to point out to him that this reasoning violated even Talmudical logic, for I feared if I received the doctrine from such mouths I should lose all my enthusiasm ere reaching the fountain-head, and hereafter in my journeyings I avoided hunting out the members of the sect, even as I strove to dismiss from my mind the malicious inuendoes and denunciations of their opponents, who said it was not without reason this sect had arisen in a country where only the eldest son in a Jewish family was allowed by the State to marry. I would keep my mind clear and free from prepossessions on either side. And thus at last, after many weary days and adventures which it boots not to recall here, such as the proposals of marriage made to me by some of my hosts—and they householders in Israel, albeit unillumined—I arrived at the goal of the first stage of my journey, the village of Mizricz.

I scarcely stayed to refresh myself after my journey, but hastened immediately to Rabbi Baer's house, which rose regal and lofty on a wooded eminence overlooking the river as it foamed through the mountain gullies on its way to the Dnieper. I crossed the broad pine-bridge without a second glance at the rushing water, but to my acute disappointment when I reached the great house I was not admitted. I was told that the Saint could not be seen of mortal eye till the Sabbath, being, I gathered, in a mystic transport. It was then Wednesday. Mine was not the only disappointment, for the door was besieged by a curious rabble of pilgrims of both sexes, some come from very far, some on foot and in rags, some in well-appointed equipages. One of the latter—a beautiful, richly dressed woman—by no means took her exclusion with good grace, bidding her coachman knock again and again at the door, and endeavoring to bribe the door-keeper with grocery, wine, and finally gold; but all in vain. I entered into conversation with members of the crowd, and discovered that some came for cures, and some for charms, and some for divine interpositions in their worldly affairs. One man, I found, desired that the price of wheat might go up, and another that it might fall. Another desired a husband for his elderly daughter, already nineteen. And an old couple were in great distress at the robbery of their jewels, and were sure the Saint would discover the thief and recover the booty. I found but one, who, like me, came from a consuming desire to hear new doctrine for the soul. And so I was to have the advantage of them, I learnt, not without chuckling; for whereas I should receive my wish on the Sabbath, being invited to attend "the Supper of the Holy Queen," these worldly matters could not be attended to till the Sunday. I whiled away the intervening days as patiently as I could, exploring the beautiful environs beyond the Saint's house, further than which nobody ever seemed to penetrate; and, indeed, it was but seldom that I had heard of a Jew's making the blessing over lofty mountains or beautiful trees. Perhaps because our country was for the most part only a great swamp. But often had I occasion in these walks to say, "Blessed art thou, O Lord our God, who hast such things in Thy world." I scarcely ever saw a human creature, which somehow comforted and uplifted me. Only once were my meditations interrupted, and that by a shout which startled me, and just enabled me to get out of the way of an elegant, glittering carriage drawn by two white horses, in which a stout-looking man lolled luxuriously, smoking a hookah. My prayerful mood was broken, and I fell upon worldly thoughts of riches and ease.

On Friday night I ate with an elder of the Chassidim, who heard of my interest in his order, but whom I could not get to understand that I was come to examine, not to accept unquestioningly. I plied him with questions as to the ideas of his sect, but he for his part could make nothing clear to me except the doctrine of self-annihilation in prayer, by which the devout worshipper was absorbed into the Godhead; a doctrine from which flowed naturally the abrogation of stated hours of prayer, since the mood of absorption could not be had at command. Sometimes, indeed, silence was the better prayer, and this was the true explanation of the Talmudical saying: "If speech is worth one piece of silver, silence is worth two." And this, likewise, was the meaning of the verse in 2 Kings ch. iii. v. 15: "When the minstrel played, the spirit of God came upon him." That is to say, when the minstrel became an instrument and uttered music, it was because the spirit of God played upon him. So long as a man is self-active, he cannot receive the Holy Ghost.

The text in Kings seemed to me rather wrenched from its context in the fashion already nauseous to me in the orthodox schools, but as I had never in my life had such moments of grace as in my mountain-walks, I expressed so hearty an acquiescence in the doctrine itself—shocking to the orthodox mind trained in elaborate codification of the time-limits of the dawn-prayer or the westering-service—that mine host was more persuaded than ever I meant to become a Chassid.

"There is no rite," said he reassuringly. "That you desire Perfection suffices to ensure your reception into our order. At the Supper of the Holy Queen you will not be asked as to your past life, or your sins, because your heart is to the Saint as an open scroll, as you will discover when you have the bliss to see him face to face, for though he will address all the pilgrims in a body, yet you will find particular references designed only for you."

"But he has never heard of me before!"

"These things would be hard for one who preaches to his own glory. But he who lets the spirit play upon him is wiser than all the preachers."

With beating heart I entered the Saint's house on the long-expected Sabbath. I was ushered, with many other men, into a dining-room, richly carpeted and tapestried, with a large oak table, laid for about a score. A liveried attendant, treading with hushed footsteps, imparted to us his own awe, and, scarcely daring to whisper, we awaited the great man. At last he appeared, tall and majestic, in a flowing caftan of white satin, cut so as to reveal his bare breast. His shoes were white, and even the snuff-box he toyed with was equally of the color of grace. As I caught my first glimpse of his face, I felt it was strangely familiar, but where or when I had seen it I could not recall, and the thought of this haunted the back of my mind throughout.

"Peace be to you," he said to each in turn. We breathed back respectful response, and took our seats at the table. The same solemn silence reigned during the meal, which was wound up by Kuggol (Sabbath-pudding). By this time the room was full of new-comers, who had gradually dropped in for the levée, and who swarmed about the table, anxious for the merest crumb of the pudding. And great was the bliss on the faces of those who succeeded in snatching a morsel, as though it secured them Paradise.

When this unseemly scramble was over, the Saint—who, leaning his brow on his hands, had appeared not to notice these proceedings—struck up a solemn hymn-tune. Then he put his hands over his eyes, as if lost in an ecstasy; after which he suddenly began to call out our names, coupled with the places we came from, astonishing us all in turn. Each guest, when thus cried, responded with a verse from the Scriptures. When it came to my turn, I was so taken aback by the Saint's knowledge of me that I could not think of a verse. But at last, blushing and confused, I fell back upon my name-verse, which began with my initial to help me to remember my name (for so I had been taught) when the angel should demand it of me in my tomb. To my astonishment the Saint then began to deliver a discourse upon all these texts, so ingeniously dovetailed that one would have sworn no better texts could have been selected. "Verily have they spoken the truth of this man's learning," I thought, with a glow. Nor did this marvellous oration fail to evince that surprising knowledge of my past—even down to my dead wife—which mine host had predicted. I left this wonder-worker's house exalted and edified, though all I remember now of the discourse was the novel interpretation of the passage in the Mishna: "Let the honor of thy neighbor be as dear to thee as thine own."

"Thine own," said Baer, "means the honor thou doest to thyself; to take pleasure in the which were ridiculous. As little pleasure should the wise man take in his neighbor's honor—that is, in the honor which his neighbor doeth him." This seemed rather inconsistent with his own pomp, and I only appreciated the sentiment months later.

After this discourse was quite over, a member of the sect arrived. "Why so late?" he was asked.

"My wife was confined," he said shamefacedly. Facetiously uproarious congratulations greeted him.

"Boy or girl?" cried many voices.

"Girl," he said more shamefacedly.

"A girl!" cried the Saint, in indignant accents. "You ought to be whipped."

Immediately the company with great glee set upon the unfortunate man, tumbled him over, and gave him an hilarious but hearty drubbing. I looked at the Saint in astonishment. His muscles were relaxed in a grin, and I had another flash of elusive recollection of his face. But ere I could fix it, he stopped the horse-play.

"Come, brethren," he said, "let us serve the Lord with gladness," and he trolled forth a jocund hymn.

On the next day, with mingled feelings, I again sought the Zaddik's doorway, through which was pouring the stream of those who had waited so long; but access to the holy man was still not easy. In the spacious antechamber sat the Saint's scribe, at a table round which the crowd clustered, each explaining his or her want, which the scribe scribbled upon a scrap of paper for them to take in to the Saint. I listened to the instructions of the clamorous applicants. "I, Rachel, daughter of Hannah, wish to have children," ran the request of the beautiful rich woman whose coachman had knocked so persistently; and her gratuity to the scribe seemed to be of gold. I myself paid only a few kreutzer, and simply desired—and was alone in desiring—"Perfection." There was another money-receiving man at the Rabbi's door; but I followed in the golden wake of the rich lady, and was just in time to witness the parting gratitude of the vociferous old couple to whom the Rabbi had restored their jewels. The Saint, with no signs of satisfaction at his miraculous success, gravely dismissed the garrulous couple, and took the folded paper which the beautiful woman handed him, and which he did not even open, placing it to his forehead and turning his eyes heavenwards.

"You wish to have a child," he said.

The woman started. "O thou man of God!" she cried, falling at his feet.

The Saint placed his hand reassuringly upon her hair. And at this moment something in his expression at length unsealed my eyes, and I recognized, with a pang of pain, the man who had driven past me in that elegant equipage, lolling luxuriously and smoking his hookah. I was so perturbed that I fled unceremoniously from the audience-chamber. Perfection, indeed! Here was a teacher of humility who sat throned amid tapestries, a preacher of righteousness who, when he feigned to be absorbed in God, was wallowing in his carriage! Yea, these Rabbis of the Chassidim were whitewashed sepulchres; and, as the orthodox communities did not fail of such, it seemed a waste of energy to go out of the fold in search of more. All that I had heard against the sect on my route swept back into my mind, and I divided its members into rogues and dupes. And in this bitter mood a dozen little threads flew together and knitted themselves into a web of wickedness. I told myself that the hamlet must be full of Baer's spies, and that my host himself had cunningly extracted from me the facts of my history; and as for the restored jewels, I felt sure his own men had stolen them. I slung my knapsack across my shoulder and started for home.

But I had not made many hundred yards when my mood softened. I remembered the wonderful sermon, with its manipulation of texts Rabbi Baer could not have foreseen, and bethought myself that he was indeed a Prince in Israel, and that King David and Solomon the Wise had not failed to live in due magnificence. "And after all," mused I, "'tis innocent enough to drive by the river-side. Who knows but even thus is his absorption in God accomplished? Do not they who smoke this tobacco aver that it soothes and purifies the soul?"

Besides, who but a fool, I reflected further, would slink back to his starting-point, his goal unvisited? I had seen the glory of the disciple, let me gaze upon the glory of the Master, and upon the purple splendors of his court.

And so I struck out again for Miedziboz, though by a side-path, so as to avoid the village of Baer.

VI

It was April ere I began to draw near my destination. The roads were still muddy and marshy; but in that happy interval between the winter gray and the summer haze the breath of spring made the world beautiful. The Stri river sparkled, even the ruined castles looked gay, while the pleasure-grounds of the lords of the soil filled the air with sweet scents. One day, as I was approaching a village up a somewhat steep road, a little gray-haired man driving a wagon holding some sacks of flour passed me, whistling cheerfully. We gave each other the "Peace" salutation, knowing ourselves brother Jews, if only by our furred caps and ear-curls. Presently, in pity of his beast, I saw him jump down and put his shoulder to the wheel; but he had not made fifty paces when his horse slipped and fell. I hastened up to help him extricate the animal; and before we had succeeded in setting the horse on his four feet again, the driver's cheeriness under difficulties had made me feel quite friendly towards him.

"Satan is evidently bent upon disturbing my Passover," Said he, "for this is the second time that I have tried to get my Passover flour home. My good wife told me that we had nothing to eat for the festival, so I felt I must give myself a counsel. Out I went with my slaughtering-knife into the villages on the north—no, don't be alarmed, not to kill the inhabitants, but to slaughter their Passover poultry."

"You are a Shochet (licensed killer)," said I.

"Yes," said he; "among other things. It would be an intolerable profession," he added reflectively, "were it not for the thought that since the poor birds have to be killed, they are better off in my hands. However, as I was saying, I killed enough poultry to buy Passover flour; but before I got it home the devil sent such a deluge that it was all spoilt. I took my knife again and went out into the southern villages, and now, here am I in another quandary. I only hope I sha'nt have to kill my horse too."

"No, I don't think he is damaged," said I, as the event proved.

When I had helped this good-natured little man and his horse to the top of the hill, he invited me to jump into the cart if my way lay in his direction.

"I am in search of the Baal Shem," I explained.

"Indeed," said he; "he is easily to be found."

"What, do you know the Baal Shem?" I cried excitedly.

He seemed amused at my agitation. His black eyes twinkled. "Why, everybody in these parts knows the Baal Shem," said he.

"How shall I find him, then?" I asked.

He shrugged his shoulders. "You have but to step up into my cart."

"May your strength increase!" I cried gratefully; "you are going in his direction?"

He nodded his head.

I climbed up the wheel and plumped myself down between two flour-sacks. "Is it far?" I asked.

He smiled. "Nay, if it was far I should scarcely have asked you up."

Then we both fell silent. For my part, despite the jolting of the vehicle, the lift was grateful to my spent limbs, and the blue sky and the rustling leaves and the near prospect of at last seeing the Baal Shem contributed to lull me into a pleasant languor. But my torpor was not so deep as that into which my new friend appeared to fall, for though as we approached a village another vehicle dashed towards us, my shouts and the other driver's cries only roused him in time to escape losing a wheel.

"You must have been thinking of a knotty point of Torah (Holy Law)," said I.

"Knotty point," said he, shuddering; "it is Satan who ties those knots."

"Oho," said I, "though a Shochet, you do not seem fond of rabbinical learning."

"Where there is much study," he replied tersely, "there is little piety."

At this moment, appositely enough, we passed by the village Beth-Hamidrash, whence loud sounds of "pilpulistic" (wire-drawn) argument issued. The driver clapped his palms over his ears.

"It is such disputants," he cried with a grimace, "who delay the redemption of Israel from exile."

"How so?" said I.

"Satan induces these Rabbis," said he, "to study only those portions of our holy literature on which they can whet their ingenuity. But from all writings which would promote piety and fear of God he keeps them away."

I was delighted and astonished to hear the Shochet thus deliver himself, but before I could express my acquiescence, his attention was diverted by a pretty maiden who came along driving a cow.

"What a glorious creature!" said he, while his eyes shone.

"Which?" said I laughingly. "The cow?"

"Both," he retorted, looking back lingeringly.

"I understand now what you mean by pious literature," I said mischievously: "the Song of Solomon."

He turned on me with strange earnestness, as if not perceiving my irony. "Ay, indeed," he cried; "but when the Rabbis do read it, they turn it into a bloodless allegory, Jewish demons as they are! What is the beauty of yonder maiden but an emanation from the divine? The more beautiful the body, the more shiningly it leads us to the thought of God."

I was much impressed with this odd fellow, whom I perceived to be an original.

"But that's very dangerous doctrine," said I; "by parity of reasoning you would make the lust of the flesh divine."

"Everything is divine," said he.

"Then feasting would be as good for the soul as fasting."

"Better," said the driver curtly.

I was disconcerted to find such Epicurean doctrines in a district where, but for my experience of Baer, I should have expected to see the ascetic influence of the Baal Shem predominant. "Then you're not a follower of the Baal Shem?" said I tentatively.

"No, indeed," said he, laughing.

He had got me into such sympathy with him—for there was a curious attraction about the man—that I felt somehow that, even if the Baal Shem were an ascetic, I should still gain nothing from him, and that my long journey would have been made in vain, the green pastures and the living waters being still as far off as ever from my droughty soul.

We had now passed out of the village and into a thick pine-wood with a path scarcely broad enough for the cart. Of a sudden the silence into which we again fell was broken by piercing screams for "Help" coming from a copse on the right. Instantly the driver checked the horse, jumped to the ground, and drew a long knife from his girdle.

"'Tis useful to be a Shochet." he said grimly, as he darted among the bushes.

I followed in his footsteps and a strange sight burst upon us. A beautiful woman was struggling with two saturnine-visaged men dressed as Rabbis in silken hose and mantles. One held her arms pinned to her sides, while the other was about to plunge a dagger into her heart.

"Hold!" cried the Shochet.

The would-be assassin fell back, a startled look on his narrow fanatical face.

"Let the woman go!" said the driver sternly.

In evident consternation the other obeyed. The woman fell forward, half-fainting, and the driver caught her.

"Be not afraid," he said. "And you, murderers, down at my feet and thank me that I have saved you your portion in the World-To-Come."

"Nay, you have lost it to us," said the one with the dagger. "For it was the vengeance of Heaven we were about to execute. Know that this is our sister, whom we have discovered to be a wanton creature, that must bring shame upon our learned house and into our God-fearing town. Whereupon we and her husband held a secret Beth-Din, and resolved, according to the spirit of our ancient Law, that this plague-spot must be cleansed out from Israel for the glory of the Name."

"The glory of the Name!" repeated the driver, and his eyes flamed. "What know you of the glory of the Name?"

Both brothers winced before the passion of his words. They looked at each other strangely and uneasily, but answered nothing.

"How dare you call any Jewess a plague-spot?" went on the driver. "Is any sin great enough to separate us irredeemably from God, who is in all things? Pray for your sister if you will, but do not dare to sit in judgment upon a fellow-creature!"

The woman burst into loud sobs and fell at his feet.

"They are right! they are right!" she cried. "I am a wicked creature. It were better to let me perish."

The driver raised her tenderly. "Nay, in that instant you repented," he said, "and one instant's repentance wins back God. Henceforward you shall live without sin."

"What! you would restore her to Brody?" cried the elder brother—"to bring the wrath of Heaven upon so godly a town. Be you who you may, saint or devil, that is beyond your power. Her husband assuredly will not take her back. With her family she cannot live."

"Then she shall live with mine," said the Shochet. "My daughter dwells in Brody. I will take her to her. Go your ways."

They stood disconcerted. Presently the younger said: "How know we are not leaving her to greater shame?"

The old man's face grew terrible.

"Go your ways," he repeated.

They slunk off, and I watched them get into a two-horsed carriage, which I now perceived on the other side of the copse. I ran forward to give an arm to the woman, who was again half-fainting.

"Said I not," said the old man musingly, "that even the worst sinners are better than these Rabbis? So blind are they in the arrogance of their self-conceit, so darkened by their pride, that their very devotion to the Law becomes a vehicle for their sin."

We helped the woman gently into the cart. I climbed in, but the old man began to walk with the horse, holding its bridle, and reversing its direction.

"Aren't you jumping up?" I asked.

"We are going up now, instead of down," he said, smiling. "Brody sits high, in the seat of the scornful."

A pang of shame traversed my breast. What! I was riding and this fine old fellow was walking! But ere I could offer to get down, a new thought increased my confusion. I, who was bent on finding the Baal Shem, was now off on a side-adventure to Brody. And yet I was loath to part so soon with my new friend. And besides, I told myself, Brody was well worth a visit. The reputation of its Talmudical schools was spread over the kingdom, and although I shared the old man's repugnance to them my curiosity was alert. And even on the Baal Shem's account I ought to go there. For I remembered now that his early life had had many associations with the town, and that it was his wife's birthplace. So I said, "How far is Brody?"

"Ten miles," he said.

"Ten miles!" I repeated in horror.

"Ten miles," he said musingly, "and ten years since I set foot in Brody."

I jumped down. "'Tis I must walk, not you," I said.

"Nay," said he good-humoredly. "I perceive neither of us can walk. Those sacks must play Jonah. Out with them."

"No," I said.

"Yes," he insisted, laughing. "Did I not say Satan was determined to spoil my Passover? The third time I shall have better luck perhaps."

I protested against thus causing him so much loss, and offered to go and find the Baal Shem alone, but he rolled out the flour-bags, laughing, leaving one for the woman to lie against.

"But your wife will be expecting them," I remarked, as the cart proceeded with both of us in our seats.

"She will be expecting me, too," he said, smiling ruefully. "However, she has faith in God. Never yet have we lacked food. Surely He who feedeth the ravens—" He broke off with a sudden thought, leapt down, and ran back.

"What is it?" I said.

I saw him draw out his knife again and slit open the sacks. "The birds shall keep Passover," he called out merrily.

The woman was still sobbing as he climbed to his place, but he comforted her with his genial and heterodox philosophy.

"'Tis a device of Satan," he said, "to drive us to despondency, so as to choke out the God-spark in us. Your sin is great, but your Father in Heaven awaits you, and will rejoice as a King rejoices over a princess redeemed from captivity. Every soul is a whole Bible in itself. Yours contains Sarah and Ruth as well as Jezebel and Michal. Hitherto you have developed the Jezebel in you; strive now to develop the Sarah." With such bold consolations he soothed her, till the monotonous movement of the cart sent her into a blessed sleep. Then he took out a pipe and, begging permission of me, lighted it. As the smoke curled up his face became ecstatic.

"I think," he observed musingly, "that God is more pleased with this incense of mine than with all the prayers of all the Rabbis."

This shocked even me, fascinated though I was. Never had I met such a man in all Israel. I shook my head in half-serious reproof. "You are a sinner," I said.

"Nay, is not smoking pleasurable? To enjoy aright aught in God's creation is to praise God. Even so, is not to pray the greatest of all pleasures?"

"To pray?" I repeated wonderingly. "Nay, methinks it is a heavy burden to get through our volumes of prayer."

"A burden!" cried the old man. "A burden to enter into relation with God, to be reabsorbed into the divine unity. Nay, 'tis a bliss as of bridegroom with bride. Whoso does not feel this joy of union—this divine kiss—has not prayed."

"Then have I never prayed," I said.

"Then 'tis you that are the sinner," he retorted, laughing.

His words struck me into a meditative silence. It was towards twilight when our oddly-encountered trio approached the great Talmudical centre. To my surprise a vast crowd seemed to be waiting at the gates.

"It is for me," said the woman hysterically, for she had now awakened. "My brothers have told the elders. They will kill you. O save yourself."

"Peace, peace," said the old man, puffing his pipe.

As we came near we heard the people shouting, and nearer still made out the sounds. Was it? Yes, I could not be mistaken. "The Baal Shem! The Baal Shem!"

My heart beat violently. What a stroke of luck was this! "The Baal Shem is there!" I cried exultantly.

The woman grew worse. "The Baal Shem!" she shrieked. "He is a holy man. He will slay us with a glance."

"Peace, my beautiful creature," said the driver. "You are more likely to slay him with a glance."

This time his levity grated on me. I peered eagerly towards the gates, striving to make out the figure of the mighty Saint!

The dense mob swayed tumultuously. Some of the people ran towards our cart. Our horse had to come to a stand-still. In a trice a dozen hands had unharnessed him, there was an instant of terrible confusion in which I felt that violence was indeed meditated, then I found our cart being drawn forward as in triumph by contesting hands, while in my ears thundered from a thousand throats, "The Baal Shem! The Baal Shem!" Suddenly I looked with an incredible suspicion at the old man, smoking imperturbably at my side.

"'Tis indeed a change for Brody," he said, with a laugh that was half a sob.

A faintness blotted out the whole strange scene—the town-gates, the eager faces, the gesticulating figures, the houses, the frightened woman at my side.

It was the greatest surprise of my life.

VII

A chaos of images clashed in my mind. I saw the mystic figure of the mighty Master of the Name standing in the cemetery judging betwixt the souls of the dead; I saw him in the upper world amid the angels; I saw him serene in the centre of his magic circle, annihilating with his glance the flaming hordes of demon boars; and even as the creatures shattered themselves into nothingness against the circle, so must these sublime visions vanish before this genial old man. And yet my disillusion was not all empty. There were still the cheers to exalt me, there was still my strange companion, to whose ideas I had already vibrated, and whose face was now transfigured to my imagination, gaining much of what the visionary figure had lost. And, amid all the tumult of the moment, there sang in my breast the divine assurance that here at last were the living waters, here the green pastures. "Master," I cried frantically, as I seized his hand and kissed it.

"My son," he said tenderly. "Those murderers have evidently informed the townspeople of my coming."

"It is well," said I, "I rejoice to witness your triumph over a town so rabbi-ridden."

"Nay, speak not of my triumph," reproved the Master. "Thank God for the change in them, if change there be. It should be indifferent to man whether he be praised or blamed, loved or hated, reputed to be the wisest of mankind or the greatest of fools."

"They wish you to address them, Master," I cried, as the cheers continued. He smiled.

"Doubtless—a sermon full of hair-splitting exegesis and devil's webs. I pray you descend and see that my horse be not stolen."

I sprang down with alacrity to obey this his first wish, and, scrambling on the animal, had again a view of the sea of faces, all turned towards the Baal Shem. From the excited talk of the crowd, I gathered that the Baal Shem had just performed one of his greatest miracles. Two brothers had been journeying with their sister in the woods, and had been attacked by robbers. They had been on the point of death when the Baal Shem miraculously appeared, and by merely mentioning the Name, had caused the robbers to sink into the earth like Korah. The sister being too terrified to return with her brothers, the Baal Shem undertook to bring her to Brody himself in his own celestial chariot, which, to those not initiated into the higher mysteries, appeared like an ordinary cart.

Meantime the Master had refilled his pipe. "Is that my old friend David," he cried, addressing one with a cobbler's apron; "and how is business?"

The cobbler, abashed by this unexpected honor, flushed and stammered: "God is good."

"A sorry answer, David; God would be as good if he sent you a-begging. Ha, ha!" he went on cheerily, "I see Joseph the innkeeper has waxed more like a barrel than ever. Peace be to you, Joseph! Have you learnt to read yet? No! Then you are still the wisest man in the town."

By this time some of the Rabbis and magnates in the forefront of the crowd had begun to look sullen at being ignored, but even more pointedly than he ignored these pillars of the commonweal, did the Baal Shem ignore his public reception, continuing to exchange greetings with humble old acquaintances, and finally begging the men between the shafts either to give place again to his horse or to draw him to his daughter's house, whither he had undertaken to convey the woman they saw (who all this time had sat as one in a dream). But on the cries for a sermon persisting, he said:

"Friends, I cannot preach to you, more than my horse yonder. Everything preaches. Call nothing common or profane; by God's presence all things are holy. See there are the first stars. Is it not a glorious world? Enjoy it; only fools and Rabbis speak of the world as vanity or emptiness. But just as a lover sees even in the jewels of his beloved only her own beauty, so in stars and waters must we see only God." He fell a-puffing again at his pipe, but the expectant crowd would not yet divide for his passage. "Ye fools," he said roughly, "you would make me as you have made the Law and the world, a place for stopping at, when all things are but on the way to God. There was once a King," he went on, "who built himself a glorious palace. The King was throned in the centre of what seemed a maze of winding corridors. In the entrance—halls was heaped much gold and silver, and here the folk were content to stay, taking their fill of pleasure. At last the vizier had compassion upon them and called out to them: 'All these treasures and all these walls and corridors do not in truth exist at all. They are magical illusions. Push forward bravely and you shall find the King.'"

But as the crowd still raged about disappointed, pleading for a miracle, the Baal Shem whistled, and his horse flew towards him so suddenly that I nearly fell off, and the crowd had to separate in haste. A paralytic cripple dropped his crutch in a flurry and fell a-running, quite cured.

"A miracle! a miracle!" cried a hundred voices. "God be praised!"

The shout was taken up all down the street, and eager spectators surrounded the joyous cripple, interrogating him and feeling his limbs.

"You see, you see!" I heard them say to each other. "There is witchcraft even in his horse!"

As the animal came towards the shafts the human drawers scattered hastily. I hitched the wagon to and we drove through the throng that begged the Baal Shem's blessing. But he only waved them off smilingly.

"Bless one another by your deeds," he cried from time to time. "Then Abraham, Isaac, and Jacob will bless you." And so we came to the Ring-Place, and through it, into the structure we sought—a tall two-storied stone building.

When we arrived at his daughter's house we found that she rented only an apartment, so that none of us but the woman could be lodged, though we were entertained with food and wine. After supper, when the iron shutters were closed, the Baal Shem's daughter—a beautiful black-eyed girl—danced with such fire and fervor that her crimson head-cloth nearly dropped off, and I, being now in a cheerful mood, fell to envying her husband, who for his part conversed blithely with the rescued woman. In the middle of the gaiety the Baal Sham retired to a corner, observing he wished to say his Mincha prayer, and bidding us continue our merriment and not regard him.

"Mincha!" I ejaculated unthinkingly, "why, it is too late."

"Would you give a child regulations when he may speak to his Father?" rebuked the Baal Shem.

So I went on talking with his daughter, but of a sudden a smile curved my lips at the thought of how the foolish makers of legends had feigned his praying to be so fraught with occult operations that he who looked at him might die. I turned and stole a glance at him.

Then to my amaze, as I caught sight of his face, I realized for the first time that he was, indeed, as men called him, the Master of Divine Secrets. There were on his brow great spots of perspiration, and, as if from agony, tears trickled down his cheeks, but his eyes were upturned and glazed, and his face was as that of a dead man without soul, only it seemed to me that the nimbus of which men spoke was verily round his head. His form, too, which was grown rigid, appeared strangely taller. One hand grasped the corner of the dresser. I turned away my eyes quickly, fearing lest they should be smitten with blindness. I know not how many minutes passed before I heard a great sigh, and, turning, saw the Baal Shem's figure stirring and quivering, and in another moment he was facing me with a beaming smile. "Well, my son, do you feel inclined for bed?"

His question recalled to me how much I had gone through that day, and though I was in no hurry to leave this pleasant circle, yet I replied his wish was law to me. Whereupon he said, to my content, that he would tarry yet another quarter of an hour. When we set out for the inn of Joseph where our horse and cart had preceded us, it was ten o'clock, but there was still a crowd outside the house, many of the great iron doors adown the street were still open, and men and women pressed forward to kiss the hem of the Master's garment.

On our walk I begged him to tell me what he had seen during his prayers.

"I made a soul-ascension," said he simply, "and saw more wonderful things than I have seen since I came to divine knowledge. Praise to the Unity!"

"Can I see such things?" said I breathlessly, as all I had learnt of Cabalah and all my futile attempts to work miracles came rushing back to me.

"No—not you."

I felt chilled, but he went on: "Not you—the you must be obliterated. You must be reabsorbed in the Unity."

"But how?"

"Concentrate your thought on God. Forget yourself."

"I will try, dear Master," said I. "But tell me what you saw."

"What I saw and learnt up there it is impossible to communicate by word of mouth."

But I entreated him sore, and ere we had parted for the night he delivered himself as follows, speaking of these divine things in Hebrew:—

"I may only relate what I witnessed when I descended to the lower Paradise. I saw there ever so many souls both of living and of dead people, known and unknown to me, without measure and number, coming and going from one world to the other, by means of the Pillar which is known to those who know Grace. Great was the joy which the bodily breath can neither narrate nor the bodily ear hear. Many very wicked people came back in repentance, and all their sins were forgiven them, because this was a season of great Grace in Heaven. I wondered indeed that so many were received. They all begged and entreated me to come up with them to the higher regions, and on account of the great rejoicing I saw amongst them I consented. Then I asked for my heavenly teacher to go with me because the danger of ascending such upper worlds is great, where I have never been since I exist. I thus ascended from grade to grade till I came into the Temple of the Messiah, in which the Messiah teaches Torah with all the Tanaim and the Zaddikim and the Seven Shepherds; and there I saw a great rejoicing. I did not know what this rejoicing meant. I thought at first that this rejoicing might perhaps be on account of my speedy death. But they made known to me that I shall not die yet, because there is great rejoicing in Heaven when I make celestial unions below by their holy teaching. But what the rejoicing meant, I still did not know. I asked, 'When will the Master come?' I was answered: 'When thy teaching shall be known and revealed to the world, and thy springs shall spread abroad that which I have taught thee, and that which thou hast received here, and when all men will be able to make unions and ascensions like thee. Then all the husks of worldly evil will disappear, and it will be a time of Grace and Salvation.' I wondered very much, and I felt great sorrow because the time was to be so long delayed. Because when can this be? But in this my last ascent three words that be mighty charms and three heavenly names I learnt. They are easy to learn and to explain. This cooled my mind. I believe that through them people of my genius will reach soon my degree, but I have no permission to reveal them. I have been praying at least for permission to teach them to you, but I must keep to my oath. But this I make known to you, and God will help you. Let your ways be directed towards God, let them not turn away from Him. When you pray and study, in every word and utterance of your lips direct your mind to unification, because in every letter there are worlds and souls and Deity. The letters unify and become a word, and afterwards unify in the Deity, wherefore try to have your soul absorbed in them, so that all universes become unified, which causes an infinite joy and exaltation. If you understand the joy of bride and bridegroom a little and in a material way, how much more ecstatic is the unification of this celestial sort! O the wondrous day when Evil shall at last be worked out of the universe, and God be at one with His creation. May He be your help!"

I sat a while in dazed wonder.

"Dear Master," said I at last, "you to whom are unveiled the secrets of all the universes, cannot you read my future?"

"Yes," he said. I looked at him breathlessly. "You will always be faithful to me," he said slowly.

My eyes filled with tears. I kissed his hand.

"And you will marry my daughter."

My heart beat: "Which?"

"She whom you have just seen."

"But she is married," I said, as the blood swirled deliciously in my veins.

"Her husband will give her a bill of divorcement."

"And what will become of him?"

"He will marry the woman we have saved. And she, too, will win many souls."

"But how know you?" I whispered, half incredulous.

"So it is borne in upon me," said the Baal Shem, smiling.

And so indeed after many days it came to pass. And so ended this first strange day with the beloved Master, whose light shines through the worlds.

VIII

It is now many years since I first saw the Baal Shem, and as many since I laid him in his grave, yet every word he spake to me is treasured up in my heart as gold, yea, as fine gold. But the hand of age is heavy upon me, and lest I may not live to complete even this briefer story, I shall set down here but the rough impression of his doctrine left in my mind, hoping to devote a separate volume to these conversations with my divine Master. And this is the more necessary, as I said, since every day the delusions and impostures of those who use his name multiply and grow ranker. Even in his own day, the Master's doctrine was already, as you will have seen, sufficiently distorted by souls smaller than his own, and by the refraction of distance—for how should a true image of him pass from town to town, by forest and mountain, throughout all that vast empire? The Master's life alone made clear to me what I had failed to gather from his followers. Just as their delirious dancings and shrieks and spasms were abortive attempts to produce his prayer-ecstasy, so in all things did they but caricature him. But now that he is dead, and these extravagances are no longer to be checked by his living example, so monstrous are the deeds wrought and the things taught in his name, that though the Chassidim he founded are become—despite every persecution by the orthodox Jews, despite the scourging of their bodies and the setting of them in the stocks, despite the excommunication of our order and the closing of our synagogues, and the burning of our books—a mighty sect throughout the length and the breadth of Central Europe, yet have I little pleasure in them, little joy in the spread of the teaching to which I devoted my life. And sometimes—now that my Master's face no longer shines consolingly upon me, save in dream and memory—I dare to wonder if the world is better for his having lived. And indeed at times I find myself sympathizing with our chief persecutor, the saintly and learned Wilna Gaon.

And first, since there are now, alas! followers of his who in their perverted straining after simplicity of existence wander about naked in the streets, and even attend to the wants of nature in public, let me testify that though the Master considered the body and all its functions holy, yet did he give no countenance to such exaggerations; and though in his love for the sun and the water and bodily purity—to him a celestial symbol—he often bathed in retired streams, yet was he ever clad becomingly in public; and though he regarded not money, yet did he, when necessary, strive to earn it by work, not lolling about smoking and vaunting his Perfection, pretending to be meditating upon God, while others span and toiled for him.

For in his work too, my Master lived in the hourly presence of God; and of the patriarchs and the prophets, the great men of Israel, the Tanaim and the Amoraim, and all who had sought to bring God's Kingdom upon earth, that God and Creation, Heaven and Earth, might be at one, and the Messiah might come and the divine peace fall upon all the world. And when he prayed and wept for the sins of his people, his spirit ascended to the celestial spheres and held converse with the holy ones, but this did not puff him up with vanity as it doth those who profess to-day to make soul-ascensions, an experience of which I for my own part, alas! have never yet been deemed worthy. For when he returned to earth the Baal Shem conducted himself always like a simple man who had never left his native hamlet, whereas these heavenly travellers feign to despise this lower world, nay, some in their conceit and arrogance lose their wits and give out that they have already been translated and are no longer mortal. My Master did, indeed, hope to be translated in his lifetime like Elijah, for he once said to me, weeping—'twas after we returned from his wife's funeral—"Now that my wife is dead I shall die too. Such a saint might have carried me with her to Heaven. She followed me unquestioningly into the woods, lived without society, summer and winter, endured pain and labor for me, and but for her faith in me I should have achieved naught." No man reverenced womankind more than the Master; in this, as in so much, his life became a model to mine, and his dear daughter profited by the lesson her father had taught me. We err grievously in disesteeming our women: they should be our comrades not our slaves, and our soul-ascensions—to speak figuratively—should be made in their loving companionship.

My Master believed that the breath of God vivified the universe, renewing daily the work of creation, and that hence the world of everyday was as inspired as the Torah, the one throwing light on the other.

The written Law must be interpreted in every age in accordance with the ruling attribute of God—for God governs in every age by a different attribute, sometimes by His Love, sometimes by His Power, sometimes by His Beauty. "It is not the number of ordinances that we obey that brings us into union with God," said the Master; "one commandment fulfilled in and through love of Him is as effective as all." But this did not mean that the other commandments were to be disregarded, as some have deduced; nor that one commandment should be made the centre of life, as has been done by others. For, though the Zaddik, who gave his life to helping his neighbor's or his enemy's ass lying under its burden, as enjoined in Exodus xxiii. 5, was not unworthy of admiration—indeed he was my own disciple, and desired thus to commemorate the circumstances of my first meeting with the Baal Shem,—yet he who made it his speciality never to tell the smallest falsehood was led into greater sin. For when his fame was so bruited that it reached even the Government officers, they, suspecting the Jews of the town of smuggling, said they would withdraw the charge if the Saint would declare his brethren innocent. Whereupon he prayed to God to save him from his dilemma by sending him death, and lo! when the men came to fetch him to the law-court, they found him dead. But a true follower of the Master should have been willing to testify for truth's sake even against his brethren, and in my humble judgment his death was not a deliverance, but a punishment from on high.

Had, moreover, the Saint practised the Humility—which my Master put as the first of the three cardinal virtues—he would not have deemed it so fatal to tell a lie once; for who can doubt there was in him more spiritual pride in his own record than pure love of truth? And had he practised the second of the three cardinal virtues—Cheerfulness—he would have known that God can redeem a man even from the sin of lying. And had he practised the third—Enkindlement—he would never have narrowed himself to one commandment, and that a negative one—not to lie. For where there is a living flame in the heart, it spreads to all the members.

"Service is its own reward, its own joy," said the Baal Shem. "No man should bend his mind on not doing sin: his day should be too full of joyous service." The Messianic Age would be, my Master taught, when every man did what was right and just of mere natural impulse, not even remembering that he was doing right, still less being uplifted on that account, for no man is proud because he walks or sleeps. Then would Righteousness be incarnate in the world, and the devil finally defeated, and every man would be able to make celestial unions and soul-ascensions.

Many sufferings did the Baal Shem endure in the years that I was with him. Penury and persecution were often his portion, and how his wife's death wounded him I have already intimated. But it was the revival of the Sabbatian heresy by Jacob Frank that caused him the severest perturbation. This Frank, who was by turns a Turk, a Jew, and a Catholic, played the rôle of successor of Zevi, as Messiah, ordered his followers to address him as the Holy Lord, and, later, paraded his beautiful daughter, Eve, as the female Godhead. Much of what my grandfather had told me of the first Pretender was repeated, save that as the first had made alliance with the Mohammedans, so the second coquetted with the Christians. Hence those public disputations, fostered by the Christians, in which the Frankists did battle with the Talmudists, and being accredited the victors, exulted in seeing the sacred books of the Rabbis confiscated. When a thousand copies of the Talmud were thrown into a great pit at Kammieniec, and burned by the hangman, the Baal Shem shed tears, and joined in the fast-day for the burning of the Torah. For despite his detestation of the devil's knots, he held that the Talmud represented the oral law which expressed the continuous inspiration of the leaders of Israel, and that to rely on the Bible alone was to worship the mummy of religion. Nor did he grieve less over the verbal tournament of the Talmudists and Frankists in the Cathedral of Lemberg, when the Polish nobility and burghers bought entrance tickets at high prices. "The devil, not God, is served by religious disputations," said the Master.

And when at last the Frankists were baptized in their thousands, and their Messiah in pompous Turkish robes paraded the town in a chariot drawn by six horses, and surrounded by Turkish guards, the Baal Shem was more pleased than grieved at this ending. When these Jewish Catholics, however, came to grief, and, on the incarceration of Frank by the Polish Inquisition, were reduced to asking alms at church-doors, the Baal Shem was alone in refusing to taunt them for still gazing longingly towards "the gate of Rome," as they mystically called the convent of Czenstochow, in which Frank lay imprisoned. And when their enemies said they had met with their desert, the Baal Shem said: "There is no sphere in Heaven where the soul remains a shorter time than in the sphere of merit, there is none where it abides longer than in the sphere of love." Much also in these troublous times did the Baal Shem suffer from his sympathy with the sufferings of Poland, in its fratricidal war, when the Cossacks hung up together a nobleman, a Jew, a monk, and a dog, with the inscription: "All are equal." Although these Cossacks, and later on the Turks, who, in the guise of friends of Poland, turned the Southern provinces into deserts, rather helped than hindered the cause of his followers by diverting their persecutors, the Baal Shem palpitated with pity for all—dogs, monks, noblemen, and Jews. But, howsoever he suffered, the serene cheerful faith on which these were but dark shadows, never ceased altogether to shine in his face. Even on his death-bed his three cardinal virtues were not absent. For no man could face the Angel of Death more cheerfully, or anticipate more glowingly the absorption into the Divine, and as for Humility, "O Vanity! vanity!" were his dying words; "even in this hour of death thou darest approach me with thy temptations. 'Bethink thee, Israel, what a grand funeral procession will be thine because thou hast been so wise and good,' O Vanity, vanity, beshrew thee."

Now although I was his son-in-law, and was with him in this last hour, it is known of all men that not I, but Rabbi Baer, was appointed by him to be his successor. For although my acquaintance with the Baal Shem did not tend to increase my admiration for his chief disciple, I never expressed my full mind on the subject to the Master, for he had early enjoined on me that the obverse side of the virtue of Humility is to think highly of one's fellow-man. "He who loves the Father, God, will also love the children."

But, inasmuch as he abhorred profitless learning, and all study for study's sake that does not lead to the infinite light, I did venture to ask him why he had allowed Baer, the Scholar, to go about as his lieutenant and found communities in his name.

"Because," he said with beautiful simplicity, "I saw that I had sinned in making ignorance synonymous with virtue. There are good men even among the learned—men whose hearts are uncorrupted by their brains. Baer was such a one, and since he had great repute among the learned I saw that the learned who would not listen to a simple man would listen to him."

Now, before I say aught else on this point, let this saying of the Master serve to rebuke his graceless followers who despise the learned while they themselves have not even holiness, and who boast of their ignorance as though it guaranteed illumination; but as to Rabbi Baer I will boldly say that it would have been better for the world and the Baal Shem's teachings had I been appointed to hand them down. For Baer made of the Master's living impulse a code and a creed which grew rigid and dead. And he organized his followers by external signs—noisy praying, ablutions, white Sabbath robes, and so forth—so that the spirit died and the symbols remained, and now of the tens of thousands who call themselves Chassidim and pray the prayers and perform the ceremonies and wear the robes, there are not ten that have the faintest notion of the Master's teaching. For spirit is volatile and flies away, but symbol is solid and is handed down religiously from generation to generation. But the greatest abuse has come from the doctrine of the Zaddik. Perhaps the logic of Baer is sound, that if God, as the Master taught, is in all things, then is there so much of Him in certain chosen men that they are themselves divine. I do not doubt that the Master himself was akin to divinity, for though he did not profess to perform miracles, pretending that such healing as he wrought was by virtue of his knowledge of herbs and simples, and saying jestingly that the Angel of Healing goes with the good physician, nor ever admitting to me that he had done battle with demons and magicians save figuratively; yet was there in him a strange power, which is not given to men, of soothing and redeeming by his mere touch, so that, laid upon the brow—as I can personally testify—his hands would cure headache and drive out ill-humors. And I will even believe that there was of this divinity in Rabbi Baer. But whereas the Baal Shem veiled his divinity in his manhood, Baer strove to veil his manhood in his divinity, and to eke out his power by arts and policies, the better to influence men and govern them, and gain of their gold for his further operations. Yet the lesson of his history to me is, that if Truth is not great enough to prevail alone, she shall not prevail by aid of cunning. For finally there will come men who will manifest the cunning without the Truth. So at least it has been here. First the Baal Shem, the pure Zaddik, then Rabbi Baer, the worldly Zaddik, and then a host of Zaddikim, many of them having only the outward show of Sainthood. For since our otherwise great sect is split up into a thousand little sects, each boasting its own Zaddik—superior to all the others, the only true Intermediary between God and Man, the sole source of blessing and fount of Grace—and each lodging him in a palace (to which they make pilgrimages at the Festivals as of yore to the Temple) and paying him tribute of gold and treasure; it is palpable that these sorry Saints have themselves brought about these divisions for their greater glory and profit. And I weep the more over this spoliation of my Chassidim, because there is so much perverted goodness among them, so much self-sacrifice for one another in distress, and such faithful obedience to the Zaddik, who everywhere monopolizes the service and the worship which should be given to God. Alas! that a movement which began with such pure aspiration, which was to the souls of me and so many other young students as the shadow of a great rock in a weary land, that a doctrine which opened out to young Israel such spiritual vistas and transcendent splendors of the Godhead, should end in such delusions and distortions.

Woe is me! Is it always to be thus with Israel? Are we to struggle out of one slough only to sink into another? But these doubts dishonor the Master. Let me be humbler in judging others, cheerfuller in looking out upon the future, more enkindling towards the young men who are growing up around me, and who may yet pass on the torch of the Master. For them let me recall the many souls he touched to purer flame; let me tell them of those who gave up posts and dignities to spread his gospel and endured hunger and scorn. And let me not forget to mention Rabbi Lemuel, the lover of justice, who once when his wife set out for the Judgment House in a cause against her maidservant set out with her too.

"I need you not to speak for me," she said, in ill-humor; "I can plead my own cause."

"Nay, it is not for thee I go to speak," he answered mildly; "it is the cause of thy servant I go to plead—she who hath none to defend her." And, bursting into tears, he repeated the verse of Job: "If I did despise the cause of my manservant or of my maidservant, when they contended with me, what shall I do when God riseth up?"

These and many such things, both of learned men and of simple, I hope yet to chronicle for the youths of Israel. But above all let the memory of the Master himself be to them a melody and a blessing: he whose life taught me to understand that the greatest man is not he who dwells in the purple, amid palaces and courtiers, hedged and guarded, and magnified by illusive pomp, but he who, talking cheerfully with his fellows in the market-place, humble as though he were unworshipped, and poor as though he were unregarded, is divinely enkindled, so that a light shines from him whereby men recognize the visible presence of God.

I

Happy burghers of Berlin in their Sunday best trooped through the Rosenthaler gate in the cool of the August evening for their customary stroll in the environs: few escaped noticing the recumbent ragged figure of a young man, with a long dirty beard, wailing and writhing uncouthly just outside the gate: fewer inquired what ailed him.

He answered in a strange mixture of jargons, blurring his meaning hopelessly with scraps of Hebrew, of Jewish-German, of Polish, of Russian and mis-punctuating it with choking sobs and gasps. One good soul after another turned away helpless. The stout roll of Hebrew manuscript the swarthy, unkempt creature clutched in his hand grew grimier with tears. The soldiers on guard surveyed him with professional callousness.

Only the heart of the writhing wretch knew its own bitterness, only those tear-blinded eyes saw the pitiful panorama of a penurious Jew's struggle for Culture. For, nursed in a narrow creed, he had dreamt the dream of Knowledge. To know—to know—was the passion that consumed him: to understand the meaning of life and the causes of things.

He saw himself a child again in Poland, in days of comparative affluence, clad in his little damask suit, shocking his father with a question at the very first verse of the Bible, which they began to read together when he was six years old, and which held many a box on the ear in store for his ingenuous intellect. He remembered his early efforts to imitate with chalk or charcoal the woodcuts of birds or foliage happily discovered on the title-pages of dry-as-dust Hebrew books; how he used to steal into the unoccupied, unfurnished manor-house and copy the figures on the tapestries, standing in midwinter, half-frozen, the paper in one hand, the pencil in the other; and how, when these artistic enthusiasms were sternly if admiringly checked by a father intent on siring a Rabbi, he relieved the dreary dialectics of the Talmud— so tedious to a child uninterested in divorce laws or the number of white hairs permissible in a red cow—by surreptitious nocturnal perusal of a precious store of Hebrew scientific and historical works discovered in an old cupboard in his father's study. To this chamber, which had also served as the bedroom in which the child slept with his grandmother, the young man's thoughts returned with wistful bitterness, and at the image of the innocent little figure poring over the musty volumes by the flickering firelight in the silence of the night, the mass of rags heaved yet more convulsively. How he had enjoyed putting on fresh wood after his grandmother had gone to bed, and grappling with the astronomical treatise, ignoring the grumblings of the poor old lady who lay a-cold for want of him. Ah, the lonely little boy was, indeed, in Heaven, treading the celestial circles—and by stealth, which made it all the sweeter. But that armillary sphere he had so ably made for himself out of twisted rods had undone him: his grandmother, terrified by the child's interest in these mystic convolutions, had betrayed the magical instrument to his father. Other episodes of the long pursuit of Knowledge—not to be impeded even by flogging pedagogues, diverted but slightly by marriage at the age of eleven,—crossed his mind. What ineffable rapture the first reading of Maimonides had excited, The Guide of the Perplexed supplying the truly perplexed youth with reasons for the Jewish fervor which informed him. How he had reverenced the great mediæval thinker, regarding him as the ideal of men, the most inspired of teachers. Had he not changed his own name to Maimon to pattern himself after his Master, was not even now his oath under temptation: "I swear by the reverence which I owe my great teacher, Rabbi Moses ben Maimon, not to do this act?"

But even Maimonides had not been able to allay his thirst. Maimonides was an Aristotelian, and the youth would fain drink at the fountain-head. He tramped a hundred and fifty miles to see an old Hebrew book on the Peripatetic philosophy. But Hebrew was not enough; the vast realm of Knowledge, which he divined dimly, must lie in other languages. But to learn any other language was pollution to a Jew, to teach a Jew any other was pollution to a Christian.

In his facile comprehension of German and Latin books, he had long since forgotten his first painful steps: now in his agony they recurred to mock him. He had learnt these alien alphabets by observing in some bulky Hebrew books that when the printers had used up the letters of the Hebrew alphabet to mark their sheets, they started other and foreign alphabets. How he had rejoiced to find that by help of his Jewish jargon he could worry out the meaning of some torn leaves of an old German book picked up by chance.

The picture of the innkeeper's hut, in which he had once been family-tutor, flew up irrelevantly into his mind—he saw himself expounding a tattered Pentateuch to a half-naked brood behind the stove, in a smoky room full of peasants sitting on the floor guzzling whisky, or pervaded by drunken Russian soldiery hacking the bedsteads or throwing the glasses in the faces of the innkeeper and his wife. Poor Polish Jews, cursed by poverty and tyranny! Who could be blamed for consoling himself with liquor in such a home? Besides, when one was paid only five thalers, one owed it to oneself not to refuse a dram or so. And then there came up another one-room home in which a youth with his eyes and hair had sat all night poring over Cabalistic books, much to the inconvenience of the newly married Rabbi, who had consented to teach him this secret doctrine. For this had been his Cabalistic phase, when he dreamed of conjurations and spells and the Mastership of the Name. A sardonic smile twitched the corners of his lips, as he remembered how the poor Rabbi and his pretty wife, after fruitless hints, had lent him the precious tomes to be rid of his persistent all-night sittings, and the smile lingered an instant longer as he recalled his own futile attempts to coerce the supernatural, either by the incantations of the Cabalists or the prayer-ecstasy he had learnt later from the Chassidim.

Yes, he had early discovered that all this Cabalistic mysticism was only an attempt at a scientific explanation of existence, veiled in fable and allegory. But the more reasonable he pronounced the Cabalah to be, the more he had irritated the local Cabalists who refused to have their "divine science" reduced to "reason." And so, disillusioned, he had rebounded to "human study," setting off on a pilgrimage in the depth of winter to borrow out-of-date books on optics and physics, and making more enemies by his obtrusive knowledge of how dew came and how lightning. It was not till—on the strength of a volume of Anatomical tables and a Medical dictionary—he undertook cures, that he had discovered the depths of his own ignorance, achieving only the cure of his own conceit. And it was then that Germany had begun to loom before his vision—a great, wonderful country where Truth dwelt, and Judaism was freer, grander. Yes, he would go to Germany and study medicine and escape this asphyxiating atmosphere.

His sobs, which had gradually subsided, revived at the thought of that terrible journey. First, the passage to Königsberg, accorded him by a pious merchant: then the voyage to Stettin, paid for by those young Jewish students who, beginning by laughing at his ludicrous accent in reading Herr Mendelssohn's Phœdon—the literary sensation of the hour that had dumfoundered the Voltaireans—had been thunderstruck by his instantaneous translation of it into elegant Hebrew, and had unanimously advised him to make his way to Berlin. Ah, but what a voyage! Contrary winds that protracted the journey to five weeks instead of two, the only other passenger an old woman who comforted herself by singing hymns, his own dialect and the Pomeranian German of the crew mutually unintelligible, his bed some hard stuffed bags, never anything warm to eat, and sea-sickness most of the time. And then, when set down safely on shore, without a pfennig or even a sound pocket to hold one, he had started to walk to Frankfort, oh, the wretched feeling of hopelessness that had made him cast himself down under a lime-tree in a passion of tears! Why had he resumed hope, why had he struggled on his way to Berlin, since this fate awaited him, this reception was to be meted him? To be refused admission as a rogue and a vagabond, to be rejected of his fellow-Jews, to be hustled out of his dream-city by the overseer of the Jewish gate-house!

Woe! Woe! Was this to be the end of his long aspiration? A week ago he had been so happy. After parting with his last possession, an iron spoon, for a glass of sour beer, he had come to a town where his Rabbinical diploma—to achieve that had been child's play to him—procured him the full honors of the position, despite his rags. The first seat in the synagogue had been given the tramp, and the wealthy president had invited him to his Sabbath dinner and placed him between himself and his daughter, a pretty virgin of twelve, beautifully dressed. Through his wine-glass the future had looked rosy, and his learned eloquence glowed responsively, but he had not been too drunk to miss the wry faces the girl began to make, nor to be suddenly struck dumb with shame as he realised the cause. Lying on the straw of inn-stables in garments one has not changed for seven weeks does not commend even a Rabbi to a dainty maiden. The spell of good luck was broken, and since then the learned tramp had known nothing but humiliation and hunger.

The throb of elation at the sight of the gate of Berlin had been speedily subdued by the discovery that he must bide in the poorhouse the Jews had built there till the elders had examined him. And there he had herded all day long with the sick and cripples and a lewd rabble, till evening brought the elders and his doom—a point-blank refusal to allow him to enter the city and study medicine.

Why? Why? What had they against him? He asked himself the question between his paroxysms. And suddenly, in the very midst of explaining his hard case to a new passer-by, the answer came to him and still further confused his explanations. Yes, it must have been that wolf in Rabbi's clothing he had talked to that morning in the poorhouse! the red-bearded reverend who had lent so sympathetic an ear to the tale of his life in Poland, his journey hither; so sympathetic an eye to his commentary on the great Maimonides' Guide of the Perplexed. The vile spy, the base informer! He had told the zealots of the town of the new-comer's heretical mode of thinking. They had shut him out, as one shuts out the plague.

So this was the free atmosphere, the grander Judaism he had yearned for. The town which boasted of the far-famed Moses Mendelssohn, of the paragon of wisdom and tolerance, was as petty as the Rabbi-ridden villages whose dust he had shaken off. A fierce anger against the Jews and this Mendelssohn shook him. This then was all he had gained by leaving his wife and children that he might follow only after Truth!

Perhaps herein lay his punishment. But no! He was not to blame for being saddled with a family. Marriage at eleven could by no stretch of sophism be called a voluntary act. He recalled the long, sordid, sensational matrimonial comedy of which he had been the victim; the keen competition of the parents of daughters for the hand of so renowned an infant prodigy, who could talk theology as crookedly as a graybeard. His own boyish liking for Pessel, the rich rent-farmer's daughter, had been rudely set aside when her sister fell down a cellar and broke her leg. Solomon must marry the damaged daughter, the rent-farmer had insisted to the learned boy's father, who had replied as pertinaciously, "No, I want the straight-legged sister."

The poor young man writhed afresh at the thought of his father's obstinacy. True, Rachael had a hobble in her leg, but as he had discovered years later when a humble tutor in her family, she was an amiable creature, and as her father had offered to make him joint heir to his vast fortune, he would have been settled for life, wallowing in luxury and learning. But no! his father was bent upon having Pessel, and so he, Solomon, had been beggared by his father's fastidious objection to a dislocated bone.

Alas, how misfortune had dogged him! There was that wealthy scholar of Schmilowitz who fell in love with his fame, and proposed for him by letter without ever having seen him. What a lofty epistle his father had written in reply, a pastiche of Biblical verses and Talmudical passages, the condition of consent neatly quoted from "The Song of Solomon," "Thou, O Solomon, must have a thousand pieces of silver, and those that keep the fruit thereof two hundred!" A dowry of a thousand guldens for the boy, and two hundred for the father! The terms of the Canticles had been accepted, his father had journeyed to Schmilowitz, seen his daughter-in-law, and drawn up the marriage-contract. The two hundred guldens for himself had been paid him on the nail, and he had even insisted on having four hundred.

In vain, "Here is your letter," the scholar had protested, "you only asked for two hundred."

"True," he had replied; "but that was only not to spoil the beautiful quotation."

How joyously he had returned home with the four hundred guldens for himself, the wedding-presents for his little Solomon—a cap of black velvet trimmed with gold lace, a Bible bound in green velvet with silver clasps, and the like.

The heart-broken tramp saw the innocent boy that had once been he, furtively strutting about in his velvet cap, rehearsing the theological disputation he was to hold at the wedding-table, and sniffing the cakes and preserves his mother was preparing for the feast, what time the mail was bringing the news of the sudden death of the bride from small-pox.

At the moment he had sorrowed as little for his unseen bride as his father, who, having made four hundred guldens by his son in an honorable way, might now hope to make another four hundred. "The cap and the silver-clasped Bible are already mine," the child had told himself, "and a bride will also not be long wanting, while my wedding-disputation can serve me again." The mother alone had been inconsolable, cakes and preserves being of a perishable nature, especially when there is no place to hide them from the secret attacks of a disappointed bridegroom. Only now did poor Maimon realize how his life had again missed ease! For he had fallen at last into the hands of the widow of Nesvig, with a public-house in the outskirts and an only daughter. Merely moderately prosperous but inordinately ambitious, she had dared to dream of this famous wonder-child for her Sarah. Refusal daunted her not, nor did she cease her campaign till, after trying every species of trick and manœuvre and misrepresentation, every weapon of law and illegality, she had carried home the reluctant bridegroom. By what unscrupulous warfare she had wrested him from his last chance of wealth, flourishing a prior marriage-contract in the face of the rich merchant who unluckily staying the night in her inn, had proudly shown her the document which betrothed his daughter to the renowned Solomon! The boy's mother dying at this juncture, the widow had not shrunk from obtaining from the law-courts an attachment on the dead body, by which its interment was interdicted till the termination of the suit. In vain the rich merchant had kidnapped the bridegroom in his carriage at dead of night, the boy was pursued and recaptured, to lead a life of constant quarrel with his mother-in-law, and exchange flying crockery at meal-times; to take refuge in distant tutorships, and in the course of years, after begetting several children, to drift further and further, and finally disappear beyond the frontier.

Poor Sarah! He thought of her now with softness. A likeable wench enough, active and sensible, if with something of her mother's pertinacity. No doubt she was still the widow's right hand in the public-house. Ah, how handsome she had looked that day when the drunken Prince Radziwil, in his mad freak at the inn, had set approving eyes upon her: "Really a pretty young woman! Only she ought to get a white chemise." A formula at which the soberer gentlemen of his train had given her the hint to clear out of the way.

Now in his despair, the baffled Pilgrim of Knowledge turned yearningly to her image, wept weakly at the leagues that separated him from all who cared for him. How was David growing up—his curly-haired first-born; child of his fourteenth year? He must be nearly ten by now, and in a few years he would be confirmed and become "A Son of the Commandment." A wave of his own early religious fervor came over him, bringing with it a faint flavor of festival dishes and far-away echoes of synagogue tunes. Fool, fool, not to be content with the Truth that contented his fathers, not to rest in the bosom of the wife God had given him. Even his mother-in-law was suffused with softer tints through the mist of tears. She at least appreciated him, had fought tooth and nail for him, while these gross Berliners—! He clenched his fists in fury: the full force of the injustice came home to him afresh; his palms burnt, his brow was racked with shooting pains. His mind wandered off again to Prince Radziwil and to that day in the public-house. He saw this capricious ruler marching to visit, with all the pomp of war, a village not four miles from his residence; first his battalions of infantry, artillery and cavalry, then his body-guard of volunteers from the poor nobility, then his kitchen-wagons, then his bands of music, then his royal coach in which he snored, overcome by Hungarian wine, lastly his train of lackeys. Then he saw his Serene Highness thrown on his mother-in-law's dirty bed, booted and spurred; for his gentlemen, as they passed the inn, had thought it best to give his slumbers a more comfortable posture. Here, surrounded by valets, pages, and negroes, he had snored on all night, while the indomitable widow cooked her meals and chopped her wood in the very room as usual. And here, in a sooty public-house, with broken windows, and rafters supported by undressed tree-stems, on a bed swarming with insects—the prince had awoke, and, naught perturbed, when the thing was explained, had bidden his menials prepare a banquet on the spot.

Poor Maimon's parched mouth watered now as he thought of that mad bacchanal banquet of choice wines and dishes, to which princes and lords had sat down on the dirty benches of the public-house. Goblets were drained in competition to the sound of cannon, and the judges who awarded the prize to the Prince, were presented by him with estates comprising hundreds of peasants. Maimon began to shout in imitation of the cannon, in imagination he ran amuck in a synagogue, as he had seen the prince do, smashing and wrecking everything, tearing the Holy Scrolls from the Ark and trampling upon them. Yes, they deserved it, the cowardly bigots. Down with the law, to hell with the Rabbis. A-a-a-h! He would grind the phylacteries under his heel—thus. And thus! And—

The soldiers perceiving he was in a violent fever, summoned the Jewish overseer, who carried him back into the poorhouse.

II

Maimon awoke the next morning with a clear and lively mind, and soon understood that he was sick. "God be thanked," he thought joyfully, "now I shall remain here some days, during which not only shall I eat but I may hope to prevail upon some kindly visitor to protect me. Perhaps if I can manage to send a message to Herr Mendelssohn, he will intercede for me. For a scholar must always have bowels of compassion for a scholar."

These roseate expectations were rudely dusked: the overseer felt Maimon's pulse and his forehead, and handing him his commentary on the Guide of the Perplexed, convoyed him politely without the gate. Maimon made no word of protest, he was paralyzed.

"What now, O Guide of the Perplexed?" he cried, stonily surveying his hapless manuscript. "O Moses, son of Maimon, thou by whom I have sworn so oft, canst thou help me now? See, my pockets are as empty as the heads of thy adversaries."

He turned out his pockets, and lo! several silver pieces fell out and rolled merrily in the roadway. "A miracle!" he shouted. Then he remembered that the elders had dismissed him with them, and that overcome by his sentence he had put them mechanically away. Yes, he had been treated as a mere beggar. A faint flush of shame tinged his bristly cheek at the thought. True, he had partaken of the hospitality of strangers, but that was the due meed of his position as Rabbi, as the free passages to Königsberg and Stettin were tributes to his learning. Never had he absolutely fallen to schnorring (begging). He shook his fist at the city. He would fling their money in their faces—some day. Thus swearing, he repocketed the coins, took the first turning that he met, and abandoned himself to chance. In the mean inn in which he halted for refreshment he was glad to encounter a fellow-Jew and one in companionable rags.

Maimon made inquiries from him about the roads and whither they led, and gathered with some surprise that his companion was a professional Schnorrer.

"Are not you?" asked the beggar, equally surprised.

"Certainly not!" cried Maimon angrily.

"What a waste of good rags!" said the Schnorrer.

"What a waste of good muscle!" retorted Maimon; for the beggar was a strapping fellow in rude health. "If I had your shoulders I should hold my head higher on them."

The Schnorrer shrugged them. "Only fools work. What has work brought you? Rags. You begin with work and end with rags. I begin with rags and end with meals."

"But have you no self-respect?" cried Maimon, in amaze. "No morality? No religion?"

"I have as much religion as any Schnorrer on the road," replied the beggar, bridling up. "I keep my Sabbath."

"Yes, indeed," said Maimon, smiling, "our sages say, Rather keep thy Sabbath as a week-day than beg; you say, Rather keep thy week-day as a Sabbath than be dependent on thyself." To himself he thought, "That is very witty: I must remember to tell Lapidoth that." And he called for another glass of whisky.

"Yes; but many of our sages, meseems, are dependent on their womankind. I have dispensed with woman; must I therefore dispense with support likewise?"

Maimon was amused and shocked in one. He set down his whisky, unsipped. "But he who dispenses with woman lives in sin. It is the duty of man to beget posterity, to found a home; for what is civilization but home, and what is home but religion?" The wanderer's tones were earnest; he forgot his own sins of omission in the lucidity with which his intellect saw the right thing.

"Ah, you are one of the canting ones," said the Schnorrer. "It strikes me you and I could do something better together than quarrel. What say you to a partnership?"

"In begging?"

"What else have I to offer? You are new to the country—you don't know the roads—you haven't got any money."

"Pardon me! I have a thaler left."

"No, you haven't—you pay that to me for the partnership."

The metaphysical Maimon was tickled. "But what do I gain for my thaler?"

"My experience."

"But if so, you gain nothing from my partnership."

"A thaler to begin with. Then, you see, your learning and morality will draw when I am at a loss for quotations. In small villages we go together and produce an impression of widespread misery: we speak of the destruction of our town by fire, of persecution, what you will. One beggar might be a liar: two together are martyrs."

"Then you beg only in villages?"

"Oh no. But in towns we divide. You do one half, I do another. Then we exchange halves, armed with the knowledge of who are the beneficent in either half. It is less fatiguing."

"Then the beneficent have to give twice over."

"They have double merit. Charity breeds charity."

"This is a rare fellow," thought Maimon. "How Lapidoth would delight in him! And he speaks truth. I know nothing of the country. If I travel a little with him I may learn much. And he, too, may learn from me. He has a good headpiece, and I may be able to instil into him more seemly notions of duty and virtue. Besides, what else can I do?" So, spinning his thaler in air, "Done!" he cried.

The beggar caught it neatly. "Herr Landlord," said he, "another glass of your excellent whisky!" And, raising it to his lips when it came, "Brother, here's to our partnership."

"What, none for me?" cried Maimon, crestfallen.

"Not till you had begged for it," chuckled the Schnorrer. "You have had your first lesson. Herr Landlord, yet another glass of your excellent whisky!"

And so the philosopher, whose brain was always twisting and turning the universe and taking it to pieces, started wandering about Germany with the beggar whose thoughts were bounded by his paunch. They exploited but a small area, and with smaller success than either had anticipated. Though now and then they were flush, there was never a regular meal; and too often they had to make shift with mouldly bread and water, and to lie on stale straw, and even on the bare earth.

"You don't curse enough," the beggar often protested.

"But why should one curse a man who refuses one's request?" the philosopher would persist. "Besides, he is embittered thereby, and only the more likely to refuse."

"Cork your philosophy, curse you!" the beggar would cry. "How often am I to explain to you that cursing terrifies people."

"Not at all," Maimon would mutter, terrified.

"No? What is Religion, but Fear?"

"False religion, if you will. But true religion, as Maimonides says, is the attainment of perfection through the knowledge of God and the imitation of His actions."

Nevertheless, when they begged together, Maimon produced an inarticulate whine that would do either for a plea or a curse. When he begged alone, all the glib formulæ he had learnt from the Schnorrer dried up on his tongue. But his silence pleaded more pitifully than his speech. For he was barefooted and almost naked. Yet amid all these untoward conditions his mind kept up its interminable twisting and turning of the universe; that acute analysis for which centuries of over-subtlety had prepared the Polish Jew's brain, and which was now for the first time applied scientifically to the actual world instead of fantastically to the Bible. And it was perhaps when he was lying on the bare earth that the riddle of existence—twinkling so defiantly in the stars—tortured him most keenly.

Thus passed half a year. Maimon had not learnt to beg, nor had the beggar acquired the rudiments of morality. How often the philosopher longed for his old friend Lapidoth—the grave-digger's son-in-law—to talk things over with, instead of this carnal vagabond. They had been poverty-stricken enough, those two, but oh! how differently they had taken the position. He remembered how merrily Lapidoth had pinned his dropped-off sleeve to the back of his coat, crying, "Don't I look like a Schlachziz (nobleman)?" and how he in return had vaunted the superiority of his gaping shoes: "They don't squeeze at the toes." How they had played the cynic, he and the grave-digger's son-in-law, turning up with remorseless spade the hollow bones of human virtue! As convincedly as synagogue-elders sought during fatal epidemics for the secret sins of the congregation, so had they two striven to uncover the secret sinfulness of self-deceived righteousness.

"Bad self-analysis is the foundation of contentment," Lapidoth had summed it up one day, as they lounged on the town-wall.

To which Maimon: "Then, friend, why are we so content to censure others? Let us be fair and pass judgment on ourselves. But the contemplative life we lead is merely the result of indolence, which we gloss over by reflections on the vanity of all things. We are content with our rags. Why? Because we are too lazy to earn better. We reproach the unscholarly as futile people addicted to the pleasures of sense. Why? Because, not being constituted like you and me, they live differently. Where is our superiority, when we merely follow our inclination as they follow theirs? Only in the fact that we confess this truth to ourselves, while they profess to act, not to satisfy their particular desires, but for the general utility."

"Friend," Lapidoth had replied, deeply moved, "you are perfectly right. If we cannot now mend our faults, we will not deceive ourselves about them, but at least keep the way open for amendment."

So they had encouraged each other to clearer vision and nobler living. And from such companionship to have fallen to a Schnorrer's! Oh, it was unendurable.

But he endured it till harvest-time came round, bringing with it the sacred season of New Year and Atonement, and the long chilly nights. And then he began to feel tremors of religion and cold.

As they crouched together in outhouses, the beggar snoozing placidly in a stout blouse, the philosopher shivering in tatters, Maimon saw his degradation more lucidly than ever. They had now turned their steps towards Poland, every day bringing Maimon nearer to the redeeming influence of early memories, and it was when sleeping in the Jewish poorhouse at Posen—the master of which eked out his livelihood honorably as a jobbing tailor—that Maimon at length found strength to resolve on a breach. He would throw himself before the synagogue door, and either die there or be relieved. When his companion awoke and began to plan out the day's campaign, "No, I dissolve the partnership," said he firmly.

"But how are you going to live, you good-for-nothing?" asked his astonished comrade, "you who cannot even beg."

"God will help," Maimon said stolidly.

"God help you!" said the beggar.

Maimon went off to the school-room. The master was away, and a noisy rabble of boys ceased their games or their studies to question the tatterdemalion, and to make fun of his Lithuanian accent—his s's for sh's. Nothing abashed, the philosopher made inquiries after an old friend of his who, he fortunately recollected, had gone to Posen as the Chief Rabbi's secretary. The news that the Chief Rabbi had proceeded to another appointment, taking with him his secretary, reduced him to despair. A gleam of hope broke when he learnt that the secretary's boy had been left behind in Posen with Dr. Hirsch Janow, the new Chief Rabbi.

And in the event this boy brought salvation. He informed Dr. Hirsch Janow that a great scholar and a pious man was accidentally fallen into miserable straits; and lo! in a trice the good-hearted man had sent for Maimon, sounded his scholarship and found it plumbless, approved of his desire to celebrate the sacred festivals in Posen, given him all the money in his pockets—the indurated beggar accepted it without a blush—invited him to dine with him every Sabbath, and sent the boy with him to procure him "a respectable lodging."

As he left the house that afternoon, Maimon could not help overhearing the high-pitched reproaches of the Rabbitzin (Rabbi's wife).

"There! You've again wasted my housekeeping money on scum and riff-raff. We shall never get clear of debt."

"Hush! hush!" said the Rabbi gently. "If he hears you, you will wound the feelings of a great scholar. The money was given to me to distribute."

"That story has a beard," snapped the Rabbitzin.

"He is a great saint," the boy told Maimon on the way. "He fasts every day of the week till nightfall, and eats no meat save on Sabbath. His salary is small, but everybody loves him far and wide; he is named 'the keen scholar.'" Maimon agreed with the general verdict. The gentle emaciated saint had touched old springs of religious feeling, and brought tears of more than gratitude to his eyes.

His soul for a moment felt the appeal of that inner world created by Israel's heart, that beautiful world of tenderest love and sternest law, wherein The-Holy-One-Blessed-Be-He (who has chosen Israel to preach holiness among the peoples), mystically enswathed with praying-shawl and phylacteries, prays to Himself, "May it be My will that My pity overcome My wrath."

And what was his surprise at finding himself installed, not in some mean garret, but in the study of one of the leading Jews of the town. The climax was reached when he handed some coppers to the housewife, and asked her to get him some gruel for supper.

"Nay, nay," said the housewife, smiling. "The Chief Rabbi has not recommended us to sell you gruel. My husband and my son are both scholars, and so long as you choose to tarry at Posen they will be delighted if you will honor our table."

Maimon could scarcely believe his ears; but the evidence of a sumptuous supper was irrefusable. And after that he was conducted to a clean bed! O the luxurious ache of stretching one's broken limbs on melting feathers! the nestling ecstasy of dainty-smelling sheets after half a year of outhouses!

It was the supreme felicity of his life. To wallow in such a wave of happiness had never been his before, was never to be his again. Shallow pates might prate, he told himself, but what pleasure of the intellect could ever equal that of the senses? Could it possibly pleasure him as much even to fulfil his early Maimonidean ideal—the attainment of Perfection? Perpending which problem, the philosopher fell deliciously asleep.

Late, very late, the next morning he dragged himself from his snug cocoon, and called, in response to a summons, upon his benefactor.

"Well, and how do you like your lodging?" said the gentle Rabbi.

Maimon burst into tears. "I have slept in a bed!" he sobbed, "I have slept in a bed!"

Two days later, clad—out of the Rabbitzin's housekeeping money—in full rabbinical vestments, with clean linen beneath, the metamorphosed Maimon, cheerful of countenance, and godly of mien, presented himself at the poorhouse, where the tailor and his wife, as well as his whilom mate—all of them acquainted with his good fortune—expected him with impatience. The sight of him transported them. The poor mother took her babe in her arms, and with tears in her eyes begged the Rabbi's blessings; the beggar besought his forgiveness for his rough treatment, and asked for an alms.

Maimon gave the little one his blessing, and the Schnorrer all he had in his pocket, and went back deeply affected.

Meantime his fame had spread: all the scholars of the town came to see and chop theology with this illustrious travelling Rabbi. He became a tutor in a wealthy family: his learning was accounted superhuman, and he himself almost divine. A doubt he expressed as to the healthiness of a consumptive-looking child brought him at her death the honors of a prophet. Disavowal was useless: a new prophet had arisen in Israel.

And so two happy years passed—honorably enough, unless the philosopher's forgetfulness of his family be counted against him. But little by little his restless brain and body began to weary of these superstitious surroundings.

It began to leak out that he was a heretic: his rare appearances in the synagogue were noted; daring sayings of his were darkly whispered; Persecution looked to its weapons.

Maimon's recklessness was whetted in its turn. At the entrance to the Common Hall in Posen there had been, from time immemorial, a stag-horn fixed into the wall, and an equally immemorial belief among the Jews that whoso touched it died on the spot. A score of stories in proof were hurled at the scoffing Maimon. And so, passing the stag-horn one day, he cried to his companions: "You Posen fools, do you think that any one who touches this horn dies on the spot? See, I dare to touch it."

Their eyes, dilating with horror, followed his sacrilegious hand. They awaited the thud of his body. Maimon walked on, smiling.

What had he proved to them? Only that he was a hateful heretic, a profaner of sanctuaries.

The wounded fanaticism that now shadowed him with its hatred provoked him to answering excesses. The remnant of religion that clung, despite himself, to his soul, irritated him. Would not further culture rid him of the incubus? His dream of Berlin revived. True, bigotry barked there too, but culture went on its serene course. The fame and influence of Mendelssohn had grown steadily, and it was now at its apogee, for Lessing had written Nathan Der Weise, and in the tempest that followed its production, and despite the ban placed on the play and its author in both Catholic and Protestant countries, the most fanatical Christian foes of the bold freelance could not cry that the character was impossible.

For there—in the very metropolis—lived the Sage himself, the David to the dramatist's Jonathan, the member of the Coffee-House of the Learned, the friend of Prince Lippe-Schaumberg, the King's own

Protected Jew, in every line of whose countenance Lavater kept insisting the unprejudiced phrenologist might read the soul of Socrates.

And he, Maimon, no less blessed with genius, what had he been doing, to slumber so long on these soft beds of superstition and barbarism, deaf to that early call of Truth, that youthful dream of Knowledge? Yes, he would go back to Berlin, he would shake off the clinging mists of the Ghetto, he would be the pioneer of his people's emancipation. His employers had remained throughout staunch admirers of his intellect. But despite every protest he bade them farewell, and purchasing a seat on the Frankfort post with his scanty savings set out for Berlin. No mendicity committees lay in wait for the prosperous passenger, and as the coach passed through the Rosenthaler gate, the brave sound of the horn seemed to Maimon at once a flourish of triumph over Berlin and of defiance to superstition and ignorance.

III

But superstition and ignorance were not yet unhorsed. The Jewish police-officers, though they allowed coach-gentry to enter and take up their quarters where they pleased, did not fail to pry into their affairs the next day, as well for the protection of the Jewish community against equivocal intruders as in accordance with its responsibility to the State.

In his modest lodging on the New-Market, Maimon had to face the suspicious scrutiny of the most dreaded of these detectives, who was puzzled and provoked by a belief he had seen him before, "evidently looking on me," as Maimon put it afterwards, "as a comet, which comes nearer to the earth the second time than the first, and so makes the danger more threatening."

Of a sudden this lynx-eyed bully espied a Hebrew Logic by Maimonides, annotated by Mendelssohn. "Yes! yes!" he shrieked; "that's the sort of books for me!" and, glaring threateningly at the philosopher, "Pack," he said. "Pack out of Berlin as quick as you can, if you don't wish to be led out with all the honors."

Maimon was once more in desperate case. His money was all but exhausted by the journey, and the outside of the Rosenthaler gate again menaced him. All his sufferings had availed him nothing: he was back almost at his starting-point.

But fortune favors fools. In a countryman settled at Berlin he found a protector. Then other admirers of talent and learning boarded and lodged him. The way was now clear for Culture.

Accident determined the line of march. Maimon rescued Wolff's Metaphysics from a butterman for two groschen. Wolff, he knew, was the pet philosopher of the day. Mendelssohn himself had been inspired by him—the great brother-Jew with whom he might now hope some day to talk face to face.

Maimon was delighted with his new treasure—such mathematical exposition, such serried syllogisms— till it came to theology. "The Principle of Sufficient Reason"—yes, it was a wonderful discovery. But as proving God? No—for that there was not Sufficient Reason. Nor could Maimon harmonize these new doctrines with his Maimonides or his Aristotle. Happy thought! He would set forth his doubts in Hebrew, he would send the manuscript to Herr Mendelssohn. Flushed by the hope of the great man's acquaintance, he scribbled fervidly and posted the manuscript.

He spent a sleepless night.

Would the lion of Berlin take any notice of an obscure Polish Jew? Maimon was not left in suspense. Mendelssohn replied by return. He admitted the justice of his correspondent's doubts, but begged him not to be discouraged by them, but to continue his studies with unabated zeal. O, judge in Israel! Nathan Der Weise, indeed.

Fired with such encouragement, Maimon flung himself into a Hebrew dissertation that should shatter all these theological cobwebs, that by an uncompromising Ontology should bring into doubt the foundations of Revealed as well as of Natural Theology. It was a bold thing to do, for since he was come to Berlin, and had read more of his books, he had gathered that Mendelssohn still professed Orthodox Judaism. A paradox this to Maimon, and roundly denied as impossible when he first heard of it. A man who could enter the lists with the doughtiest champions of Christendom, whose German prose was classical, who could philosophize in Socratic dialogue after the fashion of Plato—such a man a creature of the Ghetto! Doubtless he took his Judaism in some vague Platonic way; it was impossible to imagine him the literal bond-slave of that minute ritual, winding phylacteries round his left arm or shaking himself in a praying-shawl. Anyhow here—in logical lucid Hebrew—were Maimon's doubts and difficulties. If Mendelssohn was sincere, let him resolve them, and earn the blessings of a truly Jewish soul. If he was unable to answer them, let him give up his orthodoxy, or be proved a fraud and a time-server. Amicus Mendelssohn sed magis amica veritas.

In truth there was something irritating to the Polish Jew in the great German's attitude, as if it held some latent reproach of his own. Only a shallow thinker, he felt, could combine culture and spiritual comfort, to say nothing of worldly success. He had read the much-vaunted Phœdon which Lutheran Germany hailed as a counterblast to the notorious "Berlin religion," restoring faith to a despondent world mocked out of its Christian hopes by the fashionable French wits and materialists under the baneful inspiration of Voltaire, whom Germany's own Frederick had set on high in his Court. But what a curious assumption for a Jewish thinker to accept, that unless we are immortal, our acts in this world are of no consequence! Was not he, Maimon, leading a high-minded life in pursuit of Truth, with no such hope? "If our soul were mortal, then Reason would be a dream, which Jupiter has sent us in order that we might forget our misery; and we should be like the beasts, only to seek food and die." Nonsense! Rhetoric! True, his epistles to Lavater were effective enough, there was courage in his public refusal of Christianity, nobility in his sentiment that he preferred to shame anti-Jewish prejudice by character rather than by controversy. He, Maimon, would prefer to shame it by both. But this Jerusalem of Mendelssohn's! Could its thesis really be sustained? Judaism laid no yoke upon belief, only on conduct? was no reason-confounding dogma? only a revealed legislation? A Jew gave his life to the law and his heart to Germany! Or France, or Holland, or the Brazils as the case might be? Palestine must be forgotten. Well, it was all bold and clever enough, but was it more than a half-way house to assimilation with the peoples? At any rate here was a Polish brother's artillery to meet—more deadly than that of Lavater, or the stupid Christians.

Again, but with acuter anxiety, he awaited Mendelssohn's reply.

It came—an invitation for next Saturday afternoon. Aha! The outworks were stormed. The great man recognized in him a worthy foe, a brother in soul. Gratitude and vanity made the visit a delightful anticipation. What a wit-combat it would be! How he would marshal his dialectic epigrams! If only Lapidoth could be there to hear!

As the servant threw open the door for him, revealing a suite of beautiful rooms and a fine company of gentlefolks, men with powdered wigs and ladies with elegant toilettes, Maimon started back with a painful shock. An under-consciousness of mud-stained boots and a clumsily cut overcoat, mixed itself painfully with this impression of pretty, scented women, and the clatter of tongues and coffee-cups. He stood rooted to the threshold in a sudden bitter realization that the great world cared nothing about metaphysics. Ease, fine furniture, a position in the world—these were the things that counted. Why had all his genius brought him none of these things? Wifeless, childless, moneyless, he stood, a solitary soul wrestling with problems. How had Mendelssohn managed to obtain everything? Doubtless he had had a better start, a rich father, a University training. His resentment against the prosperous philosopher rekindled. He shrank back and closed the door. But it was opened instantly again from within. A little hunchback with shining eyes hurried towards him.

"Herr Maimon?" he said inquiringly, holding out his hand with a smile of welcome.

Startled, Maimon laid his hand without speaking in that cordial palm. So this was the man he had envied. No one had ever told him that "Nathan der Weise" was thus afflicted. It was as soul that he had appealed to the imagination of the world; even vulgar gossip had been silent about his body. But how this deformity must embitter his success.

Mendelssohn coaxed him within, complimenting him profusely on his writings: he was only too familiar with these half-shy, half-aggressive young Poles, whose brains were bursting with heretical ideas and sick fantasies. They brought him into evil odor with his orthodox brethren, did these "Jerusalem Werthers," but who should deal with them, if not he that understood them, that could handle them delicately? What was to Maimon a unique episode was to his host an everyday experience.

Mendelssohn led Maimon to the embrasure of a window: he brought him refreshments—which the young man devoured uncouthly—he neglected his fashionable guests, whose unceasing French babble proclaimed their ability to get on by themselves, to gain an insight into this gifted young man's soul. He regarded each new person as a complicated piece of wheelwork, which it was the wise man's business to understand and not be angry with. But having captured the secret of the mechanism, it was one's duty to improve it on its own lines.

"Your dissertation displays extraordinary acumen, Herr Maimon," he said. "Of course you still suffer from the Talmudic method or rather want of method. But you have a real insight into metaphysical problems. And yet you have only read Wolff! You are evidently not a Chamor nosé Sefarim (a donkey bearing books)." He used the Hebrew proverb to make the young Pole feel at home, and a half smile hovered around his sensitive lips. Even his German took on a winning touch of jargon in vocabulary and accentuation, though to kill the jargon was one of the ideals of his life.

"Nay, Herr Mendelssohn," replied Maimon modestly; "you must not forget The Guide of the Perplexed. It was the inspiration of my youth!"

"Was it?" cried Mendelssohn delightedly. "So it was of mine. In fact I tell the Berliners Maimonides was responsible for my hump, and some of them actually believe I got it bending over him."

This charming acceptance of his affliction touched the sensitive Maimon and put him more at ease than even the praise of his writings and the fraternal vocabulary. "In my country," he said, "a perfect body is thought to mark the fool of the family! They believe the finest souls prefer to inhabit imperfect tenements."

Mendelssohn bowed laughingly. "An excellently turned compliment! At this rate you will soon shine in our Berlin society. And how long is it since you left Poland?"

"Alas! I have left Poland more than once. I should have had the honor and the happiness of making your acquaintance earlier, had I not been stopped at the Rosenthaler gate three years ago."

"At the Rosenthaler gate! If I had only known!"

The tears came into Maimon's eyes—tears of gratitude, of self-pity, of regret for the lost years. He was on his feet now, he felt, and his feet were on the right road. He had found a powerful protector at last. "Think of my disappointment," he said tremulously, "after travelling all the way from Poland."

"Yes, I know. I was all but stopped at the gate myself," said Mendelssohn musingly.

"You?"

"Yes—when I was a lad."

"Aren't you a native of Berlin, then?"

"No, I was born in Dessau. Not so far to tramp from as Poland. But still a goodish stretch. It took me five days—I am not a Hercules like you—and had I not managed to stammer out that I wished to enrol myself among the pupils of Dr. Frankel, the new Chief Rabbi of the city, the surly Cerberus would have slammed the gate in my face. My luck was that Frankel had come from Dessau, and had been my teacher. I remember standing on a hillock crying as he was leaving for Berlin, and he took me in his arms and said I should also go to Berlin some day. So when I appeared he had to make the best of it."

"Then you had nothing from your parents?"

"Only a beautiful handwriting from my father which got me copying jobs for a few groschens and is now the joy of the printers. He was a scribe, you know, and wrote the Scrolls of the Law. But he wanted me to be a pedlar."

"A pedlar!" cried Maimon, open-eyed.

"Yes, the money would come in at once, you see. I had quite a fight to persuade him I would do better as a Rabbi. I fear I was a very violent and impatient youngster. He didn't at all believe in my Rabbinical future. And he was right after all—for a member of a learned guild, Jewish or Christian, have I never been."

"You had a hard time, then, when you came to Berlin?" said Maimon sympathetically.

Mendelssohn's eyes had for an instant an inward look, then he quoted gently, "Bread with salt shalt thou eat, water by measure shalt thou drink, upon the hard earth shalt thou sleep, and a life of anxiousness shalt thou live, and labor in the study of the law!"

Maimon thrilled at the quotation: the fine furniture and the fine company faded, and he saw only the soul of a fellow-idealist to which these things were but unregarded background.

"Ah yes," went on Mendelssohn. "You are thinking I don't look like a person who once notched his loaf into sections so as not to eat too much a day. Well, let it console you with the thought that there's a comfortable home in Berlin waiting for you, too."

Poor Maimon stole a glance at the buxom, blue-eyed matron doing the honors of her salon so gracefully, assisted by two dazzling young ladies in Parisian toilettes—evidently her daughters—and he groaned at the thought of his peasant-wife and his uncouth, superstition-swaddled children: decidedly he must give Sarah a divorce.

"I can't delude myself with such day-dreams," he said hopelessly.

"Wait! Wait! So long as you don't day-dream your time away. That is the danger with you clever young Poles—you are such dreamers. Everything in this life depends on steadiness and patience. When we first set up hospitality, Fromet—my wife—and I, we had to count the almonds and raisins for dessert. You see, we only began with a little house and garden in the outskirts, the main furniture of which," he said, laughing at the recollection, "was twenty china apes, life-size."

"Twenty china apes!"

"Yes, like every Jewish bridegroom, I had to buy a quantity of china for the support of the local manufactory, and that was what fell to me. Ah, my friend, what have not the Jews of Germany to support! The taxes are still with us, but the Rishus (malice)"—again he smiled confidentially at the Hebrew-jargon word—"is less every day. Why, a Jew couldn't walk the streets of Berlin without being hooted and insulted, and my little ones used to ask, 'Father, is it wicked to be a Jew?' I thank the Almighty that at the end of my days I have lived to see the Jewish question raised to a higher plane."

"I should rather thank you," cried Maimon, with sceptical enthusiasm.

"Me?" said Mendelssohn, with the unfeigned modesty of the man who, his every public utterance having been dragged out of him by external compulsion, retains his native shyness and is alone in ignorance of his own influence. "No, no, it is Montesquieu, it is Dohm, it is my dear Lessing. Poor fellow, the Christian bigots are at him now like a plague of stinging insects. I almost wish he hadn't written Nathan der Weise. I am glad to reflect I didn't instigate him, nay, that he had written a play in favor of the Jews ere we met."

"How did you come to know him?"

"I hardly remember. He was always fond of outcasts—a true artistic temperament, that preferred to consort with actors and soldiers rather than with the beer-swilling middle-class of Berlin. Oh yes, I think we met over a game of chess. Then we wrote an essay on Pope together. Dear Gotthold! What do I not owe him? My position in Berlin, my feeling for literature—for we Jews have all stifled our love for the beautiful and grown dead to poetry."

"Well, but what is a poet but a liar?"

"Ah, my dear Herr Maimon, you will grow out of that. I must lend you Homer. Intellectual speculation is not everything. For my part, I have never regretted withdrawing a portion of my love from the worthy matron, philosophy, in order to bestow it on her handmaid, belles-lettres. I am sorry to use a French word, but for once there's no better. You smile to see a Jew more German than the Germans."

"No, I smile to hear what sounds like French all round! I remember reading in your Philosophical Conversations your appeal to the Germans not to exchange their own gold for the tinsel of their neighbors."

"Yes, but what can one do? It is a Berlin mania; and, you know, the King himself.... Our Jewish girls first caught it to converse with the young gallants who came a-borrowing of their fathers, but the influence of my dear daughters—there, the beautiful one is Dorothea, the eldest, and that other, who takes more after me, is Henrietta—their influence is doing much to counteract the wave of flippancy and materialism. But fancy any one still reading my Philosophical Conversations—my 'prentice work. I had no idea of printing it. I lent the manuscript to Lessing, observing jestingly that I, too, could write like Shaftesbury, the Englishman. And lo! the next time I met him he handed me the proofs. Dear Gotthold."

"Is it true that the King—?"

"Sent for me to Potsdam to scold me? You are thinking of another matter. That was in my young days." He smiled and lowered his voice. "I ventured to hint in a review that His Majesty's French verses—I am glad by the way he has lived to write some against Voltaire—were not perfection. I thought I had wrapped up my meaning beyond royal comprehension. But a malicious courtier, the preacher Justi, denounced me as a Jew who had thrown aside all reverence for the most sacred person of His Majesty. I was summoned to Sans-Souci and—with a touch of Rishus (malice)—on a Saturday. I managed to be there without breaking my Shabbos (Sabbath)."

"Then he does keep Sabbath!" thought Maimon, in amaze.

"But, as you may imagine, I was not as happy as a bear with honey. However, I pleaded that he who makes verses plays at nine-pins, and he who plays at nine-pins, be he monarch or peasant, must be satisfied with the judgment of the boy who has charge of the bowls."

"And you are still alive!"

"To the annoyance of many people. I fancy His Majesty was ashamed to punish me before the French cynics of his court, and I know on good authority that it was because the Marquis D'Argens was astonished to learn that I could be driven out of Berlin at any moment by the police that the King made me a Schutz-Jude (protected Jew). So I owe something to the French after all. My friends had long been urging me to sue for protection, but I thought, as I still think, that one ought not to ask for any rights which the humblest Jew could not enjoy. However, a king's gift horse one cannot look in the mouth. And now you are to become my Schutz-Jude"—Maimon's heart beat gratefully—"and the question is, what do you propose to do in Berlin? What is the career that is to bring you a castle and a princess?"

"I wish to study medicine."

"Good. It is the one profession a Jew may enter here; though, you must know, however great a practice you may attain—even among the Christians—they will never publish your name in the medical list. Still, we must be thankful for small mercies. In Frankfort the Jewish doctors are limited to four, in other towns to none. We must hand you over to Dr. Herz—there, that man who is laughing so, over one of his own good things, no doubt—that is Dr. Herz, and the beautiful creature is his wife, Henrietta, who is founding a Goethe salon. She and my daughters are inseparable—a Jewish trinity. And so, Herr Physician, I extend to you the envious congratulations of a book-keeper."

"But you are not a book-keeper!"

"Not now, but that was what I began as—or rather, what I drifted into, for I was Talmudical tutor in his family, when my dear Herr Bernhardt proposed it to me. And I am not sorry. For it left me plenty of time to learn Latin and Greek and mathematics, and finally landed me in a partnership. Still I have always been a race-horse burdened with a pack, alas! I don't mean my hump, but the factory still steals a good deal of my time and brains, and if I didn't rise at five—But you have made me quite egoistic—it is the resemblance of our young days that has touched the spring of memories. But come! let me introduce you to my wife and my son Abraham. Ah, see, poor Fromet is signalling to me. She is tired of being left to battle single-handed. Would you not like to know M. de Mirabeau? Or let me introduce you to Wessely—he will talk to you in Hebrew. It is Wessely who does all the work for which I am praised—it is he who is elevating our Jewish brethren, with whom I have not the heart nor the courage to strive. Or there is Nicolai, the founder of 'The Library of the Fine Arts,' to which," he added with a sly smile, "I hope yet to see you contributing. Perhaps Fräulein Reimarus will convert you—that charming young lady there talking with her brother-in-law, who is a Danish state-councillor. She is the great friend of Lessing—as I live, there comes Lessing himself. I am sure he would like the pleasure of your acquaintance."

"Because he likes outcasts? No, no, not yet," and Maimon, whose mood had been growing dark again, shrank back, appalled by these great names. Yes, he was a dreamer and a fool, and Mendelssohn was a sage, indeed. In his bitterness he distrusted even his own Dissertation, his uncompromising logic, destructive of all theology. Perhaps Mendelssohn was right: perhaps he had really solved the Jewish problem. To be a Jew among Germans, and a German among Jews: to reconcile the old creed with Culture: to hold up one's head, and assert oneself as an honorable element in the nation—was not this catholic gathering a proof of the feasibility of such an ideal? Good sense! What true self-estimate as well as wit in the sage's famous retort to the swaggering German officer who asked him what commodity he dealt in. "In that which you appear to need—good sense." Maimon roused himself to listen to the conversation. It changed to German under the impulse of the host, who from his umpire's chair controlled it with play of eye, head, or hand; and when appealed to, would usually show that both parties were fighting about words, not things. Maimon noted from his semi-obscure retreat that the talk grew more serious and connected, touched problems. He saw that for Mendelssohn as for himself nothing really existed but the great questions. Flippant interruptions the sage seemed to disregard, and if the topic dribbled out into irrelevancies he fell silent. Maimon studied the noble curve of his forehead, the decided nose, the prominent lips, in the light of Herr Lavater's theories. Lessing said little: he had the air of a broken man. The brilliant life of the culture-warrior was closing in gloom—wife, child, health, money, almost reputation, gone: the nemesis of genius.

At one point a lady strove to concentrate attention upon herself by accusing herself of faults of character. Even Maimon understood she was angling for compliments. But Mendelssohn gravely bade her mend her faults, and Maimon saw Lessing's harassed eyes light up for the first time with a gleam of humor. Then the poet, as if roused to recollection, pulled out a paper, "I almost forgot to give you back Kant's letter," he said. "You are indeed to be congratulated."

Mendelssohn blushed like a boy, and made a snatch at the letter, but Lessing jestingly insisted on reading it to the company.

"I consider that in your Jerusalem you have succeeded in combining our religion with such a degree of freedom of conscience, as was never imagined possible, and of which no other faith can boast. You have at the same time so thoroughly and so clearly demonstrated the necessity of unlimited liberty of conscience, that ultimately our Church will also be led to reflect how it should remove from its midst everything that disturbs and oppresses conscience, which will finally unite all men in their view of the essential points of religion."

There was an approving murmur throughout the company. "Such a letter would compensate me for many more annoyances than my works have brought me," said Mendelssohn. "And to think," he added laughingly, "that I once beat Kant in a prize competition. A proof of the power of lucid expression over profound thought. And that I owe to your stimulus, Lessing."

The poet made a grimace. "You accuse me of stimulating superficiality!"

There was a laugh.

"Nay, I meant you have torn away the thorns from the roses of philosophy! If Kant would only write like you—"

"He might understand himself," flashed the beautiful Henrietta Herz.

"And lose his disciples," added her husband. "That is really, Herr Mendelssohn, why we pious Jews are so angry with your German translation of the Bible—you make the Bible intelligible."

"Yes, they have done their best to distort it," sighed Mendelssohn. "But the fury my translation arouses among the so-called wise men of the day, is the best proof of its necessity. When I first meditated producing a plain Bible in good German, I had only the needs of my own children at heart, then I allowed myself to be persuaded it might serve the multitude, now I see it is the Rabbis who need it most. But centuries of crooked thinking have deadened them to the beauties of the Bible: they have left it behind them as elementary, when they have not themselves coated it with complexity. Subtle misinterpretation is everything, a beautiful text, nothing. And then this corrupt idiom of theirs—than which nothing more corrupts a nation—they have actually invested this German jargon with sanctity, and I am a wolf in sheep's clothing for putting good German in Hebrew letters. Even the French Jews, Cerf Berr tells me, think bad German holy. To say nothing of Austria."

"Wait, wait!" said an eager-eyed man; "the laws of the Emperor Joseph will change all that—once the Jews of Vienna are forced to go to school with the sciences, they will become an honored element of the nation."

Mendelssohn shook a worldly-wise head. "Not so fast, my dear Wessely, not so fast. Your Hebrew Ode to the Austrian Emperor was unimpeachable as poetry, but, I fear, visionary as history. Who knows that this is more than a temporary political move?"

"And we pious Jews," put in Dr. Herz, smiling, "you forget, Herr Wessely, we are not so easily schooled. We have never forgiven our Mendelssohn for saying our glorious religion had accumulated cobwebs. It is the cobwebs we love, not the port."

"Yes, indeed," broke in Maimon, so interested that he forgot his own jargon, to say nothing of his attire. "When I was in Poland, I crawled nicely into mud, through pointing out that they ought not to turn to the east in praying, because Jerusalem, which, in accordance with Talmudic law, they turned to, couldn't lie due east of everywhere. In point of fact we were north-west, so that they should have turned"—his thumbs began to turn and his voice to take on the Talmudic sing-song—"south-east. I told them it was easy in each city to compute the exact turning, by corners and circles—"

"By spherical trigonometry, certainly," said Mendelssohn pleasantly. Maimon, conscious of a correction, blushed and awoke to find himself the centre of observation. His host made haste to add, "You remind me of the odium I incurred by agreeing with the Duke of Mecklenburg-Schwerin's edict, that we should not bury our dead before the third day. And this in spite of my proofs from the Talmud! Dear, dear, if the Rabbis were only as anxious to bury dead ideas as dead bodies!" There was a general smile, but Maimon said boldly—

"I think you treat them far too tolerantly."

"What, Herr Maimon," and Mendelssohn smiled the half-sad smile of the sage, who has seen the humors of the human spectacle and himself as part of it—"would you have me rebuke intolerance by intolerance? I will admit that when I was your age—and of an even hotter temper—I could have made a pretty persecutor. In those days I contributed to the mildest of sheets, 'The Moral Preacher,' we young blades called it. But because it didn't reek of religion, on every page the pious scented atheism. I could have whipped the dullards or cried with vexation. Now I see intolerance is a proof of earnestness as well as of stupidity. It is well that men should be alert against the least rough breath on the blossoms of faith they cherish. The only criticism that still has power to annoy me is that of the timid, who fear it is provoking persecution for a Jew to speak out. But for the rest, opposition is the test-furnace of new ideas. I do my part in the world, it is for others to do theirs. As soon as I had yielded my translation to friend Dubno, to be printed, I took my soul in my hands, raised my eyes to the mountains, and gave my back to the smiters. All the same I am sorry it is the Rabbi of Posen who is launching these old-fashioned thunders against the German Pentateuch of "Moses of Dessau," for both as a Talmudist and mathematician Hirsch Janow has my sincere respect. Not in vain is he styled 'the keen scholar,' and from all I hear he is a truly good man."

"A saint!" cried Maimon enthusiastically, again forgetting his shyness. His voice faltered as he drew a glowing panegyric of his whilom benefactor, and pictured him as about to die in the prime of life, worn out by vigils and penances. In a revulsion of feeling, fresh stirrings of doubt of the Mendelssohnian solution agitated his soul. Though he had but just now denounced the fanatics, he was conscious of a strange sympathy with this lovable ascetic who fasted every day, torturing equally his texts and himself, this hopeless mystic for whom there could be no bridge to modern thought; all the Polish Jew in him revolted irrationally against the new German rationalism. No, no; it must be all or nothing. Jewish Catholicism was not to be replaced by Jewish Protestantism. These pathetic zealots, clinging desperately to the past, had a deeper instinct, a truer prevision of the future, than this cultured philosopher.

"Yes, what you tell me of Hirsch Janow goes with all I have heard," said Mendelssohn calmly. "But I put my trust in time and the new generation. I will wager that the translation I drew up for my children will be read by his."

Maimon happened to be looking over Mendelssohn's shoulder at his charming daughters in their Parisian toilettes. He saw them exchange a curious glance that raised their eyebrows sceptically. With a flash of insight he caught their meaning. Mendelssohn seeking an epigram had stumbled into a dubious oracle.

"The translation I drew up for my children will be read by his."

By his, perhaps.

But by my own?

Maimon shivered with an apprehension of tragedy. Perhaps it was his Dissertation that Mendelssohn's children would read. He remembered suddenly that Mendelssohn had said no word to its crushing logic.

As he was taking his leave, he put the question point-blank. "What have you to say to my arguments?"

"You are not in the right road at present," said Mendelssohn, holding his hand amicably, "but the course of your inquiries must not be checked. Doubt, as Descartes rightly says, is the beginning of philosophical speculation."

He left the Polish philosopher on the threshold, agitated by a medley of feelings.

IV

This mingled attitude of Maimon the Fool towards Nathan the Wise continued till the death of the Sage plunged Berlin into mourning, and the Fool into vain regrets for his fits of disrespect towards one, the great outlines of whose character stood for ever fixed by the chisel of death. "Quis desiderio sit pudor aut modus tam cari capitis?" he wrote in his autobiography.

Too often had he lost his temper—particularly when Spinoza was the theme—and had all but accused Mendelssohn of dishonesty. Was not Truth the highest ideal? And was not Spinoza as irrefutable as Euclid. What! Could the emancipated intellect really deny that marvellous thinker, who, after a century of unexampled obloquy, was the acknowledged prophet of the God of the future, the inspirer of Goethe, and all that was best in modern thought! But no, Mendelssohn held stubbornly to his own life-system, never would admit that his long spiritual happiness had been based on a lie. It was highly unreasonable and annoying of him, and his formula for closing discussions, "We must hold fast not to words but to the things they signify," was exasperatingly answerable. How strange that after the restless Maimon had of himself given up Spinoza, the Sage's last years should have been clouded by the alleged Spinozism of his dear dead Lessing.

But now that the Sage himself was dead, the Fool remembered his infinite patience—the patience not of bloodlessness, but of a passionate soul that has conquered itself—not to be soured by a fool's disappointing career, nor even by his bursts of profligacy.

For Maimon's life held many more vicissitudes, but the profession of medicine was never of them. "I require of every man of sound mind that he should lay out for himself a plan of action," said the philosopher; and wandered to Breslau, to Amsterdam, to Potsdam, the parasite of protectors, the impecunious hack of publishers, the rebel of manners, the ingenious and honored metaphysician. When Kant declared he was the only one of his critics that understood The Critique of Pure Reason, Maimon returned to Berlin to devote himself to the philosophical work that was to give him a pinnacle apart among the Kantians. Goethe and Schiller made flattering advances to him. Berlin society was at his feet. But he remained to the end, shiftless and feckless, uncouth and unmanageable, and not seldom when the taverns he frequented were closed, he would wander tipsily through the sleeping streets meditating suicide, or arguing metaphysics with expostulant watchmen.

"For all his mathematics," a friend said of him, "he never seems to think of the difference between plus and minus in money matters." "People like you, there's no use trying to help," said another, worn-out, when Maimon pleaded for only a few coppers. Yet he never acquired the beggar's servility, nay, was often himself the patron of some poorer hanger-on, for whom he would sacrifice his last glass of beer. Curt in his manners, he refused to lift his hat or embrace his acquaintances in cold blood. Nor would he wear a wig. Pure Reason alone must rule.

So, clad in an all-concealing overcoat, the unshaven philosopher might be seen in a coffee-house or on an ale-house bench, scribbling at odd moments his profound essays on Transcendental Philosophy, the leaves flying about and losing themselves, and the thoughts as ill-arranged, for the Hebrew Talmudical manner still clung to his German writing as to his talking, so that the body swayed rhythmically, his thumb worked and his voice chanted the sing-song of piety to ideas that would have paralyzed the Talmud school. It was in like manner that when he lost a game of chess or waxed hot in argument, his old Judean-Polish mother jargon came back to him. His old religion he had shed completely, yet a synagogue-tune could always move him to tears. Sometimes he might be seen at the theatre, sobbing hysterically at tragedies or laughing boisterously over comedies, for he had long since learned to love Homer and the humane arts, though at first he was wont to contend that no vigor of literary expression could possibly excel his mother-in-law's curses. Not that he ever saw her again: his wife and eldest son tracked him to Breslau, but only in quest of ducats and divorce: the latter of which Maimon conceded after a legal rigmarole. But he took no advantage of his freedom. A home of his own he never possessed, save an occasional garret where he worked at an unsteady table—one leg usually supported by a folio volume—surrounded by the cats and dogs whom he had taken to solacing himself with. And even if lodged in a nobleman's palace, his surroundings were no cleaner. In Amsterdam he drove the Dutch to despair: even German housekeepers were stung to remonstrance. Yet the charm of his conversation, the brilliancy of his intellect kept him always well-friended. And the fortune which favors fools watched over his closing years, and sent the admiring Graf Kalkreuth, an intellectual Silesian nobleman, to dig him out of miserable lodgings, and instal him in his own castle near Freistadt.

As he lay upon his luxurious death-bed in the dreary November dusk, dying at forty-six of a neglected lung-trouble, a worthy Catholic pastor strove to bring him to a more Christian frame of mind.

"What matters it?" protested the sufferer; "when I am dead, I am gone."

"Can you say that, dear friend," rejoined the Pastor, with deep emotion. "How? Your mind, which amid the most unfavorable circumstances ever soared to higher attainments, which bore such fair flowers and fruits—shall it be trodden in the dust along with the poor covering in which it has been clothed? Do you not feel at this moment that there is something in you which is not body, not matter, not subject to the conditions of space and time?"

"Ah!" replied Maimon, "there are beautiful dreams and hopes—"

"Which will surely be fulfilled. Should you not wish to come again into the society of Mendelssohn?"

Maimon was silent.

Suddenly the dying man cried out, "Ay me! I have been a fool, the most foolish among the most foolish." The thought of Nathan the Wise was indeed as a fiery scourge. Too late he realized that the passion for Truth had destroyed him. Knowledge alone was not sufficient for life. The will and the emotions demanded their nutriment and exercise as well as the intellect. Man was not made merely to hunt an abstract formula, pale ghost of living realities.

"To seek for Truth"—yes, it was one ideal. But there remained also—as the quotation went on which Mendelssohn's disciples had chosen as their motto—"To love the beautiful, to desire the good, to do the best." Mendelssohn with his ordered scheme of harmonious living, with his equal grasp of thought and life, sanely balanced betwixt philosophy and letters, learning and business, according so much to Hellenism, yet not losing hold of Hebraism, and adjusting with equal mind the claims of the Ghetto and the claims of Culture, Mendelssohn shone before Maimon's dying eyes, as indeed the Wise.

The thinker had a last gleam of satisfaction in seeing so lucidly the springs of his failure as a human being. Happiness was the child of fixedness—in opinions, in space. Soul and body had need of a centre, a pivot, a home.

He had followed the hem of Truth to the mocking horizon: he had in turn fanatically adopted every philosophical system Peripatetic, Spinozist, Leibnozist, Leibnitzian, Kantian—and what did he know now he was going beyond the horizon? Nothing. He had won a place among the thinkers of Germany. But if he could only have had his cast-off son to close his dying eyes, and could only have believed in the prayers his David would have sobbed out, how willingly would he have consented to be blotted out from the book of fame. A Passover tune hummed in his brain, sad, sweet tears sprang to his eyes—yea, his soul found more satisfaction in a meaningless melody charged with tremulous memories of childhood, than in all the philosophies.

A melancholy synagogue refrain quavered on his lips, his soul turned yearningly towards these ascetics and mystics, whose life was a voluntary martyrdom to a misunderstood righteousness, a passionate sacrifice to a naïve conception of the cosmos. The infinite pathos of their lives touched him to forgetfulness of his own futility. His soul went out to them, but his brain denied him the comfort of their illusions.

He set his teeth and waited for death.

The Pastor spoke again: "Yes, you have been foolish. But that you say so now shows your soul is not beyond redemption. Christ is ever on the threshold."

Maimon made an impatient gesture. "You asked me if I should not like to see Mendelssohn again. How do you suppose I could face him, if I became a Christian?"

"You forget, my dear Maimon, he knows the Truth now. Must he not rejoice that his daughters have fallen upon the bosom of the Church?"

Maimon sat up in bed with a sudden shock of remembrance that set him coughing.

"Dorothea, but not Henrietta?" he gasped painfully.

"Henrietta too. Did you not know? And Abraham Mendelssohn also has just had his boy Felix baptized— a wonder-child in music, I hear."

Maimon fell back on his pillow, overcome with emotions and thoughts. The tragedy latent in that smile of the sisters had developed itself.

He had long since lost touch with Berlin, ceased to interest himself in Judaism, its petty politics, but now his mind pieced together vividly all that had reached him of the developments of the Jewish question since Mendelssohn's death: the battle of old and new, grown so fierce that the pietists denied the reformers Jewish burial; young men scorning their fathers and crying, "Culture, Culture; down with the Ghetto"; many in the reaction from the yoke of three thousand years falling into braggart profligacy, many more into fashionable Christianity. And the woman of the new generation no less apostate, Henrietta Herz bringing beautiful Jewesses under the fascination of brilliant Germans and the romantic movement, so that Mendelssohn's own daughter, Dorothea, had left her husband and children to live with Schlegel, and the immemorial chastity of the Jewess was undermined. And instead of the honorable estimation of his people Mendelssohn had worked for, a violent reaction against the Jews, fomented spiritually by Schleiermacher with his "transcendental Christianity," and politically by Gentz with his cry of "Christian Germany": both men lions of the Jewish-Christian Salon which Mendelssohn had made possible. And the only Judaism that stood stable amid this flux, the ancient rock of Rabbinism he had sought to dislodge, the Amsterdam Jewry refusing even the civil rights for which he had fought.

"Poor Mendelssohn!" thought the dying Maimon. "Which was the Dreamer after all, he or I? Well for him, perhaps, that his Phœdon is wrong, that he will never know."

The gulf between them vanished, and in a last flash of remorseless insight he saw himself and Mendelssohn at one in the common irony of human destiny.

He murmured: "And how dieth the wise? As the fool."

"What do you say?" said the Pastor.

"It is a verse from the Bible."

"Then are you at peace?"

"I am at peace."

FROM A MATTRESS GRAVE

["I am a Jew, I am a Christian. I am tragedy, I am comedy—Heraclitus and Democritus in one: a Greek, a Hebrew: an adorer of despotism as incarnate in Napoleon, an admirer of communism as embodied in Proudhon; a Latin, a Teuton; a beast, a devil, a god."

"God's satire weighs heavily upon me. The Great Author of the Universe, the Aristophanes of Heaven, was bent on demonstrating with crushing force to me, the little earthly so-called German Aristophanes, how my weightiest sarcasms are only pitiful attempts at jesting in comparison with His, and how miserably I am beneath Him in humor, in colossal mockery."]

The carriage stopped, and the speckless footman, jumping down, inquired: "Monsieur Heine?"

The concierge, knitting beside the porte cochère, looked at him, looked at the glittering victoria he represented, and at the grande dame who sat in it, shielding herself with a parasol from the glory of the Parisian sunlight. Then she shook her head.

"But this is number three, Avenue Matignon?"

"Yes, but Monsieur receives only his old friends. He is dying."

"Madame knows. Take up her name.'"

The concierge glanced at the elegant card. She saw "Lady"—which she imagined meant an English Duchesse—and words scribbled on it in pencil.

"It is au cinquième," she said, with a sigh.

"I will take it up."

Ere he returned, Madame descended and passed from the sparkling sunshine into the gloom of the portico, with a melancholy consciousness of the symbolic. For her spirit, too, had its poetic intuitions and insights, and had been trained by friendship with one of the wittiest and tenderest women of her time to some more than common apprehension of the greater spirit at whose living tomb she was come to worship. Hers was a fine face, wearing the triple aristocracy of beauty, birth, and letters. The complexion was of lustreless ivory, the black hair wound round and round. The stateliness of her figure completed the impression of a Roman matron.

"Monsieur Heine begs that your ladyship will do him the honor of mounting, and will forgive him the five stories for the sake of the view."

Her ladyship's sadness was tinctured by a faint smile at the message, which the footman delivered without any suspicion that the view in question meant the view of Heine himself. But then that admirable menial had not the advantage of her comprehensive familiarity with Heine's writings. She crossed the blank stony courtyard and curled up the curving five flights, her mind astir with pictures and emotions.

She had scribbled on her card a reminder of her identity; but could he remember, after all those years, and in his grievous sickness, the little girl of eleven who had sat next to him at the Boulogne table d'hôte? And she herself could now scarcely realize at times that the stout, good-natured, short-sighted little man with the big white brow, who had lounged with her daily at the end of the pier, telling her stories, was the most mordant wit in Europe, "the German Aristophanes"; and that those nursery tales, grotesquely compact of mermaids, water-sprites, and a funny old French fiddler with a poodle that diligently took three baths a day, were the frolicsome improvisations of perhaps the greatest lyric poet of his age. She recalled their parting: "When you go back to England, you can tell your friends that you have seen Heinrich Heine!"

To which the little girl: "And who is Heinrich Heine?"

A query which had set the blue-eyed little man roaring with laughter.

These things might be vivid still to her vision: they colored all she had read since from his magic pen— the wonderful poems interpreting with equal magic the romance of strange lands and times, or the modern soul, naked and unashamed, as if clothed in its own complexity; the humorous-tragic questionings of the universe; the delicious travel-pictures and fantasies; the lucid criticisms of art, and politics, and philosophy, informed with malicious wisdom, shimmering with poetry and wit. But, as for him, doubtless she and her ingenuous interrogation had long since faded from his tumultuous life.

The odors of the sick-room recalled her to the disagreeable present. In the sombre light she stumbled against a screen covered with paper painted to look like lacquer-work, and, as the slip-shod old nurse in her serre-tête motioned her forward, she had a dismal sense of a lodging-house interior, a bourgeois barrenness enhanced by two engravings after Léopold Robert, depressingly alien from that dainty boudoir atmosphere of the artist-life she knew.

But this sordid impression was swallowed up in the vast tragedy behind the screen. Upon a pile of mattresses heaped on the floor lay the poet. He had raised himself a little on his pillows, amid which showed a longish, pointed, white face with high cheek-bones, a Grecian nose, and a large pale mouth, wasted from the sensualism she recollected in it to a strange Christ-like beauty. The outlines of the shrivelled body beneath the sheet seemed those of a child of ten, and the legs looked curiously twisted. One thin little hand, as of transparent wax, delicately artistic, upheld a paralyzed eyelid, through which he peered at her.

"Lucy Liebchen!" he piped joyously. "So you have found out who Heinrich Heine is!"

He used the familiar German "du"; for him she was still his little friend. But to her the moment was too poignant for speech. The terrible passages in the last writings of this greatest of autobiographers, which she had hoped poetically colored, were then painfully, prosaically true.

"Can it be that I still actually exist? My body is so shrunk that there is hardly anything left of me but my voice, and my bed makes me think of the melodious grave of the enchanter Merlin, which is in the forest of Broceliand in Brittany, under high oaks whose tops shine like green flames to heaven. Oh, I envy thee those trees, brother Merlin, and their fresh waving. For over my mattress grave here in Paris no green leaves rustle, and early and late I hear nothing but the rattle of carriages, hammering, scolding, and the jingle of pianos. A grave without rest, death without the privileges of the departed, who have no longer any need to spend money, or to write letters, or to compose books...."

And then she thought of that ghastly comparison of himself to the ancient German singer—the poor clerk of the Chronicle of Limburg—whose sweet songs were sung and whistled from morning to night all through Germany; while the Minnesinger himself, smitten with leprosy, hooded and cloaked, and carrying the lazarus-clapper, moved through the shuddering city. God's satire weighed heavily upon him, indeed. Silently she held out her hand, and he gave her his bloodless fingers; she touched the strangely satin skin, and felt the fever beneath.

"It cannot be my little Lucy," he said reproachfully. "She used to kiss me. But even Lucy's kiss cannot thrill my paralyzed lips."

She stooped and kissed his lips. His little beard felt soft and weak as the hair of a baby.

"Ah, I have made my peace with the world and with God. Now He sends me His death-angel."

She struggled with the lump in her throat. "You must be indeed a prey to illusions, if you mistake an Englishwoman for Azrael."

"Ach, why was I so bitter against England? I was only once in England, years ago. I knew nobody, and London seemed so full of fog and Englishmen. Now England has avenged herself beautifully. She sends me you. Others too mount the hundred and five steps. I am an annexe to the Paris Exhibition. Remains of Heinrich Heine. A very pilgrimage of the royal demi-monde! A Russian princess brings the hateful odor of her pipe," he said with scornful satisfaction, "an Italian princess babbles of her aches and pains, as if in competition with mine. But the gold medal would fall to my nerves, I am convinced, if they were on view at the Exhibition. No, no, don't cry; I meant you to laugh. Don't think of me as you see me now; pretend to me I am as you first knew me. But how fine and beautiful you have grown; even to my fraction of an eye, which sees the sunlight as through black gauze. Fancy little Lucy has a husband; a husband—and the poodle still takes three baths a day. Are you happy, darling? are you happy?"

She nodded. It seemed a sacrilege to claim happiness.

"Das ist schön! Yes, you were always so merry. God be thanked! How refreshing to find one woman with a heart, and that her husband's. Here the women have a metronome under their corsets, which beats time, but not music. Himmel! What a whiff of my youth you bring me! Does the sea still roll green at the end of Boulogne pier, and do the sea-gulls fly? while I lie here, a Parisian Prometheus, chained to my bed-post. Ah, had I only the bliss of a rock with the sky above me! But I must not complain; for six years before I moved here I had nothing but a ceiling to defy. Now my balcony gives sideways on the Champs-Elysées, and sometimes I dare to lie outside on a sofa and peer at beautiful, beautiful Paris, as she sends up her soul in sparkling fountains, and incarnates herself in pretty women, who trip along like dance music. Look!"

To please him she went to a window and saw, upon the narrow iron-grilled balcony, a tent of striped chintz, like the awning of a café, supported by a light iron framework. Her eyes were blurred by unshed tears, and she divined rather than saw the far-stretching Avenue, palpitating with the fevered life of the Great Exhibition year; the intoxicating sunlight, the horse-chestnut trees dappling with shade the leafy footways, the white fountain-spray and flaming flower-beds of the Rond Point, the flashing flickering stream of carriages flowing to the Bois with their freight of beauty and wealth and insolent vice.

"The first time I looked out of that window," he said, "I seemed to myself like Dante at the end of the Divine Comedy, when once again he beheld the stars. You cannot know what I felt when after so many years I saw the world again for the first time, with half an eye, for ever so little a space. I had my wife's opera-glass in my hand, and I saw with inexpressible pleasure a young vagrant vendor of pastry offering his goods to two ladies in crinolines, with a small dog. I closed the glass; I could see no more, for I envied the dog. The nurse carried me back to bed and gave me morphia. That day I looked no more. For me the Divine Comedy was far from ended. The divine humorist has even descended to a pun. Talk of Mahomet's coffin. I lie between the two Champs-Elysées, the one where warm life palpitates, and that other, where the pale ghosts flit."

Then it was not a momentary fantasy of the pen, but an abiding mood that had paid blasphemous homage to the "Aristophanes of Heaven." Indeed, had it not always run through his work, this conception of humor in the grotesqueries of history, "the dream of an intoxicated divinity"? But his amusement thereat had been genial. "Like a mad harlequin," he had written of Byron, the man to whom he felt himself most related, "he strikes a dagger into his own heart, to sprinkle mockingly with the jetting black blood the ladies and gentlemen around.... My blood is not so splenetically black; my bitterness comes only from the gall-apples of my ink." But now, she thought, that bitter draught always at his lips had worked into his blood at last.

"Are you quite incurable?" she said gently, as she returned from the window to seat herself at his mattress graveside.

"No, I shall die some day. Gruby says very soon. But doctors are so inconsistent. Last week, after I had had a frightful attack of cramp in the throat and chest, 'Pouvez-vous siffler?' he said. 'Non, pas méme une comédie de M. Scribe,' I replied. So you may see how bad I was. Well, even that, he said, wouldn't hasten the end, and I should go on living indefinitely! I had to caution him not to tell my wife. Poor Mathilde! I have been unconscionably long a-dying. And now he turns round again and bids me order my coffin. But I fear, despite his latest bulletin, I shall go on some time yet increasing my knowledge of spinal disease. I read all the books about it, as well as experiment practically. What clinical lectures I will give in heaven, demonstrating the ignorance of doctors!"

She was glad to note the more genial nuance of mockery. Raillery vibrated almost in the very tones of his voice, which had become clear and penetrating under the stimulus of her presence, but it passed away in tenderness, and the sarcastic wrinkles vanished from the corners of his mouth as he made the pathetic jest anent his wife.

"So you read as well as write," she said.

"Oh, well, De Zichlinsky, a nice young refugee, does both for me most times. My mother, poor old soul, wrote the other day to know why I only signed my letters, so I had to say my eyes pained me, which was not so untrue as the rest of the letter."

"Doesn't she know?"

"Know? God bless her, of course not. Dear old lady, dreaming so happily at the Dammthor, too old and wise to read newspapers. No, she does not know that she has a dying son, only that she has an undying! Nicht Wahr?"

He looked at her with a shade of anxiety; that tragic anxiety of the veteran artist scenting from afar the sneers of the new critics at his life-work, and morbidly conscious of his hosts of enemies.

"As long as the German tongue lives."

"Dear old Germany," he said, pleased. "Yes, as I wrote to you, for you are the liebe Kleine of the poem,

'Nennt man die besten Namen,
So wird auch der meine genannt.'"

She was flattered, but thought sadly of the sequel:

"'Nennt man die schlimmsten Schmerzen,
So wird auch der meine genannt'"

as he went on:—

"That was why, though the German censorship forbade or mutilated my every book, which was like sticking pins into my soul, I would not become naturalized here. Paris has been my new Jerusalem, and I crossed my Jordan at the Rhine; but as a French subject I should be like those two-headed monstrosities they show at the fairs. Besides, I hate French poetry. What measured glitter! Not that German poetry has ever been to me more than a divine plaything. A laurel-wreath on my grave, place or withhold, I care not; but lay on my coffin a sword, for I was as brave a soldier as your Canning in the Liberation War of Humanity. But my Thirty Years' War is over, and I die 'with sword unbroken, and a broken heart.'" His head fell back in ineffable hopelessness. "Ah," he murmured, "it was ever my prayer, 'Lord, let me grow old in body, but let my soul stay young; let my voice quaver and falter, but never my hope.' And this is how I end."

"But your work does not end. Your fight was not vain. You are the inspirer of young Germany. And you are praised and worshipped by all the world. Is that no pleasure?"

"No, I am not le bon Dieu!" He chuckled, his spirits revived by the blasphemous mot." Ah, what a fate! To have the homage only of the fools, a sort of celestial Victor Cousin. One compliment from Hegel now must be sweeter than a churchful of psalms." A fearful fit of coughing interrupted further elaboration of the blasphemous fantasia. For five minutes it rent and shook him, the nurse bending fruitlessly over him; but at its wildest he signed to his visitor not to go, and when at last it lulled he went on calmly: "Donizetti ended mad in a gala dress, but I end at least sane enough to appreciate the joke—a little long-drawn out, and not entirely original, yet replete with ingenious irony. Little Lucy looks shocked, but I sometimes think, little Lucy, the disrespect is with the goody-goody folks, who, while lauding their Deity's strength and hymning His goodness, show no recognition at all of His humor. Yet I am praised as a wit as well as a poet. If I could take up my bed and walk, I would preach a new worship—the worship of the Arch-Humorist. I should draw up the Ritual of the Ridiculous. Three times a day, when the muezzin called from the Bourse-top, all the faithful would laugh devoutly at the gigantic joke of the cosmos. How sublime, the universal laugh! at sunrise, noon, and sunset; those who did not laugh would be persecuted; they would laugh, if only on the wrong side of the mouth. Delightful! As most people have no sense of humor, they will swallow the school catechism of the comic as stolidly as they now swallow the spiritual. Yes, I see you will not laugh. But why may I not endow my Deity—as everybody else does—with the quality which I possess or admire most?"

She felt some truth in his apology. He was mocking, not God, but the magnified man of the popular creeds; to him it was a mere intellectual counter with which his wit played, oblivious of the sacred aura that clung round the concept for the bulk of the world. Even his famous picture of Jehovah dying, or his suggestion that perhaps dieser Parvenu des Himmels was angry with Israel for reminding Him of his former obscure national relations—what was it but a lively rendering of what German savants said so unreadably about the evolution of the God-Idea? But she felt also it would have been finer to bear unsmiling the smileless destinies; not to affront with the tinkle of vain laughter the vast imperturbable. She answered gently, "You are talking nonsense."

"I always talked nonsense to you, little Lucy, for

'My heart is wise and witty And it bleeds within my breast.'

Will you hear its melodious drip-drip, my last poem?—My manuscript, Catherine; and then you can go take a nap. I am sure I gave you little rest last night."

The old woman brought him some folio sheets covered with great pathetically sprawling letters, and when she had retired, he began—

"Wie langsam kriechet sie dahin, Die Zeit, die schauderhafte Schnecke...?"

His voice went on, but after the first lines the listener's brain was too troubled to attend. It was agitated with whirling memories of those earlier outcries throbbing with the passion of life, flaming records of the days when every instant held not an eternity of ennui, but of sensibility. "Red life boils in my veins.... Every woman is to me the gift of a world.... I hear a thousand nightingales.... I could eat all the elephants of Hindostan and pick my teeth with the spire of Strasburg Cathedral.... Life is the greatest of blessings, and death the worst of evils...." But the poet was still reading—she forced herself to listen.

"'Perhaps with ancient heathen shapes, Old faded gods, this brain is full; Who, for their most unholy rites, Have chosen a dead poet's skull.'"

He broke off suddenly. "No, it is too sad. A cry in the night from a man buried alive; a new note in German poetry—was sage ich?—in the poetry of the world. No poet ever had such a lucky chance before—voyez-vous—to survive his own death, though many a one has survived his own immortality. Dici miser ante obitum nemo debet—call no man wretched till he's dead. 'Tis not till the journey is over that one can see the perspective truthfully and the tombstones of one's hopes and illusions marking the weary miles. 'Tis not till one is dead that the day of judgment can dawn; and when one is dead one cannot see or judge at all. An exquisite irony. Nicht Wahr? The wrecks in the Morgue, what tales they could tell! But dead men tell no tales. While there's life there's hope; and so the worst cynicisms have never been spoken. But I—I alone—have dodged the Fates. I am the dead-alive, the living dead. I hover over my racked body like a ghost, and exist in an interregnum. And so I am the first mortal in a position to demand an explanation. Don't tell me I have sinned, and am in hell. Most sins are sins of classification by bigots and poor thinkers. Who can live without sinning, or sin without living? All very well for Kant to say: 'Act so that your conduct may be a law for all men under similar conditions.' But Kant overlooked that you are part of the conditions. And when you are a Heine, you may very well concede that future Heines should act just so. It is easy enough to be virtuous when you are a professor of pure reason, a regular, punctual mechanism, a thing for the citizens of Königsberg to set their watches by. But if you happen to be one of those fellows to whom all the roses nod and all the stars wink ... I am for Schelling's principle: the highest spirits are above the law. No, no, the parson's explanation won't do. Perhaps heaven holds different explanations, graduated to rising intellects, from parsons upwards. Moses Lump will be satisfied with a gold chair, and the cherubim singing, 'holy! holy! holy!' in Hebrew, and ask no further questions. Abdullah Ben Osman's mouth will be closed by the kisses of houris. Surely Christ will not disappoint the poor old grandmother's vision of Jerusalem the Golden seen through tear-dimmed spectacles as she pores over the family Bible. He will meet her at the gates of death with a wonderful smile of love; and, as she walks upon the heavenly Jordan's shining waters, hand in hand with Him, she will see her erst-wrinkled face reflected from them in angelic beauty. Ah, but to tackle a Johann Wolfgang Goethe or a Gotthold Ephraim Lessing—what an ordeal for the celestial Professor of Apologetics! Perhaps that's what the Gospel means—only by becoming little children can we enter the kingdom of heaven. I told my little god-daughter yesterday that heaven is so pure and magnificent that they eat cakes there all day—it is only what the parson says, translated into child-language—and that the little cherubs wipe their mouths with their white wings. 'That's very dirty,' said the child. I fear that unless I become a child myself I shall have severer criticisms to bring against the cherubs. O God," he broke off suddenly, letting fall the sheets of manuscript and stretching out his hands in prayer, "make me a child again, even before I die; give me back the simple faith, the clear vision of the child that holds its father's hand. Oh, little Lucy, it takes me like that sometimes, and I have to cry for mercy. I dreamt I was a child the other night, and saw my dear father again. He was putting on his wig, and I saw him as through a cloud of powder. I rushed joyfully to embrace him; but, as I approached him, everything seemed changing in the mist. I wished to kiss his hands, but I recoiled with mortal cold. The fingers were withered branches, my father himself a leafless tree, which the winter had covered with hoar-frost. Ah, Lucy, Lucy, my brain is full of madness and my heart of sorrow. Sing me the ballad of the lady who took only one spoonful of gruel, 'with sugar and spices so rich.'"

Astonished at his memory, she repeated the song of Ladye Alice and Giles Collins, the poet laughing immoderately till at the end,

"The parson licked up the rest,"

in his effort to repeat the line that so tickled him, he fell into a fearful spasm, which tore and twisted him till his child's body lay curved like a bow. Her tears fell at the sight.

"Don't pity me too much," he gasped, trying to smile with his eyes; "I bend, but I do not break."

But she, terrified, rang the bell for aid. A jovial-looking woman—tall and well-shaped—came in, holding a shirt she was sewing. Her eyes and hair were black, and her oval face had the rude coloring of health. She brought into the death-chamber at once a whiff of ozone, and a suggestion of tragic incongruity. Nodding pleasantly at the visitor, she advanced quickly to the bedside, and laid her hand upon the forehead, sweating with agony.

"Mathilde," he said, when the spasm abated, "this is little Lucy of whom I have never spoken to you, and to whom I wrote a poem about her dark-brown eyes which you have never read."

Mathilde smiled amiably at the Roman matron.

"No, I have never read it," she said archly. "They tell me that Heine is a very clever man, and writes very fine books; but I know nothing about it, and must content myself with trusting to their word."

"Isn't she adorable?" cried Heine delightedly. "I have only two consolations that sit at my bedside, my French wife and my German muse, and they are not on speaking terms. But it has its compensations, for she is unable also to read what my enemies in Germany say about me, and so she continues to love me."

"How can he have enemies?" said Mathilde, smoothing his hair. "He is so good to everybody. He has only two thoughts—to hide his illness from his mother, and to earn enough for my future. And as for having enemies in Germany, how can that be, when he is so kind to every poor German that passes through Paris?"

It moved the hearer to tears—this wifely faith. Surely the saint that lay behind the Mephistopheles in his face must have as real an existence, if the woman who knew him only as man, undazzled by the glitter of his fame, unwearied by his long sickness, found him thus without flaw or stain.

"Delicious creature," said Heine fondly. "Not only thinks me good, but thinks that goodness keeps off enemies. What ignorance of life she crams into a dozen words. As for those poor countrymen of mine, they are just the people that carry back to Germany all the awful tales of my goings-on. Do you know, there was once a poor devil of a musician who had set my Zwei Grenadiere, and to whom I gave no end of help and advice, when he wanted to make an opera on the legend of the Flying Dutchman, which I had treated in one of my books. Now he curses me and all the Jews together, and his name is Richard Wagner."

Mathilde smiled on vaguely. "You would eat those cutlets," she said reprovingly.

"Well, I was weary of the chopped grass cook calls spinach. I don't want seven years of Nebuchadnezzardom."

"Cook is angry when you don't eat her things, chéri. I find it difficult to get on with her, since you praised her dainty style. One would think she was the mistress and I the servant."

"Ah, Nonotte, you don't understand the artistic temperament." Then a twitch passed over his face. "You must give me a double dose of morphia to-night, darling."

"No, no; the doctor forbids."

"One would think he were the employer and I the employee," he grumbled smilingly. "But I daresay he is right. Already I spend 500 francs a year on morphia, I must really retrench. So run away, dearest, I have a good friend here to cheer me up."

She stooped down and kissed him.

"Ah, madame," she said, "it is very good of you to come and cheer him up. It is as good as a new dress to me, to see a new face coming in, for the old ones begin to drop off. Not the dresses, the friends," she added gaily, as she disappeared.

"Isn't she divine?" cried Heine enthusiastically.

"I am glad you love her," his visitor replied simply.

"You mean you are astonished. Love? What is love? I have never loved."

"You!" And all those stories those countrymen of his had spread abroad, all his own love-poems were in that exclamation.

"No—never mortal woman. Only statues and the beautiful dead dream-women, vanished with the neiges d'antan. What did it matter whom I married? Perhaps you would have had me aspire higher than a grisette? To a tradesman's daughter? Or a demoiselle in society? 'Explain my position?'—a poor exile's position—to some double-chinned bourgeois papa who can only see that my immortal books are worth exactly two thousand marks banco; yes, that's the most I can wring out of those scoundrels in wicked Hamburg. And to think that if I had only done my writing in ledgers, the 'prentice millionaire might have become the master millionaire, ungalled by avuncular advice and chary cheques. Ah, dearest Lucy, you can never understand what we others suffer—you into whose mouths the larks drop roasted. Should I marry fashion and be stifled? Or money and be patronized? And lose the exquisite pleasure of toiling to buy my wife new dresses and knick-knacks? Après tout, Mathilde is quite as intelligent as any other daughter of Eve, whose first thought when she came to reflective consciousness was a new dress. All great men are mateless, 'tis only their own ribs they fall in love with. A more cultured woman would only have misunderstood me more pretentiously. Not that I didn't, in a weak moment, try to give her a little polish. I sent her to a boarding-school to learn to read and write; my child of nature among all the little school-girls—ha! ha! ha!—and I only visited her on Sundays, and she could rattle off the Egyptian Kings better than I, and once she told me with great excitement the story of Lucretia, which she had heard for the first time. Dear Nonotte! You should have seen her dancing at the school ball, as graceful and maidenly as the smallest shrimp of them all. What gaieté de cœur! What good humor! What mother-wit! And such a faithful chum. Ah, the French women are wonderful. We have been married fifteen years, and still, when I hear her laugh come through that door, my soul turns from the gates of death and remembers the sun. Oh, how I love to see her go off to Mass every morning with her toilette nicely adjusted and her dainty prayer-book in her neatly gloved hand, for she's adorably religious, is my little Nonotte. You look surprised; did you then think religious people shock me!"

She smiled a little. "But don't you shock her?"

"I wouldn't for worlds utter a blasphemy she could understand. Do you think Shakespeare explained himself to Ann Hathaway? But she doubtless served well enough as artist's model; raw material to be worked up into Imogens and Rosalinds. Enchanting creatures! How you foggy islanders could have begotten Shakespeare! The miracle of miracles. And Sterne! Mais non, an Irishman like Swift, Ça s'explique. Is Sterne read?"

"No; he is only a classic."

"Barbarians! Have you read my book on Shakespeare's heroines? It is good; nicht wahr?"

"Admirable."

"Then, why shouldn't you translate it into English?"

"It is an idea."

"It is an inspiration. Nay, why shouldn't you translate all my books? You shall; you must. You know how the French edition fait fureur. French, that is the European hall-mark, for Paris is Athens. But English will mean fame in ultima Thule; the isles of the sea, as the Bible says. It isn't for the gold pieces, though, God knows, Mathilde needs more friends, as we call them—perhaps because they leave us so soon. I fear she doesn't treat them too considerately, the poor little featherhead. Heaven preserve you from the irony of having to earn your living on your death-bed! Ach, my publisher, Campe, has built himself a new establishment; what a monument to me! Why should not some English publisher build me a monument in London? The Jew's books, like the Jew, should be spread abroad, so that in them all the nations of the earth shall be blessed. For the Jew peddles, not only old clo', but new ideas. I began life—tell it not in Gath—as a commission agent for English goods; and I end it as an intermediary between France and Germany, trying to make two great nations understand each other. To that not unworthy aim has all my later work been devoted."

"So you really consider yourself a Jew still?"

"Mein Gott! have I ever been anything else but an enemy of the Philistines?"

She smiled: "Yes; but religiously?"

"Religiously! What was my whole fight to rouse Hodge out of his thousand years' sleep in his hole? Why did I edit a newspaper, and plague myself with our time and its interests? Goethe has created glorious Greek statues, but statues cannot have children. My words should find issue in deeds. Put me rather with poor Lessing. I am no true Hellenist. I may have snatched at pleasure, but self-sacrifice has always called to the depths of me. Like my ancestor, David, I have been not only a singer, I have slung my smooth little pebbles at the forehead of Goliath."

"Yes; but haven't you turned Catholic?"

"Catholic!" he roared like a roused lion, "they say that again! Has the myth of death-bed conversion already arisen about me? How they jump, the fools, at the idea of a man's coming round to their views when his brain grows weak!"

"No, not death-bed conversion. Quite an old history. I was assured you had married in a Catholic Church."

"To please Mathilde. Without that the poor creature wouldn't have thought herself married in a manner sufficiently pleasing to God. It is true we had been living together without any Church blessing at all, but que voulez-vous? Women are like that. But for a duel I had to fight, I should have been satisfied to go on as we were. I understand by a wife something nobler than a married woman chained to me by money-brokers and parsons, and I deemed my faux ménage far firmer than many a "true" one. But since I was to be married, I could not leave my beloved Nonotte a dubious widowhood. We even invited a number of Bohemian couples to the wedding-feast, and bade them follow our example in daring the last step of all. Ha! ha! there is nothing like a convert's zeal, you see. But convert to Catholicism, that's another pair of sleeves. If your right eye offends you, pluck it out; if your right arm offends you, cut it off. And if your reason offends you, become a Catholic. No, no, Lucy, I may have worshipped the Madonna in song, for how can a poet be insensible to the beauty of Catholic symbol and ritual? But a Jew I have always been."

"Despite your baptism?"

The sufferer groaned, but not from physical pain.

"Ah, cruel little Lucy, don't remind me of my youthful folly. Thank your stars you were born an Englishwoman. I was born under the fearful conjunction of Christian bigotry and Jewish, in the Judenstrasse. In my cradle lay my line of life marked out from beginning to end. My God, what a life! You know how Germany treated her Jews—like pariahs and wild beasts. At Frankfort for centuries the most venerable Rabbi had to take off his hat if the smallest gamin cried: 'Jud', mach mores!' I have myself been shut up in that Ghetto, I have witnessed a Jew-riot more than once in Hamburg. Ah, Judaism is not a religion, but a misfortune. And to be born a Jew and a genius! What a double curse! Believe me, Lucy, a certificate of baptism was a necessary card of admission to European culture. Neither my mother nor my money-bag of an uncle sympathized with my shuddering reluctance to wade through holy water to my doctor's degree. And yet no sooner had I taken the dip than a great horror came over me. Many a time I got up at night and looked in the glass, and cursed myself for my want of backbone! Alas! my curses were more potent than those of the Rabbis against Spinoza, and this disease was sent me to destroy such backbone as I had. No wonder the doctors do not understand it. I learnt in the Ghetto that if I didn't twine the holy phylacteries round my arm, serpents would be found coiled round the arm of my corpse. Alas! serpents have never failed to coil themselves round my sins. The Inquisition could not have tortured me more, had I been a Jew of Spain. If I had known how much easier moral pain was to bear than physical, I would have saved my curses for my enemies, and put up with my conscience—twinges. Ah, truly said your divine Shakespeare that the wisest philosopher is not proof against a toothache. When was any spasm of pleasure so sustained as pain? Certain of our bones, I learn from my anatomy books, only manifest their existence when they are injured. Happy are the bones that have no history. Ugh! how mine are coming through the skin, like ugly truth through fair romance. I shall have to apologize to the worms for offering them nothing but bones. Alas, how ugly bitter it is to die; how sweet and snugly we can live in this snug, sweet nest of earth. What nice words; I must start a poem with them. Yes, sooner than die I would live over again my miserable boyhood in my uncle Salomon's office, miscalculating in his ledgers like a Trinitarian, while I scribbled poems for the Hamburg Wächter. Yes, I would even rather learn Latin again at the Franciscan cloister, and grind law at Göttingen. For, after all, I shouldn't have to work very hard; a pretty girl passes, and to the deuce with the Pandects! Ah, those wild University days, when we used to go and sup at the 'Landwehr,' and the rosy young Kellnerin, who brought us our duck mit Apfelkompot, kissed me alone of all the Herren Studenten, because I was a poet, and already as famous as the professors. And then, after I should be re-rusticated from Göttingen, there would be Berlin over again, and dear Rahel Levin and her salon, and the Tuesdays at Elise von Hohenhausen's (at which I would read my Lyrical Intermezzo), and the mad literary nights with the poets in the Behrenstrasse. And balls, theatres, operas, masquerades—shall I ever forget the ball when Sir Walter Scott's son appeared as a Scotch Highlander, just when all Berlin was mad about the Waverley Novels! I, too, should read them over again for the first time, those wonderful romances; yes, and I should write my own early books over again—oh, the divine joy of early creation!—and I should set out again with bounding pulses on my Harzreise: and the first night of Freischütz would come once more, and I should be whistling the Jungfern and sipping punch in the Casino, with Lottchen filling up my glass." His eyes oozed tears, and suddenly he stretched out his arms and seized her hand and pressed it frantically, his face and body convulsed, his paralyzed eyelids dropping. "No, no!" he pleaded, in a hoarse, hollow voice, as she strove to withdraw it, "I hear the footsteps of death, I must cling on to life; I must, I must. O the warmth and the scent of it!"

She shuddered. For an instant he seemed a vampire with shut eyes sucking at her life-blood to sustain his; and when that horrible fantasy passed, there remained the overwhelming tragedy of a dead man lusting for life. Not this the ghost, who, as Berlioz put it, stood at the window of his grave, regarding and mocking the world in which he had no further part. But his fury waned, he fell back as in a stupor, and lay silent, little twitches passing over his sightless face.

She bent over him, terribly distressed. Should she go? Should she ring again? Presently words came from his lips at intervals, abrupt, disconnected, and now a ribald laugh, and now a tearful sigh. And then he was a student humming:

"Gaudeamus igitur, juvenes dum sumus,"

and his death-mask lit up with the wild joys of living. And then earlier memories still—of his childhood in Düsseldorf—seemed to flow through his comatose brain; his mother and brothers and sisters; the dancing-master he threw out of the window; the emancipation of the Jewry by the French conquerors; the joyous drummer who taught him French; the passing of Napoleon on his white horse; the atheist school-boy friend with whom he studied Spinoza on the sly, and the country louts from whom he bought birds merely to set them free, and the blood-red hair of the hangman's niece who sang him folk-songs. And suddenly he came to himself, raised his eyelid with his forefinger and looked at her.

"Catholic!" he cried angrily. "I never returned to Judaism, because I never left it. My baptism was a mere wetting. I have never put Heinrich—only H—on my books, and never have I ceased to write 'Harry' to my mother. Though the Jews hate me even more than the Christians, yet I was always on the side of my brethren."

"I know, I know," she said soothingly. "I am sorry I hurt you. I remember well the passage in which you say that your becoming a Christian was the fault of the Saxons who changed sides suddenly at Leipzig; or else of Napoleon who had no need to go to Russia; or else of his school-master who gave him instruction at Brienne in geography, and did not tell him that it was very cold at Moscow in winter."

"Very well, then," he said, pacified. "Let them not say either that I have been converted to Judaism on my death-bed. Was not my first poem based on one in the Passover night Hagadah? Was not my first tragedy, Almansor, really the tragedy of down-trodden Israel, that great race which from the ruins of its second Temple knew to save, not the gold and the precious stones, but its real treasure, the Bible—a gift to the world that would make the tourist traverse oceans to see a Jew, if there were only one left alive. The only people that preserved freedom of thought through the middle ages, they have now to preserve God against the free-thought of the modern world. We are the Swiss guards of Deism. God was always the beginning and end of my thought. When I hear His existence questioned, I feel as I felt once in your Bedlam when I lost my guide, a ghastly forlornness in a mad world. Is not my best work, The Rabbi of Bacharach, devoted to expressing the 'vast Jewish sorrow,' as Börne calls it?"

"But you never finished it?"

"I was a fool to be persuaded by Moser. Or was it Gans? Ah, will not Jehovah count it to me for righteousness, that New Jerusalem Brotherhood with them in the days when I dreamt of reconciling Jew and Greek—the goodness of beauty with the beauty of goodness! Oh, those days of youthful dreams, whose winters are warmer than the summers of the after years. How they tried to crush us, the Rabbis and the State alike! O the brave Moser, the lofty-souled, the pure-hearted, who passed from counting-house to laboratory, and studied Sanscrit for recreation, moriturus te saluto. And thou, too, Markus, with thy boy's body, and thy old man's look, and thy encyclopædic, inorganic mind; and thou, O Gans, with thy too organic Hegelian hocus-pocus. Yes, the Rabbis were right, and the baptismal font had us at last; but surely God counts the will to do, and is more pleased with great-hearted dreams than with the deeds of the white-hearted burghers of virtue, whose goodness is essence of gendarmerie. And where, indeed—if not in Judaism, broadened by Hellenism—shall one find the religion of the future? Be sure of this, anyhow, that only a Jew will find it. We have the gift of religion, the wisdom of the ages. You others—young races fresh from staining your bodies with woad—have never yet got as far as Moses. Moses—that giant figure—who dwarfs Sinai when he stands upon it, the great artist in life, who, as I point out in my Confessions built human pyramids; who created Israel; who took a poor shepherd family, and created a nation from it—a great, eternal, holy people, a people of God, destined to outlive the centuries, and to serve as a pattern to all other nations—a statesman, not a dreamer, who did not deny the world and the flesh, but sanctified it. Happiness, is it not implied in the very aspiration of the Christian for postmundane bliss? And yet, 'the man Moses was very meek'; the most humble and lovable of men. He too—though it is always ignored—was ready to die for the sins of others, praying, when his people had sinned, that his name might be blotted out instead; and though God offered to make of him a great nation, yet did he prefer the greatness of his people. He led them to Palestine, but his own foot never touched the promised land. What a glorious, Godlike figure, and yet so prone to wrath and error, so lovably human. How he is modelled all round like a Rembrandt—while your starveling monks have made of your Christ a mere decorative figure with a gold halo. O Moshé Rabbenu, Moses our teacher indeed! No, Christ was not the first nor the last of our race to wear a crown of thorns. What was Spinoza but Christ in the key of meditation?"

"Wherever a great soul speaks out his thoughts, there is Golgotha," quoted the listener.

"Ah, you know every word I have written," he said, childishly pleased. "Decidedly, you must translate me. You shall be my apostle to the heathen. You are good apostles, you English. You turned Jews under Cromwell, and now your missionaries are planting our Palestinian doctrines in the South Seas, or amid the josses and pagodas of the East, and your young men are colonizing unknown continents on the basis of the Decalogue of Moses. You are founding a world-wide Palestine. The law goes forth from Zion, but by way of Liverpool and Southampton. Perhaps you are indeed the lost Ten Tribes."

"Then you would make me a Jew, too," she laughed.

"Jew or Greek, there are only two religious possibilities—fetish-dances and spinning dervishes don't count—the Renaissance meant the revival of these two influences, and since the sixteenth century they have both been increasing steadily. Luther was a child of the Old Testament. Since the Exodus, Freedom has always spoken with a Hebrew accent. Christianity is Judaism run divinely mad, a religion without a drainage system, a beautiful dream dissevered from life, soul cut adrift from body, and sent floating through the empyrean, when it can only at best be a captive balloon. At the same time, don't take your idea of Judaism from the Jews. It is only an apostolic succession of great souls that understands anything in this world. The Jewish mission will never be over till the Christians are converted to the religion of Christ. Lassalle is a better pupil of the Master than the priests who denounce socialism. You have met Lassalle! No? You shall meet him here one day. A marvel. Me plus Will. He knows everything, feels everything, yet is a sledge-hammer to act. He may yet be the Messiah of the nineteenth century. Ah! when every man is a Spinoza, and does good for the love of good, when the world is ruled by justice and brotherhood, reason and humor, then the Jews may shut up shop, for it will be the Holy Sabbath. Did you mark, Lucy, I said, reason and humor? Nothing will survive in the long run but what satisfies the sense of logic, and the sense of humor. Logic and laughter—the two trumps of doom! Put not your trust in princes—the really great of the earth are always simple. Pomp and ceremonial, popes and kings, are toys for children. Christ rode on an ass, now the ass rides on Christ."

"And how long do you give your trumps to sound before your Millennium dawns?" said "little Lucy," feeling strangely old and cynical beside this incorrigible idealist.

"Alas, perhaps I am only another dreamer of the Ghetto, perhaps I have fought in vain. A Jewish woman once came weeping to her Rabbi with her son, and complained that the boy, instead of going respectably into business like his sires, had developed religion, and insisted on training for a Rabbi. Would not the Rabbi dissuade him? 'But,' said the Rabbi, chagrined, 'why are you so distressed about it? Am I not a Rabbi?' 'Yes,' replied the woman, 'but this little fool takes it seriously,' Ach, every now and again arises a dreamer who takes the world's lip-faith seriously, and the world tramples on another fool. Perhaps there is no resurrection for humanity. If so, if there's no world's Saviour coming by the railway, let us keep the figure of that sublime Dreamer whose blood is balsam to the poor and the suffering."

Marvelling at the mental lucidity, the spiritual loftiness of his changed mood, his visitor wished to take leave of him with this image in her memory; but just then a half-paralyzed Jewish graybeard made his appearance, and Heine's instant dismissal of him on her account made it difficult not to linger a little longer.

"My chef de police!" he said, smiling. "He lives on me and I live on his reports of the great world. He tells me what my enemies are up to. But I have them in there," and he pointed to an ebony box on a chest of drawers, and asked her to hand it to him.

"Pardon me before I forget," he said; and, seizing a pencil like a dagger, he made a sprawling note, laughing venomously. "I have them here!" he repeated, "they will try to stop the publication of my Memoirs, but I will outwit them yet. I hold them! Dead or alive, they shall not escape me. Woe to him who shall read these lines, if he has dared attack me. Heine does not die like the first comer. The tiger's claws will survive the tiger. When I die, it will be for them the Day of Judgment."

It was a reminder of the long fighting life of the freelance, of all the stories she had heard of his sordid quarrels, of his blackmailing his relatives, and besting his uncle. She asked herself his own question, "Is genius, like the pearl in the oyster, only a splendid disease?"

Aloud she said, "I hope you are done with Börne!"

"Börne?" he said, softening. "Ach, what have I against Börne? Two baptized German Jews exiled in Paris should forgive each other in death. My book was misunderstood. I wish to heaven I hadn't written it. I always admired Börne, even if I could not keep up the ardor of my St. Simonian days when my spiritual Egeria was Rahel von Varnhagen. I had three beautiful days with him in Frankfort when he was full of Jewish wit, and hadn't yet shrunk to a mere politician. He was a brave soldier of humanity, but he had no sense of art, and I could not stand the dirty mob around him with its atmosphere of filthy German tobacco and vulgar tirades against tyrants. The last time I saw him he was almost deaf, and worn to a skeleton by consumption. He dwelt in a vast, bright silk dressing-gown, and said that if an Emperor shook his hand he would cut it off. I said if a workman shook mine I should wash it. And so we parted, and he fell to denouncing me as a traitor and a persifleur, who would preach monarchy or republicanism, according to which sounded better in the sentence. Poor Lob Baruch! Perhaps he was wiser than I in his idea that his brother Jews should sink themselves in the nations. He was born, by the way, in the very year of old Mendelssohn's death. What an irony! But I am sorry for those insinuations against Mme. Strauss. I have withdrawn them from the new edition, although, as you perhaps know, I had already satisfied her husband's sense of justice by allowing him to shoot at me, whilst I fired in the air. What can I more?"

"I am glad you have withdrawn them," she said, moved.

"Yes; I have no Napoleonic grip, you see. A morsel of conventional conscience clings to me."

"Therefore I could never understand your worship of Napoleon."

"There speaks the Englishwoman. You Pharisees—forgive me—do not understand great men, you and your Wellington! Napoleon was not of the wood of which kings are made, but of the marble of the gods. Let me tell you the "code Napoleon" carried light not only into the Ghettos, but into many another noisome spider-clot of feudalism. The world wants earthquakes and thunderstorms, or it grows corrupt and stagnant. This Paris needs a scourge of God, and the moment France gives Germany a pretext, there will be sackcloth and ashes, or prophecy has died out of Israel."

"Qui vivra verra," ran heedlessly off her tongue. Then, blushing painfully, she said quickly, "But how do you worship Napoleon and Moses in the same breath?"

"Ah, my dear Lucy, if your soul was like an Aladdin's palace with a thousand windows opening on the human spectacle! Self-contradiction the fools call it, if you will not shut your eyes to half the show. I love the people, yet I hate their stupidity and mistrust their leaders. I hate the aristocrats, yet I love the lilies that toil not, neither do they spin, and sometimes bring their perfume and their white robes into a sick man's chamber. Who would harden with work the white fingers of Corysande, or sacrifice one rustle of Lalage's silken skirts? Let the poor starve; I'll have no potatoes on Parnassus. My socialism is not barracks and brown bread, but purple robes, music, and comedies.

"Yes, I was born for Paradox. A German Parisian, a Jewish German, a hated political exile who yearns for dear homely old Germany, a sceptical sufferer with a Christian patience, a romantic poet expressing in classic form the modern spirit, a Jew and poor—think you I do not see myself as lucidly as I see the world? 'My mind to me a kingdom is' sang your old poet. Mine is a republic, and all moods are free, equal and fraternal, as befits a child of light. Or if there is a despot, 'tis the king's jester, who laughs at the king as well as all his subjects. But am I not nearer Truth for not being caged in a creed or a clan? Who dares to think Truth frozen—on this phantasmagorical planet, that whirls in beginningless time through endless space! Let us trust, for the honor of God, that the contradictory creeds for which men have died are all true. Perhaps humor—your right Hegelian touchstone to which everything yields up its latent negation, passing on to its own contradiction—gives truer lights and shades than your pedantic Philistinism. Is Truth really in the cold white light, or in the shimmering interplay of the rainbow tints that fuse in it? Bah! Your Philistine critic will sum me up after I am dead in a phrase; or he will take my character to pieces and show how they contradict each other, and adjudge me, like a schoolmaster, so many good marks for this quality, and so many bad marks for that. Biographers will weigh me grocerwise, as Kant weighed the Deity. Ugh! You can only be judged by your peers or by your superiors, by the minds that circumscribe yours, not by those that are smaller than yours. I tell you that when they have written three tons about me, they shall as little understand me as the Cosmos I reflect. Does the pine contradict the rose or the lotusland the iceberg? I am Spain, I am Persia, I am the North Sea, I am the beautiful gods of old Greece, I am Brahma brooding over the sun-lands, I am Egypt, I am the Sphinx.

But oh, dear Lucy, the tragedy of the modern, all-mirroring consciousness that dares to look on God face to face, not content, with Moses, to see the back parts; nor, with the Israelites, to gaze on Moses. Ach, why was I not made four-square like Moses Mendelssohn, or sublimely one-sided like Savonarola; I, too, could have died to save humanity, if I did not at the same time suspect humanity was not worth saving. To be Don Quixote and Sancho Panza in one, what a tragedy! No, your limited intellects are happier: those that see life in some one noble way, and in unity find strength. I should have loved to be a Milton—like one of your English cathedrals, austere, breathing sacred memories, resonant with the roll of a great organ, with painted windows, on which the shadows of the green boughs outside wave and flicker, and just hint of Nature. Or one of your aristocrats with a stately home in the country, and dogs and horses, and a beautiful wife. In short, I should like to be your husband. Or, failing that, my own wife, a simple, loving creature, whose idea of culture is cabbages. Ach, why was my soul wider than the Ghetto I was born in? why did I not mate with my kind?" He broke into a fit of coughing, and "little Lucy" thought suddenly of the story that all his life-sadness and song-sadness was due to his rejection by some Jewish girl in his own family circle.

"I tire you," she said. "Do not talk to me. I will sit here a little longer."

"Nay, I have tired you. But I could not but tell you my thoughts; for you are at once a child who loves and a woman who understands me. And to be understood is rarer than to be loved. My very parents never understood me. Nay, were they my parents—the mild man of business, the clever, clear-headed, romance-disdaining Dutchwoman, God bless her? No, my father was Germany, my mother was the Ghetto. The brooding spirit of Israel breathes through me that engendered the tender humor of her sages, the celestial fantasies of her saints. Perhaps I should have been happier had I married the first black-eyed Jewess whose father would put up with a penniless poet. I might have kept a kitchen with double crockery and munched Passover cakes at Easter. Every Friday night I should have come home from the labors of the week and found the table-cloth shining like my wife's face, and the Sabbath candles burning, and the Angels of Peace sitting hidden beneath their great invisible wings, and my wife, piously conscious of having thrown the dough on the fire, would have kissed me tenderly, and I should have recited in an ancient melody: 'A virtuous woman, who can find her? Her price is far above rubies.' There would have been little children with great candid eyes, on whose innocent heads I should have laid my hands in blessing, praying that God might make them like Ephraim and Manasseh, Rachel and Leah—persons of dubious exemplariness—and we should have sat down and eaten Schalet, which is the divinest dish in the world, pending the Leviathan that awaits the blessed at Messiah's table. And, instead of singing of cocottes and mermaids, I should have sung, like Jehuda Halévi, of my Herzensdame, Jerusalem. Perhaps—who knows?—my Hebrew verses would have been incorporated in the festival liturgy, and pious old men would have snuffled them helter-skelter through their noses. The letters of my name would have run acrosticwise down the verses, and the last verse would have inspired the cantor to jubilant roulades or tremolo wails while the choir boomed in 'Pom'; and perhaps many a Jewish banker, to whom my present poems make so little appeal, would have wept and beat his breast and taken snuff to the words of them. And I should have been buried honorably in the 'House of Life,' and my son would have said Kaddish. Ah me, it is, after all, so much better to be stupid and walk in the old laid-out, well-trimmed paths, than to wander after the desires of your own heart and your own eyes over the blue hills. True, there are glorious vistas to explore, and streams of living silver to bathe in, and wild horses to catch by the mane, but you are in a chartless land without stars and compass. One false step and you are over a precipice, or up to your neck in a slough. Ah, it is perilous to throw over the old surveyors. I see Moses ben Amram, with his measuring-chain and his graving-tools, marking on those stone tables of his the deepest abysses and the muddiest morasses. When I kept swine with the Hegelians, I used to say, or rather, I still say, for, alas! I cannot suppress what I have published: 'teach man he's divine; the knowledge of his divinity will inspire him to manifest it.' Ah me, I see now that our divinity is like old Jupiter's, who made a beast of himself as soon as he saw pretty Europa. Would to God I could blot out all my book on German Philosophy! No, no, humanity is too weak and too miserable. We must have faith, we cannot live without faith, in the old simple things, the personal God, the dear old Bible, a life beyond the grave."

Fascinated by his talk, which seemed to play like lightning round a cliff at midnight, revealing not only measureless heights and soundless depths, but the greasy wrappings and refuse bottles of a picnic, the listener had an intuition that Heine's mind did indeed, as he claimed, reflect or rather refract the All. Only not sublimely blurred as in Spinoza's, but specifically colored and infinitely interrelated, so that he might pass from the sublime to the ridiculous with an equal sense of its value in the cosmic scheme. It was the Jewish artist's proclamation of the Unity, the humorist's "Hear, O Israel."

"Will it never end, this battle of Jew and Greek?" he said, half to himself, so that she did not know whether he meant it personally or generally. Then, as she tore herself away, "I fear I have shocked you," he said tenderly. "But one thing I have never blasphemed—Life. Is not enjoyment an implicit prayer, a latent grace? After all, God is our Father, not our drill-master. He is not so dull and solemn as the parsons make out. He made the kitten to chase its tail and my Nonotte to laugh and dance. Come again, dear child, for my friends have grown used to my dying, and expect me to die for ever—an inverted immortality. But one day they will find the puppet-show shut up and the jester packed in his box. Good-bye. God bless you, little Lucy, God bless you."

The puppet-show was shut up sooner than he expected; but the jester had kept his most wonderful mot for the last.

"Dieu me pardonnera," he said. "C'est son métier."

THE PEOPLE'S SAVIOUR

I

"Der Bahn, der kühnen, folgen wir, Die uns geführt Lassalle."

Such is the Marseillaise the Social Democrats of Germany sing, as they troop out when the police break up their meetings.

This Lassalle, whose bold lead they profess to follow, lies at rest in the Jewish cemetery of his native Breslau under the simple epitaph "Thinker and Fighter," and at his death the extraordinary popular manifestations seemed to inaugurate the cult of a modern Messiah—the Saviour of the People.

II

But no man is a hero to his valet or his relatives, and on the spring morning when Lassalle stood at the parting of the ways—where the Thinker's path debouched on the Fighter's—his brother-in-law from Prague, being in Berlin on business, took the opportunity of remonstrating.

"I can't understand what you mean by such productions," he cried, excitedly waving a couple of pamphlets.

"That is not my fault, my dear Friedland," said Lassalle suavely. "It takes some brain to follow even what I have put so clearly. What have you there?"

"The lecture to the artisans, for which you have to go to gaol for four months," said the outraged ornament of Prague society, which he illumined as well as adorned, having, in fact, the town's gas-contract.

"Not so fast. There is my appeal yet before the Kammergericht. And take care that you are not in gaol first; that pamphlet is either one of the suppressed editions, or has been smuggled in from Zürich, a proof in itself of that negative concept of the State which the pamphlet aims at destroying. Your State is a mere night-watchman—it protects the citizen but it does nothing to form him. It keeps off ideas, but it has none of its own. But the State, as friend Bœckh puts it, should be the institution in which the whole virtue of mankind realizes itself. It should sum up human experience and wisdom, and fashion its members in accordance therewith. What is history but the story of man's struggle with nature? And what is a State but the socialization of this struggle, the stronger helping the weaker?"

"Nonsense! Why should we help the lower classes?"

"Pardon me," said Lassalle, "it is they who help us. We are the weaker, they are the stronger. That is the point of the other pamphlet you have there, explaining what is a Constitution."

"Don't try your legal quibbles on me."

"Legal quibbles! Why the very point of my pamphlet is to ignore verbal definitions. A Constitution is what constitutes it, and the working-class being nine-tenths of the population must be nine-tenths of the German Constitution."

"Then it's true what they say, that you wish to lead a Revolution!" exclaimed Friedland, raising his coarse glittering hands in horror.

"Follow a Revolution, you mean," said Lassalle. "Here again I do away with mere words. Real Revolutions make themselves, and we only become conscious of them. The introduction of machinery was a greater Revolution than the French, which, since it did not express ideals that were really present among the masses, was bound to be followed by the old thing over again. Indeed, sometimes, as I showed in Franz von Sickingen (my drama of the sixteenth-century war of the Peasants), a Revolution may even be reactionary, an attempt to re-establish an order of things that has hopelessly passed away. Hence it is your sentiments that are revolutionary."

Friedland's face had the angry helplessness of a witness in the hands of a clever lawyer. "A pretty socialist you are!" he broke out, as his arm swept with an auctioneer's gesture over the luxurious villa in the Bellevuestrasse. "Why don't you call in the first sweep from the street and pour him out your champagne?"

"My dear Friedland! Delighted. Help yourself," said Lassalle imperturbably.

The Prague dignitary purpled.

"You call your sister's husband a sweep!"

"Forgive me. I should have said 'gas-fitter.'"

"And who are you?" shrieked Friedland; "you gaol-bird!"

"The honor of going to gaol for truth and justice will never be yours, my dear brother-in-law."

Although he was scarcely taller than the gross-paunched parvenu who had married his only sister, his slim form seemed to tower over him in easy elegance. An aristocratic insolence and intelligence radiated from the handsome face that so many women had found irresistible, uniting, as it did, three universal types of beauty—the Jewish, the ancient Greek, and the Germanic. The Orient gave complexion and fire, the nose was Greek, the shape of the head not unlike Goethe's. The spirit of the fighter who knows not fear flashed from his sombre blue eyes. The room itself—Lassalle's cabinet—seemed in its simple luxuriousness to give point at once to the difference between the two men and to the parvenu's taunt. It was of moderate size, with a large work-table thickly littered with papers, and a comfortable writing-chair, on the back of which Lassalle's white nervous hand rested carelessly. The walls were a mass of book-cases, gleaming with calf and morocco, and crammed with the literature of many ages and races. Precious folios denoted the book-lover, ancient papyri the antiquarian. It was the library of a seeker after the encyclopædic culture of the Germany of his day. The one lighter touch in the room was a small portrait of a young woman of rare beauty and nobility. But this sober cabinet gave on a Turkish room—a divan covered with rich Oriental satins, inlaid whatnots, stools, dainty tables, all laden with costly narghiles, chibouques, and opium-pipes with enormous amber tips, Damascus daggers, tiles, and other curios brought back by him from the East—and behind this room one caught sight of a little winter-garden full of beautiful plants.

"Truth and justice!" repeated Friedland angrily. "Fiddlesticks! A crazy desire for notoriety. That's the truth. And as for justice—well, that was what was meted out to you."

"Prussian justice!" Lassalle's hand rose dramatically heavenwards. His brow grew black and his voice had the vibration of the great orator or the great actor. "When I think of this daily judicial murder of ten long years that I passed through, then waves of blood seem to tremble before my eyes, and it seems as if a sea of blood would choke me. Galley-slaves appear to me very honorable persons compared with our judges. As for our so-called Liberal press, it is a harlot masquerading as the goddess of liberty."

"And what are you masquerading as?" retorted Friedland. "If you were really in earnest, you would share all your fine things with dirty working-men, and become one of them, instead of going down to their meetings in patent-leather boots."

"No, my dear man, it is precisely to show the dirty working-man what he has missed that I exhibit to him my patent-leather boots. Humility, contentment, may be a Christian virtue, but in economics 'tis a deadly sin. What is the greatest misfortune for a people? To have no wants, to be lazzaroni sprawling in the sun. But to have the greatest number of needs, and to satisfy them honestly, is the virtue of to-day, of the era of political economy. I have always been careful about my clothes, because it is our duty to give pleasure to other people. If I went down to my working-men in a dirty shirt, they would be the first to cry out against my contempt for them. And as for becoming a working-man, I choose to be a working-man in that sphere in which I can do most good, and I keep my income in order to do it. At least it was honorably earned."

"Honorably earned!" sneered Friedland. "That is the first time I have heard it described thus." And he looked meaningly at the beautiful portrait.

"I am quite aware you have not the privilege of conversing with my friends," retorted Lassalle, losing his temper for the first time. "I know I am kept by my mistress, the Countess Hatzfeldt; that all the long years, all the best years of my life, I chivalrously devoted to championing an oppressed woman count for nothing, and that it is dishonorable for me to accept a small commission on the enormous estates I won back for her from her brutal husband! Why, my mere fees as lawyer would have come to double. But pah! why do I talk with you?" He began to pace the room. "The fact that I have such a delightful home to exchange for gaol is just the thing that should make you believe in my sincerity. No, my respected brother-in-law"—and he made a sudden theatrical gesture, and his voice leapt to a roar,—"understand I will carry on my life-mission as I choose, and never—never to satisfy every fool will I carry the ass." His voice sank. "You know the fable."

"Your mission! The Public Prosecutor was right in saying it was to excite the non-possessing classes to hatred and contempt of the possessing class."

"He was. I live but to point out to the working-man how he is exploited by capitalists like you."

"And ruin your own sister!"

"Ha, ha! So you're afraid I shall succeed. Good!" His blue eyes blazed. He stood still, an image of triumphant Will.

"You will succeed only in disgracing your relatives," said Friedland sullenly.

His brother-in-law broke into Homeric laughter. "Ho, ho," he cried. "Now I see. You are afraid that I'll come to Prague, that I'll visit you and cry out to your fashionable circle: 'I, Ferdinand Lassalle, the pernicious demagogue of all your journals, Governmental and Progressive alike, the thief of the casket-trial, the Jew-traitor, the gaol-bird, I am the brother-in-law of your host,' And so you've rushed to Berlin to break off with me. Ho, ho, ho!"

Friedland gave him a black look and rushed from the room. Lassalle laughed on, scarcely noticing his departure. His brain was busy with that comical scene, the recall of which had put the enemy to flight. On his migration from Berlin to Prague, when he got the gas-contract, Friedland, by a profuse display of his hospitality, and a careful concealment of his Jewish birth, wormed his way among families of birth and position, and finally into the higher governmental circles. One day, when he was on the eve of dining the élite of Prague, Lassalle's old father turned up accidentally on a visit to his daughter and son-in-law. Each in turn besought him hurriedly not to let slip that they were Jews. The old man was annoyed, but made no reply. When all the guests were seated, old Lassalle rose to speak, and when silence fell, he asked if they knew they were at a Jew's table. "I hold it my duty to inform you," he said, "that I am a Jew, that my daughter is a Jewess, and my son-in-law a Jew. I will not purchase by deceit the honor of dining with you." The well-bred guests cheered the old fellow, but the host was ghastly with confusion, and never forgave him.

But Lassalle's laughter soon ceased. Another recollection stabbed him to silence. The old man was dead—that beautiful, cheerful old man. Never more would his blue eyes gaze in proud tenderness on his darling brilliant boy. But a few months ago and he had seemed the very type of ruddy old age. How tenderly he had watched over his poor broken-down old wife, supporting her as she walked, cutting up her food as she ate, and filling her eyes with the love-light, despite all her pain and weakness. And now this poor, deaf, shrivelled little mother, had to totter on alone. "Father, what have you to do to-day?" he remembered asking him once. "Only to love you, my child," the old man had answered cheerily, laying his hand on his son's shoulder.

Yes, he had indeed loved him. What long patience from his childhood upwards; patience with the froward arrogant boy, a law to himself even in forging his parents' names to his school-notes, and meditating suicide because his father had beaten him for demanding more elegant clothes; patience with the emotional volcanic youth to whose grandiose soul a synod of professors reprimanding him seemed unclean crows and ravens pecking at a fallen eagle that had only to raise quivering wings to fly towards the sun; patience with his refusal to enter a commercial career, and carry on the prosperous silk business; patience even with his refusal to study law and medicine. "But what then do you wish to study, my boy? At sixteen one must choose decisively."

"The vastest study in the world, that which is most closely bound up with the most sacred interests of humanity—History."

"But what will you live on, since, as a Jew, you can't get any post or professorship in Prussia?"

"Oh, I shall live somehow."

"But why won't you study medicine or law?"

"Doctors, lawyers, and even savants, make a merchandise of their knowledge. I will have nothing of the Jew. I will study for the sake of knowledge and action."

"Do you think you are a poet?"

"No, I wish to devote myself to public affairs. The time approaches when the most sacred ends of humanity must be fought for. Till the end of the last century the world was held in the bondage of the stupidest superstition. Then rose, at the mighty appeal of intellect, a material force which blew the old order into bloody fragments. Intellectually this revolt has gone on ever since. In every nation men have arisen who have fought by the Word, and fallen or conquered. Börne says that no European sovereign is blind enough to believe his grandson will have a throne to sit on. I wish I could believe so. For my part, father, I feel that the era of force must come again, for these folk on the thrones will not have it otherwise. But for the moment it is ours not to make the peoples revolt, but to enlighten and raise them up."

"What you say may not be altogether untrue, but why should you be a martyr,—you, our hope, our stay? Spare us. One human being can change nothing in the order of the world. Let those fight who have no parents' hearts to break."

"Yes, but if every one talked like that—! Why offer myself as a martyr? Because God has put in my breast a voice which calls me to the struggle, has given me the strength that makes fighters. Because I can fight and suffer for a noble cause. Because I will not disappoint the confidence of God, who has given me this strength for His definite purpose. In short, because I cannot do otherwise."

Yes, looking back, he saw he could not have done otherwise, though for that old voice of God in his heart he now substituted mentally the Hegelian concept of the Idea trying to realize itself through him, Shakespeare's "prophetic soul of the wide world dreaming on things to come." The Will of God was the Will of the Time-spirit, and what was True for the age was whatever its greatest spirits could demonstrate to it by reason and history. The world had had enough of merely dithyrambic prophets, it was for the Modern Prophet to heat with his fire the cannon-balls of logic and science; he must be a thinker among prophets and a prophet among thinkers. Those he could not inspire through emotion must be led through reason. There must be not one weak link in his close-meshed chain of propositions. And who could doubt that what the Time-spirit was working towards among the Germans—the Chosen People in the eternal plan of the universe for this new step in human evolution—was the foundation of a true Kingdom of right, a Kingdom of freedom and equality, a State which should stand for justice on earth, and material and spiritual blessedness for all? But his father had complained not unjustly. Why should he have been chosen for the Man—the Martyr—through whom the Idea sought self-realization? It was a terrible fate to be Moses, to be Prometheus. No doubt that image of himself he read in the faces of his friends, and in the loving eyes of the Countess Hatzfeldt—that glorious wonder-youth gifted equally with genius and beauty—must seem enviable enough, yet to his own heart how chill was this lonely greatness. And youth itself was passing—was almost gone.

IV

But he shook off this rare sombre mood, and awoke to the full consciousness that Friedland was fled. Well, better so. The stupid fool would come back soon enough, and to-day, with Prince Puckler-Muskau, Baron Korff, General de Pfuel, and von Bülow the pianist, coming to lunch, and perhaps Wagner, if he could finish his rehearsal of "Lohengrin" in time, he was not sorry to see his table relieved of the dull pomposity and brilliant watch-chain of the pillar of Prague society. How mean to hide one's Judaism! What a burden to belong to such a race, degenerate sons of a great but long-vanished past, unable to slough the slave traits engendered by centuries of slavery! How he had yearned as a boy to shake off the yoke of the nations, even as he himself had shaken off the yoke of the Law of Moses. Yes, the scaffold itself would have been welcome, could he but have made the Jews a respected people. How the persecution of the Jews of Damascus had kindled the lad of fifteen! A people that bore such things was hideous. Let them suffer or take vengeance. Even the Christians marvelled at their sluggish blood, that they did not prefer swift death on the battle-field to the long torture. Was the oppression against which the Swiss had rebelled one whit greater? Cowardly people! It merited no better lot. And he recalled how, when the ridiculous story that the Jews make use of Christian blood cropped up again at Rhodes and Lemnos, he had written in his diary that the universal accusation was a proof that the time was nigh when the Jews in very sooth would help themselves with Christian blood. Aide-toi, le ciel t'aidera. And ever in his boyish imagination he had seen himself at the head of an armed nation, delivering it from bondage, and reigning over a free people. But these dreams had passed with childhood. He had found a greater, grander cause, that of the oppressed German people, ground down by capitalists and the Iron Law of Wages, and all that his Judaism had brought him was a prejudice the more against him, a cheap cry of Jew-demagogue, to hamper his larger fight for humanity. And yet was it not strange?—they were all Jews, his friends and inspirers; Heine and Börne in his youth, and now in his manhood, Karl Marx. Was it perhaps their sense of the great Ghetto tragedy that had quickened their indignation against all wrong?

Well, human injustice was approaching its term at last. The Kingdom of Heaven on earth was beginning to announce itself by signs and portents. The religion of the future was dawning—the Church of the People. "O father, father!" he cried, "if you could have lived to see my triumph!"

V

There was a knock at the door.

His man appeared, but, instead of announcing the Countess Hatzfeldt, as Lassalle's face expected, he tendered a letter.

Lassalle's face changed yet again, and the thought of the Countess died out of it as he caught sight of the graceful writing of Sophie de Solutzew. What memories it brought back of the first real passion of his life, when, whirled off his feet by an unsuspected current, enchanted yet astonished to be no longer the easy conqueror throwing crumbs of love to poor fluttering woman, he had asked the Russian girl to share his strife and triumphs. That he should want to marry her had been as amazing to him as her refusal. What talks they had had in this very room, when she passed through Berlin with her ailing father! How he had suffered from the delay of her decision, foreseen, yet none the less paralyzing when it came. And yet no, not paralyzing; he could not but recognize that the shock had in reality been a stimulation. It was in the reaction against his misery, in the subtle pleasure of a temptation escaped despite himself, and of regained freedom to work for his great ideals, that he had leapt for the first time into political agitation. The episode had made him reconsider, like a great sickness or a bereavement. It had shown him that life was slipping, that afternoon was coming, that in a few more years he would be forty, that the "Wonder-Child," as Humboldt had styled him, was grown to mature man, and that all the vent he had as yet found for his great gifts was a series of scandalous law-suits and an esoteric volume of the philosophy of Heraclitus the Dark. And now, coming to him in the midst of his great spurt, this letter from the quieter world of three years ago—though he himself had provoked it—seemed almost of dreamland. Its unexpected warmth kindled in him something of the old glow. Brussels! She was in western Europe again, then. Yes, she still possessed the Heine letter he required; only it was in her father's possession, and she had written to him to Russia to send it on. Her silence had been due to pique at the condition Lassalle had attached to acceptance of the mere friendship she offered him, to wit, that, like all his friends, she must write him two letters to his one. "Inconsiderate little creature!" he thought, smiling but half resentful. But, though she had now only that interest for him which the woman who has refused one never quite loses, she stirred again his sense of the foolish emptiness of loveless life. His brilliant reputation as scholar and orator and potential leader of men; his personal fascination, woven of beauty, wit, elegance, and a halo of conquest, that made him the lion of every social gathering, and his little suppers to celebrities the talk of Berlin—what a hollow farce it all was! And his thoughts flew not to Sophie but to the new radiance that had flitted across his life. He called up the fading image of the brilliant Helene von Dönniges whom he had met a year before at the Hirsemenzels.

He lived again through that wonderful evening, that almost Southern episode of mutual love at first sight.

He saw himself holding the salon rapt with his wonderful conversation. A silvery voice says suddenly, "No, I don't agree with you." He turns his head in astonishment. O the piquante, golden-haired beauty, adorably white and subtle, the dazzling shoulders, the coquettish play of the lorgnette, the wit, the daring, the diablerie. "So it's a no, a contradiction, the first word I hear of yours. So this is you. Yes, yes, it is even thus I pictured you." She is rising to beg the hostess to introduce them, but he places his hand gently on her arm. "Why? We know each other. You know who I am, and you are Brunehild, Adrienne Cardoville of the Wandering Jew, the gold chestnut hair that Captain Korff has told me of, in a word—Helene!" The whole salon regards them, but what are the others but the due audience to this splendid couple taking the centre of the stage by the right divine of a love too great for drawing-room conventions, calling almost for orchestral accompaniment by friend Wagner! He talks no more save to her, he sups at her side, he is in boyish ecstasies over her taste in wines. And when, at four in the morning, he throws her mantle over her shoulders and carries her down the three flights of stairs to her carriage, even her prudish cousinly chaperon seems to accept this as but the natural manner in which the hero takes possession of his heaven-born bride.

So rousing to his sleeping passion was his sudden abandonment to this old memory, that he now went to a drawer and rummaged for her photograph. After the Baron, her father, that ultra-respectable Bavarian diplomatist, had refused to hear her speak of the Jew-demagogue, Lassalle had asked her to send him her portrait, as he wished to build a house adorned with frescoes, and the artist was to seek in her the inspiration of his Brunehild. In the rush of his life, project and photograph had been alike neglected. He had let her go without much effort—in a way he still considered her his, since the opposition had not come from her. But had he been wise to allow this drifting apart? Great political events might be indeed maturing, but oh, how slowly, and there was always that standing danger of her "Moorish Prince"—the young Wallachian student, Janko von Racowitza, the "dragon who guards my treasure," as he had once called him, and who, though betrothed to her, was the slave of her caprices, ready to sacrifice himself if she loved another better, a gentle, pliant creature Lassalle could scarcely understand, especially considering his princely blood.

When he at last came upon the photograph, he remembered with a thrill that her birthday was at hand. She would be of age in a day or two, no longer the puppet of her father's will.

VI

When a little later the Countess Hatzfeldt was announced, he had forgotten he was expecting her. He slipped the photograph back among the papers, and moved forward hurriedly to greet her.

Her face was the face of the beautiful portrait on the wall, grown twice as old, but with the lines of beauty still clear under the unnecessary touches of rouge, so that sometimes, despite her frosted hair, one could imagine her life at its spring-tide. This was especially so when the sunshine leapt into her eyes. But, at her oldest, there remained to her the dignity of the Princess born, the charm of the woman of virile intellect and vast social experience.

"Something is troubling you," she said.

He smiled reassuringly. "My brother-in-law popped in from Prague. He read me a sermon."

"That would not trouble you, Ferdinand."

Lassalle was silent.

"You have heard again from that Sophie de Solutzew!"

"Divinatrix! After three years! You are wonderful as ever, Countess."

The compliment did not lighten her features. They looked haggard, almost their real age.

"It is not the moment for petticoats—with the chance of your life before you and months of imprisonment hanging over your head."

"Oh, I am certain my appeal will get me off with a fine at most. You must remember, Countess, that only once in my life, despite incessant snares, have the fowlers really caged me. And even then I was let out every time I had to plead in one of your cases. It was quite illegal," and he laughed at the recollection of the many miracles his eloquence, now insinuating, now menacing, had achieved.

"Yes, you are marvellous."

"I marvel at myself."

"Let me see your new 'Open Sesame.' Is it ready?"

"No, no, Sophie," he said banteringly. "You know you mean you want to see your namesake's letter."

"That is not my concern."

"O Countess!" He tendered the letter.

"Hum," she said, casting a rapid eye over it. "Then you wrote her first."

"Only because the letter was wanted for the new edition of Heine, and I had no copy of it.".

"But I have a copy."

"You? Where?"

"In my heart, mon cher enfant. Why should I not remember the great poet's words? 'Dearest brother-in-arms—Never have I found in any other but you so much passion united with so much clairvoyance in action. You have truly the divine right of autocracy. I only feel a humble fly....'" She paused and smiled at him. "You see."

"Perfect," cried Lassalle, who had been listening complacently. "But it's not that letter. The letter of introduction he gave me to Varnhagen von Ense when I was a boy of twenty—in the year we met."

"How should I not remember that? Was it not the first you showed me?"

A sigh escaped her. In that year when he had won her love, she had been just twice as old as he. Now, despite arithmetic, she felt three times his age.

"I will dictate it to you," she went on; "and you can send it to the publisher and be done with it."

"My rare Countess, my more than mother," he said, touched, "that you should have carried all that in your dear, wise head."

"'My friend, Herr Lassalle, the bearer of this letter, is a young man of extraordinary talent. To the most profound erudition and the greatest insight and the richest gifts of expression, he unites—'"

"Doesn't it also say, 'that I have ever met?'"

"Yes, yes; my head is leaving me. Put it in after 'insight.' 'He unites an energy of will and an attitude for action which plunge me into astonishment.'"

"You see," interrupted Lassalle, looking up; "Heine saw at once the difference between me and Karl Marx. Marx is, when all is said and done, a student, and his present address is practically the British Museum. In mere knowledge I do not pretend to superiority. What language, what art, what science, is unknown to him? But he has run almost entirely to brain. He works out his thoughts best in mathematics—the Spinoza of socialism. But fancy Spinoza leading a people; and even Spinoza had more glow. When I went to see him in London in the winter to ask him to head the movement with me, he objected to my phraseology, dissected my battle-cries in cold blood. I preach socialism as a religion, the Church of the People—he won't even shout 'Truth and Justice!' He will only prove you scientifically that the illusion of the masses that Right is not done them will goad them to express their Might. And his speeches! Treatises, not trumpets! Once after one of his speeches in the prisoner's box, a juror shook hands with him, and thanked him for his instructive lecture. Ha! ha! ha! Take my System of Acquired Rights, now."—Lassalle was now launched on one of his favorite monologues, and the Countess at least never desired to interrupt him—"There you have learning and logic that has forced the most dry-as-dust to hail it as a masterpiece of Jurisprudence. But it is enrooted in life, and drew its sustenance from my actual practice in fighting my dear Countess's battles. As Heine goes on to say, savoir and pouvoir are rarely united. Luther was a man of action, but his thought was not the widest. Lessing was a man of thought, but he died broken on the wheel of fortune. It was a combination of the two I tried to paint in my Ulrich von Hutten—the Humanist who transcended Luther and who was the morning star of the true Reformation. You remember his Frankfort student who, having mistakenly capped a Jew, could not decide whether the sin was mortal or venial. But though I put my own self into him, I shall not be beaten like him." He jumped to his feet and threw down his pen so that it stood quivering in the table. "For surely it was of me that Heine was thinking when he wrote: 'Yes, a third man will come'"—and Lassalle's accent became dramatically sonorous—"'and he will conclude what Luther began, what Lessing continued, a man of whom the Fatherland stands in such need, The Third Liberator.'"

"The Third Liberator," passionately echoed the Countess.

"Do you know," he went on, "I've often fancied it was I who gave Heine the line of thought he developed in his sketch of German philosophy, that our revolution will be the outcome of our Philosophy, that in the earthquake will be heard the small still voice of Kant and Hegel. It is what I tried to say the other day in my address on Fichte. It is pure thought that will build up the German Empire. Reality—with its fragments, Prussia, Saxony, etc—will have to remould itself after the Idea of a unified German—Republic. Why do you smile?" he broke off uneasily, with a morbid memory of his audience drifting away into the refreshment room.

"I was thinking of Heine's saying that we Germans are a methodical nation, to take our thinking first and our revolution second, because the heads that have been used for thinking may be afterwards used for chopping off. But if you chopped off heads first, like the French, they could not be of much use to philosophy."

Lassalle laughed. "I love Heine. He seemed my soul's brother. I loved him from boyhood, only regretting he wasn't a republican like Börne. Would he could have lived to see the triumph of his prediction, the old wild Berserker rage that will arise among us Teutons when the Talisman of the Cross breaks at last, as break it must, and the old gods come to their own again. A tooth for a tooth, an eye for an eye. The canting tyrants shall bite the dust, the false judges shall be judged."

"That is how I like you to talk."

He smote the table with his fist. His own praises had fired him, though his marvellous memory that could hold even the complete libretti of operas had been little in doubt as to Heine's phrasing.

"Yes, the holy alliance of Science and the People—those opposite poles! They will crush between their arms of steel all that opposes the higher civilization. The State, the immemorial vestal fire of all civilization—what a good phrase! I must write that down for my Kammergericht speech."

"And at the same time finish this Heine business, please, and be done with that impertinent demoiselle. What! she must have letter for letter! Of course it's a blessing she ceased to correspond with you. But all the same, just see what these creatures are. No sympathy with the wear and tear of your life. All petty egotisms and vanities! What do they care about your world-reaching purposes? Yes, they'll sit at your feet, but their own enjoyment or mental development is all they're thinking of. These Russian girls are the most dreadful. I know hundreds like your Sophie. They're a typical development of our new-fangled age. They even take nominal husbands, merely to emancipate themselves from the parental roof. I wonder she didn't play you that trick. And now she's older and has got over her pique, she sees what she has lost. But you will not be drawn in again?"

"No; you may rely on that," said Lassalle.

Her face became almost young.

"You are so ignorant of woman, mon cher enfant," she said, smoothing his brown curly hair; "you are really an infant, without judgment or reason where they are concerned."

"And you are so ignorant of man," thought Lassalle, for his repudiation of the Russian girl had brought up vividly the vision of his enchanting Brunehild. Did the Countess then think that a man could feed for ever on memories? True, she had gracefully declined into a quasi-maternal position, but a true mother would have felt more strongly that the relation was not so sufficing to him as to her.

The Countess seemed to divine what was passing through his mind. "If you could get a wife worthy of you," she cried. "A brain to match yours, a soul to feel yours, a heart to echo the drum-beat of yours, a mate for your dungeon or your throne, ready for either—but where is this paragon?"

"You are right," cried Lassalle, subtly gratified. After all Helene was a child with a child's will, broken by the first obstacle. "Never have I met a woman I could really feel my mate. If ever I have kindled a soul in one, it has been for a moment. No, I have always known I must live and die alone. I have told you of my early love for the beautiful Rosalie Zander, my old comrade's sister, who still lives unmarried for love of me. But I knew that to marry her would mean crippling myself through my tenderness. Alone I can suffer all, but how drag a weaker than myself into the tragic circle of my destinies? No, Curtius must leap into his gulf alone."

His words soothed her, but had a sting in them.

"But your happiness must be before all," she said, not without meaning it. "Only convince me that you have found your equal, and she shall be yours in the twinkling of an eye. I shouldn't even allow love-letters to intervene—you are so colossal. Your Titanic emotions overflow into hundreds of pages. You are the most uneconomical man I ever met."

He smiled.

"A volcano is not an ant-heap. But I know you are right. For Lassalle the Fighter the world holds no wife. If I could only be sure that the victory will come in my day."

"Remember what your own Heraclitus said: 'The best follow after fame.'"

"Yes, Fame is the Being of Man in Non-Being. It is the immortality of man made real," he quoted himself. "But—"

She hastened to continue his quotation. "'Hence it has always so mightily stirred the greatest souls and lifted them beyond all petty and narrow ends.'"

"The ends are great—but the means, how petty! The Presidency of a Working-Men's Union, one not even to be founded in Berlin."

"But yet a General German Working-Men's Union. Who knows what it may grow to! The capture of Berlin will be a matter of days."

"I had rather capture it with the sword. Bismarck is right. The German question can only be solved by blood and iron."

"Is it worth while going over that ground again? Did we not agree last year in Caprera when Garibaldi would not see his way to invading Austria for us, that we must put our trust in peaceful methods. You have as yet no real following at all. The Progressists will never make a Revolution, for all their festivals and fanfaronades. This National League of theirs is only a stage-threat."

"Yes, Bismarck knows our weak-kneed, white-livered bourgeois too well to be taken in by it. The League talks and Bismarck is silent. Oh, if I had a majority in the Chamber, as they have, I'd leave him to do the talking."

"But even if their rant was serious, they would allow you no leadership in their revolution. Have they not already rejected your overtures? Therefore this deputation to you of the Leipzig working-men (whom they practically rejected by offering them honorary membership) is simply providential. The conception of a new and real Progressive Party that is seething in their minds under the stimulus of their contact with socialism in London—you did write that they had been in London?"

"Yes; they went over to see the Exhibition. But they also represent, I take it, the old communistic and revolutionary traditions, that have never been wholly lulled to sleep by our pseudo-Liberalism. But that is how history repeats itself. When the middle classes oppose the upper classes, they always have the air of fighting for the whole majority. But the day soon comes, especially if the middle classes get into power, when the lower classes discover there never was any real union of interests!"

"Well, that's just your chance!" cried the Countess. "Here is a new party waiting to be called out of chaos, nay, calling to you. An unformed party is just what you want. You give it the impress of your own personality. Remember your own motto: Si superos nequeo movere Acheronta movebo."

Lassalle shook his head doubtfully. He had from the first practically resolved on developing the vague ideas of the Deputation, but he liked to hear his own reasons in the mouth of the Countess.

"The headship of a party not even in existence," he murmured. "That doesn't seem a very short cut to the German Republic."

"Do you doubt yourself? Think of what you were when you took up my cause—a mere unknown boy. Think how you fought it from court to court, picking up your Law on the way, a Demosthenes, a Cicero, till all the world wondered and deemed you a demigod. You did that because I stood for Injustice. You were the Quixote to right all wrong. You saw the universal in the individual. My case was but a prefiguration of your real mission. Now it is the universal that calls to you. See in your triumph for me your triumph for that suffering humanity, with which you have taught me to sympathize."

"My noble Countess!"

"What does your own Franz von Sickingen say of history?

"'And still its Form remains for ever Force.'

The Force of the modern world is the working-man. And as you yourself have taught me that there are no real revolutions except those that formally express what is already a fact, there wants then only the formal expression of the working-man's Force. To this Force you will now give Form."

"What an apt pupil!" He stooped and kissed her lips. Then, walking about agitatedly: "Yes," he cried; "I will weld the workers of Germany—to gain their ends they must fuse all their wills into one—none of these acrid, petty, mutually-destructive individualities of the bourgeois—one gigantic hammer, and I will be the Thor who wields it." His veins swelled, he seemed indeed a Teutonic god. "And therefore I must have Dictator's rights," he went on. "I will not accept the Presidency to be the mere puppet of possible factions."

"There speaks Ferdinand Lassalle! And now, mon cher enfant, you deserve to hear my secret."

She smiled brilliantly.

His heart beat a little quicker as he bent his ear to her customary whisper. Her secrets were always interesting, sometimes sensational, and there was always a pleasure in the sense of superiority that knowledge conferred, and in the feeling of touching, through his Princess-Countess, the inmost circles of European diplomacy. He was of the gods, and should know whatever was on the knees of his fellow-gods.

"Bismarck is thinking of granting Universal Suffrage!"

"Universal Suffrage!" he shouted.

"Hush, hush! Walls have ears."

"Then I must have inspired him."

"No; but you will have."

"How do you mean? Is it not my idea?"

"Implicitly, perhaps, but you have never really pressed for it specifically. Your only contribution to practical politics is a futile suggestion that the Diet should refuse to sit, and so cut off supplies. Now of course Universal Suffrage is the first item of the programme of your Working-Men's Union."

"Sophie!"

She smiled and nodded. "Why should Bismarck have the credit," she whispered, "for what is practically your idea? You will seem to exact it from him by the force of your new party, which will peg away at that one point like the Anti-Corn-Law people in England."

"Yes; but I'll have no Manchester state-concepts."

"I know, I know. Now even if Bismarck hesitates,"—she made her whisper still lower—"there are foreign complications looming that will make it impossible for him to ignore the masses. Now I understand that what the Leipzig working-men suggest is that you shall write them an Open Letter."

"Yes. In it I shall counsel the creation of the Fourth Party, I shall declare that the Progressists do not represent the People at all, that their pretensions are as impertinent as their threats are hollow, that there is no People behind them. It will be a thunderbolt! Like Luther's nailing his theses to the church-door at Wittenberg. And to the real masses themselves I shall declare: 'You are the rock on which the Church of the Present is to be built. Steep yourselves in the thought of this, your mission. The vices of the oppressed, the idle indifference of the thoughtless, and even the harmless frivolity of the unimportant no longer become you.' And I shall teach them how to exact from the State the capital for co-operative associations that will oust the capitalist."

"And make them capitalists themselves?"

"That is what Rodbertus and Marx object. But you must give the working-man something definite, you must educate him gradually."

"Put that second if you will, but Universal Suffrage must be first."

"Naturally. It will be the instrument to force the second."

"It will be the instrument to force you to the front. Bismarck will appear the mere tool of your will. Who knows but that the King himself may be a pawn on your board!"

Lassalle seized her hands. "There I recognize my soul's mate."

"And I recognize the voice of the von Bulows," she said, with a half-sob in her laughter, as she drew back.

The lunch was brilliant, blending the delicate perfume of aristocracy with free-and-easy Bohemianism, and enhanced by the artistic background of pictures, bric-à-brac, and marble facsimiles of the masterpieces of statuary, including the Venus of Milo and the Apollo Belvedere.

The Countess stayed only long enough to smoke a couple of cigarettes, but the other guests were much longer in shaking off the fascination of Lassalle's boyish spirits and delightful encyclopædic monologues. When the last guest was gone, Lassalle betook himself to the best florist in Berlin, composing a birthday poem on the way. At the shop he wrote it down, and, signing it "F.L.," placed it in the most beautiful basket of flowers he could find. The direction was Fräulein Helene von Dönniges.

VII

The "Open Reply Letter" did not thrill the world like a Lutheran thesis, but it made the Progressists very angry. What! they had not the People behind them! They were only exploiting, not representing the People! And while the Court organs chuckled over this flank attack on their bragging foes, the Liberal organs denounced Lassalle as the catspaw of reaction. The whilom "friends of the working-man," in their haste to overturn Lassalle's position, tumbled into their own pits. Schulze-Delitzsch himself, founder of co-operative working-men's societies, denouncer of the middleman, now found himself—in the face of Lassalle's uncompromising analysis—praising the Law of Competition, while that Iron Law of Wages, their tendency to fall to the minimum of subsistence (which was in the canon of all orthodox economists), was denied the moment it was looked at resentfully from the wage-earner's standpoint. Herculean labors now fell upon Lassalle—a great speech of four hours at Frankfort-on-the-Main, the founding of the General German Working-Men's Union, with himself as dictator for five years, the delivery of inflammatory speeches in town after town, the publishing of pamphlets against the Progressists, attempts to capture Berlin for the cause, the successful fighting of his own law-case. And amid all this, the writing of one of his most wonderful and virulent books, at once deeply instructing and passionately inflaming the German working-man.

And always the same sledge-hammer hitting at the same nail—Universal Suffrage. Get that and you may get everything. Nourish no resentment against the capitalists. They are the product of history as much as your happier children will be. But on the other hand, no inertia, no submission! Wake up! English or French working-men would follow me in a trice. You are a pack of valets.

In such a whirl Helene von Dönniges was shot off from his mind as a spinning-top throws off a straw.

But when, after a couple of months of colossal activity, incessant correspondence, futile attempts to convert friends, quarrels with the authorities, grapplings with the internal cabals of the Union itself, he fled on his summer tour—where was the great new Party? He had hoped to have five hundred thousand men at his back, but they had come in by beggarly hundreds. There was even talk of an insurance bonus to attract them. Lassalle had exaggerated both the magnetism of his personality and the intelligence and discontent of the masses. His masterful imagination had made the outer world a mere reflection of his inner world. Even in those early days, when he was scarcely known, and that favorably rather than otherwise, he had imagined himself the pet aversion of the comfortable classes. Knowing the rôle he purposed to play, his dramatic self-consciousness had reaped in anticipation the rebel's reward. And now, though he was nearer detestation than before, there was still no Party of revolt for him to lead. But he worked on undaunted, Titanic, spending his money to subsidize tottering democratic papers, using his summer journeyings to try to attach not abilities in the countries he passed through, and his stay at the waters to draw up a great speech, with which he toured on his return. And now a new cry! The cowardly venal Press must be swept away. "As true as you are here, hanging on my lips, eager and transported, as true as my soul trembles with the purest enthusiasm in pouring itself wholly into yours, so truly does the certainty penetrate me that a day will come when we shall launch the thunderbolt which will bury that Press in eternal night." He proposed that the newspapers should therefore be deprived of their advertisement columns. What wonder if they accused him of playing Bismarck's game! And, indeed, there was not wanting direct mention of Bismarck in the speech. He at least was a man, while the Progressists were old women. The orator mocked their festive demonstrations. They were like the Roman slaves who, during the Saturnalia, played at being free. To spare themselves a real battle, the defeated were intoning among the wines and the victuals a hymn of victory. "Let us lift up our arms and pledge ourselves, if this Revolution should come about, whether in this way or in that, to remember that the Progressists and members of the National League to the last declared they wanted no revolution! Pledge yourselves to do this, raise your hands on high!" At the Sonningen meeting in the great shooting-gallery, they not only raised their hands, but their knives, against interrupting Progressists. The Burgomaster, a Progressist, at the head of ten gendarmes armed with bayonets, and policemen with drawn swords, dissolved the meeting. Lassalle, half followed, half borne onward by six thousand cheering men, strode to the telegraph office, and sent off a telegram to Bismarck. His working-men's meeting had been dissolved by a Progressist Burgomaster without any legal justification. "I ask for the severest, promptest legal satisfaction."

VIII

Bismarck took no official notice. But it was not long before the Countess succeeded in bringing the two men together. The way had indeed been paved. If Lassalle's idealism had survived the experience of the Hatzfeldt law-suits, if he had yet to learn that the Fighter cannot pick his steps as cleanly and logically as the Thinker, those miry law-suits, waged unscrupulously on both sides, had prepared him to learn the lesson readily and to apply it unflinchingly. Without Force behind one, victory must be sought more circuitously. But to a man who represents no Force, how shall Bismarck listen? What have you to offer? "Do ut des" is his overt motto. To poor devils I have nothing to say. Lassalle must therefore needs magnify his office of President, wave his arm with an air of vague malcontent millions. Was Bismarck taken in? Who shall say? In after-years, though he had in the meantime granted Universal Suffrage in Prussia, he told the Reichstag he was merely fascinated by this marvellous conversationalist, who delighted him for hours, without his being able to get a word in; by this grandiloquent Demagogue without a Demos, who plainly loved Germany, yet was uncertain whether the German Empire would be formed by a Hohenzollern dynasty or a Lassalle dynasty. And, in truth, since extremes meet, there was much in Lassalle's conception of the State, and in his German patriotism, which made him subtly akin to the Conservative Chancellor. They walked arm-in-arm in the streets of Berlin, Bismarck parading heart on sleeve; they discussed the annexation of Schleswig-Holstein. Bismarck promised both Universal Suffrage and State-Capitalized Associations—"only let us wait till the war is done with!" En attendant, the profit of his strange alliance with this thorn in his enemies' flesh, was wholly to the Minister. But Lassalle, exalted to forgetfulness of the pettiness of the army at his back, almost persuaded himself to believe as he believed Bismarck believed. "Bismarck is my tool, my plenipotentiary," he declared to his friends. And to his judges: "I play cards on table, gentlemen, for the hand is strong enough. Perhaps before a year is over Universal Suffrage will be the law of the land, and Bismarck will have enacted the rôle of Sir Robert Peel." He even gave his followers to understand that the King of Prussia's promise to consider the condition of the Silesian weavers was the result of his pressure. And was not the Bishop of Mayence an open partisan? Church, King, and Minister, do you not see them all dragged at my chariot wheels? Nevertheless, he failed completely to organize a branch at Berlin. And new impeachments for inciting to hatred and contempt, and for high-treason, came to cripple his activity. "If I have glorified political passion," he cried in his defence, "I have only followed Hegel's maxim: 'Nothing great has ever been done in the world without passion.'"

He was in elegant evening dress, with patent-leather boots, the one cool person in the stifling court. For hours and hours he spoke, with the perpetually changing accents of the great orator who has so studied his art that it has become nature. Now he was winning, persuasive, now menacing, terrible, now with disdainful smile and half-closed eyes of contempt. And ever and anon he threw back his head with the insolent majesty of a Roman Emperor. Even when there was a touch of personal pathos, defiance followed on its heels. "I used to go to gaol as others go to the ball, but I am no longer young. Prison is hard for a mature man, and there is no article of the code that entitles you to send me there." Yet six months' imprisonment was adjudged him, and the most he could obtain by his ingeniously inexhaustible technical pleas was deferment of his punishment.

But there was consolation in the memories of his triumphal tour through the Rhenish provinces, where the Union had struck widest root. Town after town sent its whole population to greet him. Roaring thousands met him at the railway stations, and he passed under triumphal arches and through streets a-flutter with flags, where working-girls welcomed him with showers of roses. "Such scenes as these," he wrote to the Countess, "must have attended the foundation of new religions." And, indeed, as weeping working-men fought to draw his carriage, and as he looked upon the vast multitudes surging around him, he could not but remember Heine's prophecy: "You will be the Messiah of the nineteenth century."

"I have not grasped this banner," he cried at Ronsdorf, "without knowing quite clearly that I myself may fall. But in the words of the Roman poet:

"'Exoriare aliquis nostris ex ossibus ultor.'

May some avenger and successor arise out of my bones! May this great and national movement of civilization not fall with my person. But may the conflagration which I have kindled spread farther and farther as long as one of you still breathes!"

Those were his last words to the working-men of Germany.

For beneath all the flowers and the huzzahing what a tragedy of broken health and broken hopes! Each glowing speech represented a victory over throat-disease and over his own fits of scepticism. His nerves, shattered by the tremendous strain of the year, the fevers, the disillusions, the unprofitable shiftings of standpoint, painted the prospect as black as they had formerly ensanguined it. And the six months' imprisonment hanging over him gained added terrors from his physical breakdown. Even on his eider-down bed he could not woo sleep—how then on a prison pallet?

When he started the Union he had imagined he could bring the Socialistic movement to a head in a year. When, after a year as crammed as many a lifetime, he went down at the Countess's persuasion to take the milk-cure at Kaltbad on the Righi, he confessed to his friend Becker that he saw no near hope save from a European war.

IX

One stormy day at the end of July, a bovine-eyed Swiss boy, dripping with rain, appeared at the hygienic hotel, where Lassalle sat brooding with his feet on the mantelpiece, to tell him that a magnificent lady wanted to see him. She was with a party that had taken refuge in a mountain-side shed. A great coup his resurging energy was meditating at Hamburg, was swept clean from his mind.

He dashed down, his heart beating with a hopeless surmise, and saw, amid a strange group, the golden hair of Helene von Dönniges shining like a star. He accepted it at once as the star of his destiny. His strength seemed flowing back in swift currents of glowing blood.

"By all the gods of Greece," he cried, "'tis she!"

In an instant they were lovers again, and her American friend and confidante, Mrs. Arson, was enchanted by this handsome apparition, which, Helene protested, she had only summoned up half laughingly. Dear old Holthoff had written her that Lassalle was somewhere on the Righi, but she had not really believed she would stumble on him. She was suffering from nervous prostration, and it was only the accident of Mrs. Arson's holiday plan for her children that had enabled her to obey the doctor's advice to breathe mountain air.

"I breathe it for the first time," said Lassalle. "Do you know what I was doing when your boy-angel came? Writing to Holthoff and old Bœckh the philologist for introductions to your father. The game has dallied on long enough. We must finish."

Helene blushed charmingly, and looked at Mrs. Arson with a glance that sought protection against and admiration for his audacity.

"I guess you're made for each other," said Mrs. Arson, carried off her feet. "Why, you're like twins. Are you relatives?"

"That's what everybody asks," said Helene. "Why, even before I met him, people piqued my curiosity about him by saying I talked like him."

"It was the best compliment I had ever received—said behind my back too. But people are right for once. Do you know that the painter to whom I gave your portrait to inspire him for the Brunehild fresco said that in drawing our two faces he discovered that they have exactly the same anatomical structure."

Her face took on that fascinating diablerie which men found irresistible.

"Then your compliments to me are only boomerangs."

"Boomerangs only return when they miss."

The storm abating, they moved up the mountain, talking gaily. Mrs. Arson and her children kept considerately in the rear with their guide. Helene admired Lassalle's stick. He handed it to her.

"It was Robespierre's. Förster the historian gave it me. That repoussé gold-work on the handle is of course the Bastille."

"How appropriate!" she laughed.

"Which? The Bastille to the stick, or the stick to me?"

"Both."

He grew serious.

"What would you do if I lost my head?"

"I should stand by till your head was severed in order that you might look on your beloved to the last. Then I should take poison."

"My Cleopatra!"

Her fitful face changed.

"Or marry Janko!"

"That weakling—is he still hovering?"

"He passed the winter with us. He looks upon me as his," she said dolefully.

"I flick him away. Do not try to belong to another. I tell you solemnly I claim you as mine. We cannot resist destiny. Our meeting to-day proves it. To-morrow we climb to see the sunrise together,—the sunrise over the mountains. Symbol of our future that begins. The heavens opening in purple and gold over the white summits—love breaking upon your virginal purity."

Already she felt, as of yore, swept off on roaring seas. But the rush and the ecstasy had their alloy of terror. To be with him was to be no longer herself, but a hypnotized stranger. Perhaps she was unwise to have provoked this meeting. She should have remembered he was not to be coquetted with. As well put a match to a gunpowder barrel to warm your fingers. Every other man could be played with. This one swallowed you up.

"But Prince Janko has no one but me," she tried to protest. "My little Moorish page, my young Othello!"

"Keep him a page. Othellos are best left bachelors. Remember the fate of Desdemona."

"I'll give you both up," she half whimpered. "I'll go on the stage."

"You!"

"Yes. Everybody says I'm splendid at burlesque. You should see me as a boy."

"You baby! You need no triumphs in the mimic world. Your rôle is grander."

"Oh, please let us wait for Mrs. Arson. You go too fast."

"I don't. I have waited a year for you. When shall we marry?"

"Not before our wedding-day."

"Evasive Helene!"

"Cruel Ferdinand! Ask anything of me, but not will-power."

A little cough came to accentuate her weakness.

"My darling!" he cried in deep emotion. "We'll fly to Egypt or the Indies. I'll hang up politics and all that frippery. My books and science shall claim me again, and I will watch over my ailing little girl till she becomes the old splendid Brunehild again!"

"No, no, I am no Brunehild; only a modern woman with nerves—the most feminine woman in the world, irresponsible, capricious—please, please remember."

"If you were not yourself I should not love you."

"But it cannot come to anything."

"Cannot? The word is for pigmies."

"But my mother?"

"She is a woman—I will talk to her."

"My father!"

"He is a man, with men one can always get on. They are reasonable. Besides, you tell me he is an author, and I will read his famous books."

She smiled faintly. "But there is myself."

"You are myself—and I never doubt myself."

"Oh, but there are heaps of other difficulties."

"There are none other."

She pouted deliciously. "You don't know everything under the sun."

"Under your aureole of hair, do you mean?"

"What if I do?" she smiled back. "You must not trust me too far. I am a spoilt child—wild, unbridled, unaccustomed to please others except by pleasing myself."

Her actress-nature enjoyed the picture of herself. She felt that Baudelaire himself would have admired it. Lassalle's answer was subtly attuned:

"My Satanic enchantress! my bewitching child of the devil."

"Bien fou qui s'y fie. When I lived at Nice in that royal Bohemia, where musicians rubbed shoulders with grand-duchesses, and the King of Bavaria exchanged epigrams with Bulwer Lytton, do you know what they called me?"

"The Queen of all the Follies!"

"You know?"

"Did I not love my Brunehild ere we met?"

"Yes, and I—knew of you. Only I didn't recognize you at first, because they told me you were a frightful demagogue and—a—a—Jew!"

He laughed. "And so you expected a gaberdine. And yet surely Bulwer Lytton gave you a presentation copy of Leila. Don't you remember the Jew in it? As a boy I had his ideal—to redeem my people. But if my Judaism offends you, I can become a Christian—not in belief of course, but—"

"Oh, not for worlds. I believe too little myself to bother about religion. My friends call me the Greek, because I can readily believe in many gods, but only with difficulty in one."

He laughed. "Is it the same in love?"

Her eyes gleamed archly.

"Yes. Hitherto, at least, a single man has never sufficed. With only one I had time to see all his faults, and since my first love, a Russian officer, I would always have preferred to keep three knives dancing in the air. But as that was impossible, I generally halved my loaf."

The mountains rang with his laughter.

"Well. I haven't lived a saint, and I can't expect my wife to bring more than I."

"You bring too much. You bring that Countess."

"My dear Helene," he said, struck serious. "I am entirely free in regard to the Countess, as she is long since as regards me. Of course she will, at the first shock, feel opposed to my marriage with a distinguished young girl on the same intellectual level as herself. That is human, feminine, natural. But when she knows you she will adore you, and you will repay her in kind, since she is my second mother. You do not understand her. The dear Countess desires no other happiness than to see me happy."

"And therefore," said Helene cynically, "she will warn you to beware. She will hunt up all my offences against holy German morals—"

"I don't care what she hunts up. All I ask is, be a monotheist henceforwards."

"Now you are asking me to become a Jewess."

"I ask you only to become my wife."

He caught her hands passionately. His eyes seemed to drink her in. She fluttered, enjoying her bird-like helplessness.

"Turn your eyes away, my royal eagle!"

"You are mine! you are mine!" he cried.

"I am my father's—I am Janko's," she panted.

"They are shadows. Listen to yourself. Be true to yourself."

"I have no self. It seems so selfish to have one. I am anything—a fay, a sprite, an elf." She freed her hands with a sudden twist and ran laughing up the mountain.

"To the sunrise!" she cried. "To the sunrise!"

He gave chase: "To the sunrise! To the symbol!"

X

But the next morning the symbolic sunrise they rose to see was hidden by fog and rain.

And—what was still more disappointing to Lassalle—Mrs. Arson insisted on escaping with her charges from this depressing climate and re-descending to Wabern, the village near Berne, where they had been staying.

Not even Lassalle's fascinations and persuasions could counteract the pertinacious plash-plash of the rain, and the chilling mist, and perhaps the uneasy pricks of her awakening chaperon-conscience. Nor could he extract a decisive "Yes" from his fluttering volatile enchantress. At Kaltbad, where they said farewell, he pressed her hands with passion. "For a little while! Be prudent and strong! You have the goodness of a child—and a child's will. Oh, if I could pour into these blue veins"—he kissed them fiercely—"only one drop of my giant's will, of my Titanic energy. Grip my hands; perhaps I can do it by magnetism. I will to join our lives. You must will too. Then there are no difficulties. Only say 'Yes'—but definitely, unambiguously, of your own free will—and I answer for the rest."

The thought of Janko resurged painfully when his giant's will was left behind on the heights. How ill she would be using him—her pretty delicate boy!

The giant's will left behind her? Never had Helene been more mistaken. The very reverse! It went before her all day like a pillar of fire. At the first stopping-place a letter already awaited her, brought by a swift courier; lower down a telegram; as she got off her horse another letter; at her hotel two copious telegrams; as she stepped on board the lake steamer a final letter—all breathing passion, encouragement, solicitous instructions to wrap up well.

Wrap up well! He wrapped one up in himself!

Half fascinated, half panting for free air, but wholly flattered and enamoured, she wrote at once to break off with Janko and surrender to her Satanic Ferdinand.

"Yes, friend Satan, the child wills! A drop of your diabolical blood has passed into her veins. I am yours for life. But first try reasonable means. Make my parents' acquaintance, cover up your horns and tail, try and win me like a bourgeois. If that fails, there is always Egypt. But quick, quick: I cannot bear scenes and delays and comments. Once we are married, let society stare. With you to lean on I snap my fingers at the world. The obstacles are gigantic, but you are also a giant, who with God's help smashes rocks to sand, that even my breath can blow away. I must stab the beautiful dream of a noble youth, but even this—frightfully painful for me as it is—I do for you. I say nothing of the disappointment to my parents, of the pain of all I love and respect. I am writing to Holthoff, my father-confessor. We must have him for us, with us, near us. God has destined us for each other."

A telegram replied: "Bravissimo! I am on my way to join you."

And to the Countess, fighting rheumatism at the waters of Wildbad in the Black Forest, he wrote: "The rain has passed, the long fog has gone. The mountains stand out mighty and dazzling, peak beyond peak, like the heights of a life. What a sunset! The Eiger seemed wrapped in a vapor of burning gold. My sufferings are nearly all wiped out. I am joyous, full of life and love. And I have also finished at last with that terrible correspondence for the Union. Seventy-six pages of minute writing have I sent to Berlin yesterday and to-day, and I breathe again. In my yesterday's letter I broke Helene to you. It is extraordinarily fortunate that on the verge of forty I should be able to find a wife so beautiful, so sympathetic, who loves me so much, and who, as you and I agreed was indispensable, is entirely absorbed in my personality. In your last letter you throw cold water on my proposed journey to

Hamburg; and perhaps you are right in thinking the coup I planned not so great and critical as I have been imagining. But how you misunderstand my motives when you write: 'Cannot you, till your health is re-established, find contentment for a while in science, in friendship, in Nature?' You think politics the breath of my nostrils. Ah, how little you are au fait with me! I desire nothing more ardently than to be quite rid of all politics, and to devote myself to science, friendship, and Nature. I am sick and tired of politics. Truly I would burn as passionately for them as any one, if there were anything serious to be done, or if I had the power or saw the means, a means worthy of me; for without supreme power nothing can be done. For child's play, however, I am too old and too great. That is why I very reluctantly undertook the Presidentship. I only yielded to you, and that is why it now weighs upon me terribly. If I were but rid of it, this were the moment I should choose to go to Naples with you. But how to get rid of it? For events, I fear, will develop slowly, so slowly, and my burning soul finds no interest in these children's maladies and petty progressions. Politics means actual, immediate activity. Otherwise one can work just as well for humanity by writing. I shall still try to exercise at Hamburg a pressure upon events. But up to what point it will be effective I cannot say. Nor do I promise myself much from it. Ah, could I but get out of it!

"Helene is a wonderful creature, the only personality I could wed. She looks forward to your friendship. I know it. For I am a good observer of women without seeming to be. That dear enfant du diable, as everybody calls her at Geneva, has a deep sympathy for you, because she is, as Goethe puts it, an original nature. Only one fault—but gigantic. She has no Will. But if we became husband and wife, that would cease to be a fault. I have enough Will for two, and she would be the flute in the hands of the artist. But till then—"

The Countess showed herself a kind Cassandra. His haste, she replied, would ruin his cause. He had to deal with Philistines. The father was a man of no small self-esteem—he had been the honored tutor of Maximilian II., and was now in high favor at the Bavarian court, even controlling university and artistic appointments. A Socialist would be especially distasteful to him. Twenty years ago Varnhagen von Ense had heard him lecture on Communism—good-humoredly, wittily, shrugging shoulders at these poor, fantastic fools who didn't understand that the world was excellently arranged centuries before they were born. Helene herself, with her weak will, would be unable to outface her family. Before approaching the parents, had he not better wait the final developments of his law-case? If he had to leave Germany temporarily to escape the imprisonment, would not that be a favorable opportunity for prosecuting his love-affairs in Switzerland? And what a pity to throw up his milk-cure! "Enfin, I wish you success, mon cher enfant, though I will only put complete trust in my own eyes. In feminine questions you have neither reason nor judgment."

Lassalle's response was to enclose a pretty letter from Helene, pleading humbly for the Countess's affection. Together let them nurse the sick eagle. She herself was but a child, and would lend herself to any childish follies to drive the clouds from his brow. She would try to comprehend his magnificent soul, his giant mind, and in happiness or in sorrow would remain faithful and firm at his side.

The Countess knit her brow. Then Lassalle was already with this Helena in Berne.

XI

It was a week of delicious happiness, niched amid the eternal mountains, fused with skies and waters.

With an accommodating chaperon who knew no German, the couple could do and say what they pleased. Lassalle, throwing off the heavy burdens of prophet and politician, alternated between brilliant lover and happy-hearted boy. It was almost a honeymoon. Now they were children with all the overflowing endearments of plighted lovers. Now they were on the heights of intellect, talking poetry and philosophy, and reading Lassalle's works; now they were discussing Balzac's Physiologie du Mariage. Anon Lassalle was a large dog, gambolling before his capricious mistress. "Lie down, sir," she cried once, as he was reading a poem to her. And with peals of Homeric laughter Ferdinand declared she had found the only inoffensive way of silencing him. "If ever I displease you in future, you have only to say, 'Lie down, sir!'" And he began barking joyously.

And in the glow of this happiness his sense of political defeat evaporated. He burgeoned, expanded, flung back his head in the old, imperial way. "By God!" he said, marching up and down the room feverishly, "you have chosen no mean destiny. Have you any idea of what Ferdinand Lassalle's wife will be? Look at me!" He stood still. "Do I look a man to be content with the second rôle in the State? Do you think I give the sleep of my nights, the marrow of my bones, the strength of my lungs, to draw somebody else's chestnuts out of the fire? Do I look like a political martyr? No! I wish to act, to fight, and also to enjoy the crown of victory, to place it on your brow."

A vision of the roaring streets and floral arches of the Rhenish cities flashed past him. "Chief of the People, President of the German Republic,—there's the only true sovereignty. That was what kings were once—giants of brain and brawn. King—one who knows, one who can! Headship is for the head. What is this mock dignity that stands on the lying breaths of winking courtiers? What is this farcical, factitious glamour that will not bear the light of day? The Grace of God? Ay, give me god-like manhood, and I will bend the knee. But to ask me to worship a stuffed purple robe on a worm-eaten throne! 'Tis an insult to manhood and reason. Hereditary kingship! When you can breed souls as you breed racehorses it will be time to consider that. Stand here by my side before this mirror. Is not that a proud, a royal couple? Did not Nature fashion these two creatures in a holiday mood of joy and intoxication? Vive la République and its Queen with the golden locks!"

"Vive la République and its eagle King!" she cried, intoxicated, yet with more of dramatic enjoyment than of serious conviction.

"Bravo! You believe in our star! Since I met you I see it shining clearer over the heights. We mount, we mount, peak beyond peak. We have enemies enough now, thick as the serpents in tropic forests. Well, let them soil with their impure slaver the hem of our garments. But how they will crawl fangless when Ferdinand—the Elect of the People—makes his solemn entry into Berlin. And at his side, drawn by six white horses, his blonde darling, changed into the first woman of Germany." He, too, though to him the fancy was real enough for the moment, enjoyed it with a certain artistic aloofness.

XII

In honor of the fiancés—for such they openly avowed themselves, Geneva and Helene's family being sufficiently distant to be temporarily forgotten—the American Consul at Berne gave a charming dinner. There was a gallant old Frenchman, a honey-tongued Italian, a pervasive air of complimentary congratulation. Helene returned to her hotel, thrilling with pleasure and happy auguries. The night was soft and warm. Before undressing she leaned out of the window of her room on the ground floor, and gazed upon the eternal glaciers, sparkling like silver under the full moon. Through every sense she drank in the mystery and perfume of the night, till her spirit seemed at one with the stars and the mountains. Suddenly she felt two mighty arms clasped about her. Lassalle stood outside. Her heart throbbed violently.

"Hush!" he said, "don't be frightened. I will stay outside here, good and quiet, till you are tired and say, 'Lie down, sir!' Then I will go!"

"My gentle Romeo!" she whispered, and bent her fragrant lips to meet his—the divine kiss of god and goddess in the divine night. "My Ferdinand!" she breathed. "If we should be parted after all. I tremble to think of it. My father will never consent."

"He shall consent. And you don't even need his consent. You are of age."

"Then take me now, dear heart. I am yours—your creature, your thing. Fly away with me, my beautiful eagle, to Paris, to Egypt, where you will. Let us be happy Bohemians. We do not need the world. We have ourselves, and the moonlight, and the mountains."

She was maddening to-night, his enfant du diable. But he kept a last desperate grip upon his common sense. What would his friends say if he involved Helene in the scandal of an elopement? What would Holthoff say, what Baron Korff? Surely this was not the conduct that would commend itself to the chivalry and nobility of Berlin! And besides, how could his political career survive a new scandal? He was already sufficiently hampered by his old connection with the Countess, and not even a public acquittal and twenty years had sufficed to lay that accusation of instigating the stealing of a casket of papers from her husband's mistress, which was perhaps the worst legacy of the great Hatzfeldt case. No, he must win his bride honorably: the sanctities and dignities of wedlock were seductive to the Bohemian in love.

"We shall have ourselves and the world, too," he urged gently. "Let us enter our realm with the six white horses, not in a coach with drawn blinds. Your father shall give you to me, I tell you, in the eye of day. What, am I an advertisement canvasser to be shown the door? Shall my darling not have as honorable nuptials as her father's wife. Shall the Elect of the People confess that a petty diplomatist didn't consider him good enough for a son-in-law? Think how Bismarck would chuckle. After all I have said to him!"

Her confidence came back. Yes, one might build one's house on the rock of such a Will! "What have you said to him?"

He laughed softly. "I've let slip a secret, little girl."

"Tell me."

"Incredible! That baby with her little fingers,"—he seized them—"with her fairy paws, she plunges boldly into my most precious secrets, into my heart's casket, picks out the costliest jewel, and asks for it."

"Well, do you like him? Is he an intellectual spirit?"

"Hum! If he is, we are not. He is iron, and of iron we make steel, and of steel pretty weapons; but one can make nothing but weapons. I prefer gold. Gold like my darling's hair"—he caressed it—"like my own magic power over men. You shall see, darling, how your gold and mine will triumph."

"But you also are always speaking of arms, of blood, of battles; and Revolutions are scarcely forged without arms and iron."

"Child, child," he answered, drawing her golden locks to his lips, "why do you wish to learn all in this beautiful starry night? The conquests of thousands of years, the results of profound studies, you ask for as for toys. To speak of battles, to call to arms, is by no means the same thing as to sabre one's fellow, one's brother, with icy heart and bloodstained hand. Don't you understand, sly little thing, of what arms I speak, of the golden weapons of the spirit, eloquence, the love of humanity, the effort to raise to manly dignity the poor, the unfortunate, the workers. Above all, I mean—Will. These noble weapons, these truly golden weapons, I count higher and more useful than the rusted swords of Mediævalism."

Her eyes filled with tears. She felt herself upborne on waves of religious emotion towards those shining stars. The temptation was over.

"Good-night, my love," she said humbly.

He drew her face to his in passionate farewell, and seemed as if he would never let her go. When her window closed he strode towards the glaciers.

An adventure next day came to show the conquered Helena that her spiritual giant was no less king of men physically. At the American Consul's dinner an expedition on the Niessen had been arranged. But as the party was returning at nightfall across the fields, and laughing over Lassalle's sprightly anecdotes, suddenly a dozen diabolical gnomes burst upon them with savage roars and incomprehensible inarticulate jabberings, and began striking at hazard with their short, solid cudgels, almost ere the startled picnickers could recognize in these bestial creatures, with their enormously swollen heads and horrible hanging goitres, the afflicted idiot peasants of the valley. The gallant Frenchman and the honey-tongued Italian screamed with the women, and made even less play with umbrellas and straps; but Lassalle fell like a thunderbolt with his Robespierre stick upon the whole band of cretins, and reduced them to howls and bloodstained tears. It was only then that Lassalle was able to extract from them that the party had trampled over the hay in their fields, and that they demanded compensation. Being given money, they departed, growling and waving their cudgels. When the excursionists looked at one another they found themselves all in rags, and Lassalle's face disfigured by two heavy blows. Helene ran to him with a cry.

"You are wounded, bruised!"

"No, only one of the towers of the Bastille," he said, ruefully surveying the stick; "the brutes have dinted it."

"And there are people who call him coward because he won't fight duels," thought Helene adoringly.

XIII

The drama shifted to Geneva, where heroine preceded hero by a few hours, charged to be silent till her parents had personally experienced Lassalle's fascinations. He had scarcely taken possession of his room in the Pension Bovet when a maidservant brought in a letter from Helene, and ere he had time to do more than break the envelope, Helene herself burst in.

"Take me away, take me away," she cried hysterically.

He flew to support her.

"What has happened?"

"I cannot bear it. I cannot fight them. Save me, my king, my master. Let us fly across the frontier—to Paris." She clung to him wildly.

Sternness gathered on his brow.

"Then you have disobeyed me!" he said. "Why?"

"I have written you," she sobbed.

He laid her gently on the bed, and ran his eye through the long, hysteric letter.

Unhappy coincidence! At Helene's arrival, her whole family had met her joyously at the railway station, overbrimming with the happy news that her little sister, Marguerite, had just been proposed to by Count Kayserling.

Helene had thought this a heaven-sent opportunity of breaking her own happiness to her radiant mother, foolishly forgetting that the Count Kayserling would be the last man in the world to endure a Jew and a demagogue as a brother-in-law. Terrible scenes had followed—the mother's tears, the father's thunders, the general family wail and supplication, sisters trembling for their prospects, brothers anticipating the sneers of club-land. What! exchange Prince Janko for a thief!

Cross-examined by Lassalle, Helene admitted her mother was not so furious as her father, and had even, weeping on her bosom, promised to try and smooth the Baron down. But she knew that was impossible—her father considered nothing but his egoistic plans. And so, when the dinner-bell was sounding, informed with a mad courage by the thought of her hero's proximity, she had flown to him.

Lassalle felt that the test-moment of his life had come, and the man of action must rise to it. He scribbled three telegrams—one to his mother, one to his sister, Frau Friedland, and one to the Countess, asking all to come at once.

"You must have a chaperon," he interjected. "And till one of the three arrives, who is there here?"

She sobbed out the address of Madame Rognon. Lassalle opened the door to hand over the telegrams, and saw the woman who had brought Helene's letter lingering uneasily, and he had the unhappiest yet not least characteristic inspiration of his life. "These to the telegraph office," he said aloud, and in a whisper: "Tell the Baroness von Dönniges that we shall be at Madame Rognon's."

For, with lightning rapidity, his brain had worked out a subtle piece of heroic comedy. He would restore Helene to her mother, he would play the grand seigneur, the spotless Bayard, he, the Jew, the thief, the demagogue, the Don Juan; his chivalry would shame this little diplomatist. In no case could they refuse him the girl, she was too hopelessly compromised. All the Pension had seen her—the mother would be shrewd enough to understand that. She must allow the renunciation to remain merely verbal, but the words would sound how magnificent!

The scene was duly played. The bewildered Helene, whom he left in the dark, confused by the unexpected appearance of her mother, was thrown into the last stage of dazed distress by being recklessly restored to the maternal bosom. He kissed her good-bye, and she vanished from his sight for ever.

XIV

For he had reckoned without his Janko, always at hand to cover up a scandal. The Will he had breathed into Helene had been exhausted in the one supreme effort of her life. Sucked up again into the family egotism, kept for weeks under a régime of terror and intercepted letters, hurried away from Geneva; chagrined and outraged, too, by her lover's incomprehensible repudiation of her, which only success could have excused, and which therefore became more unpardonable as day followed day without rescue from a giant, proved merely windbag; she fell back with compunction into the tender keeping of the ever-waiting Janko. The one letter her father permitted her to send formally announced her eternal love and devotion for her former fiancé. Profitless to tell the story of how the stricken giant, raving in outer darkness, this Polyphemus who had gouged out his own eye, this Hercules self-invested in the poisoned robe of Nessus, moved heaven and earth to see her again. It was an earthquake, a tornado, a nightmare. He had frenzies of tears, his nights were sleepless reviews of his folly in throwing her away, and vain phantasms of her eyes and lips. He poured out torrents of telegrams and letters, in which cries of torture mingled with minute legal instructions. The correspondence of the Working-Men's Union alone was neglected. He pressed everybody and anybody into his feverish service—musicians, artists, soldiers, antiquarians, aristocrats. Would not Wagner induce the King of Bavaria to speak to von Dönniges? Would not the Catholic Bishop Ketteler help him?—he would become a Catholic. And ever present an insane belief in the reality of her faithlessness, mockingly accompanied by a terribly lucid recognition of the instability of character that made it certain. The "No"—her first word to him at their first meeting—resounded in his ears, prophetically ominous. The sunrise, hidden by rain and mist, added its symbolic gloom. But he felt her lips on his in the marvellous moonlight; a thousand times she clung to him crying, "Take me away!" And now she was to be another's. She refused even to see him. Incredible! Monstrous! If he could only get an interview with her face to face. Then they would see if she was resisting him of her own free will or under pressure illegal for an adult. It was impossible his will-power over her should fail.

Helene evidently thought so too. By fair means and foul, by spies and lawyers and friendly agents, Lassalle's frenzied energy had penetrated through every defence to the inmost entrenchment where she sat cowering. He had exacted the father's consent to an interview. Only Helene's own consent was wanting. His friend Colonel Rustow brought the sick Hercules the account of her refusal—a refusal which made ridiculous his moving of mountains.

"But surely you owe Lassalle some satisfaction," he had protested.

"To what? To his wounded vanity?"

It was the last straw.

"Harlot!" cried Lassalle, and as in a volcanic jet, hurled her from his burning heart.

A terrible calm settled upon him. It was as if fire should become ice. Yes, he understood at last what Destiny had always been trying to tell him—that love and happiness were not for him. He was consecrate to great causes: His Will, entangled with that of others, grew feeble, fruitless. Women were truly enfants du diable. He had been within an ace of abandoning his historical mission. Now he would arise, strong, sublime: a mighty weapon forged by the gods, and tempered by fire and tears.

Only, one thing must first be done. The past must be wiped off. He must recommence with a clean sheet. True, he had always refused duels. But now he saw the fineness, the necessity of them. In a world of chicanery and treachery the sword alone cut clean.

He sent a challenge to the father, a message of goodwill to the lover. But it was Janko who took up the challenge.

The weapon chosen was the pistol.

Lassalle's friends begged him to practise.

"Useless! I know what is destined."

Never had he been so colossal, so assured. His nerves seemed to have regained their tone. The night before the duel he slept like a tranquil child.

In the early morn, on the way to the field outside Geneva, he begged his second to arrange the duel on the French side of the frontier, so that he might remain in Geneva and settle his account with the father. At the word of command, "One!" Janko's shot rang out. Lassalle's was not a second later, but he had already received his death-wound.

He lay three days, dying in terrible agony, relieved only by copious opium. Between the spasms, surprise possessed his mind that his Will should have counted for nothing before the imperturbable march of the universe. "There will never be Justice for the People," he thought bitterly. "I was a dreamer. Heine was right. A mad world, my masters." But sometimes he had a gleam of suspicion that it was he that had lacked sanity. His Will had become mere wilfulness. In his love as in his crusade he had shut his eyes to the brute facts; had precipitated what could only be coaxed. "I die by my own hand," he said. If he had only married Rosalie Zander, who still lived on, loving him! These Russian and Bavarian minxes were neurotic, fickle, shifting as sand; the daughters of Judæa were sane, cheerful, solid. Then he thought of his own sister married to that vulgarian, Friedland. He saw her, a rosy-cheeked girl, sitting at the Passover table, with its picturesque ritual. How happy were those far-off pious days! And then he felt a cold wind, remembering how Riekchen had hidden her face to laugh at these mediæval mummeries, and to spit out the bitter herbs, so meaningless to her.

O terrible tragi-comedy of life, O strange, tangled world, in which poor, petty man must walk, tripped by endless coils—religion, race, sex, custom, wealth, poverty! World that from boyhood he had seemed to see stretching so clearly before him, to be mapped out with lucid logic, to be bestridden with triumphant foot by men become as gods, knowing good and evil.

Only one thing was left—to die unbroken.

He had his lawyer brought to his bedside, went through his last testament again, left money for the Union, recommended it to the workers as their one sure path of salvation. Moses had only been permitted to gaze upon the Promised Land, but the Chosen People—the Germans—should yet luxuriate in its milk and honey.

A month after his meeting with Helene on the Righi—a month after his glad shout, "By all the gods of Greece, 'tis she!"—he was a corpse, the magic voice silent for ever; while the woman he had sought was to give herself to his slayer, and the movement he had all but abandoned for her was to become a great power in the State, under the ever-growing glamour of his memory.

The Countess bent over the body. A strange, grim joy mingled with her rage and despair. None of all these women had the right to share in her grief. He belonged to her—to her and the People. Yes, she would bear the body of her cher enfant through the provinces of the Rhine—he had been murdered by a cunning political plot, the People who loved him should rise and avenge their martyred Messiah.

And suddenly she remembered with a fresh pang the one woman who had a right to share her grief, nay, to call him—in no figurative sense—"enfant"; the wrinkled old Jewess, palsied and deaf and peevish, who lived on in a world despoiled of his splendid fighting strength, of his superb fore-visionings.

THE PRIMROSE SPHINX

I

In the choir of the old-fashioned church of Hughenden, that broods amid the beautiful peace of English meadows, there stands, on the left hand of the aisle, a black high-backed stall of polished oak, overhung by the picturesque insignia of the Order of the Garter.

In the pavement behind it gleams a square slab, dedicated by "his grateful sovereign and friend" to her great Prime Minister, and heaped in the spring with primroses.

And on this white memorial is sculptured in bas-relief the profile of the head of a Semitic Sphinx, round whose mute lips flickers in a faint sardonic smile the wisdom of the ages.

II

I see him, methinks, in life, Premier of England, Lord Privy Seal, Earl Beaconsfield of Beaconsfield, Viscount Hughenden of Hughenden, sitting in his knightly stall, listening impassibly to the country parson's sermon. His head droops on his breast, but his coal-black inscrutable eyes are open.

It is the hour of his star.

He is just back from the Berlin Congress, bringing "Peace with Honor." The Continent has stood a-tiptoe to see the wonderful English Earl pass and repass. He has been the lion of a congress that included Bismarck. The laurels and the Oriental palm placed by his landlord on the hotel-balcony have but faintly typified the feeling of Europe. His feverous reception in England, from Dover pier onwards, has recalled an earlier, a more romantic world. Fathers have brought their little ones to imprint upon their memories the mortal features of this immortal figure, who passes through a rain of flowers to his throne in Downing Street. The London press, with scarce an exception, is in the dust at his feet—with the proud English nobles and all that has ever flouted or assailed him.

The sunshine comes floridly through the stained-glass windows, and lies upon the austere crucifix.

III

By what devious ways has he wandered hither—from that warm old Portuguese synagogue in Bevis Marks, whence his father withdrew under the smart of a fine from "the gentlemen of the Mahamad?"

But hark! The parson—as paradoxically—is reading a Jewish psalm.

"'The Lord said unto my lord: Sit thou on my right hand, until I make thine enemies thy footstool. The Lord shall send the rod of thy power out of Zion: be thou ruler in the midst of thine enemies. In the day of thy power shall the people offer thee freewill offerings with a holy worship: the dew of thy birth is of the womb of the morning.'"

The Earl remains impassive.

"Half Christendom worships a Jewess, and the other half a Jew."

Whom does he worship?

"Sensible men never tell."

IV

Yet in that facial mask I seem to read all the tale of the long years of desperate waiting, only half sweetened by premature triumphs of pen and person; all the rancorous energies of political strife.

And as I gaze, a sense of something shoddy oppresses me, of tinsel and glitter and flamboyance: a feeling that here is no true greatness, no sphinx-like sublimity. A shadow of the world and the flesh falls across the brooding figure, a Napoleonic vulgarity coarsens the features, there is a Mephistophelian wrinkle in the corner of the lips.

I think of his books, of his grandiose style, gorgeous as his early waistcoats and gold chains, the prose often made up of bad blank verse, leavings from his long coxcombical strain to be a poet; of his false-sublime and his false-romantic, of his rococo personages, monotonously magnificent; of his pseudo-Jewish stories, and his braggart assertions of blood, played off against the insulting pride of the proudest aristocracy in the world, and combined with a politic perseverance to be more English than the English;

of his naïve delight in fine clothes and fine dishes and fine company; of his nice conduct of a morning and evening cane; of his morbid self-consciousness of his gifts and his genius; of his unscrupulous chase of personal success and of Fame—that shadow which great souls cast, and little souls pursue as substance; of his scrupulous personal rejection of Love—Love, the one touch of true romance in his novels—and his pecuniary marriage for his career's sake, after the manner of his tribe; of his romanesque conception of the British aristocracy, which he yet dominates, because he is not really rooted in the social conceptions which give it its prestige, and so is able to manœuvre it artistically from without, intellect detached from emotion: to play English politics like a game of chess, moving proud peers like pawns, with especial skill in handling his Queen; his very imperturbability under attack, only the mediæval Jew's self-mastery before the grosser-brained persecutor.

I think these things and the Sphinx yields up his secret—the open secret of the Ghetto parvenu.

V

But as I look again upon his strange Eastern face, so deep-lined, so haggard, something subtler and finer calls to me from the ruins of its melancholy beauty.

Into this heavy English atmosphere he brings not only the shimmer of ideas and wit, but—a Heine of action—the fantasy of personal adventure, and—when audacity has been crowned by empery—of dramatic surprises of policy. A successful Lassalle, he flutters the stagnant castes of aristocracy by the supremacy of the individual Will.

To a country that lumbers on from precedent to precedent, and owes its very constitution to the pinch of practical exigencies, he brings the Jew's unifying sweep of idea. First, he is the encourager of the Young England party, for, conceiving himself child of a race of aristocrats whose mission is to civilize the world, he feels the duty of guidance to which these young English squires and nobles are born. The bourgeois he hates—only the pomp of sovereignty and the pathos of poverty move his soul; his lifelong dream is of a Tory democracy, wherein the nobles shall make happy the People that is exploited by the middle classes. Product of a theocratic state, where the rich and the poor are united in God, he is shocked by "the Two Nations" into which, by the gradual break-up of the feudal world, this England is split. The cry of the Chartists does not leave him cold. He is one in revolt with Byron and Shelley against a Philistine world. And later, to a mighty empire that has grown fortuitously, piecemeal, by the individual struggles of independent pioneers or isolated filibusters, he gives a unifying soul, a spirit, a mission. He perceives with Heine that as Puritan Britain is already the heir of ancient Palestine, and its State Church only the guardian of the Semitic principle, popularized, so is it by its moral and physical energy, the destined executant of the ideals of Zion; that it is planting the Law like a great shady tree in the tropic deserts and arid wastes of barbarism. That grandeur and romance of their empire, of which the English of his day are only dimly aware, because like their constitution it has evolved without a conscious principle, he, the outsider, sees. He is caught by the fascination of its vastness, of its magnificent possibilities. And in very deed he binds England closer to her colonies, and restores her dwindled prestige in the Parliament of Nations. He even proclaims her an Asiatic power.

For his heart is always with his own people—its past glories, its persistent ubiquitous potency, despite ubiquitous persecution. He sees himself the appointed scion of a Chosen Race, the only race to which God has ever spoken, and perhaps the charm of acquired Cyprus is its propinquity to Palestine, the only soil on which God has ever deigned to reveal Himself.

And, like his race, he has links with all the human panorama.

He is in touch with the humors and graces of European courts and cities, has rapport with the rich-dyed, unchanging, double-dealing East, enjoys the picaresque life of the Spanish mountains: he feels the tragedy of vanished Rome, the marble appeal of ancient Athens, the mystery of the Pyramids, the futility of life; his books palpitate with world-problems.

And, as I think these things, his face is transfigured and he becomes—beneath all his dazzle of deed—a Dreamer of the Ghetto.

VI

So think I. But what—as the country parson's sermon drones on—thinks the Sphinx?

Who shall tell?

DREAMERS IN CONGRESS

"By the rivers of Babylon, there we sat down; yea, we wept, when we remembered Zion." By the river of Bâle we sit down, resolved to weep no more. Not the German Rhine, but the Rhine ere it leaves the land of liberty; where, sunning itself in a glory of blue sky and white cloud, and overbrooded by the eternal mountains; it swirls its fresh green waves and hurries its laden rafts betwixt the quaint old houses and dreaming spires, and under the busy bridges of the Golden Gate of Switzerland.

In the shady courtyard of the Town Hall are sundry frescoes testifying to the predominant impress on the minds of its citizens of the life and thoughts of a little people that flourished between two and three thousand years ago in the highlands of Asia Minor. But, amid these suggestive illustrations of ancient Jewish history, the strangest surely is that of Moses with a Table of the Law, on which are written the words: "Who brought thee out of the land of Egypt, out of the house of bondage."

For here, after all this travail of the centuries, a very modern Moses—in the abstract-concrete form of a Congress—is again meditating the deliverance of Israel from the house of bondage.

Not in the Town Hall, however, but in the Casino the Congress meets, and, where Swiss sweethearts use to dance, are debated the tragic issues of an outcast nation. An oblong hall, of drab yellow, with cane chairs neatly parted in the middle, and green-baized tables for reporters, and a green-baized rostrum, and a green-baized platform, over which rise the heads and festal shirt-fronts of the leaders.

A strangely assorted set of leaders, but all with that ink-mark on the brow which is as much on the Continent the badge of action, as it is in England the symbol of sterility; all believing more or less naïvely that the pen is mightier than the millionaire's gold.

Only one of them hitherto has really stirred the world with his pen-point—a prophet of the modern, preaching "Woe, woe" by psycho-physiology; in himself a breezy, burly undegenerate, with a great gray head marvellously crammed with facts and languages; now to prove himself golden-hearted and golden-mouthed, an orator touching equally to tears or laughter. In striking contrast with this quasi-Teutonic figure shows the leonine head, with its tossing black mane and shoulders, of the Russian leader, Apollo turned Berserker, beautiful, overpowering, from whose resplendent mouth roll in mountain thunder the barbarous Russian syllables.

And even as no two of the leaders are alike, so do the rank and file fail to resemble one another. Writers and journalists, poets and novelists and merchants, professors and men of professions—types that once sought to slough their Jewish skins, and mimic, on Darwinian principles, the colors of the environment, but that now, with some tardy sense of futility or stir of pride, proclaim their brotherhood in Zion—they are come from many places; from far lands and from near, from uncouth, unknown villages of Bukowina and the Caucasus, and from the great European capitals; thickliest from the pales of persecution, in rare units from the free realms of England and America—a strange phantasmagoria of faces. A small, sallow Pole, with high cheek-bones; a blond Hungarian, with a flaxen moustache; a brown, hatchet-faced Roumanian; a fresh-colored Frenchman, with eye-glasses; a dark, Marrano-descended Dutchman; a chubby German; a fiery-eyed Russian, tugging at his own hair with excitement, perhaps in prescience of the prison awaiting his return; a dusky Egyptian, with the close-cropped, curly black hair, and all but the nose of a negro; a yellow-bearded Swede; a courtly Viennese lawyer; a German student, with proud duel-slashes across his cheek; a Viennese student, first fighter in the University, with a colored band across his shirt-front; a dandy, smelling of the best St. Petersburg circles; and one solitary caftan-Jew, with ear-locks and skull-cap, wafting into the nineteenth century the cabalistic mysticism of the Carpathian Messiah.

Who speaks of the Jewish type? One can only say negatively that these faces are not Christian. Is it the stamp of a longer, more complex heredity? Is it the brand of suffering? Certainly a stern Congress, the speeches little lightened by humor, the atmosphere of historic tragedy too overbrooding for intellectual dalliance. Even the presence of the gayer sex—for there are a few ladies among the delegates, and more peep down from the crowded spectators' gallery that runs sideways along the hall—only makes a few shots of visual brightness in the sober scene. Seriousness is stamped everywhere; on the broad-bulging temples of the Russian oculist, on the egg-shaped skull and lank white hair of the Heidelberg professor, on the open countenance of the Hungarian architect, on the weak, narrow lineaments of the neurotic Hebrew poet; it gives dignity to red hair and freckles, tones down the grossness of too-fleshy cheeks, and lends an added beauty to finely-cut features.

Superficially, then, they have little in common, and if almost all speak German—the language of the Congress—it is only because they are all masters of three or four tongues. Yet some subtle instinct links them each to each; presage, perhaps, of some brotherhood of mankind, of which ingathered Israel—or even ubiquitous Israel—may present the type.

Through the closed red-curtained windows comes ever and anon the sharp ting of the bell of an electric car, and the President, anxiously steering the course of debate through difficult international cross-roads, rings his bell almost as frequently.

A majestic Oriental figure, the President's—not so tall as it appears when he draws himself up and stands dominating the assembly with eyes that brood and glow—you would say one of the Assyrian Kings, whose sculptured heads adorn our Museums, the very profile of Tiglath-Pileser. In sooth, the beautiful sombre face of a kingly dreamer, but of a Jewish dreamer who faces the fact that flowers are grown in dung. A Shelley "beats in the air his luminous wings in vain"; our Jewish dreamer dreams along the lines of life; his dream but discounts the future, his prophecy is merely fore-speaking, his vision prevision. He talks agriculture, viticulture, subvention of the Ottoman Empire, both by direct tribute and indirect enrichment; stocks and shares, railroads, internal and to India; natural development under expansion—all the jargon of our iron age. Let not his movement be confounded with those petty projects for helping Jewish agriculturists into Palestine. What! Improve the Sultan's land without any political equivalent guaranteed in advance! Difficulty about the holy places of Christianity and Islam? Pooh! extra-territorial.

A practised publicist, a trained lawyer, a not unsuccessful comedy writer, converted to racial self-consciousness by the "Hep, Hep" of Vienna, and hurried into unforeseen action by his own paper-scheme of a Jewish State, he has, perhaps, at last—and not unreluctantly—found himself as a leader of men.

In a Congress of impassioned rhetoricians he remains serene, moderate; his voice is for the more part subdued; in its most emotional abandonments there is a dry undertone, almost harsh. He quells disorder with a look, with a word, with a sharp touch of the bell. The cloven hoof of the Socialist peeps out from a little group. At once "The Congress shall be captured by no party!" And the Congress is in roars of satisfaction.

'Tis the happy faculty of all idealists to overlook the visible—the price they pay for seeing the unseen. Even our open-eyed Jewish idealist has been blest with ignorance of the actual. But, in his very ignorance of the people he would lead and the country he would lead them to, lies his strength, just as in his admission that his Zionist fervor is only that second-rate species produced by local anti-Semitism, lies a powerful answer to the dangerous libel of local unpatriotism. Of the real political and agricultural conditions of Palestine he knows only by hearsay. Of Jews he knows still less. Not for him the paralyzing sense of the humors of his race, the petty feud of Dutchman and Pole, the mutual superiorities of Sephardi and Ashkenazi, the grotesque incompatibility of Western and Eastern Jew, the cynicism and snobbery of the prosperous, the materialism of the uneducated adventurers in unexploited regions. He stands so high and aloof that all specific colorings and markings are blurred for him into the common brotherhood, and, if he is cynic enough to suspect them, he is philosopher enough to recognize that all nations are compact of incongruites, vitalized by warring elements. Nor has he any sympathetic perception of the mystic religious hopes of generations of zealots, of the great swirling spiritual currents of Ghetto life. But in a national movement—which appears at first sight hopeless, because it lacks the great magnetizer, religion—lies a chance denied to one who should boldly proclaim himself the evangel of a modern Judaism, the last of the Prophets. Political Zionism alone can transcend and unite: any religious formula would disturb and dissever. Along this line may all travel to Jerusalem. And, as the locomotive from Jaffa draws all alike to the sacred city, and leaves them there to their several matters, so may the pious concern themselves not at all with the religion of the engineer.

Not this the visionary figure created by the tear-dimmed yearning of the Ghetto; no second Sabbataï Zevi, master of celestial secrets, divine reincarnation, come with signs and wonders to lead back Israel to the Promised Land. Still less the prophet prefigured by Christian visionaries, some of whom, fevered nevertheless, press upon the Congress itself complex collations of texts, or little cards with the sign of the cross. Palestine, indeed, but an afterthought: an aspiration of unsuspected strength, to be utilized—like all human forces—by the maker of history. States are the expression of souls; in any land the Jewish soul could express itself in characteristic institutions, could shake off the long oppression of the ages, and renew its youth in touch with the soil. Yet since there is this longing for Palestine, let us make capital of it—capital that will return its safe percentage. A rush to Palestine will mean all that seething medley of human wants and activities out of which profits are snatched by the shrewd—gold-rush and God-rush, they are both one in their economic working. May not the Jews themselves take shares in so promising a project? May not even their great bankers put their names to such a prospectus? The shareholders incur no liability beyond the extent of their shares; there shall be no call upon them to come to Palestine—let them remain in their snug nests; the Jewish Company, Limited, seeks a home only for the desolate dove that finds no rest for the sole of her feet.

And yet beneath all this statesmanlike prose, touched with the special dryness of the jurist, lurk the romance of the poet and the purposeful vagueness of the modern evolutionist; the fantasy of the Hungarian, the dramatic self-consciousness of the literary artist, the heart of the Jew.

Is one less a poet because he regards the laws of reality, less religious because he accepts them, less a Jew because he will live in his own century? Our dreamer will have none of the Mediæval, is enamoured of the Modern; has lurking admiration of the "over-man" of Nietzsche, even to be overpassed by the coming Jerusalem Jew; the psychical Eurasian, the link and interpreter between East and West—nay, between antiquity and the modern spirit; the synthesis of mankind, saturated with the culture of the nations, and now at last turning home again, laden with the spiritual spoils of the world—for the world's benefit. He shall found an ideal modern state, catholic in creed, righteous in law, a centre of conscience—even geographically—in a world relapsing to Pagan chaos. And its flag shall be a "shield of David," with the Lion of Judah rampant, and twelve stars for the Tribes. No more of the cringing and the whispering in dark corners; no surreptitious invasion of Palestine. The Jew shall demand right, not tolerance. Israel shall walk erect. And he, Israel's spokesman, will not juggle with diplomatic combinations—he will play cards on table. He has nothing to say to the mob, Christian or Jewish, he will not intrigue with political underlings. He is no demagogue; he will speak with kings in their palaces, with prime ministers in their cabinets. There is a touch of the ὕβρισ of Lassalle, of the magnificence of Manasseh Bueno Barzillai Azevedo Da Costa, King of the question-beggars.

Do you object that the poor will be the only ones to immigrate to Palestine? Why, it is just those that we want. Prithee, how else shall we make our roads and plant our trees? No mention now of the Eurasian exemplar, the synthetic "over-man." Perhaps he is only to evolve. Do you suggest that an inner ennobling of scattered Israel might be the finer goal, the truer antidote to anti-Semitism? Simple heart, do you not see it is just for our good—not our bad—qualities that we are persecuted? A jugglery— specious enough for the moment—with the word "good"; forceful "struggle-for-life" qualities substituted for spiritual, for ethical. And yet to doubt that the world would—and does—respond sympathetically to the finer elements so abundantly in Israel, is it not to despair of the world, of humanity? In such a world, what guarantee against the pillage of the Third Temple? And in such a world were life worth living at all? And, even with Palestine for ultimate goal, do you counsel delay, a nursing of the Zionist flame, a gradual education and preparation of the race for a great conscious historic rôle in the world's future, a forty years' wandering in the wilderness to organize or kill off the miscellaneous rabble—then will you, dreamer, turn a deaf ear to the cry of millions oppressed to-day? Would you ignore the appeals of these hundreds of telegrams, of these thousands of petitions with myriads of signatures, for the sake of some visionary perfection of to-morrow? Nay, nay, the cartoon of the Congress shall bring itself to pass. Against the picturesque wailers at the ruins of the Temple wall shall be set the no less picturesque peasants sowing the seed, whose harvest is at once waving grain and a regenerated Israel. The stains of sordid traffic shall be cleansed by the dews and the rains. In the Jewish peasant behold the ideal plebeian of the future; a son of the soil, yet also a son of the spirit. And what fair floriage of art and literature may not the world gain from this great purified nation, carrying in its bosom the experience of the ages?

Not all his own ideas, these; some perhaps only half-consciously present to him, so that even in this very Congress the note of jealousy is heard, the claim of an earlier prophet insisted on fiercely. For a moment the dignified assembly, becomes a prey to atavism, reproduces the sordid squabbles of the Kahal. As if every movement was not fed by subterranean fires, heralded by obscure rumblings, though 'tis only the earthquake or the volcanic jet which leaps into history!

But the President is finely impersonal. Not he, but the Congress. The Bulgarians have a tradition that the Messiah will be born on August 29. He shares this belief. To-day the Messiah has been born—the Congress. "In this Congress we procure for the Jewish people an organ which till now it did not possess, and of which it was so sadly in want. Our cause is too great for the ambition and wilfulness of a single person. It must be lifted up to something impersonal if it is to succeed. And our Congress shall be lasting, not only until we are redeemed from the old state, but still more so afterwards ... serious and lofty, a blessing for the unfortunate, noxious to none, to the honor of all Jews, and worthy of a past, the glory of which is far off, but everlasting."

And, as he steps from the tribune, amid the roar of "Hochs," and the thunder of hands and feet and sticks, and the flutter of handkerchiefs, with men precipitating themselves to kiss his hand, and others weeping and embracing, be sure that no private ambition possesses him, be sure that his heart swells only with the presentiment of great events and with uplifting thoughts of the millions who will thrill to the distant echo of this sublime moment.

What European parliament could glow with such a galaxy of intellect? Is not each man a born orator, master of arts or sciences? Has not the very caftan-Jew from the Carpathians published his poetry and his philosophy, gallantly championing "The Master of the Name" against a Darwinian world? Heine had figured the Jew as a dog, that at the advent of the Princess Sabbath is changed back to a man. More potent than the Princess, the Congress has shown the Jew's manhood to the world. That old painter, whose famous Dance of Death drew for centuries the curious to Bâle, could not picture the Jew save as the gaberdined miser, only dropping his money-bag at Death's touch. Well, here is another sight for him—could Death, that took him too, bring him back for a moment—these scholars, thinkers, poets, from all the lands of the Exile, who stand up in honor of the dead pioneers of Zionism, and, raising their right hands to heaven, cry, "If I forget thee, O Jerusalem, let my right hand forget its cunning!" Yes, the dream still stirs at the heart of the mummied race, the fire quenched two thousand years ago sleeps yet in the ashes. And if our President forgets that the vast bulk of his brethren are unrepresented in his Congress, that they are content with the civic rights so painfully won, and have quite other conceptions of their creed's future, who will grudge him this moment of fine rapture?

Or, when at night, in the students' Kommers, with joyful weeping and with brotherly kisses, sages and gray-beards join in the gaudeamus igitur, who shall deny him grounds for his faith that juvenes sumus yet, that the carking centuries have had no power over our immortal nation. "Age cannot wither her, nor custom stale her infinite variety."

The world in which prophecies are uttered cannot be the world in which prophecies are fulfilled. And yet when—at the wind-up of this memorable meeting—the Rabbi of Bâle, in the black skull-cap of sanctity, ascending the tribune amid the deafening applause of a catholic Congress, expresses the fears of the faithful, lest in the new Jewish State the religious Jew be under a ban; and when the President gravely gives the assurance, amid enthusiasm as frantic, that Judaism has nothing to fear—Judaism, the one cause and consolation of the ages of isolation and martyrdom—does no sense of the irony of history intrude upon his exalted mood?

THE PALESTINE PILGRIM

A vast, motley crowd of poor Jews and Jewesses swayed outside the doors of the great Manchester synagogue, warmed against the winter afternoon by their desperate squeezing and pushing. They stretched from the broad-pillared portico down the steps and beyond the iron railings, far into the street. The wooden benches of the sacred building were already packed with a perspiring multitude, seated indiscriminately, women with men, and even men in the women's gallery, resentfully conscious—for the first time—of the grating. The hour of the address had already struck, but the body of police strove in vain to close the doors against the mighty human stream that pressed on and on, frenzied with the fear of disappointment and the long wait.

A policeman, worming his way in by the caretaker's entrance, bore to the hero of the afternoon the superintendent's message that unless he delayed his speech till the bulk of the disappointed could be got inside, a riot could not be staved off. And so the stream continued to force itself slowly forward, flowing into every nook and gangway, till it stood solid and immovable, heaped like the waters of the Red Sea. And when at last the doors were bolted, and thousands of swarthy faces, illumined faintly by clusters of pendent gas-globes, were turned towards the tall pulpit where the speaker stood, dominant, against the mystic background of the Ark-curtain, it seemed as if the whole Ghetto of Manchester—the entire population of Strange-ways and Redbank—had poured itself into this one synagogue in a great tidal wave, moved by one of those strange celestial influences which have throughout all history disturbed the torpor of the Jewries.

Of these poverty-stricken thousands, sucked hither by the fame of a soldier rumored to represent a Messianic millionaire bent on the restoration and redemption of Israel, Aaron the Pedlar was an atom—ugly, wan, and stooping, with pious ear-locks, and a long, fusty coat, little regarded even by those amid whom he surged and squeezed for hours in patience. Aaron counted for less than nothing in a world he helped to overcrowd, and of which he perceived very little. For, although he did not fail to make a profit on his gilded goods, and knew how to wheedle servants at side-doors, he was far behind his fellows in that misapprehension of the human hurly-burly which makes your ordinary Russian Jew a political oracle. Aaron's interest in politics was limited to the wars of the Kings of Israel and the misdeeds of Titus and Antiochus Epiphanes. To him the modern world was composed of Jews and heathen; and society had two simple sections—the rich and the poor.

"Don't you enjoy travelling?" one of the former section once asked him affably. "Even if it's disagreeable in winter you must pass through a good deal of beautiful scenery in summer."

"If I am on business," replied the pedlar, "how can I bother about the beautiful?"

And, flustered though he was by the condescension of the great person, his naïve counter-query expressed a truth. He lived, indeed, in a strange dream-world, and had no eyes for the real except in the shape of cheap trinkets. He was happier in the squalid streets of Strange-ways, where strips of Hebrew patched the windows of cook-shops, and where a synagogue was ever at hand, than when striding across the purple moors under an open blue sky, or resting with his pack by the side of purling brooks.

Stupid his enemies would have called him, only he was too unimportant to have enemies, the roughs and the children who mocked his passage being actuated merely by impersonal malice. To his friends—if the few who were aware of his existence could be called friends—he was a Schlemihl (a luckless fool).

"A man who earns a pound a week live without a wife!" complained the Shadchan (marriage-broker) to a group of sympathetic cap-makers.

"I suppose he's such a Schlemihl no father would ever look at him!" said a father, with a bunch of black-eyed daughters.

"Oh, but he was married in Russia," said another; "but just as he sent his wife the money to come over, she died."

"And yet you call him a Schlemihl!" cried Moshelé, the cynic.

"Ah, but her family stuck to the money!" retorted the narrator, and captured the laugh.

It was true. After three years of terrible struggle and privation, Aaron had prepared an English home for his Yenta, but she slept instead in a Russian grave. Perhaps if his friends had known how he had thrown away the chance of sending for her earlier, they would have been still more convinced that he was a born Schlemihl. For within eighteen months of his landing in London docks, Aaron, through his rapid mastery of English and ciphering at the evening classes for Hebrew adults, had found a post as book-keeper to a clothes-store in Ratcliff Highway. But he soon discovered that he was expected to fake the invoices, especially when drunken sailors came to rig themselves up in mufti.

"Well, we'll throw the scarf in," the genial salesman would concede cheerily. "And the waistcoat? One-and-three—a good waistcoat, as clean as new, and dirt cheap, so 'elp me."

But when Aaron made out the bill he was nudged to put the one-and-three in the column for pounds and shillings respectively, and even, if the buyer were sufficiently in funds and liquor, to set down the date of the month in the same pecuniary partitions, and to add it up glibly with the rest, calendar and coin together. But Aaron, although he was not averse from honestly misrepresenting the value of goods, drew the line at trickery, and so he was kicked out. It took him a year of nondescript occupations to amass a little stock of mock jewellery wherewith to peddle, and Manchester he found a more profitable centre than the metropolis. Yenta dead, profit and holy learning divided his thoughts, and few of his fellows achieved less of the former or more of the latter than our itinerant idealist.

Such was one of the thousands of souls swarming that afternoon in the synagogue, such was one despised unit of a congregation itself accounted by the world a pitiable mass of superstitious poverty, and now tossing with emotion in the dim spaces of the sacred building.

The Oriental imagination of the hearers magnified the simple soldierly sentences of the orator, touched them with color and haloed them with mystery, till, as the deep gasps and sobs of the audience struck back like blows on the speaker's chest, the contagion of their passion thrilled him to responsive emotion. And, seen through tears, arose for him and them a picture of Israel again enthroned in Palestine, the land flowing once more with milk and honey, rustling with corn and vines planted by their own hands, and Zion—at peace with all the world—the recognized arbitrator of the nations, making true the word of the Prophet: "For from Zion shall go forth the Law, and the word of God from Jerusalem."

To Aaron the vision came like a divine intoxication. He stamped his feet, clapped, cried, shouted. He felt tears streaming down his cheeks like the rivers that watered Paradise. What! This hope that had haunted him from boyhood, wafting from the pages of the holy books, was not then a shadowy splendor on the horizon's rim. It was a solidity, within sight, almost within touch. He himself might hope to sit in peace under his own fig-tree, no more the butt of the street boys. And the vague vision, though in becoming definite it had been transformed to earthliness, was none the less grand for that. He had always dimly expected Messianic miracles, but in that magic afternoon the plain words of the soldier unsealed his eyes, and suddenly he saw clearly that just as, in Israel, every man was his own priest, needing no mediator, so every man was his own Messiah.

And as he squeezed out of the synagogue, unconscious of the chattering, jostling crowd, he saw himself in Zion, worshipping at the Holy Temple, that rose spacious and splendid as the Manchester Exchange. Yes; the Jews must return to Palestine, there must be a great voluntary stream—great, if gradual. Slowly but surely the Jews must win back their country; they must cease trafficking with the heathen and return to the soil, sowing and reaping, so that the Feast of the Ingathering might become a reality instead of a prayer-service. Then should the atonement of Israel be accomplished, and the morning stars sing together as at the first day.

As he walked home along the squalid steeps of Fernie Street and Verdon Street, and gazed in at the uncurtained windows of the one-story houses, a new sense of their sordidness, as contrasted with that bright vision, was borne in upon him. Instead of large families in one ragged room, encumbered with steamy washing, he saw great farms and broad acres; and all that beauty of the face of earth, to which he had been half blind, began to appeal to him now that it was mixed up with religion. In this wise did Aaron become a politician and a modern.

Passing through the poulterer's on his way to his room—the poulterer and he divided the house between them, renting a room each—he paused to talk with the group of women who were plucking the fowls, and told them glad tidings of great fowl-rearing farms in Palestine. He sat down on the bed, which occupied half the tiny shop, and became almost eloquent upon the great colonization movement and the "Society of Lovers of Zion," which had begun to ramify throughout the world.

"Yes; but if all Israel has farms, who will buy my fowls?" said the poulterer's wife.

"You will not need to sell fowls," Aaron tried to explain.

The poulterer shook his head. "The whole congregation is gone mad," he said. "For my part I believe that when the Holy One, blessed be He, brings us back to Palestine, it will be without any trouble of our own. As it is written, I will bear thee upon eagles' wings."

Aaron disputed this notion—which he had hitherto accepted as axiomatic—with all the ardor of the convert. It was galling to find, as he discussed the thing during the next few weeks, that many even of those present at the speech read miracle into the designs of Providence and the millionaire. But Aaron was able to get together a little band of brother souls bent on emigrating together to Palestine, there to sow the seeds of the Kingdom, literally as well as metaphorically. This enthusiasm, however, did not wear well. Gradually, as the memory of the magnetic meeting faded, the pilgrim brotherhood disintegrated, till at last only its nucleus—Aaron—was left in solitary determination.

"You have only yourself," pleaded the backsliders. "We have wife and children."

"I have more than myself," retorted Aaron bitterly. "I have faith."

And, indeed, his faith in the vision was unshakable. Every man being his own Messiah, he, at least, would not draw back from the prospective plough to which he had put his hand. He had been saving up for the great voyage and a little surplus wherewith to support him in Palestine while looking about him. Once established in the Holy Land, how forcibly he would preach by epistle to the men of little faith! They would come out and join him. He—the despised Aaron—the least of the House of Israel—would have played a part in the restoration of his people.

"You will come back," said the poulterer sceptically, when his fellow-tenant bade him good-bye; and parodying the sacred aspiration—"Next year in Manchester," he cried, in genial mockery. The fowl-plucking females laughed heartily, agitating the feathery fluff in the air.

"Not so," said Aaron. "I cannot come back. I have sold the goodwill of my round to Joseph Petowski, and have transferred to him all my customers."

Some of the recreant brotherhood, remorsefully admiring, cheered him up by appearing on the platform of the station to wish him God-speed.

"Next year in Jerusalem!" he prophesied for them, too, recouping himself for the poulterer's profane scepticism.

He went overland to Marseilles, thence by ship to Asia Minor. It was a terrible journey. Piety forebade him to eat or drink with the heathen, or from their vessels. His portmanteau held a little store of provisions and crockery, and dry bread was all he bought on the route.

Fleeced and bullied by touts and cabmen, he found himself at last on board a cheap Mediterranean steamer which pitched and rolled through a persistent spell of stormy weather. His berth was a snatched corner of the bare deck, where heaps of earth's failures, of all races and creeds and colors, grimily picturesque, slept in their clothes upon such bedding as they had brought with them. There was a spawn of babies, a litter of animals and fowls in coops, a swarm of human bundles, scarcely distinguishable from bales except for a protruding hand or foot. There were Bedouins, Armenians, Spaniards, a Turk with several wives in an improvised tent, some Greek women, a party of Syrians from Mount Lebanon. There were also several Jews of both sexes. But Aaron did not scrape acquaintance with these at first—they lay yards away, and he was half dead with sea-sickness and want of food. He had counted on making tea in his own cup with his own little kettle, but the cook would not trouble to supply him with hot water. Only the great vision drawing hourly nearer and nearer sustained him.

It was the attempt of a half-crazy Egyptian Jewess to leap overboard with her new-born child that brought him into relation with the other Jewish passengers. He learnt her story: the everyday story of a woman divorced in New York, after the fashion of its Ghetto, and sent back with scarcely a penny to her native Cairo, while still lightheaded after childbirth. He heard also the story of the buxom, kind-hearted Jewess who now shadowed her protectingly; the no less everyday story of the good-looking girl inveigled by a rascally Jew to a situation in Marseilles. They contributed with the men, a Russian Jew from Chicago, and a German from Brindisi, to give Aaron of Manchester a new objective sense of the tragedy of wandering Israel, interminably tossed betwixt persecution and poverty, perpetually tempted by both to be false to themselves: the tragedy that was now—thank God!—to have its end. Egyptians, Americans, Galicians, Englishmen, Russians, Dutchmen, they had only one last migration before them— that which he, Aaron, was now accomplishing. To his joy one of his new acquaintances—the Russian— shared the dream of a Palestine flowing once more with milk and honey and holy doctrine, was a member of a "Lovers of Zion" society. He was a pasty-faced young man with gray eyes and eyebrows and a reddish beard. He wore frowsy clothes, with an old billy-cock and a dingy cotton shirt, but he combined all the lore of the old-fashioned, hard-shell Jew with a living realization of what his formulæ meant, and so the close of Aaron's voyage—till the Russian landed at Alexandria—was softened and shortened by sitting worshipfully at this idealist's feet, drinking in quotations from Bachja's Duties of the Heart or Saadja Gaon's Book of the Faith. There was not wanting some one to play Sancho Panza, for the German Jew, while binding his arm piously with phylacteries in the publicity of the swarming deck, loved to pose as a man of common sense, free from superstition.

"The only reason men go to Palestine," he maintained, "is because they think, as the psalm says, the land forgives sin. And they believe, too, that those bodies which are not burned in Palestine, when the Messiah's last trump sounds, will have to roll under lands and seas to get to Jerusalem. So they go to die there, so as to escape the underground route. Besides, Maimonides says the Messianic period will only last forty years. So perhaps they are afraid all the fun will be over and the Leviathan eaten up before they arrive."

"Fools there are always in the world," replied the Russian, "and their piety cannot give them brains. These literal folk are the sort who imagine that the Temple expanded miraculously, because the Talmud says howsoever great a multitude flocked to worship therein, there was always room for them. Do you not see what a fine metaphor that is! Even so the Third Temple will be of the Spirit, not of Fire, as these literal materialists translate the prophecy. As the prophet Joel says, 'I will pour out my Spirit. Your old men shall dream dreams, your young men shall see visions,' And this Spirit is working to-day. But through our own souls. No Messiah will ever come from a split heaven. If a Christian does anything wrong, it is the individual; if a Jew, it is the nation. Why? Because we have no country, and hence are set apart in all countries. But a country we must and shall have. The fact that we still dream of our land shows that it is to be ours again. Without a country we are dead. Without us the land is dead. It has been waiting for us. Why has no other nation possessed it and cultivated it?"

"Why? Why do the ducks go barefoot?" The German quoted the Yiddish proverb with a sneer.

"The land waits for us," replied the young Russian fervidly, "so that we may complete our mission. Jerusalem—whose very name means the heritage of double Peace—must be the watch-tower of Peace on earth. The nations shall be taught to compete neither with steel weapons nor with gold, but with truth and purity. Every man shall be taught that he exists for another man, else were men as the beasts. And thus at last 'the knowledge of God shall cover the earth as the waters cover the sea.'"

"If they would only remain covering the sea!" said the German irreverently, as the spray of a wave swept over his mattress.

"Those who have lost this faith are no longer Jews," curtly replied the Russian. "Without this hope the preservation of the Jewish race is a superstition. Let the Jews be swallowed up in the nations—and me in the sea. If I thought that Israel's hope was a lie I should jump overboard."

The German shrugged his shoulders good-humoredly. "You and the Egyptian woman are a pair."

At Alexandria, where some of the cargo and his Jewish fellow-passengers were to be landed, Aaron was tantalized for days by the quarantine, so that he must needs fret amid the musty odors long after he had thought to tread the sacred streets of Jerusalem. But at last he found himself making straight for the Holy Land; and one magic day, the pilgrim, pallid and emaciated, gazed in pious joy upon the gray line of rocks that changed gradually into terraces of red sloping roofs overbrooded by a palm-tree. Jaffa! But a cruel, white sea still rolled and roared betwixt him and these holy shores, guarded by the rock of Andromeda and tumbling and leaping billows; and the ship lay to outside the ancient harbor, while heavy boats rowed by stalwart Arabs and Syrians, in red fez and girdle, clamored for the passengers. Aaron was thrown unceremoniously over the ship's side at the favorable moment when the boat leapt up to meet him; he fell into it, soused with spray, but glowing at heart. As his boat pitched and tossed along, a delicious smell of orange-blossom wafted from the orange-groves, and seemed to the worn pilgrim a symbol of the marriage betwixt him and Zion. The land of his fathers—there it lay at last, and in a transport of happiness the wanderer had, for the first time in his life, a sense of the restful dignity of an ancestral home. But as the boat labored without apparent progress towards the channel betwixt the black rocks, over which the spray flew skywards, a foreboding tortured him that some ironic destiny would drown him in sight of his goal. He prayed silently with shut eyes and his petition changed to praise as the boat bumped the landing-stage and he opened them on a motley Eastern crowd and the heaped barrels of a wharf. Shouldering his portmenteau, which, despite his debilitated condition, felt as light as the feathers at the poulterer's, he scrambled ecstatically up some slippery steps on to the stone platform, and had one foot on the soil of the Holy Land, when a Turkish official in a shabby black uniform stopped him.

"Your passport," he said, in Arabic. Aaron could not understand. Somebody interpreted.

"I have no passport," he answered, with a premonitory pang.

"Where are you going?"

"To live in Palestine."

"Where do you come from?"

"England," he replied triumphantly, feeling this was a mighty password throughout the world.

"You are not an Englishman?"

"No-o," he faltered. "I have lived in England some—many years."

"Naturalized?"

"No," said Aaron, when he understood.

"What countryman are you?"

"Russian."

"And a Jew, of course?"

"Yes."

"No Russian Jews may enter Palestine."

Aaron was hustled back into the boat and restored safely to the steamer.

THE CONCILIATOR OF CHRISTENDOM

I

The Red Beadle shook his head. "There is nothing but Nature," he said obstinately, as his hot iron polished the boot between his knees. He was called the Red Beadle because, though his irreligious opinions had long since lost him his synagogue appointment and driven him back to his old work of bootmaking, his beard was still ruddy.

"Yes, but who made Nature?" retorted his new employer, his strange, scholarly face aglow with argument, and the flame of the lamp suspended over his bench by strings from the ceiling. The other clickers and riveters of the Spitalfields workshop, in their shocked interest in the problem of the origin of Nature, ceased for an instant breathing in the odors of burnt grease, cobbler's wax, and a coke fire replenished with scraps of leather.

"Nature makes herself," answered the Red Beadle. It was his declaration of faith—or of war. Possibly it was the familiarity with divine things which synagogue beadledom involves that had bred his contempt for them. At any rate, he was not now to be coerced by Zussmann Herz, even though he was fully alive to the fact that Zussmann's unique book-lined workshop was the only one that had opened to him, when the more pious shoemakers of the Ghetto had professed to be "full up." He was, indeed, surprised to find Zussmann a believer in the Supernatural, having heard whispers that the man was as great an "Epicurean" as himself. Had not Zussmann—ay, and his wigless wife, Hulda, too—been seen emerging from the mighty Church that stood in frowsy majesty amid its tall, neglected box-like tombs, and was to the Ghetto merely a topographical point and the chronometric standard? And yet, here was Zussmann an assiduous attendant at the synagogue of the first floor—nay, a scholar so conversant with Hebrew, not to mention European, lore, that the Red Beadle felt himself a Man-of-the-Earth, only retaining his superiority by remembering that learning did not always mean logic.

"Nature make herself!" Zussmann now retorted, with a tolerant smile. "As well say this boot made itself! The theory of Evolution only puts the mystery further back, and already in the Talmud we find—"

"Nature made the boot," interrupted the Red Beadle. "Nature made you, and you made the boot. But nobody made Nature."

"But what is Nature?" cried Zussmann. "The garment of God, as Goethe says. Call Him Noumenon with Kant or Thought and Extension with Spinoza—I care not."

The Red Beadle was awed into temporary silence by these unknown names and ideas, expressed, moreover, in German words foreign to his limited vocabulary of Yiddish.

The room in which Zussmann thought and worked was one of two that he rented from the Christian corn-factor who owned the tall house—a stout Cockney who spent his life book-keeping in a little office on wheels, but whom the specimens of oats and dog-biscuits in his window invested with an air of roseate rurality. This personage drew a little income from the population of his house, whose staircases exhibited strata of children of different social developments, and to which the synagogue on the first floor added a large floating population. Zussmann's attendance thereat was not the only thing in him that astonished the Red Beadle. There was also a gentle deference of manner not usual with masters, or with pious persons. His consideration for his employés amounted, in the Beadle's eyes, to maladministration, and the grave loss he sustained through one of his hands selling off a crate of finished goods and flying to America was deservedly due to confidence in another pious person.

II

Despite the Red Beadle's Rationalism, which, basing itself on the facts of life, was not to be crushed by high-flown German words, the master-shoemaker showed him marked favor and often invited him to stay on to supper. Although the Beadle felt this was but the due recognition of one intellect by another, if an inferior intellect, he was at times irrationally grateful for the privilege of a place to spend his evenings in. For the Ghetto had cut him—there could be no doubt of that. The worshippers in his old synagogue whom he had once dominated as Beadle now passed him by with sour looks—"a dog one does not treat thus," the Beadle told himself, tugging miserably at his red beard.

"It is not as if I were a Meshummad—a convert to Christianity." Some hereditary instinct admitted that as a just excuse for execration. "I can't make friends with the Christians, and so I am cut off from both."

When after a thunderstorm two of the hands resigned their places at Zussmann's benches on the avowed ground that atheism attracts lightning, Zussmann's loyalty to the freethinker converted the Beadle's gratitude from fitfulness into a steady glow.

And, other considerations apart, those were enjoyable suppers after the toil and grime of the day. The Beadle especially admired Zussmann's hands when the black grease had been washed off them, the fingers were so long and tapering. Why had his own fingers been made so stumpy and square-tipped? Since Nature made herself, why was she so uneven a worker? Nay, why could she not have given him white teeth like Zussmann's wife? Not that these were ostentatious—you thought more of the sweetness of the smile of which they were part. Still, as Nature's irregularity was particularly manifest in his own teeth, he could not help the reflection.

If the Red Beadle had not been a widower, the unfeigned success of the Herz union might have turned his own thoughts to that happy state. As it was, the sight of their happiness occasionally shot through his breast renewed pangs of vain longing for his Leah, whose death from cancer had completed his conception of Nature. Lucky Zussmann, to have found so sympathetic a partner in a pretty female! For Hulda shared Zussmann's dreams, and was even copying out his great work for the press, for business was brisk and he would soon have saved up enough money to print it. The great work, in the secret of which the Red Beadle came to participate, was written in Hebrew, and the elegant curves and strokes would have done honor to a Scribe. The Beadle himself could not understand it, knowing only the formal alphabet such as appears in books and scrolls, but the first peep at it which the proud Zussmann permitted him removed his last disrespect for the intellect of his master, without, however, removing the mystery of that intellect's aberrations.

"But you dream with the eyes open," he said, when the theme of the work was explained to him.

"How so?" asked Hulda gently, with that wonderful smile of hers.

"Reconcile the Jews and the Christians! Meshuggas—madness." He laughed bitterly. "Do you forget what we went through in Poland? And even here in free England, can you walk in the street without every little shegetz calling after you and asking, 'Who killed Christ?'"

"Yes, but herein my husband explains that it was not the Jews who killed Christ, but Herod and Pilate."

"As it says in Corinthians," broke in Zussmann eagerly: "'We speak the wisdom of God in a mystery, which none of the princes of this world knew; for had they known it, they would not have crucified the Lord of Glory.'"

"So," said the Red Beadle, visibly impressed.

"Assuredly," affirmed Hulda. "But, as Zussmann explains here, they threw the guilt upon the Jews, who were too afraid of the Romans to deny it."

The Beadle pondered.

"Once the Christians understand that," said Zussmann, pursuing his advantage, "they will stretch out the hand to us."

The Beadle had a flash. "But how will the Christians read you? No Christian understands Hebrew."

Zussmann was taken momentarily aback. "But it is not so much for the Christians," he explained. "It is for the Jews—that they should stretch out the hand to the Christians."

The Red Beadle stared at him in shocked silent amaze. "Still greater madness!" he gasped at length. "They will treat you worse than they treat me."

"Not when they read my book."

"Just when they read your book."

Hulda was smiling serenely. "They can do nothing to my husband; he is his own master, God be thanked; no one can turn him away."

"They can insult him."

Zussmann shook his head gently. "No one can insult me!" he said simply. "When a dog barks at me I pity it that it does not know I love it. Now draw to the table. The pickled herring smells well."

But the Red Beadle was unconvinced. "Besides, what should we make it up with the Christians for—the stupid people?" he asked, as he received his steaming coffee cup from Frau Herz.

"It is a question of the Future of the World," said Zussmann gravely, as he shared out the herring, which had already been cut into many thin slices by the vendor and pickler. "This antagonism is a perversion of the principles of both religions. Shall we allow it to continue for ever?"

"It will continue till they both understand that Nature makes herself," said the Red Beadle.

"It will continue till they both understand my husband's book," corrected Hulda.

"Not while Jews live among Christians. Even here they say we take the bread out of the mouths of the Christian shoemakers. If we had our own country now—"

"Hush!" said Zussmann. "Do you share that materialistic dream? Our realm is spiritual. Nationality—the world stinks with it! Germany for the Germans, Russia for the Russians. Foreigners to the devil—pah! Egomania posing as patriotism. Human brotherhood is what we stand for. Have you forgotten how the Midrash explains the verse in the Song of Solomon: 'I charge you, O ye daughters of Jerusalem, by the roes, and by the hinds of the field, that ye stir not up, nor awake my love till he please'?"

The Red Beadle, who had never read a line of the Midrash, did not deny that he had forgotten the explanation, but persisted: "And even if we didn't kill Christ, what good will it do to tell the Jews so? It will only make them angry."

"Why so?" said Zussmann, puzzled.

"They will be annoyed to have been punished for nothing."

"But they have not been punished for nothing!" cried Zussmann, setting down his fork in excitement. "They have denied their greatest son. For, as He said in Matthew, 'I come to fulfil the Law of Moses,' Did not all the Prophets, His predecessors, cry out likewise against mere form and sacrifice? Did not the teachers in Israel who followed Him likewise insist on a pure heart and a sinless soul? Jesus must be restored to His true place in the glorious chain of Hebrew Prophets. As I explain in my chapter on the Philosophy of Religion, which I have founded on Immanuel Kant, the ground-work of Reason is—"

But here the Red Beadle, whose coffee had with difficulty got itself sucked into the right channel, gasped—"You have put that into your book?"

The wife touched the manuscript with reverent pride. "It all stands here," she said.

"What! Quotations from the New Testament?"

"From our Jewish Apostles!" said Zussmann. "Naturally! On every page!"

"Then God help you!" said the Red Beadle.

III

The Brotherhood of the Peoples was published. Though the bill was far heavier than the Hebrew printer's estimate—there being all sorts of mysterious charges for corrections, which took away the last Groschen of their savings, Hulda and her husband were happy. They had sown the seed, and waited in serene faith the ingathering, the reconciliation of Israel with the Gentiles.

The book, which was in paper covers, was published at a shilling; five hundred copies had been struck off for the edition. After six months the account stood thus: Sales, eighty-four copies; press notices, two in the jargon papers (printed in the same office as his book and thus amenable to backstairs influence). The Jewish papers written in English, which loomed before Zussmann's vision as world-shaking, did not even mention its appearance; perhaps it had been better if the jargon papers had been equally silent, for, though less than one hundred copies of The Brotherhood of the Peoples were in circulation, the book was in everybody's mouth—like a piece of pork to be spat out again shudderingly. The Red Beadle's instinct had been only too sound. The Ghetto, accustomed by this time to insidious attacks on its spiritual citadel, feared writers even bringing Hebrew. Despite the Oriental sandal which the cunning shoemaker had fashioned, his fellow-Jews saw the cloven hoof. They were not to be deceived by the specious sanctity which Darwin and Schopenhauer—probably Bishops of the Established Church—borrowed from their Hebrew lettering. Why, that was the very trick of the Satans who sprinkled the sacred tongue freely about handbills inviting souls that sought for light to come and find it in the Whitechapel Road between three and seven. It had been abandoned as hopeless even by the thin-nosed gentlewomen who had begun by painting a Hebrew designation over their bureau of beneficence. But the fact that the Ghetto was perspicacious did not mitigate the author's treachery to his race and faith. Zussmann was given violently to understand that his presence in the little synagogue would lead to disturbances in the service. "The Jew needs no house of prayer," he said; "his life is a prayer, his workshop a temple."

His workmen deserted him one by one as vacancies occurred elsewhere.

"We will get Christians," he said.

But the work itself began to fail. He was dependent upon a large firm whose head was Parnass of a North London congregation, and when one of Zussmann's workers, anxious to set up for himself, went to him with the tale, the contract was transferred to him, and Zussmann's security-deposit returned. But far heavier than all these blows was Hulda's sudden illness, and though the returned trust-money came in handy to defray the expense of doctors, the outlook was not cheerful. But "I will become a hand myself," said Zussmann cheerfully. "The annoyance of my brethren will pass away when they really understand my Idea; meantime it is working in them, for even to hate an Idea is to meditate upon it."

The Red Beadle grunted angrily. He could hear Hulda coughing in the next room, and that hurt his chest.

But it was summer now, and quite a considerable strip of blue sky could be seen from the window, and the mote-laden sun-rays that streamed in encouraged Hulda to grow better. She was soon up and about again, but the doctor said her system was thoroughly upset and she aught to have sea air. But that, of course, was impossible now. Hulda herself declared there was much better air to be got higher up, in the garret, which was fortunately "to let." It is true there was only one room there. Still, it was much cheaper. The Red Beadle's heart was heavier than the furniture he helped to carry upstairs. But the unsympathetic couple did not share his gloom. They jested and laughed, as light of heart as the excited children on the staircases who assisted at the function. "My Idea has raised me nearer heaven," said

Zussmann. That night, after the Red Beadle had screwed up the four-poster, he allowed himself to be persuaded to stay to supper. He had given up the habit as soon as Zussmann's finances began to fail.

By way of house-warming, Hulda had ordered in baked potatoes and liver from the cook-shop, and there were also three tepid slices of plum-pudding.

"Plum-pudding!" cried Zussmann in delight, as his nostrils scented the dainty. "What a good omen for the Idea!"

"How an omen?" inquired the Red Beadle.

"Is not plum-pudding associated with Christmas, with peace on earth?"

Hulda's eyes flashed. "Yes, it is a sign—the Brotherhood of the Peoples! The Jew will be the peace-messenger of the world." The Red Beadle ate on sceptically. He had studied The Brotherhood of the Peoples to the great improvement of his Hebrew but with little edification. He had even studied it in Hulda's original manuscript, which he had borrowed and never intended to return. But still he could not share his friends' belief in the perfectibility of mankind. Perhaps if they had known how he had tippled away his savings after his wife's death, they might have thought less well of humanity and its potentialities of perfection. After all, Huldas were too rare to make the world sober, much less fraternal. And, charming as they were, honesty demanded one should not curry favor with them by fostering their delusions.

"What put such an idea into your head, Zussmann!" he cried unsympathetically. Zussmann answered naïvely, as if to a question—

"I have had the idea from a boy. I remember sitting stocking-footed on the floor of the synagogue in Poland on the Fast of Ab, wondering why we should weep so over the destruction of Jerusalem, which scattered us among the nations as fertilizing seeds. How else should the mission of Israel be fulfilled? I remember"—and here he smiled pensively—"I was awakened from my day-dream by a Patsch (smack) in the face from my poor old father, who was angry because I wasn't saying the prayers."

"There will be always somebody to give you that Patsch," said the Red Beadle gloomily. "But in what way is Israel dispersed? It seems to me our life is everywhere as hidden from the nations as if we were all together in Palestine."

"You touch a great truth! Oh, if I could only write in English! But though I read it almost as easily as the German, I can write it as little. You know how one has to learn German in Poland—by stealth—the Christians jealous on one hand, the Jews suspicious on the other. I could not risk the Christians laughing at my bad German—that would hurt my Idea. And English is a language like the Vale of Siddim—full of pits."

"We ought to have it translated," said Hulda. "Not only for the Christians, but for the rich Jews, who are more liberal-minded than those who live in our quarter."

"But we cannot afford to pay for the translating now," said Zussmann.

"Nonsense; one has always a jewel left," said Hulda.

Zussmann's eyes grew wet. "Yes," he said, drawing her to his breast, "one has always a jewel left."

"More meshuggas!" cried the Red Beadle huskily. "Much the English Jews care about ideas! Did they even acknowledge your book in their journals? But probably they couldn't read it," he added with a laugh. "A fat lot of Hebrew little Sampson knows! You know little Sampson—he came to report the boot-strike for The Flag of Judah. I got into conversation with him—a rank pork-gorger. He believes with me that Nature makes herself."

But Zussmann was scarcely eating, much less listening.

"You have given me a new scheme, Hulda," he said, with exaltation. "I will send my book to the leading English Jews—yes, especially to the ministers. They will see my Idea, they will spread it abroad, they will convert first the Jews and then the Christians."

"Yes, but they will give it as their own Idea," said Hulda.

"And what then? He who has faith in an Idea, his Idea it is. How great for me to have had the Idea first! Is not that enough to thank God for? If only my Idea gets spread in English! English! Have you ever thought what that means, Hulda? The language of the future! Already the language of the greatest nations, and the most on the lips of men everywhere—in a century it will cover the world." He murmured in Hebrew, uplifting his eyes to the rain-streaked sloping ceiling. "And in that day God shall be One and His name One."

"Your supper is getting cold," said Hulda gently.

He began to wield his knife and fork as hypnotized by her suggestion, but his vision was inwards.

IV

Fifty copies of The Brotherhood of the Peoples went off by post the next day to the clergy and gentry of the larger Jewry. In the course of the next fortnight seventeen of the recipients acknowledged the receipt with formal thanks, four sent the shilling mentioned on the cover, and one sent five shillings. This last depressed Zussmann more than all the others. "Does he take me for a Schnorrer?" he said, almost angrily, as he returned the postal order.

He did not forsee the day when, a Schnorrer indeed, he would have taken five shillings from anybody who could afford it: had no prophetic intuition of that long, slow progression of penurious days which was to break down his spirit. For though he managed for a time to secure enough work to keep himself and the Red Beadle going, his ruin was only delayed. Little by little his apparatus was sold off, his benches and polishing-irons vanished from the garret, only one indispensable set remaining, and master and man must needs quest each for himself for work elsewhere. The Red Beadle dropped out of the ménage, and was reduced to semi-starvation. Zussmann and Hulda, by the gradual disposition of their bits of jewellery and their Sabbath garments, held out a little longer, and Hulda also got some sewing of children's under-garments. But with the return of winter, Hulda's illness returned, and then the beloved books began to leave bare the nakedness of the plastered walls. At first, Hulda, refusing to be visited by doctors who charged, struggled out bravely through rain and fog to a free dispensary, where she was jostled by a crowd of head-shawled Polish crones, and where a harassed Christian physician, tired of jargon-speaking Jewesses, bawled and bullied. But at last Hulda grew too ill to stir out, and Zussmann, still out of employment, was driven to look about him for help. Charities enough there were in the Ghetto, but to charity, as to work, one requires an apprenticeship. He knew vaguely that there were persons who had the luck to be ill and to get broths and jellies. To others, also, a board of guardian angels doled out payments, though some one had once told him you had scant chance unless you were a Dutchman. But the inexperienced in begging are naturally not so successful as those always at it. 'Twas vain for Zussmann to kick his heels among the dismal crowd in the corridor, the whisper of his misdeeds had been before him, borne by some competitor in the fierce struggle for assistance. What! help a hypocrite to sit on the twin stools of Christendom and Judaism, fed by the bounty of both! In this dark hour he was approached by the thin-nosed gentlewomen, who had got wind of his book and who scented souls. Zussmann wavered. Why, indeed, should he refuse their assistance? He knew their self-sacrificing days, their genuine joy in salvation. On their generosities he was far better posted than on Jewish—the lurid legend of these Mephistophelian matrons included blankets, clothes, port wine, and all the delicacies of the season. He admitted that Hulda had indeed been brought low, and permitted them to call. Then he went home to cut dry bread for the bedridden, emaciated creature who had once been beautiful, and to comfort her—for it was Friday evening—by reading the Sabbath prayers; winding up, "A virtuous woman who can find? For her price is far above rubies."

On the forenoon of the next day arrived a basket, scenting the air with delicious odors of exquisite edibles.

Zussmann received it with delight from the boy who bore it. "God bless them!" he said. "A chicken—grapes—wine. Look, Hulda!"

Hulda raised herself in bed; her eyes sparkled, a flush of color returned to the wan cheeks.

"Where do these come from?" she asked.

Zussmann hesitated. Then he told her they were the harbingers of a visit from the good sisters.

The flush in her cheek deepened to scarlet.

"My poor Zussmann!" she cried reproachfully. "Give them back—give them back at once! Call after the boy."

"Why?" stammered Zussmann.

"Call after the boy!" she repeated imperatively. "Good God! If the ladies were to be seen coming up here, it would be all over with your Idea. And on the Sabbath, too! People already look upon you as a tool of the missionaries. Quick! quick!"

His heart aching with mingled love and pain, he took up the basket and hurried after the boy. Hulda sank back on her pillow with a sigh of relief.

"Dear heart!" she thought, as she took advantage of his absence to cough freely. "For me he does what he would starve rather than do for himself. A nice thing to imperil his Idea—the dream of his life! When the Jews see he makes no profit by it, they will begin to consider it. If he did not have the burden of me he would not be tempted. He could go out more and find work farther afield. This must end—I must die or be on my feet again soon."

Zussmann came back, empty-handed and heavy-hearted.

"Kiss me, my own life!" she cried. "I shall be better soon."

He bent down and touched her hot, dry lips. "Now I see," she whispered, "why God did not send us children. We thought it was an affliction, but lo! it is that your Idea shall not be hindered."

"The English Rabbis have not yet drawn attention to it," said Zussmann huskily.

"All the better," replied Hulda. "One day it will be translated into English—I know it, I feel it here." She touched her chest, and the action made her cough.

Going out later for a little fresh air, at Hulda's insistence, he was stopped in the broad hall on which the stairs debouched by Cohen, the ground-floor tenant, a black-bearded Russian Jew, pompous in Sabbath broadcloth.

"What's the matter with my milk?" abruptly asked Cohen, who supplied the local trade besides selling retail. "You might have complained, instead of taking your custom out of the house. Believe me, I don't make a treasure heap out of it. One has to be up at Euston to meet the trains in the middle of the night, and the competition is so cut-throat that one has to sell at eighteen pence a barn gallon. And on Sabbath one earns nothing at all. And then the analyst comes poking his nose into the milk."

"You see—my wife—my wife—is ill," stammered Zussmann. "So she doesn't drink it."

"Hum!" said Cohen. "Well, you might oblige me then. I have so much left over every day, it makes my reputation turn quite sour. Do, do me a favor and let me send you up a can of the leavings every night. For nothing, of course; would I talk business on the Sabbath? I don't like to be seen pouring it away. It would pay me to pay you a penny a pint," he wound up emphatically.

Zussmann accepted unsuspiciously, grateful to Providence for enabling him to benefit at once himself and his neighbor. He bore a can upstairs now and explained the situation to the shrewder Hulda, who, however, said nothing but, "You see the Idea commences to work. When the book first came out, didn't he—though he sells secretly to the trade on Sabbath mornings—call you an Epicurean?"

"Worse," said Zussmann joyously, with a flash of recollection.

He went out again, lightened and exalted. "Yes, the Idea works," he said, as he came out into the gray street. "The Brotherhood of the Peoples will come, not in my time, but it will come." And he murmured again the Hebrew aspiration: "In that day shall God be One and His name One."

"Whoa, where's your—eyes?"

Awakened by the oath, he just got out of the way of a huge Flemish dray-horse dragging a brewer's cart. Three ragged Irish urchins, who had been buffeting each other with whirling hats knotted into the ends of dingy handkerchiefs, relaxed their enmities in a common rush for the projecting ladder behind the dray and collided with Zussmann on the way. A one-legged, misery-eyed hunchback offered him penny diaries. He shook his head in impotent pity, and passed on, pondering.

"In time God will make the crooked straight," he thought.

Jews with tall black hats and badly made frock-coats slouched along, their shoulders bent. Wives stood at the open doors of the old houses, some in Sabbath finery, some flaunting irreligiously their every-day shabbiness, without troubling even to arrange their one dress differently, as a pious Rabbi recommended. They looked used-up and haggard, all these mothers in Israel. But there were dark-eyed damsels still gay and fresh, with artistic bodices of violet and green picked out with gold arabesque.

He turned a corner and came into a narrow street that throbbed with the joyous melody of a piano-organ. His heart leapt up. The roadway bubbled with Jewish children, mainly girls, footing it gleefully in the graying light, inventing complex steps with a grace and an abandon that lit their eyes with sparkles and painted deeper flushes on their olive cheeks. A bounding little bow-legged girl seemed unconscious of her deformity; her toes met each other as though in merry dexterity.

Zussmann's eyes were full of tears. "Dance on, dance on," he murmured. "God shall indeed make the crooked straight."

Fixed to one side of the piano-organ on the level of the handle he saw a little box, in which lay, as in a cradle, what looked like a monkey, then like a doll, but on closer inspection turned into a tiny live child, flaxen-haired, staring with wide gray eyes from under a blue cap, and sucking at a milk-bottle with preternatural placidity, regardless of the music throbbing through its resting-place.

"Even so shall humanity live," thought Zussmann, "peaceful as a babe, cradled in music. God hath sent me a sign."

He returned home, comforted, and told Hulda of the sign.

"Was it an Italian child?" she asked.

"An English child," he answered. "Fair-eyed and fair-haired."

"Then it is a sign that through the English tongue shall the Idea move the world. Your book will be translated into English—I shall live to see it."

V

A few afternoons later the Red Beadle, his patched garments pathetically spruced up, came to see his friends, goaded by the news of Hulda's illness. There was no ruddiness in his face, the lips of which were pressed together in defiance of a cruel and credulous world. That Nature in making herself should have produced creatures who attributed their creation elsewhere, and who refused to allow her one acknowledger to make boots, was indeed a proof, albeit vexatious, of her blind workings.

When he saw what she had done to Hulda and to Zussmann, his lips were pressed tighter, but as much to keep back a sob as to express extra resentment.

But on parting he could not help saying to Zussmann, who accompanied him to the dark spider-webbed landing, "Your God has forgotten you."

"Do you mean that men have forgotten Him?" replied Zussmann. "If I am come to poverty, my suffering is in the scheme of things. Do you not remember what the Almighty says to Eleazar ben Pedos, in the Talmud, when the Rabbi complains of poverty? 'Wilt thou be satisfied if I overthrow the universe, so that perhaps thou mayest be created again in a time of plenty?' No, no, my friend, we must trust the scheme."

"But the fools enjoy prosperity," said the Red Beadle.

"It is only a fool who would enjoy prosperity," replied Zussmann. "If the righteous sometimes suffer and the wicked sometimes flourish, that is just the very condition of virtue. What! would you have righteousness always pay and wickedness always fail! Where then would be the virtue in virtue? It would be a mere branch of commerce. Do you forget what the Chassid said of the man who foreknew in his lifetime that for him there was to be no heaven? 'What a unique and enviable chance that man had of doing right without fear of reward!'"

The Red Beadle, as usual, acquiesced in the idea that he had forgotten these quotations from the Hebrew, but to acquiesce in their teachings was another matter. "A man who had no hope of heaven would be a fool not to enjoy himself," he said doggedly, and went downstairs, his heart almost bursting. He went straight to his old synagogue, where he knew a Hesped or funeral service on a famous Maggid (preacher) was to be held. He could scarcely get in, so dense was the throng. Not a few eyes, wet with tears, were turned angrily on him as on a mocker come to gloat, but he hastened to weep too, which was easy when he thought of Hulda coughing in her bed in the garret. So violently did he weep that the Gabbai or treasurer—one of the most pious master-bootmakers—gave him the "Peace" salutation after the service.

"I did not expect to see you weeping," said he.

"Alas!" answered the Red Beadle. "It is not only the fallen Prince in Israel that I weep; it is my own transgressions that are brought home to me by his sudden end. How often have I heard him thunder and lighten from this very pulpit!" He heaved a deep sigh at his own hypocrisy, and the Gabbai sighed in response. "Even from the grave the Tsaddik (saint) works good," said the pious master-bootmaker. "May my latter end be like his!"

"Mine, too!" suspired the Red Beadle. "How blessed am I not to have been cut off in my sin, denying the Maker of Nature!" They walked along the street together.

The next morning, at the luncheon-hour, a breathless Beadle, with a red beard and a very red face, knocked joyously at the door of the Herz garret.

"I am in work again," he explained.

"Mazzeltov!" Zussmann gave him the Hebrew congratulation, but softly, with finger on lip, to indicate Hulda was asleep. "With whom?"

"Harris the Gabbai."

"Harris! What, despite your opinions?"

The Red Beadle looked away.

"So it seems!"

"Thank God!" said Hulda. "The Idea works."

Both men turned to the bed, startled to see her sitting up with a rapt smile.

"How so?" said the Red Beadle uneasily. "I am not a Goy (Christian) befriended by a Gabbai."

"No, but it is the brotherhood of humanity."

"Bother the brotherhood of humanity, Frau Herz!" said the Red Beadle gruffly. He glanced round the denuded room. "The important thing is that you will now be able to have a few delicacies."

"I?" Hulda opened her eyes wide.

"Who else? What I earn is for all of us."

"God bless you!" said Zussmann; "but you have enough to do to keep yourself."

"Indeed he has!" said Hulda. "We couldn't dream of taking a farthing!" But her eyes were wet.

"I insist!" said the Red Beadle.

She thanked him sweetly, but held firm.

"I will advance the money on loan till Zussmann gets work."

Zussmann wavered, his eyes beseeching her, but she was inflexible.

The Red Beadle lost his temper. "And this is what you call the brotherhood of humanity!"

"He is right, Hulda. Why should we not take from one another? Pride perverts brotherhood."

"Dear husband," said Hulda, "it is not pride to refuse to rob the poor. Besides, what delicacies do I need? Is not this a land flowing with milk?"

"You take Cohen's milk and refuse my honey!" shouted the Red Beadle unappeased.

"Give me of the honey of your tongue and I shall not refuse it," said Hulda, with that wonderful smile of hers which showed the white teeth Nature had made; the smile which, as always, melted the Beadle's mood. That smile could repair all the ravages of disease and give back her memoried face.

After the Beadle had been at work a day or two in the Gabbai's workshop, he broached the matter of a fellow-penitent, one Zussmann Herz, with no work and a bedridden wife.

"That Meshummad!" (apostate) cried the Gabbai." He deserves all that God has sent him."

Undaunted, the Red Beadle demonstrated that the man could not be of the missionary camp, else had he not been left to starve, one converted Jew being worth a thousand pounds of fresh subscriptions. Moreover he, the Red Beadle, had now convinced the man of his spiritual errors, and The Brotherhood of the Peoples was no longer on sale. Also, being unable to leave his wife's bedside, Zussmann would do the work at home below the Union rates prevalent in public. So, trade being brisk, the Gabbai relented and bargained, and the Red Beadle sped to his friend's abode and flew up the four flights of stairs.

"Good news!" he cried. "The Gabbai wants another hand, and he is ready to take you."

"Me?" Zussmann was paralyzed with joy and surprise.

"Now will you deny that the Idea works?" cried Hulda, her face flushed and her eyes glittering. And she fell a-coughing.

"You are right, Hulda; you are always right," cried Zussmann, in responsive radiance. "Thank God! Thank God!"

"God forgive me," muttered the Red Beadle.

"Go at once, Zussmann," said Hulda. "I shall do very well here—this has given me strength. I shall be up in a day or two."

"No, no, Zussmann," said the Beadle hurriedly. "There is no need to leave your wife. I have arranged it all. The Gabbai does not want you to come there or to speak to him, because, though the Idea works in him, the other 'hands' are not yet so large-minded: I am to bring you the orders, and I shall come here to fetch them."

The set of tools to which Zussmann clung in desperate hope made the plan both feasible and pleasant.

And so the Red Beadle's visits resumed their ancient frequency even as his Sabbath clothes resumed their ancient gloss, and every week's-end he paid over Zussmann's wages to him—full Union rate.

But Hulda, although she now accepted illogically the Red Beadle's honey in various shapes, did not appear to progress as much as the Idea, or as the new book which she stimulated Zussmann to start for its further propagation.

VI

One Friday evening of December, when miry snow underfoot and grayish fog all around combined to make Spitalfields a malarious marsh, the Red Beadle, coming in with the week's wages, found to his horror a doctor hovering over Hulda's bed like the shadow of death.

From the look that Zussmann gave him he saw a sudden change for the worse had set in. The cold of the weather seemed to strike right to his heart. He took the sufferer's limp chill hand.

"How goes it?" he said cheerily.

"A trifle weak. But I shall be better soon."

He turned away. Zussmann whispered to him that the doctor who had been called in that morning had found the crisis so threatening that he was come again in the evening.

The Red Beadle, grown very white, accompanied the doctor downstairs, and learned that with care the patient might pull through.

The Beadle felt like tearing out his red beard. "And to think that I have not yet arranged the matter!" he thought distractedly.

He ran through the gray bleak night to the office of The Flag of Judah; but as he was crossing the threshold he remembered that it was the eve of the Sabbath, and that neither little Sampson nor anybody else would be there. But little Sampson was there, working busily.

"Hullo! Come in," he said, astonished.

The Red Beadle had already struck up a drinking acquaintanceship with the little journalist, in view of the great negotiation he was plotting. Not in vain did the proverbial wisdom of the Ghetto bid one beware of the red-haired.

"I won't keep you five minutes," apologized little Sampson. "But, you see, Christmas comes next week, and the compositors won't work. So I have to invent the news in advance."

Presently little Sampson, lighting an unhallowed cigarette by way of Sabbath lamp, and slinging on his shabby cloak, repaired with the Red Beadle to a restaurant, where he ordered "forbidden" food for himself and drinks for both.

The Red Beadle felt his way so cautiously and cunningly that the negotiation was unduly prolonged. After an hour or two, however, all was settled. For five pounds, paid in five monthly instalments, little Sampson would translate The Brotherhood of the Peoples into English, provided the Beadle would tell him what the Hebrew meant. This the Beadle, from his loving study of Hulda's manuscript, was now prepared for. Little Sampson also promised to run the translation through The Flag of Judah, and thus the Beadle could buy the plates cheap for book purposes, with only the extra cost of printing such passages, if any, as were too dangerous for The Flag of Judah. This unexpected generosity, coupled with the new audience it offered the Idea, enchanted the Red Beadle. He did not see that the journalist was getting gratuitous "copy," he saw only the bliss of Hulda and Zussmann, and in some strange exaltation, compact of whisky and affection, he shared in their vision of the miraculous spread of the Idea, once it had got into the dominant language of the world.

In his gratitude to little Sampson he plied him with fresh whisky; in his excitement he drew the paper-covered book from his pocket, and insisted that the journalist must translate the first page then and there, as a hansel. By the time it was done it was near eleven o'clock. Vaguely the Red Beadle felt that it was too late to return to Zussmann's to-night. Besides, he was liking little Sampson very much. They did not separate till the restaurant closed at midnight.

Quite drunk, the Red Beadle staggered towards Zussmann's house. He held the page of the translation tightly in his hand. The Hebrew original he had forgotten on the restaurant table, but he knew in some troubled nightmare way that Zussmann and Hulda must see that paper at once, that he had been charged to deliver it safely, and must die sooner than disobey.

The fog had lifted, but the heaps of snow were a terrible hindrance to his erratic progression. The cold air and the shock of a fall lessened his inebriety, but the imperative impulse of his imaginary mission still hypnotized him. It was past one before he reached the tall house. He did not think it at all curious that the great outer portals should be open; nor, though he saw the milk-cart at the door, and noted Cohen's uncomfortable look, did he remember that he had discovered the milk-purveyor nocturnally infringing the Sabbath. He stumbled up the stairs and knocked at the garret door, through the chinks of which light streamed. The thought of Hulda smote him almost sober. Zussmann's face, when the door opened, restored him completely to his senses. It was years older.

"She is not dead?" the visitor whispered hoarsely.

"She is dying, I fear—she cannot rouse herself." Zussmann's voice broke in a sob.

"But she must not die—I bring great news—The Flag of Judah has read your book—it will translate it into English—it will print it in its own paper—and then it will make a book of it for you. See, here is the beginning!"

"Into English!" breathed Zussmann, taking the little journalist's scrawl. His whole face grew crimson, his eye shone as with madness. "Hulda! Hulda!" he cried, "the Idea works! God be thanked! English! Through the world! Hulda! Hulda!" He was bending over her, raising her head.

She opened her eyes.

"Hulda! the Idea wins. The book is coming out in English. The great English paper will print it. In that day God shall be One and His name One. Do you understand?" Her lips twitched faintly, but only her eyes spoke with the light of love and joy. His own look met hers, and for a moment husband and wife were one in a spiritual ecstasy.

Then the light in Hulda's eyes went out, and the two men were left in darkness.

The Red Beadle turned away and left Zussmann to his dead, and, with scalding tears running down his cheek, pulled up the cotton window blind and gazed out unseeing into the night.

Presently his vision cleared: he found himself watching the milk-cart drive off, and, following it towards the frowsy avenue of Brick Lane, he beheld what seemed to be a drunken fight in progress. He saw a policeman, gesticulating females, the nondescript nocturnal crowd of the sleepless city. The old dull hopelessness came over him. "Nature makes herself," he murmured in despairing resignation.

Suddenly he became aware that Zussmann was beside him, looking up at the stars.

"Well, what are you gaping at? Why the devil don't you say something?" And all the impatience of the rapt artist at being interrupted by anything but praise was in the outburst.

"Holy Moses!" I gasped. "Give a man a chance to get his breath. I fall through a dark antechamber over a bicycle, stumble round a screen, and—smack! a glare of Oriental sunlight from a gigantic canvas, the vibration and glow of a group of joyous figures, reeking with life and sweat! You the Idealist, the seeker after Nature's beautiful moods and Art's beautiful patterns!"

"Beautiful moods!" he echoed angrily. "And why isn't this a beautiful mood? And what more beautiful pattern than this—look! this line, this sweep, this group here, this clinging of the children round this mass—all in a glow—balanced by this mass of cool shadow. The meaning doesn't interfere with the pattern, you chump!"

"Oh, so there is a meaning! You've become an anecdotal painter."

"Adjectives be hanged! I can't talk theory in the precious daylight. If you can't see—!"

"I can see that you are painting something you haven't seen. You haven't been in the East, have you?"

"If I had, I haven't got time to jaw about it now. Come and have an absinthe at the Café Victor—in memory of old Paris days—Sixth Avenue—any of the boys will tell you. Let me see, daylight till six—half-past six. Au 'voir, au 'voir."

As I went down the steep, dark stairs, "Same old Dan," I thought. "Who would imagine I was a stranger in New York looking up an old fellow-struggler on his native heath? If I didn't know better, I might fancy his tremendous success had given him the same opinion of himself that America has of him. But no, nothing will change him; the same furious devotion to his canvas once he has quietly planned his picture, the same obstinate conviction that he is seeing something in the only right way. And yet something has changed him. Why has his brush suddenly gone East? Why this new kind of composition crowded with figures—ancient Jews, too? Has he been taken with piety, and is he going henceforward ostentatiously to proclaim his race? And who is the cheerful central figure with the fine, open face? I don't recollect any such scene in Jewish history, or anything so joyous. Perhaps it's a study of modern Jerusalem Jews, to show their life is not all Wailing Wall and Jeremiah. Or perhaps it's only decorative. America is great on decoration just now. No; he said the picture had a meaning. Well, I shall know all about it to-night. Anyhow, it's a beautiful thing."

"Same old Dan!" I thought even more decisively as, when I opened the door of the little café, a burly, black-bearded figure with audacious eyes came at me with a grip and a slap and a roar of welcome, and dragged me to the quiet corner behind the billiard tables.

"I've just been opalizing your absinthe for you," he laughed, as we sat down. "But what's the matter? You look kind o' scared."

"It's your Inferno of a city. As I turned the corner of Sixth Avenue, an elevated train came shrieking and rumbling, and a swirl of wind swept screeching round and round, enveloping me in a whirlpool of smoke and steam, until, dazed and choked in what seemed the scalding effervescence of a collision, I had given up all hope of ever learning what your confounded picture meant."

"Aha!" He took a complacent sip. "It stayed with you, did it?" And the light of triumph, flushing for an instant his rugged features, showed when it waned how pale and drawn they were by the feverish tension of his long day's work.

"Yes it did, old fellow," I said affectionately. "The joy and the glow of it, and yet also some strange antique simplicity and restfulness you have got into it, I know not how, have been with me all day, comforting me in the midst of the tearing, grinding life of this closing nineteenth century after Christ."

A curious smile flitted across Dan's face. He tilted his chair back, and rested his head against the wall.

"There's nothing that takes me so much out of the nineteenth century after Christ," he said dreamily, "as this little French café. It wafts me back to my early student days, that lie somewhere amid the enchanted mists of the youth of the world; to the zestful toil of the studios, to the careless trips in quaint, gray Holland or flaming, devil-may-care Spain. Ah! what scenes shift and shuffle in the twinkle of the gas-jet in this opalescent liquid; the hot shimmer of the arena at the Seville bull-fight, with its swirl of color and movement; the torchlight procession of pilgrims round the church at Lourdes, with the one black nun praying by herself in a shadowy corner; the lovely valley of the Tauba, where the tinkle of the sheep-bells mingles with the Lutheran hymn blown to the four winds from the old church tower; wines that were red—sunshine that was warm—mandolines—!" His voice died away as in exquisite reverie.

"And the East?" I said slily.

A good-natured smile dissipated his delicious dream.

"Ah, yes," he said. "My East was the Tyrol."

"The Tyrol? How do you mean?"

"I see you won't let me out of that story."

"Oh, there's a story, is there?"

"Oh, well, perhaps not what you literary chaps would call a story! No love-making in it, you know."

"Then it can wait. Tell me about your picture."

"But that's mixed up with the story."

"Didn't I say you had become an anecdotal artist?"

"It's no laughing matter," he said gravely. "You remember when we parted at Munich, a year ago last spring, you to go on to Vienna and I to go back to America. Well, I had a sudden fancy to take one last European trip all by myself, and started south through the Tyrol, with a pack on my back. The third day out I fell and bruised my thigh severely, and could not make my little mountain town till moonlight. And I tell you I was mighty glad when I limped across the bridge over the rushing river and dropped on the hotel sofa. Next morning I was stiff as a poker, but I struggled up the four rickety flights to the local physician, and being assured I only wanted rest, I resolved to take it with book and pipe and mug in a shady beer-garden on the river. I had been reading for about an hour when five or six Tyrolese, old men and young, in their gray and green costumes and their little hats, trooped in and occupied the large table near the inn-door. Presently I was startled by the sound of the zither; they began to sing songs; the pretty daughter of the house came and joined in the singing. I put down my book.

"The old lady who served me with my Maass of beer, seeing my interest, came over and chatted about her guests. Oh no, they were not villagers; they came from four hours away. The slim one was a school-teacher, and the dicker was a tenor, and sang in the chorus of the Passion-Spiel; the good-looking young man was to be the St. John. Passion play! I pricked up my ears. When? Where? In their own village, three days hence; only given once every ten years—for hundreds and hundreds of years. Could strangers see it? What should strangers want to see it for? But could they see it? Gewiss. This was indeed a stroke of luck. I had always rather wanted to see the Passion play, but the thought of the fashionable Ober-Ammergau made me sick. Would I like to be vorgestellt? Rather! It was not ten minutes after this introduction before I had settled to stay with St. John, and clouds of good American tobacco were rising from six Tyrolese pipes, and many an "Auf Ihr Wohl" was busying the pretty Kellnerin. They trotted out all their repertory of quaint local songs for my benefit. It sounded bully, I tell you, out there with the sunlight, and the green leaves, and the rush of the river; and in this aroma of beer and brotherhood I blessed my damaged thigh. Three days hence! Just time for it to heal. A providential world, after all.

"And it was indeed with a buoyant step and a gay heart that I set out over the hills at sunrise on that memorable morning. The play was to begin at ten, and I should just be on time. What a walk! Imagine it! Clear coolness of dawn, fresh green, sparkling dew, the road winding up and down, round hills, up cliffs, along valleys, through woods, where the green branches swayed in the morning wind and dappled the grass fantastically with dancing sunlight. And as fresh as the morning, was, I felt, the artistic sensation awaiting me. I swung round the last hill-shoulder; saw the quaint gables of the first house peeping through the trees, and the church spire rising beyond, then groups of Tyrolese converging from all the roads; dipped down the valley, past the quiet lake, up the hills beyond; found myself caught in a stream of peasants, and, presto! was sucked from the radiant day into the deep gloom of the barn-like theatre.

"I don't know how it is done in Ober-Ammergau, but this Tyrolese thing was a strange jumble of art and naïveté, of talent and stupidity. There was a full-fledged stage and footlights, and the scenery, some one said, was painted by a man from Munich. But the players were badly made up; the costumes, if correct, were ill-fitting; the stage was badly lighted, and the flats didn't 'jine.' Some of the actors had gleams of artistic perception. St. Mark was beautiful to look on, Caiaphas had a sense of elocution, the Virgin was tender and sweet, and Judas rose powerfully to his great twenty minutes' soliloquy. But the bulk of the players, though all were earnest and fervent, were clumsy or self-conscious. The crowds were stiff and awkward, painfully symmetrical, like school children at drill. A chorus of ten or twelve ushered in each episode with song, and a man further explained it in bald narrative. The acts of the play proper were interrupted by tableaux vivants of Old Testament scenes, from Adam and Eve onwards. There was much, you see, that was puerile, even ridiculous; and every now and then some one would open the door of the dusky auditorium, and a shaft of sunshine would fly in from the outside world to remind me further how unreal was all this gloomy make-believe. Nay, during the entr'acte I went out, like everybody else, and lunched off sausages and beer.

"And yet, beneath all this critical consciousness, beneath even the artistic consciousness that could not resist jotting down a face or a scene in my sketch-book, something curious was happening in the depths of my being. The play exercised from the very first a strange magnetic effect on me; despite all the primitive humors of the players, the simple, sublime tragedy that disengaged itself from their uncouth but earnest goings-on, began to move and even oppress my soul. Christ had been to me merely a theme for artists; my studies and travels had familiarized me with every possible conception of the Man of Sorrows. I had seen myriads of Madonnas nursing Him, miles of Magdalens bewailing Him. Yet the sorrows I had never felt. Perhaps it was my Jewish training, perhaps it was that none of the Christians I lived with had ever believed in Him. At any rate, here for the first time the Christ story came home to me as a real, living fact—something that had actually happened. I saw this simple son of the people—made more simple by my knowledge that His representative was a baker—moving amid the ancient peasant and fisher life of Galilee; I saw Him draw men and women, saints and sinners, by the magic of His love, the simple sweetness of His inner sunshine; I saw the sunshine change to lightning as He drove the money-changers from the Temple; I watched the clouds deepen as the tragedy drew on; I saw Him bid farewell to His mother; I heard suppressed sobs all around me. Then the heavens were overcast, and it seemed as if earth held its breath waiting for the supreme moment. They dragged Him before Pilate; they clothed Him in scarlet robe, and plaited His crown of thorns, and spat on Him; they gave Him vinegar to drink mixed with gall; and He so divinely sweet and forgiving through all. A horrible oppression hung over the world. I felt choking; my ribs pressed inwards, my heart seemed contracted. He was dying for the sins of the world, He summed up the whole world's woe and pitifulness—the two ideas throbbed and fused in my troubled soul. And I, a Jew, had hitherto ignored Him. What would they say, these simple peasants sobbing all around, if they knew that I was of that hated race? Then something broke in me, and I sobbed too—sobbed with bitter tears that soon turned sweet in strange relief and glad sympathy with my rough brothers and sisters." He paused a moment, and sipped silently at his absinthe. I did not break the silence. I was moved and interested, though what all this had to do with his glowing, joyous picture I could only dimly surmise. He went on—

"When it was all over, and I went out into the open air, I did not see the sunlight. I carried the dusk of the theatre with me, and the gloom of Golgotha brooded over the sunny afternoon. I heard the nails driven in; I saw the blood spurting from the wounds—there was realism in the thing, I tell you. The peasants, accustomed to the painful story, had quickly recovered their gaiety, and were pouring boisterously down the hill-side, like a glad, turbulent mountain stream, unloosed from the dead hand of frost. But I was still ice-bound and fog-wrapped. Outside the Gasthaus where I went to dine, gay groups assembled, an organ played, some strolling Italian girls danced gracefully, and my artistic self was aware of a warmth and a rush. But the inmost Me was neck-deep in gloom, with which the terribly pounded steak they gave me, fraudulently overlaid with two showy fried eggs, seemed only in keeping. St. John came in, and Christ and the schoolmaster—who had conducted the choir—and the thick tenor and some supers, and I congratulated them one and all with a gloomy sense of dishonesty. When, as evening fell, I walked home with St. John, I was gloomily glad to find the valley shrouded in mist and a starless heaven sagging over a blank earth. It seemed an endless uphill drag to my lodging, and though my bedroom was unexpectedly dainty, and a dear old woman—St. John's mother—metaphorically tucked me in, I slept ill that night. Formless dreams tortured me with impalpable tragedies and apprehensions of horror. In the morning—after a cold sponging—the oppression lifted a little from my spirit, though the weather still seemed rather gray. St. John had already gone off to his field-work, his mother told me. She was so lovely, and the room in which I ate breakfast so neat and demure with its whitewashed walls—pure and stainless like country snow—that I managed to swallow everything but the coffee. O that coffee! I had to nibble at a bit of chocolate I carried to get the taste of it out of my mouth. I tried hard not to let the blues get the upper hand again. I filled my pipe and pulled out my sketch-book. My notes of yesterday seemed so faint, and the morning to be growing so dark, that I could scarcely see them. I thought I would go and sit on the little bench outside. As I was sauntering through the doorway, my head bending broodingly over the sketch-book, I caught sight out of the corner of my eye of a little white match-stand fixed up on the wall. Mechanically I put out my left hand to take a light for my pipe. A queer, cold wetness in my fingers and a little splash woke me to the sense of some odd mistake, and in another instant I realized with horror that I had dipped my fingers into holy water and splashed it over that neat, demure, spotless, whitewashed wall."

I could not help smiling. "Ah, I know; one of those porcelain things with a crucified Saviour over a little font. Fancy taking heaven for brimstone!"

"It didn't seem the least bit funny at the time. I just felt awful. What would the dear old woman say to this profanation? Why the dickens did people have whitewashed walls on which sacrilegious stains were luridly visible? I looked up and down the hall like Moses when he slew that Egyptian, trembling lest the old woman should come in. How could I make her understand I was so ignorant of Christian custom as to mistake a font for a matchbox? And if I said I was a Jew, good heavens! she might think I had done it of fell design. What a wound to the gentle old creature who had been so sweet to me! I could not stay in sight of that accusing streak, I must walk off my uneasiness. I threw open the outer door; then I stood still, paralyzed. Monstrous evil-looking gray mists were clumped at the very threshold. Sinister formless vapors blotted out the mountain; everywhere vague, drifting hulks of malarious mist. I sought to pierce them, to find the landscape, the cheerful village, the warm human life nesting under God's heaven, but saw only—way below—as through a tunnel cut betwixt mist and mountain, a dead, inverted world of houses and trees in a chill, gray lake. I shuddered. An indefinable apprehension possessed me, something like the vague discomfort of my dreams; then, almost instantly, it crystallized into the blood-curdling suggestion: What if this were divine chastisement? what if all the outer and inner dreariness that had so steadily enveloped me since I had witnessed the tragedy were punishment for my disbelief? what if this water were really holy, and my sacrilege had brought some grisly Nemesis?"

"You believed that?"

"Not really, of course. But you, as an artist, must understand how one dallies with an idea, plays with a mood, works oneself up imaginatively into a dramatic situation. I let it grow upon me till, like a man alone in the dark, afraid of the ghosts he doesn't believe in, I grew horribly nervous."

"I daresay you hadn't wholly recovered from your fall, and your nerves were unstrung by the blood and the nails, and that steak had disagreed with you, and you had had a bad night, and you were morbidly uneasy about annoying the old woman, and all those chunks of mist got into your spirits. You are a child of the sun!"

"Of course I knew all that, down in the cellars of my being, but upstairs, all the same, I had this sense of guilt and expiation, this anxious doubt that perhaps all that great, gloomy, mediæval business of saints and nuns, and bones, and relics, and miracles, and icons, and calvaries, and cells, and celibacy, and horsehair shirts, and blood, and dirt, and tears, was true after all! What if the world of beauty I had been content to live in was a Satanic show, and the real thing was that dead, topsy-turvy world down there in the cold, gray lake under the reeking mists? I sneaked back into the house to see if the streak hadn't dried yet; but no! it loomed in tell-tale ghastliness, a sort of writing on the wall announcing the wrath and visitation of heaven. I went outside again and smoked miserably on the little bench. Gradually I began to feel warmer, the mists seemed clearing. I rose and stretched myself with an ache of luxurious languor. Encouraged, I stole within again to peep at the streak. It was dry—a virgin wall, innocently white, met my delighted gaze. I opened the window; the draggling vapors were still rising, rising, the bleakness was merging in a mild warmth. I refilled my pipe, and plunged down the yet gray hill. I strode past the old saw-mill, skirted the swampy border of the lake, came out on the firm green, when bing! zim! br-r-r! a heavenly bolt of sunshine smashed through the raw mists, scattering them like a bomb to the horizon's rim; then with sovereign calm the sun came out full, flooding hill and dale with luminous joy; the lake shimmered and flashed into radiant life, and gave back a great white cloud-island on a stretch of glorious blue, and all that golden warmth stole into my veins like wine. A little goat came skipping along with tinkling bell, a horse at grass threw up its heels in ecstasy, an ox lowed, a dog barked. Tears of exquisite emotion came into my eyes; the beautiful soft warm light that lay over all the happy valley seemed to get into them and melt something. How unlike those tears of yesterday, wrung out of me as by some serpent coiled round my ribs! Now my ribs seemed expanding—to hold my heart—and all the divine joy of existence thrilled me to a religious rapture. And with the lifting of the mists all that ghastly mediæval nightmare was lifted from my soul; in that sacred moment all the lurid tragedy of the crucified Christ vanished, and only Christ was left, the simple fellowship with man and beast and nature, the love of life, the love of love, the love of God. And in that yearning ecstasy my picture came to me—The Joyous Comrade. Christ—not the tortured God, but the joyous comrade, the friend of all simple souls; the joyous comrade, with the children clinging to him, and peasants and fishers listening to his chat; not the theologian spinning barren subtleties, but the man of genius protesting against all forms and dogmas that would replace the direct vision and the living ecstasy; not the man of sorrows loving the blankness of underground cells and scourged backs and sexless skeletons, but the lover of warm life, and warm sunlight, and all that is fresh and simple and pure and beautiful."

"Every man makes his God in his own image," I thought, too touched to jar him by saying it aloud.

"And so—ever since—off and on—I have worked at this human picture of him—The Joyous Comrade—to restore the true Christ to the world."

"Which you hope to convert?"

"My business is with work, not with results. 'Whatsoever thy hand findeth to do, do with all thy might.' What can any single hand, even the mightiest, do in this great weltering world? Yet, without the hope and the dream, who would work at all? And so, not without hope, yet with no expectation of a miracle, I give the Jews a Christ they can now accept, the Christians a Christ they have forgotten. I rebuild for my beloved America a type of simple manhood, unfretted by the feverish lust for wealth or power, a simple lover of the quiet moment, a sweet human soul never dispossessed of itself, always at one with the essence of existence. Who knows but I may suggest the great question: What shall it profit a nation to gain the whole world and lose its own soul?"

His voice died away solemnly, and I heard only the click of the billiard-balls and the rumble and roar of New York.

CHAD GADYA

"And it shall be when thy son asketh thee in time to come, saying: What is this? that thou shalt say unto him, By strength of hand the Lord brought us out from Egypt, from the house of bondage. And ... the Lord slew all the first-born in the land of Egypt, ... but all the first-born of my children I redeem."—EXODUS xiii. 14, 15.

Chad Gadya! Chad Gadya! One only kid of the goat.

At last the Passover family service was drawing to an end. His father had started on the curious Chaldaic recitative that wound it up:

One only kid, one only kid, which my father bought for two zuzim. Chad Gadya! Chad Gadya!

The young man smiled faintly at the quaintness of an old gentleman in a frock-coat, a director of the steamboat company in modern Venice, talking Chaldaic, wholly unconscious of the incongruity, rolling out the sonorous syllables with unction, propped up on the prescribed pillows.

And a cat came and devoured the kid which my father bought for two zuzim. Chad Gadya! Chad Gadya!

He wondered vaguely what his father would say to him when the service was over. He had only come in during the second part, arriving from Vienna with his usual unquestioned unexpectedness, and was quite startled to find it was Passover night, and that the immemorial service was going on just as when he was a boy. The rarity of his visits to the old folks made it a strange coincidence to have stumbled upon them at this juncture, and, as he took his seat silently in the family circle without interrupting the prayers by greetings, he had a vivid artistic perception of the possibilities of existence—the witty French novel that had so amused him in the train, making him feel that, in providing raw matter for esprit, human life had its joyous justification; the red-gold sunset over the mountains; the floating homewards down the Grand Canal in the moonlight, the well-known palaces as dreamful and mysterious to him as if he had not been born in the city of the sea; the gay reminiscences of Goldmark's new opera last night at the Operntheater that had haunted his ear as he ascended the great staircase; and then this abrupt transition to the East, and the dead centuries, and Jehovah bringing out His chosen people from Egypt, and bidding them celebrate with unleavened bread throughout the generations their hurried journey to the desert.

Probably his father was distressed at this glaring instance of his son's indifference to the traditions he himself held so dear; though indeed the old man had realized long ago the bitter truth that his ways were not his son's ways, nor his son's thoughts his thoughts. He had long since known that his first-born was a sinner in Israel, an "Epikouros," a scoffer, a selfish sensualist, a lover of bachelor quarters and the feverish life of the European capitals, a scorner of the dietary laws and tabus, an adept in the forbidden. The son thought of himself through his father's spectacles, and the faint smile playing about the sensitive lips became bitterer. His long white fingers worked nervously.

And yet he thought kindly enough of his father; admired the perseverance that had brought him wealth, the generosity with which he expended it, the fidelity that resisted its temptations and made this Seder service, this family reunion, as homely and as piously simple as in the past when the Ghetto Vecchio, and not this palace on the Grand Canal, had meant home. The beaker of wine for the prophet Elijah stood as naïvely expectant as ever. His mother's face, too, shone with love and goodwill. Brothers and sisters—shafts from a full quiver—sat around the table variously happy and content with existence. An atmosphere of peace and restfulness and faith and piety pervaded the table.

And a dog came and bit the cat which had devoured the kid which my father bought for two zuzim. Chad Gadya! Chad Gadya!

And suddenly the contrast of all these quietudes with his own restless life overwhelmed him in a great flood of hopelessness. His eyes filled with salt tears. He would never sit at the head of his own table, carrying on the chain of piety that linked the generations each to each; never would his soul be lapped in this atmosphere of faith and trust; no woman's love would ever be his; no children would rest their little hands in his; he would pass through existence like a wraith, gazing in at the warm firesides with hopeless eyes, and sweeping on—the wandering Jew of the world of soul. How he had suffered—he, modern of moderns, dreamer of dreams, and ponderer of problems! Vanitas Vanitatum! Omnia Vanitas! Modern of the moderns? But it was an ancient Jew who had said that, and another who had said "Better is the day of a man's death than the day of a man's birth." Verily an ironical proof of the Preacher's own maxim that there is nothing new under the sun. And he recalled the great sentences:

"Vanity of vanities, saith the Preacher, vanity of vanities; all is vanity.

"One generation passeth away and another generation cometh: but the earth abideth for ever.

"All the rivers run into the sea; yet the sea is not full; unto the place from whence the rivers come, thither they return again.

"The thing that hath been, it is that which shall be; and that which is done is that which shall be done: and there is no new thing under the sun.

"That which is crooked cannot be made straight; and that which is wanting cannot be numbered.

"For in much wisdom is much grief; and he that increaseth knowledge increaseth sorrow."

Yes, it was all true, all true. How the Jewish genius had gone to the heart of things, so that the races that hated it found comfort in its Psalms. No sense of form, the end of Ecclesiastes a confusion and a weak repetition like the last disordered spasms of a prophetic seizure. No care for art, only for reality. And yet he had once thought he loved the Greeks better, had from childhood yearned after forbidden gods, thrilled by that solitary marble figure of a girl that looked in on the Ghetto alley from a boundary wall. Yes; he had worshipped at the shrine of the Beautiful; he had prated of the Renaissance. He had written—with the multiform adaptiveness of his race—French poems with Hellenic inspiration, and erotic lyrics—half felt, half feigned, delicately chiselled. He saw now with a sudden intuition that he had never really expressed himself in art, save perhaps in that one brutal Italian novel written under the influence of Zola, which had been so denounced by a world with no perception of the love and the tears that prompted the relentless unmasking of life.

And a staff came and smote the dog which had bitten the cat, which had devoured the kid, which my father bought for two zuzim. Chad Gadya! Chad Gadya!

Yes, he was a Jew at heart. The childhood in the Ghetto, the long heredity, had bound him in emotions and impulses as with phylacteries. Chad Gadya! Chad Gadya! The very melody awakened associations innumerable. He saw in a swift panorama the intense inner life of a curly-headed child roaming in the narrow cincture of the Ghetto, amid the picturesque high houses. A reflex of the child's old joy in the

Festivals glowed in his soul. How charming this quaint sequence of Passover and Pentecost, New Year and Tabernacles; this survival of the ancient Orient in modern Europe, this living in the souls of one's ancestors, even as on Tabernacles one lived in their booths. A sudden craving seized him to sing with his father, to wrap himself in a fringed shawl, to sway with the rhythmic passion of prayer, to prostrate himself in the synagogue. Why had his brethren ever sought to emerge from the joyous slavery of the Ghetto? His imagination conjured it up as it was ere he was born: the one campo, bordered with a colonnade of shops, the black-bearded Hebrew merchants in their long robes, the iron gates barred at midnight, the keepers rowing round and round the open canal-sides in their barca. The yellow cap? The yellow O on their breasts? Badges of honor; since to be persecuted is nobler than to persecute. Why had they wished for emancipation? Their life was self-centred, self-complete. But no; they were restless, doomed to wander. He saw the earliest streams pouring into Venice at the commencement of the thirteenth century, German merchants, then Levantines, helping to build up the commercial capital of the fifteenth century. He saw the later accession of Peninsular refugees from the Inquisition, their shelter beneath the lion's wing negotiated through their fellow-Jew, Daniel Rodrigues, Consul of the Republic in Dalmatia. His mind halted a moment on this Daniel Rodrigues, an important skeleton. He thought of the endless shifts of the Jews to evade the harsher prescriptions, their subtle, passive refusal to live at Mestre, their final relegation to the Ghetto. What well-springs of energy, seething in those paradoxical progenitors of his, who united the calm of the East with the fever of the West; those idealists dealing always with the practical, those lovers of ideas, those princes of combination, mastering their environment because they never dealt in ideas except as embodied in real concrete things. Reality! Reality!

That was the note of Jewish genius, which had this affinity at least with the Greek. And he, though to him his father's real world was a shadow, had yet this instinctive hatred of the cloud-spinners, the word-jugglers, his idealisms needed solid substance to play around. Perhaps if he had been persecuted, or even poor, if his father had not smoothed his passage to a not unprosperous career in letters, he might have escaped this haunting sense of the emptiness and futility of existence. He, too, would have found a joy in outwitting the Christian persecutor, in piling ducat on ducat. Ay, even now he chuckled to think how these strazzaroli—these forced vendors of second-hand wares—had lived to purchase the faded purple wrappings of Venetian glory.

He remembered reading in the results of an ancient census: Men, women, children, monks, nuns—and Jews! Well, the Doges were done with, Venice was a melancholy ruin, and the Jew—the Jew lived sumptuously in the palaces of her proud nobles. He looked round the magnificent long-stretching dining-room, with its rugs, oil-paintings, frescoed ceiling, palms; remembered the ancient scutcheon over the stone portal—a lion rampant with an angel volant—and thought of the old Latin statute forbidding the Jews to keep schools of any kind in Venice, or to teach anything in the city, under penalty of fifty ducats' fine and six months' imprisonment. Well, the Jews had taught the Venetians something after all—that the only abiding wealth is human energy. All other nations had had their flowering time and had faded out. But Israel went on with unabated strength and courage. It was very wonderful. Nay, was it not miraculous? Perhaps there was, indeed, "a mission of Israel," perhaps they were indeed God's "chosen people." The Venetians had built and painted marvellous things and died out and left them for tourists to gaze at. The Jews had created nothing for ages, save a few poems and a few yearning synagogue melodies; yet here they were, strong and solid, a creation in flesh and blood more miraculous and enduring than anything in stone and bronze. And what was the secret of this persistence and strength? What but a spiritual? What but their inner certainty of God, their unquestioning trust in Him, that He would send His Messiah to rebuild the Temple, to raise them to the sovereignty of the peoples? How typical his own father—thus serenely singing Chaldaic—a modern of moderns without, a student and saint at home! Ah, would that he, too, could lay hold on this solid faith! Yes, his soul was in sympathy with the brooding immovable East; even with the mysticisms of the Cabalists, with the trance of the ascetic, nay, with the fantastic frenzy-begotten ecstasy of the Dervishes he had seen dancing in Turkish mosques,—that intoxicating sense of a satisfying meaning in things, of a unity with the essence of existence, which men had doubtless sought in the ancient Eleusinian mysteries, which the Mahatmas of India had perhaps found, the tradition of which ran down through the ages, misconceived by the Western races, and for lack of which he could often have battered his head against a wall, as in literal beating against the baffling mystery of existence. Ah! there was the hell of it! His soul was of the Orient, but his brain was of the Occident. His intellect had been nourished at the breast of Science, that classified everything and explained nothing. But explanation! The very word was futile! Things were. To explain things was to state A in terms of B, and B in terms of A. Who should explain the explanation? Perhaps only by ecstasy could one understand what lay behind the phenomena. But even so the essence had to be judged by its manifestations, and the manifestations were often absurd, unrighteous, and meaningless. No, he could not believe. His intellect was remorseless. What if Israel was preserved? Why should the empire of Venice be destroyed?

And a fire came and burnt the staff, which had smitten the dog, which had bitten the cat, which had devoured the kid, which my father bought for two zuzim. Chad Gadya! Chad Gadya!

He thought of the energy that had gone to build this wonderful city; the deep sea-soaked wooden piles hidden beneath; the exhaustless art treasures—churches, pictures, sculptures—no less built on obscure human labor, though a few of the innumerable dead hands had signed names. What measureless energy petrified in these palaces! Carpaccio's pictures floated before him, and Tintoretto's—record of dead generations; and then, by the link of size, those even vaster paintings—in gouache—of Vermayen in Vienna: old land-fights with crossbow, spear, and arquebus, old sea-fights with inter-grappling galleys. He thought of galley-slaves chained to their oar—the sweat, the blood that had stained history. "So I returned and considered all the oppressions that are done under the sun: and behold the tears of such as were oppressed, and they had no comforter." And then he thought of a modern picture with a beautiful nude female figure that had cost the happiness of a family; the artist now dead and immortal, the woman, once rich and fashionable, on the streets. The futility of things—love, fame, immortality! All roads lead nowhere! What profit shall a man have from all his labor which he hath done under the sun?

No; it was all a flux—there was nothing but flux. Παντα ρει. The wisest had always seen that. The cat which devoured the kid, and the dog which bit the cat, and the staff which smote the dog, and the fire which burnt the staff, and so on endlessly. Did not the commentators say that that was the meaning of this very parable—the passing of the ancient empires, Egypt, Assyria, Persia, Greece, Rome? Commentators! what curious people! What a making of books to which there was no end! What a wilderness of waste logic the Jewish intellect had wandered in for ages! The endless volumes of the Talmud and its parasites! The countless codes, now obsolescent, over which dead eyes had grown dim! As great a patience and industry as had gone to build Venetian art, and with less result. The chosen people, indeed! And were they so strong and sane? A fine thought in his brain, forsooth!

He, worn out by the great stress of the centuries, such long in-breeding, so many ages of persecution, so many manners and languages adopted, so many nationalities taken on! His soul must be like a palimpsest with the record of nation on nation. It was uncanny, this clinging to life; a race should be content to die out. And in him it had perhaps grown thus content. He foreshadowed its despair. He stood for latter-day Israel, the race that always ran to extremes, which, having been first in faith, was also first in scepticism, keenest to pierce to the empty heart of things; like an orphan wind, homeless, wailing about the lost places of the universe. To know all to be illusion, cheat—itself the most cheated of races; lured on to a career of sacrifice and contempt. If he could only keep the hope that had hallowed its sufferings. But now it was a viper—not a divine hope—it had nourished in its bosom. He felt so lonely; a great stretch of blackness, a barren mere, a gaunt cliff on a frozen sea, a pine on a mountain. To be done with it all—the sighs and the sobs and the tears, the heart-sinking, the dull dragging days of wretchedness and the nights of pain. How often he had turned his face to the wall, willing to die.

Perhaps it was this dead city of stones and the sea that wrought so on his spirit. Tourgénieff was right; only the young should come here, not those who had seen with Virgil the tears of things. And then he recalled the lines of Catullus—the sad, stately plaint of the classic world, like the suppressed sob of a strong man:

"Soles occidere et redire possunt,
Nobis cum semel occidit brevis lux,
Nox est perpetuo una dormienda."

And then he thought again of Virgil, and called up a Tuscan landscape that expressed him, and lines of cypresses that moved on majestic like hexameters. He saw the terrace of an ancient palace, and the grotesque animals carven on the balustrade; the green flicker of lizards on the drowsy garden-wall; the old-world sun-dial and the grotto and the marble fountain, and the cool green gloom of the cypress-grove with its delicious dapple of shadows. An invisible blackbird fluted overhead. He walked along the great walk under the stone eyes of sculptured gods, and looked out upon the hot landscape taking its siesta under the ardent blue sky—the green sunlit hills, the white nestling villas, the gray olive-trees. Who had paced these cloistral terraces? Mediæval princesses, passionate and scornful, treading delicately, with trailing silks and faint perfumes. He would make a poem of it. Oh, the loveliness of life! What was it a local singer had carolled in that dear soft Venetian dialect?

"Belissimo xe el mondo perchè l' è molto vario. nè omo ghe xe profondo che dir possa el contrario."

Yes, the world was indeed most beautiful and most varied. Terence was right: the comedy and pathos of things was enough. We are a sufficient spectacle to one another. A glow came over him; for a moment he grasped hold on life, and the infinite tentacles of things threw themselves out to entwine him.

And a water came and extinguished the fire, which had burnt the staff, which had smitten the dog, which had bitten the cat, which had devoured the kid, which my father bought for two zuzim. Chad Gadya! Chad Gadya!

But the glow faded, and he drew back sad and hopeless. For he knew now what he wanted. Paganism would not suffice. He wanted—he hungered after—God. The God of his fathers. The three thousand years of belief could not be shaken off. It was atavism that gave him those sudden strange intuitions of God at the scent of a rose, the sound of a child's laughter, the sight of a sleeping city; that sent a warmth to his heart and tears to his eyes, and a sense of the infinite beauty and sacredness of life. But he could not have the God of his fathers. And his own God was distant and dubious, and nothing that modern science had taught him was yet registered in his organism. Could he even transmit it to descendants? What was it Weismann said about acquired characteristics? No, certain races put forth certain beliefs, and till you killed off the races, you could never kill off the beliefs. Oh, it was a cruel tragedy, this Western culture grafted on an Eastern stock, untuning the chords of life, setting heart and brain asunder. But then Nature was cruel. He thought of last year's grape-harvest ruined by a thunderstorm, the frightful poverty of the peasants under the thumb of the padrones. And then the vision came up of a captured cuttle-fish he had seen gasping, almost with a human cough, on the sands of the Lido. It had spoilt the sublimity of that barren stretch of sand and sea, and the curious charm of the white sails that seemed to glide along the very stones of the great breakwater. His soul demanded justice for the uncouth cuttle-fish. He did not understand how people could live in a self-centred spiritual world that shut out the larger part of creation. If suffering purified, what purification did overdriven horses undergo, or starved cats? The miracle of creation—why was it wrought for puppies doomed to drown? No; man had imposed morality on a non-moral universe, anthropomorphizing everything, transferring into the great remorseless mechanism the ethical ideals that governed the conduct of man to man. Religion, like art, focussed the universe round man, an unimportant by-product: it was bad science turned into good art. And it was his own race that had started the delusion! "And Abraham said unto God: 'Shall not the Judge of all the earth do right?'" Formerly the gods had meant might, but man's soul had come to crave for right. From the welter of human existence man had abstracted the idea of goodness and made a god of it, and then foolishly turned round and asked why it permitted the bad without which the idea of it could never have been formed. And because God was goodness, therefore He was oneness—he remembered the acute analysis of Kuenen. No, the moral law was no more the central secret of the universe than color or music. Religion was made for man, not man for religion. Even justice was a meaningless concept in the last analysis: What was, was. The artist's view of life was the only true one: the artist who believes in everything and in nothing.

The religions unconsciously distorted everything. Life itself was simple enough: a biological phenomenon that had its growth, its maturity, its decay. Death was no mystery, pain no punishment, nor sin anything but the survival of lower attributes from a prior phase of evolution, or not infrequently the legitimate protest of the natural self against artificial social ethics. It was the creeds that tortured things out of their elemental simplicity. But for him the old craving persisted. That alone would do. God, God—he was God-intoxicated, without Spinoza's calm or Spinoza's certainty. Justice, Pity, Love—something that understood. He knew it was sheer blind heredity that spoilt his life for him—oh, the irony of it—and that, if he could forget his sense of futility, he could live beautifully unto himself. The wheels of chance had ground well for him. But his soul rejected all the solutions and self-equations of his friends—the all-sufficiency of science, of art, of pleasure, of the human spectacle; saw with inexorable insight through the phantasmal optimisms, refused to blind itself with Platonisms and Hegelisms, refused the positions of æsthetes and artists and self-satisfied German savants, equally with the positions of conventional preachers, demanded justice for the individual down to the sparrow, two of which were sold in the market-place for a farthing, and a significance and a purpose in the secular sweep of destiny; yet knew all the while that Purpose was as anthropomorphic a conception of the essence of things as justice or goodness. But the world without God was a beautiful, heartless woman—cold, irresponsive. He needed the flash of soul. He had experimented in Nature—as color, form, mystery—what had he not experimented in? But there was a want, a void. He had loved Nature, had come very near finding peace in the earth-passion, in the intoxicating smell of grass and flowers, in the scent and sound of the sea, in the rapture of striking through the cold, salt waves, tossing green and white-flecked; ill exchanged for any heaven. But the passion always faded and the old hunger for God came back.

He had found temporary peace with Spinoza's God: the eternal infinite-sided Being, of whom all the starry infinities were but one poor expression, and to love whom did not imply being loved in return. 'Twas magnificent to be lifted up in worship of that supernal splendor. But the splendor froze, not scorched. He wanted the eternal Being to be conscious of his existence; nay, to send him a whisper that He was not a metaphysical figment. Otherwise he found himself saying what Voltaire has made Spinoza say: "Je crois, entre nous, que vous n'existez pas." Obedience? Worship? He could have prostrated himself for hours on the flags, worn out his knees in prayer. O Luther, O Galileo, enemies of the human race! How wise of the Church to burn infidels, who would burn down the spirit's home—the home warm with the love and treasures of the generations—and leave the poor human soul naked and shivering amid the cold countless worlds. O Napoleon, arch-fiend, who, opening the Ghettos, where the Jews crouched in narrow joy over the Sabbath fire, let in upon them the weight of the universe.

And an ox came and drank the water, which had extinguished the fire, which had burnt the staff, which had smitten the dog, which had bitten the cat, which had devoured the kid, which my father bought for two zuzim. Chad Gadya! Chad Gadya!

In Vienna, whence he had come, an Israelite, on whom the modern universe pressed, yet dreamed the old dream of a Jewish State—a modern State, incarnation of all the great principles won by the travail of the ages. The chameleon of races should show a specific color: a Jewish art, a Jewish architecture would be born, who knew? But he, who had worked for Mazzini, who had seen his hero achieve that greatest of all defeats, victory, he knew. He knew what would come of it, even if it came. He understood the fate of Christ and of all idealists, doomed to see themselves worshipped and their ideas rejected in a religion or a State founded like a national monument to perpetuate their defeat. But the Jewish State would not even come. He had met his Viennese brethren but yesterday; in the Leopoldstadt, frowsy with the gaberdines and side-curls of Galicia; in the Prater, arrogantly radiant in gleaming carriages with spick-and-span footmen—that strange race that could build up cities for others but never for itself; that professed to be both a religion and a nationality, and was often neither. The grotesquerie of history! Moses, Sinai, Palestine, Isaiah, Ezra, the Temple, Christ, the Exile, the Ghettos, the Martyrdoms—all this to give the Austrian comic papers jokes about stockbrokers with noses big enough to support unheld opera—glasses. And even supposing another miraculous link came to add itself to that wonderful chain, the happier Jews of the new State would be born into it as children to an enriched man, unconscious of the struggles, accepting the luxuries, growing big-bellied and narrow-souled. The Temple would be rebuilt. Et après? The architect would send in the bill. People would dine and dig one another in the ribs and tell the old smoking-room stories. There would be fashionable dressmakers. The synagogue would persecute those who were larger than it, the professional priests would prate of spiritualities to an applausive animal world, the press would be run in the interests of capitalists and politicians, the little writers would grow spiteful against those who did not call them great, the managers of the national theatre would advance their mistresses to leading parts. Yes, the ox would come and drink the water, and Jeshurun would wax fat and kick. "For that which is crooked cannot be made straight." Menander's comedies were fresh from the mint, the Book of Proverbs as new as the morning paper. No, he could not dream. Let the younger races dream; the oldest of races knew better. The race that was first to dream the beautiful dream of a Millennium was the first to discard it. Nay, was it even a beautiful dream? Every man under his own fig-tree, forsooth, obese and somnolent, the spirit disintegrated! Omnia Vanitas, this too was vanity.

And the slaughterer came and slaughtered the ox, which had drunk the water, which had extinguished the fire, which had burnt the staff, which had smitten the dog, which had bitten the cat, which had devoured the kid, which my father bought for two zuzim. Chad Gadya! Chad Gadya!

Chad Gadya! Chad Gadya! He had never thought of the meaning of the words, always connected them with the finish of the ceremony. "All over! All over!" they seemed to wail, and in the quaint music there seemed a sense of infinite disillusion, of infinite rest; a winding-up, a conclusion, things over and done with, a fever subsided, a toil completed, a clamor abated, a farewell knell, a little folding of the hands to sleep.

Chad Gadya! Chad Gadya! It was a wail over the struggle for existence, the purposeless procession of the ages, the passing of the ancient empires—as the commentators had pointed out—and of the modern empires that would pass on to join them, till the earth itself—as the scientists had pointed out—passed away in cold and darkness. Flux and reflux, the fire and the water, the water and the fire! He thought of the imperturbable skeletons that still awaited exhumation in Pompeii, the swaddled mummies of the Pharaohs, the undiminished ashes of forgotten lovers in old Etruscan tombs. He had a flashing sense of the great pageant of the Mediæval—popes, kings, crusaders, friars, beggars, peasants, flagellants, schoolmen; of the vast modern life in Paris, Vienna, Rome, London, Berlin, New York, Chicago; the brilliant life of the fashionable quarters, the babble of the Bohemias, the poor in their slums, the sick on their beds of pain, the soldiers, the prostitutes, the slaveys in lodging-houses, the criminals, the lunatics; the vast hordes of Russia, the life pullulating in the swarming boats on Chinese rivers, the merry butterfly life of Japan, the unknown savages of mid-Africa with their fetishes and war-dances, the tribes of the East sleeping in tents or turning uneasily on the hot terraces of their houses, the negro races growing into such a terrible problem in the United States, and each of all these peoples, nay, each unit of any people, thinking itself the centre of the universe, and of its love and care; the destiny of the races no clearer than the destiny of the individuals and no diviner than the life of insects, and all the vast sweep of history nothing but a spasm in the life of one of the meanest of an obscure group of worlds, in an infinity of vaster constellations. Oh, it was too great! He could not look on the face of his own God and live. Without the stereoscopic illusions which made his father's life solid, he could not continue to exist. His point of view was hopelessly cosmic. All was equally great and mysterious? Yes; but all was equally small and commonplace. Kant's Starry Infinite Without? Bah! Mere lumps of mud going round in a tee-totum dance, and getting hot over it; no more than the spinning of specks in a drop of dirty water. Size was nothing in itself. There were mountains and seas in a morsel of wet mud, picturesque enough for microscopic tourists. A billion billion morsels of wet mud were no more imposing than one. Geology, chemistry, astronomy—they were all in the splashes of mud from a passing carriage. Everywhere one law and one futility. The human race? Strange marine monsters crawling about in the bed of an air-ocean, unable to swim upwards, oddly tricked out in the stolen skins of other creatures. As absurd, impartially considered, as the strange creatures quaintly adapted to curious environments one saw in aquaria. Kant's Moral Law Within! Dissoluble by a cholera germ, a curious blue network under the microscope, not unlike a map of Venice. Yes, the cosmic and the comic were one. Why be bullied into the Spinozistic awe? Perhaps Heine—that other Jew—saw more truly, and man's last word on the universe into which he had been projected unasked, might be a mockery of that which had mocked him, a laugh with tears in it.

And he, he foreshadowed the future of all races, as well as of his own. They would all go on struggling, till they became self-conscious; then, like children grown to men, the scales falling from their eyes, they would suddenly ask themselves what it was all about, and, realizing that they were being driven along by blind forces to labor and struggle and strive, they too would pass away; the gross childish races would sweep them up, Nature pouring out new energies from her inexhaustible fount. For strength was in the unconscious, and when a nation paused to ask of itself its right to Empire, its Empire was already over. The old Palestine Hebrew, sacrificing his sheep to Yahweh, what a granite figure compared with himself, infinitely subtle and mobile! For a century or two the modern world would take pleasure in seeing itself reflected in literature and art by its most decadent spirits, in vibrating to the pathos and picturesqueness of all the periods of man's mysterious existence on this queer little planet; while the old geocentric ethics, oddly clinging on to the changed cosmogony, would keep life clean. But all that would pall—and then the deluge!

There was a waft of merry music from without. He rose and went noiselessly to the window and looked out into the night. A full moon hung in the heavens, perpendicularly and low, so that it seemed a terrestrial object in comparison with the stars scattered above, glory beyond glory, and in that lucent Italian atmosphere making him feel himself of their shining company, whirling through the infinite void on one of the innumerable spheres. A broad silver green patch of moonlight lay on the dark water, dwindling into a string of dancing gold pieces. Adown the canal the black gondolas clustered round a barca lighted by gaily colored lanterns, whence the music came. Funiculi, Funicula—it seemed to dance with the very spirit of joyousness. He saw a young couple holding hands. He knew they were English, that strange, happy, solid, conquering race. Something vibrated in him. He thought of bridegrooms, youth, strength; but it was as the hollow echo of a far-off regret, some vague sunrise of gold over hills of dream. Then a beautiful tenor voice began to sing Schubert's Serenade. It was as the very voice of hopeless passion; the desire of the moth for the star, of man for God. Death, death, at any cost, death to end this long ghastly creeping about the purlieus of life. Life even for a single instant longer, life without God, seemed intolerable. He would find peace in the bosom of that black water. He would glide downstairs now, speaking no word.

And the Angel of Death came and slew the slaughterer, which had slaughtered the ox, which had drunk the water, which had extinguished the fire, which had burnt the staff, which had smitten the dog, which had bitten the cat, which had devoured the kid, which my father bought for two zuzim. Chad Gadya! Chad Gadya!

When they should find him accidentally drowned, for how could the world understand, the world which yet had never been backward to judge him, that a man with youth, health, wealth, and a measure of fame should take his own life; his people would think, perhaps, that it was a ghost that had sat at the Seder table so silent and noiseless. And, indeed, what but a ghost? One need not die to hover outside the warm circle of life, stretching vain arms. A ghost? He had always been a ghost. From childhood those strange solid people had come and talked and walked with him, and he had glided among them, an unreal spirit, to which they gave flesh-and-blood motives like their own. As a child death had seemed horrible to him; red worms crawling over white flesh. Now his thoughts always stopped at the glad moment of giving up the ghost. More lives beyond the grave? Why, the world was not large enough for one life. It had to repeat itself incessantly. Books, newspapers, what tedium! A few ideas deftly re-combined. For there was nothing new under the sun. Life like a tale told by an idiot, full of sound and fury, and signifying nothing. Shakespeare had found the supreme expression for it as for everything in it.

He stole out softly through the half-open door, went through the vast antechamber, full of tapestry and figures of old Venetians in armor, down the wide staircase, into the great courtyard that looked strange and sepulchral when he struck a match to find the water-portal, and saw his shadow curving monstrous along the ribbed roof, and leering at the spacious gloom. He opened the great doors gently, and came out into the soft spring night air. All was silent now. The narrow side-canal had a glimmer of moonlight, the opposite palace was black, with one spot of light where a window shone: overhead in the narrow rift of dark-blue sky a flock of stars flew like bright birds through the soft velvet gloom. The water lapped mournfully against the marble steps, and a gondola lay moored to the posts, gently nodding to its black shadow in the water.

He walked to where the water-alley met the deeper Grand Canal, and let himself slide down with a soft, subdued splash. He found himself struggling, but he conquered the instinctive will to live.

But as he sank for the last time, the mystery of the night and the stars and death mingled with a strange whirl of childish memories instinct with the wonder of life, and the immemorial Hebrew words of the dying Jew beat outwards to his gurgling throat: "Hear, O Israel, the Lord our God, the Lord is One."

Through the open doorway floated down the last words of the hymn and the service:—

And the Holy One came, blessed be He, and slew the Angel of Death, who had slain the slaughterer, who had slaughtered the ox, which had drunk the water, which had extinguished the fire, which had burnt the staff, which had smitten the dog, which had bitten the cat, which had devoured the kid, which my father bought for two zuzim. Chad Gadya! Chad Gadya!

EPILOGUE

A MODERN SCRIBE IN JERUSALEM

I

Outside the walls of Jerusalem, on the bleak roadless way to the Mount of Olives, within sight of the domes and minarets of the sacred city, and looking towards the mosque of Omar—arrogantly a-glitter on the site of Solomon's Temple—there perches among black, barren rocks a colony of Arabian Jews from Yemen.

These all but cave-dwellers, grimy caftaned figures, with swarthy faces, coal-black ringlets, and hungry eyes, have for sole public treasure a synagogue, consisting of a small room, furnished only with an Ark, and bare even of seats.

In this room a Scribe of to-day, humblest in Israel, yet with the gift of vision, stood turning over the few old books that lay about, strange flotsam and jetsam of the great world-currents that have drifted Israel to and fro. And to him bending over a copy of the mystic Zohar,—that thirteenth century Cabalistic classic, forged in Chaldaic by a Jew of Spain, which paved the way for the Turkish Messiah—was brought a little child.

A little boy in his father's arms, his image in miniature, with a miniature grimy caftan and miniature coal-black ringlets beneath his little black skull-cap. A human curiosity brought to interest the stranger and increase his bakhshísh.

For lo! the little boy had six fingers on his right hand! The child held it shyly clenched, but the father forcibly parted the fingers to exhibit them.

And the child lifted up his voice and wept bitterly.

And so, often in after days when the Scribe thought of Jerusalem, it was not of what he had been told he would think; not of Prophets and Angels and Crusaders—only of the crying of that little six-fingered Jewish child, washed by the great tides of human history on to the black rocks near the foot of the Mount of Olives.

II

Jerusalem—centre of pilgrimage to three great religions—unholiest city under the sun!

"For from Zion the Law shall go forth and the Word of God from Jerusalem." Gone forth of a sooth, thought the Scribe, leaving in Jerusalem itself only the swarming of sects about the corpse of Religion.

No prophetic centre, this Zion, even for Israel; only the stagnant, stereotyped activity of excommunicating Rabbis, and the capricious distribution of the paralyzing Chalukah, leaving an appalling multitudinous poverty agonizing in the steep refuse-laden alleys. The faint stirrings of new life, the dim desires of young Israel to regenerate at once itself and the soil of Palestine, the lofty patriotism of immigrant Dreamers as yet unable to overcome the long lethargy of holy study and of prayers for rain. A city where men go to die, but not to live.

An accursèd city, priest-ridden and pauperized, with cripples dragging about its shrines and lepers burrowing at the Zion gate; but a city infinitely pathetic, infinitely romantic withal, a centre through which pass all the great threads of history, ancient and mediæval, and now at last quivering with the telegraphic thread of the modern, yet only the more charged with the pathos of the past and the tears of things; symbol not only of the tragedy of the Christ, but of the tragedy of his people, nay of the great world-tragedy.

III

On the Eve of the Passover and Easter, the Scribe arrived at the outer fringe of the rainbow-robed, fur-capped throng that shook in passionate lamentation before that Titanic fragment of Temple Wall, which is the sole relic of Israel's national glories. Roaring billows of hysterical prayer beat against the monstrous, symmetric blocks, quarried by King Solomon's servants and smoothed by the kisses of the generations. A Fatherland lost eighteen hundred years ago, and still this strange indomitable race hoped on!

"Hasten, hasten, O Redeemer of Zion."

And from amid the mourners, one tall, stately figure, robed in purple velvet, turned his face to the Scribe, saying, with out-stretched hand and in a voice of ineffable love—

"Shalom Aleichem."

And the Scribe was shaken, for lo! it was the face of the Christ.

IV

Did he haunt the Wailing Wall, then, sharing the woe of his brethren? For in the Church of the Holy Sepulchre the Scribe found him not.

The Scribe had slipt in half disguised: no Jew being allowed even in the courtyard or the precincts of the sacred place. His first open attempt had been frustrated by the Turkish soldiers who kept the narrow approach to the courtyard. "Rüh! Emshi!" they had shouted fiercely, and the Scribe recklessly refusing to turn back had been expelled by violence. A blessing in disguise, his friends had told him, for should the Greek-Church fanatics have become aware of him, he might have perished in a miniature Holy War. And as he fought his way through the crowd to gain the shelter of a balcony, he felt indeed that one ugly rush would suffice to crush him.

VI

In the sepulchral incense-laden dusk of the uncouth Church, in the religious gloom punctuated by the pervasive twinkle of a thousand hanging lamps of silver, was wedged and blent a suffocating mass of palm-bearing humanity of all nations and races, the sumptuously clothed and the ragged, the hale and the unsightly; the rainbow colors of the East relieved by the white of the shrouded females, toned down by the sombre shabbiness of the Russian moujiks and peasant-women, and pierced by a vivid circular line of red fezzes on the unbared, unreverential heads of the Turkish regiment keeping order among the jostling jealousies of Christendom, whose rival churches swarm around the strange, glittering, candle-illumined Rotunda that covers the tomb of Christ. Not an inch of free space anywhere under this shadow of Golgotha: a perpetual sway to and fro of the human tides, seething with sobs and quarrels; flowing into the planless maze of chapels and churches of all ages and architectures, that, perched on rocks or hewn into their mouldy darkness, magnificent with untold church-treasure—Armenian, Syrian, Coptic, Latin, Greek, Abyssinian—add the resonance of their special sanctities and the oppression of their individual glories of vestment and ceremonial to the surcharged atmosphere palpitant with exaltation and prayer and mystic bell-tinklings; overspreading the thirty-seven sacred spots, and oozing into the holy of holies itself, towards that impassive marble stone, goal of the world's desire in the blaze of the ever burning lamps; and overflowing into the screaming courtyard, amid the flagstone stalls of chaplets and crosses and carven-shells, and the rapacious rabble of cripples and vendors.

And amid the frenzied squeezing and squabbling, way was miraculously made for a dazzling procession of the Only Orthodox Church, moving statelily round and round, to the melting strains of unseen singing boys and preceded by an upborne olive-tree; seventy priests in flowering damask, carrying palms or swinging censers, boys in green, uplifting silken banners richly broidered with sacred scenes, archimandrites attended by deacons, and bearing symbolic trinitarian candlesticks, bishops with mitres, and last and most gorgeous of all, the sceptred Patriarch bowing to the tiny Coptic Church in the corner, as his priests wheel and swing their censers towards it—all the elaborately jewelled ritual evolved by alien races from the simple life and teaching of Jesus of Nazareth.

"O Jesus, brother in Israel, perhaps only those excluded from this sanctuary of thine can understand thee!"

VII

So thought the Scribe, as from the comparative safety of an upper monastery where no Jewish foot had ever trod, he looked down upon the glowing, heaving mass. The right emotion did not come to him. He was irritated; the thought of entering so historic and so Jewish a shrine only at peril of his life, recalled the long intolerance of mediæval Christendom, the Dark Ages of the Ghettos. His imagination conjured up an ironic vision of himself as the sport of that seething mob, saw himself seeking a last refuge in the Sepulchre, and falling dead across the holy tomb. And then the close air charged with all those breaths and candles and censers, the jewelled pageantry flaunted in that city of squalor and starvation, the military line of contemptuous Mussulmen complicating the mutual contempt of the Christian sects, and reminding him of the obligation on a new Jewish State, if it ever came, to safeguard these divine curios; the grotesque incongruity of all this around the tomb of the Prince of Peace, the tomb itself of very dubious authenticity, to say nothing of the thirty-six parasitical sanctities!...

He thought of the even more tumultuous scene about to be enacted here on the day of the Greek fire: when in the awful darkness of extinguished lamps, through a rift in the Holy Sepulchre within which the Patriarch prayed in solitude and darkness, a tongue of heavenly flame would shoot, God's annual witness to the exclusive rightness of the Greek Church, and the poor foot-sore pilgrims, mad with ecstasy, would leap over one another to kindle their candles and torches at it, while a vessel now riding at anchor would haste with its freight of sacred flame to kindle the church-lamps of Holy Russia.

And then the long historic tragi-comedy of warring sects swept before him, the Greek Church regarding the Roman as astray in the sacraments of Baptism and the Lord's Supper; at one with the Protestant only in not praying to the Virgin; every new misreading of human texts sufficing to start a new heresy.

VIII

He hated Palestine: the Jordan, the Mount of Olives, the holy bazaars, the geographical sanctity of shrines and soils, the long torture of prophetic texts and apocalyptic interpretations, all the devotional maunderings of the fool and the Philistine. He would have had the Bible prohibited for a century or two, till mankind should be able to read it with fresh vision and true profit. He wished that Christ had crucified the Jews and defeated the plan for the world's salvation. O happy Christ, to have died without foresight of the Crusades or the Inquisition!

IX

Irritation passed into an immense pity for humanity, crucified upon the cross whose limbs are Time and Space. Those poor Russian pilgrims faring foot-sore across the great frozen plains, lured on by this mirage of blessedness, sleeping by the wayside, and sometimes never waking again! Poor humanity, like a blind Oriental beggar on the deserted roadway crying Bakhshísh to vain skies, from whose hollow and futile spaces floats the lone word, Mâfísh—"there is nothing." At least let it be ours to cover the poorest life with that human love and pity which is God's vicegerent on earth, and to pass it gently into the unknown.

X

But since Christianity already covered these poor lives with love and pity, let them live in the beautiful illusion, so long as the ugly facts did not break through! What mattered if these sites were true or false—the believing soul had made them true. All these stones were holy, if only with the tears of the generations. The Greek fire might be a shameless fraud, but the true heavenly flame was the faith in it. The Christ story might be false, but it had idealized the basal things—love, pity, self-sacrifice, purity, motherhood. And if any divine force worked through history, then must the great common illusions of mankind also be divine. And in a world—itself an illusion—what truths could there be save working truths, established by natural selection in the spiritual world, varying for different races, and maintaining themselves by correspondence with the changing needs of the spirit?

XI

Absolute religious truth? How could there be such a thing? As well say German was truer than French, or that Greek was more final than Arabic. Its religion like its speech was the way the deepest instincts of a race found expression, and like a language a religion was dead when it ceased to change. Each religion gave the human soul something great to love, to live by, and to die for. And whosoever lived in joyous surrender to some greatness outside himself had religion, even though the world called him atheist. The finest souls too easily abandoned the best words to the stupidest people.

The time had come for a new religious expression, a new language for the old everlasting emotions, in terms of the modern cosmos; a religion that should contradict no fact and check no inquiry; so that children should grow up again with no distracting divorce from their parents and their past, with no break in the sweet sanctities of childhood, which carry on to old age something of the freshness of early sensation, and are a fount of tears in the desert of life.

The ever-living, darkly-laboring Hebraic spirit of love and righteous aspiration, the Holy Ghost that had inspired Judaism and Christianity, and moved equally in Mohammedanism and Protestantism, must now quicken and inform the new learning, which still lay dead and foreign, outside humanity.

XII

If Evolution was a truth, what mystic force working in life! From the devil-fish skulking towards his prey to the Christian laying down his life for his fellow, refusing the reward of the stronger; from the palpitating sac—all stomach—of embryonic life to the poet, the musician, the great thinker. The animality of average humanity made for hope rather than for despair, when one remembered from what it had developed. It was for man in this laboring cosmos to unite himself with the stream that made for goodness and beauty.

XIII

A song came to him of the true God, whose name is one with Past, Present, and Future.

YAHWEH

I sing the uplift and the upwelling, I sing the yearning towards the sun, And the blind sea that lifts white hands of prayer. I sing the wild battle-cry of warriors and the sweet whispers   of lovers, The dear word of the hearth and the altar, Aspiration, Inspiration, Compensation, God!

The hint of beauty behind the turbid cities, The eternal laws that cleanse and cancel, The pity through the savagery of nature, The love atoning for the brothels, The Master-Artist behind his tragedies, Creator, Destroyer, Purifier, Avenger, God!

Come into the circle of Love and Justice,
Come into the brotherhood of Pity,
Of Holiness and Health!
Strike out glad limbs upon the sunny waters,
Or be dragged down amid the rotting weeds,
The festering bodies.
Save thy soul from sandy barrenness,
Let it blossom with roses and gleam with the living waters.

Blame not, nor reason of, your Past,
Nor explain to Him your congenital weakness,
But come, for He is remorseless,
Call Him unjust, but come,
Do not mock or defy Him, for he will prevail.
He regardeth not you, He hath swallowed the worlds and the nations,
He hath humor, too: disease and death for the smugly prosperous.

For such is the Law, stern, unchangeable, shining;
Making dung from souls and souls from dung;
Thrilling the dust to holy, beautiful spirit,
And returning the spirit to dust.
Come and ye shall know Peace and Joy.
Let what ye desire of the Universe penetrate you,
Let Loving-kindness and Mercy pass through you,
And Truth be the Law of your mouth.
For so ye are channels of the divine sea,
Which may not flood the earth but only steal in
Through rifts in your souls.

Israel Zangwill – A Short Biography

Israel Zangwill was born in London on 21st January 1864, to a family of Jewish immigrants from the Russian Empire. His father, Moses, was from modern-day Latvia, and his mother, Ellen Hannah Marks Zangwill, from modern-day Poland.

Zangwill was initially educated in Plymouth and Bristol. At age 9 he was enrolled into the Jews' Free School in Spitalfields in east London. The school was for the children of Jewish immigrants and added to its teaching, of both secular and religious matters, with supplies of clothing, food, and health care. Zangwill excelled here. He began to teach part-time at the school and eventually full time. Whilst teaching he also studied with the University of London and by 1884 had earned his BA with triple honours in philosophy, history, and the sciences.

He had already co-written a tale entitled 'The Premier and the Painter' when he resigned as a teacher owing to differences with the managers of the school. Zangwill now turned to journalism for his new career path, initiating Ariel, The London Puck, as well as working in various capacities for the London press.

His writing earned him the sobriquet "the Dickens of the Ghetto" primarily based on his much lauded novel 'Children of the Ghetto: A Study of a Peculiar People' in 1892 and its glimpse of the poverty-stricken life in London's Jewish quarter.

As a writer he was keen to reflect on his political and social outlooks. His simulation of Yiddish sentence structure in English aroused great interest. His mystery work, 'The Big Bow Mystery' (1892) was the first locked room mystery novel. Social satire flowed with 'The King of Schnorrers' (1894). A follow up to 'Children of the Ghetto' was 'Ghetto Tragedies' in 1894 and 'Dreamers of the Ghetto' in 1898 which included essays on famous Jews such as Baruch Spinoza, Heinrich Heine and Ferdinand Lassalle.

Zangwill was also involved with narrowly focused Jewish issues as an assimilationist, an early Zionist, and later a territorialist. In the early 1890s he had joined the Lovers of Zion movement in England. A few years later, in 1897, he took part in the "pilgrimage" of English Jews to Palestine. That same year he also joined Theodor Herzl (considered the father of modern political Zionism) in founding the World Zionist Organization and would take part in the first seven Zionist congresses. Zangwill was much admired as an orator and spoke movingly and eloquently on the issues he was passionate on.

In 1901 he had written that "Palestine is a country without a people; the Jews are a people without a country". On Herzl's visits to London, they worked closely together. In a debate at the Article Club in November 1901 however Zangwill was still mis-using the facts: "Palestine has but a small population of Arabs and fellahin and wandering, lawless, blackmailing Bedouin tribes." And made a direct plea to "restore the country without a people to the people without a country. For we have something to give as well as to get. We can sweep away the blackmailer—be he Pasha or Bedouin—we can make the wilderness blossom as the rose, and build up in the heart of the world a civilisation that may be a mediator and interpreter between the East and the West."

In 1902, Zangwill wrote that Palestine "remains at this moment an almost uninhabited, forsaken and ruined Turkish territory". But from this point on Zangwill began to see things differently which would, in 1905, result in his breakaway from Zionism.

Zangwill quit the established philosophy of Zionism when his plan for a homeland in Uganda was rejected and instead founded his own organisation; the Jewish Territorialist Organization. Its stated goal was to create a Jewish homeland in whatever territory in the world could be found for them. At that point in time suggestions were as varied as Canada, Australia, Mesopotamia, Argentina, Uganda and Cyrenaica.

Amongst the challenges in his life he found time to write poetry. He had translated a medieval Jewish poet in 1903 and his own volume 'Blind Children' in 1908 shows his promise in this new endeavour.

In 1908, Zangwill told a London court that he had been naive when he made his 1901 speech and had since recognised that the Arab population was twice that of the United States.

Zangwill was a supporter of both feminism and pacifism, but his greatest effect was as a writer who gained a wide audience with the idea of combining ethnicities into a single, American nation. The hero of 'The Melting Pot', proclaims: "America is God's Crucible, the great Melting-Pot where all the races of Europe are melting and reforming... Germans and Frenchmen, Irishmen and Englishmen, Jews and Russians – into the Crucible with you all! God is making the American."'

'The Melting Pot' made Zangwill's name as an admired playwright. The title itself was popularised as the phrase to use to describe American absorption of immigrants when it ran in the United States.

When the play opened in Washington D.C. on 5th October 1909, former President Theodore Roosevelt leaned over the edge of his box and shouted, "That's a great play, Mr. Zangwill, that's a great play." In a later letter in 1912 Roosevelt went further "That particular play I shall always count among the very strong and real influences upon my thought and my life."

'The Melting Pot' shone a spotlight on America's growth through the input of its new waves of immigrants. Zangwill was writing as "a Jew who no longer wanted to be a Jew. His real hope was for a world in which the entire lexicon of racial and religious difference is thrown away."

According to Ze'ev Jabotinsky, Zangwill told him in 1916 that, "If you wish to give a country to a people without a country, it is utter foolishness to allow it to be the country of two peoples. This can only cause trouble. The Jews will suffer and so will their neighbours. One of the two: a different place must be found either for the Jews or for their neighbours".

In 1917 he wrote "'Give the country without a people,' magnanimously pleaded Lord Shaftesbury, 'to the people without a country.' Alas, it was a misleading mistake. The country holds 600,000 Arabs."

With the end of World War I, and a more clearly defined idea of a Jewish settlement in Palestine, Zangwill once more returned to the Zionist effort and made efforts on behalf of the Balfour Declaration, proclaiming the right of a Jewish homeland in Palestine

In 1921 Zangwill wrote "If Lord Shaftesbury was literally inexact in describing Palestine as a country without a people, he was essentially correct, for there is no Arab people living in intimate fusion with the country, utilizing its resources and stamping it with a characteristic impress: there is at best an Arab encampment, the break-up of which would throw upon the Jews the actual manual labor of regeneration and prevent them from exploiting the fellahin, whose numbers and lower wages are moreover a considerable obstacle to the proposed immigration from Poland and other suffering centers".

Despite his advocacy on Jewish matters he would be disappointed to know that despite Israel now being established the quarrels of the Middle East continue to divide.

Israel Zangwill died on 1st August 1926 in Midhurst, West Sussex.

Israel Zangwill – A Concise Bibliography

The Bachelors' Club (1891)

The Old Maid's Club (1892)
Children of the Ghetto: A Study of a Peculiar People (1892)
Grandchildren of the Ghetto (1892)
The Big Bow Mystery (1892)
Merely Mary Ann (1893)
The King of Schnorrers (1894)
The Master (1895) (based on the life of George Wylie Hutchinson)
Without Prejudices (1896)
Dreamers of the Ghetto (1898)
Ghetto Tragedies, (1899)
"The Return to Palestine", New Liberal Review, (Dec. 1901)
Children of the Ghetto (1902)
"Providence, Palestine and the Rothschilds", The Speaker, vol. 4, no. 125 (22 February 1902)
Selected Religious Poems (1903) Translation of the Jewish Medieval Poet Solomon in Cabirol.
The Grey Wig: Stories and Novelettes (1903)
The Serio-Comic Governess (1904)
Merely Mary Ann (1904)
Ghetto Comedies, (1907)
Blind Children (1908) Poetry
The Melting Pot (1909)
Italian Fantasies (1910) Travel
Chosen Peoples, (1919)
The War For The World (1916)
The Principle of Nationalities (1917)
Chosen Peoples (1918)
Hands Off Russia: Speech by Mr. Israel Zangwill at the Albert Hall, February 8th, 1919. London: Workers'
Socialist Federation, n.d. (1919)
The Voice of Jerusalem. (1921)

Filmography

Children of the Ghetto (1915, based on the play Children of the Ghetto)
The Melting Pot (1915, based on the play The Melting Pot)
Merely Mary Ann (1916, based on the play Merely Mary Ann)
The Moment Before (1916, based on the play The Moment of Death)
Mary Ann (1918, based on the play Merely Mary Ann)
Nurse Marjorie (1920, based on the play Nurse Marjorie)
Merely Mary Ann (1920, based on the play Merely Mary Ann)
The Bachelor's Club (1921, based on the novel We Moderns)
We Moderns (1925, based on the play We Moderns)
Too Much Money (1926, based on the play Too Much Money)
Perfect Crime (1928, based on the novel The Big Bow Mystery)
Merely Mary Ann (1931, based on the play Merely Mary Ann)
The Crime Doctor (1934, based on the novel The Big Bow Mystery)
The Verdict (1946, based on the novel The Big Bow Mystery)